BELGRAVE SQUARE

BELGRAVE SQUARE

Anne Perry

FAWCETT COLUMBINE

New York

A Fawcett Columbine Book
Published by Ballantine Books
Copyright © 1992 by Anne Perry

All rights reserved under International and Pan-American Copyright Conventions. Published in the United States by Ballantine Books, a division of Random House, Inc., New York, and simultaneously in Canada by Random House of Canada Limited, Toronto.

Library of Congress Cataloging-in-Publication Data
Perry, Anne.
Belgrave Square / Anne Perry. — 1st ed.
p. cm.
ISBN 0-449-90678-7
I. Title.
PR6066.E693B45 1992
823'.914—dc20   91-73144
                                          CIP

Design by Holly Johnson

Manufactured in the United States of America

First Edition: April 1992
10 9 8 7 6 5 4 3 2 1

To my friend, Cathy Ross

BELGRAVE
SQUARE

CHAPTER
ONE

Pitt stood on the river steps, the water slurping from the wakes of the barges as they passed close in shore on their way up from the Pool of London. It was lunchtime. In one hand he had a little pot of jellied eels from the stall near Westminster Bridge, and in the other a thick slice of bread. The summer sun was bright and hot on his face and the air was salt and a little sharp. Behind and above him he could hear the carts and carriages clopping along the Embankment taking gentlemen to the City for business, or to their clubs for pleasure, and ladies to make their afternoon calls, swap visiting cards and gossip, and make arrangements for the endless social whirl of the season.

The terror and the outrage of the Whitechapel murders had died down, although the police were still viewed as a failure for not having caught the worst murderer in London's history, whom the newspapers had called "Jack the Ripper." Indeed the commissioner had resigned. The Queen mourned in Windsor, as she had done for the last twenty-eight years, or as some said sulked, but altogether the outlook was fair, and improving. Personally Pitt had never been happier. He had a wife he loved and whose companionship he enjoyed, and two children who were healthy, and it was a keen pleasure to watch them grow. He was good at his work and it provided him with sufficient money to have a comfortable home, and even the occasional luxury, if he were careful between times.

"Inspector!" The voice was urgent and breathless and the feet loud on the steps. "Inspector Pitt—sir!" The constable lumbered down noisily, clattering his boots on the stairs. "Inspector Pitt, ah!" He stopped and gasped in satisfaction. "Mr. Drummond sent me ter find yer. 'E needs ter see yer, important like, as quick as yer can."

Reluctantly Pitt turned around and looked at the hot and uncomfortable young man, pink-faced above his tunic with its bright buttons, his eyes filled with anxiety in case he should not have carried out his duty rapidly enough. Micah Drummond was the most senior man in Bow Street and unmistakably a gentleman, and Pitt was an inspector at last gathering some of the credit he deserved.

Pitt ate the last of the eels, stuffed the carton in his pocket and threw the crust of bread onto the water for the birds. Immediately a dozen appeared and swooped down for it, their wings flashing in the sun.

"Thank you, Constable," he acknowledged. "Is he in his office?"

"Yes sir." He seemed about to add something more, then changed his mind. "Yes sir," he repeated, following Pitt up onto the Embankment.

"All right, you can go back to patrol," Pitt directed him, and set out with a long stride towards Bow Street. It was close enough to be faster walking than looking for a cab free to pick up a fare at this unlikely spot, and on a day when the air was so mild and people were out driving for pleasure.

He strode into the station to the visible relief of the desk sergeant, and went straight up to Drummond's office and knocked.

"Yes?" Drummond's voice was sharp with expectation.

Pitt went in and closed the door behind him automatically. Drummond was standing by the window, as immaculately dressed as always, with the effortlessness of those born to good taste without ostentation, but his long, lean face was tense and anxiety was written in the angle of his body, and the tightness of his shoulders.

"Ah Pitt! Good." He smiled with a flash of warmth, and then the concern replaced it instantly. "I've told Parfitt to take over your fraud case, I've got something more important. It's delicate—" He hesitated, seemed to consider something and then discard it, which was unlike him. Pitt had found him direct, without flattery or evasion, and always without that manipulation which marked so many lesser men. It was indicative of the degree of pressure he now felt that the right words should be so difficult for him to find.

Pitt waited in silence.

Drummond came to the point. "Pitt, there is a case I want you to handle." They had worked together with mutual respect, even friendship. He allowed that to guide his speech now. "A very important man has just called me, in the name of . . . friendship." He hesitated only an instant over the word, but Pitt noticed it with surprise, and saw the faintest of color in his cheeks.

Drummond moved away from the window overlooking the street and stood behind the large, leather-topped desk.

"He has asked me to preempt the local police," he went on, "and possibly the newspapers, by handling the investigation. You have more skill than anyone else in dealing with cases like this. In fact I have had it in mind to promote you to political cases from now on—and those that look like becoming political. I know you refused promotion before because you didn't want to sit behind a desk . . ." He tailed off, looking at Pitt's face.

Pitt would have helped him if he could, but he had no idea what the situation involved, or whom, or why it should cause Drummond to exhibit such an uncharacteristic loss of composure and obvious unease.

"I'll tell you as we go." Drummond shrugged and walked over, taking his hat from the stand, and opened the door. Pitt followed with a simple nod of assent.

In the street below it took only a moment to hail a hansom cab. As soon as Drummond had given the driver instructions and they were both seated he began his explanation, not looking at Pitt, but staring straight ahead of him, his hat balanced on his knees.

"Today I received a call on the telephone from Lord Sholto Byam, whom I know slightly. We have friends in common." His voice was curiously on edge. "He was in some distress because he had just heard of the murder of a man of his acquaintance, a most unsavory man." He breathed in and out slowly, still without looking at Pitt. "And for reasons he will explain to us, he fears he himself may come under suspicion for the crime."

Questions leaped to Pitt's mind. How had Lord Byam heard of

the murder? It could not yet be in the newspapers. How did he know a man of such a nature? And why should he be suspected? But more powerful than these was his awareness of Drummond's acute discomfort, almost embarrassment. The conciseness of his account suggested a prepared speech, and he had gone straight through it without deviation or a glance at Pitt to see his response.

"Who is the victim, sir?" he said aloud.

"A man called William Weems, a petty usurer from Clerkenwell," Drummond replied.

"Where was he found?"

"In his home, in Cyrus Street, shot through the head." Drummond winced as he said it. He hated guns and Pitt knew it.

"We're going west," Pitt pointed out. Clerkenwell was to the east.

"We're going to see Lord Byam," Drummond answered. "In Belgravia. I want you to know all you can about it before you go to Clerkenwell. It will be hard enough to take over another man's investigation without going in ignorant of what you face or why you are there."

Pitt felt his first really sharp misgiving. Now he could no longer put off the questions.

"Who is Lord Sholto Byam, sir, apart from being one of your acquaintances?"

Drummond looked less uncomfortable. Now he was in the realm of ordinary fact.

"The Byams are a very distinguished family, generations of service to the Board of Trade and in the Foreign Office. Money, of course. The present Lord Byam is in the Treasury, especially concerned with foreign loans and trade alliances. A brilliant man."

"How does he come to know a petty usurer in Clerkenwell?" Pitt asked with as much tact in his voice as he could manage. The question sounded ridiculous even so.

A bleak smile flickered across Drummond's face and died again.

"I don't know. That is what we are going to learn in Belgravia."

Pitt remained silent for a few moments, his mind filled with questions and uncertainties. The cab was moving at a brisk trot, threading its way up Eccleston Street and across Eaton Square to where it changed into Belgrave Place, passing carriages with matched pairs and coats of arms on the doors. This was the beginning of the high season, and everyone who was anyone was out and about.

"Is it in the newspapers yet?" Pitt asked finally.

Drummond knew what he was reaching towards and smiled with self-mocking humor.

"I doubt it will be. What is one usurer more or less? It is not a spectacular murder, simply a shooting in a back office in Clerkenwell, by person or persons unknown." He shifted his position a trifle. "I suppose the use of a gun is unusual. Few people have them. But nothing else is worthy of comment."

"Then how does Lord Byam come to know of it so rapidly?" Pitt had to say it.

Again Drummond stared ahead of him.

"He has friends in the police—"

"I can imagine he might in Belgravia." Pitt could not let it go so blindly. "But in Clerkenwell?"

"Apparently."

"And why do they suppose that he should be interested in the murder of a usurer? Why this man?"

"I don't know," Drummond said unhappily. "I can only assume someone knew of Byam's connection with the man, and chose to forewarn him."

Pitt allowed the matter to drop for the time being, and rode the few moments more in silence until the cab stopped and they alighted in the bright leafy sunshine of Belgrave Square. The houses were huge, of pale stone, and classic Georgian in style, their front doors flanked by Doric pillars, areaways bounded by wrought-iron rails, the balconies bright with boxes of potted plants.

Drummond walked slowly up the steps of number 21, shoulders stiff, head high, back straight, and Pitt followed him two paces behind, gangling, pockets full, tie a trifle too loose and hat on crooked. Only his boots, a gift from his sister-in-law, were immaculately polished and quite beautiful.

The door was opened by the usual supercilious kind of footman in such an area. He saw Drummond and made an instant judgment, as was part of his trade. Then he saw Pitt behind him and changed his mind. His deferential half bow vanished.

"Yes sir?" he inquired dubiously.

"Micah Drummond," Drummond said with dignity. "Lord Byam is expecting me."

"And the other . . . gentleman?" The footman barely raised his eyebrows but his expression was an exquisite mixture of pained civility and distaste.

"You have it precisely," Drummond said with a chill. "He is a gentleman who is with me. That will satisfy Lord Byam, I assure you. Please inform him of our presence."

The footman was put in his place. "Yes sir." He retreated before further discomfort and invited them in. The entrance hall was large and surprisingly old-fashioned in its decoration, harking back to the simplicity of the late Georgian period, quite unlike the cluttered and rather ponderous fashion of the present time. The walls were dark but very simple and the woodwork was all white. The mahogany table was of Adam design, clean legged and finely polished, and a large bowl of summer roses shone with a blaze of color, reflected in the rich wood in reds and golds. Pitt's opinion of Lord Byam rose immediately—or perhaps of Lady Byam?

They were shown into the morning room and left there while the footman informed his master of their arrival. He returned within moments to conduct them to the library, where Lord and Lady Byam were standing in the bright sun streaming through the window. He was in the center of the room; slender, a little more than average height, dark hair graying at the temples and a sensitive, almost dreaming face lit by the most magnificent dark eyes. Only on second glance did one see an underlying determination, a weight in the jaw and a thickening of the flesh. Now he was obviously troubled, his fine hands moved nervously and the muscles of his neck were tight.

Lady Byam, standing to his right, was equally dark, and almost as tall, but the balance of her features was entirely different, less mercurial, reflective; untried as to strength or passion, or perhaps merely concealed.

"Ah, Drummond!" Byam's face relaxed and some of the tension slipped out of him as if the mere sight of Micah Drummond had brought him relief. Then his eyes moved to Pitt and the question was implicit.

"Good afternoon, my lord, Lady Byam." Drummond insisted

on the courtesies first. It was probably a habit so deeply ingrained he did it without thinking. "I have brought Inspector Pitt with me to save having to explain the situation twice, and it is better he should hear it from you, and ask what he needs, than have to do it indirectly later on. He is the best man I know for a delicate investigation."

Byam regarded Pitt dubiously. Pitt looked back at him with interest. Perhaps the situation and Drummond's nervousness inclined him to prejudice, but the man in front of him was not what he had expected. There was acute intelligence in his face, and imagination and subtlety, and he thought perhaps considerable capacity for humor.

And on the other hand, Drummond refused to explain Pitt, or recommend him further, as if he were a commodity he was selling. He had said enough, and Byam could accept him on that, or look elsewhere for help.

Byam appreciated it without further words. "Then I am obliged to you for coming." He turned to Lady Byam. "Eleanor, my dear, there is no need for you to be harrowed by having to listen yet again. But I am sensible of your kindness in remaining with me until Drummond should arrive."

Eleanor smiled graciously and accepted her dismissal. Perhaps indeed she had already heard the story and would find it distressing to hear it again.

Drummond bowed very slightly and she inclined her head in acknowledgment, then walked gracefully from the room, closing the door behind her.

Byam invited them to be seated, which out of politeness they both accepted, but he himself seemed unable to relax. He walked slowly back and forth across the cream-and-pink Chinese carpet and without waiting to be asked, began his explanation for having sent for them.

"I learned this morning from a friend in the Clerkenwell police station . . ." He looked down at the floor, his expression hidden from them, his fingers locked behind his back. "A man for whom I had done some small service . . ." He turned and began back again, still not looking at them. "That the body of one William Weems had been found dead in his rooms in Cyrus Street. He was shot, I believe;

at this point they have no idea with what manner of gun, except that it was at close quarters, and some type of large-barrelled weapon." He breathed in and out. "A sporting gun seems possible."

Drummond opened his mouth, perhaps to ask why anyone should suppose Byam to be interested in the death of Weems, or to suggest he leave the forensic facts, which would be better expounded in Clerkenwell, and continue with his own connection. In the event Byam was standing with his back half to them, staring at the sunlight on the spines of the leather-bound, gold-tooled books on the shelf, and Drummond said nothing.

"Normally it would be a sordid crime which would have no interest to me, except to deplore it," Byam went on with obvious effort, turning again and beginning his way back to the far table. "But in this case I am acquainted with Weems in the most unpleasant circumstances. Through a servant, with whom he had some relationship—" he stopped and touched an ornament as if straightening it "—he learned of a tragedy in the past in which I played a regrettable part, and he was blackmailing me over it." He stood rigid, his back to them, the light so bright it shone on his hair and picked out the fabric of his jacket, making it look faintly dusty in the brilliant room.

Drummond was obviously stunned. He sat motionless in the green leather sofa, his face stiff with amazement. Pitt guessed he had been expecting a quarrel, or at worst a debt, and this both startled and embarrassed him.

"For money?" he asked quietly.

"Of course," Byam replied, then immediately seemed to recollect himself. "I'm sorry, yes indeed for money. Thank God he did not want favors of any other kind." He hesitated, and neither Pitt nor Drummond interrupted the prickling silence. Byam kept his back to them.

"I presume you are going to ask me what the matter was for which I was willing to pay a man like Weems to keep his silence. You have a right to know, if you are to help me." He took a deep breath; Pitt saw his slender shoulders rise and fall. "Twenty years ago, before I was married, I spent some time at the country home of Lord Frederick Anstiss, and his wife, Laura." His beautiful, well-modulated voice was husky. "Anstiss and I were good friends, indeed I may say we still are." He swallowed. "But at that time we were almost as close as brothers. We had many interests in common, both in pursuits of the mind and in such physical pleasures as shooting, riding to hounds, and the raising of good horses."

No one in the room moved. The clock on the mantel chimed the quarter hour, its intrusion making Pitt start.

"Laura, Lady Anstiss, was the most beautiful woman I have ever seen," Byam went on. "She had skin as pale as a lily, indeed an artist painting her portrait entitled it *The Moonflower*. I've never seen a woman move with such grace as she had." He hesitated again, obviously finding the words with which to tear open so old and private a wound difficult. "I was very foolish. Anstiss was my friend, and my host, and I betrayed him—only in word, you understand, never deed!" His voice was urgent, as though he cared intensely that they believe him, and there was a ring of candor in it that surpassed even his present anxiety and self-conscious discomfort.

Drummond murmured something inaudible.

"I suppose I paid court to her," Byam continued, staring out of the window at the trees and the rhododendrons beyond. "I can hardly remember now, but I must have spent more time with her than was appropriate, and certainly I told her she was beautiful— she was, quite incredibly so." He hesitated. "Only when it was too late did I realize she returned what she thought was my feeling for her, with a passion quite out of proportion to anything I had encouraged."

He began to speak more rapidly, his voice a little breathless. "I had been foolish, extremely foolish, and far worse than that, I was betraying my friend and my host. I was horrified by what I had done, quite thoughtlessly. I had been flattered because she liked me, what young man would not be? I had allowed her to think I meant far more by my attentions than a slight romance, a few rather silly dreams. She was in love, and expected something dramatic to come of it." He still had his back to them. "I told her it was not only hopeless, but quite morally wrong. I imagined she had accepted it—I suppose because I knew it so surely myself." He stopped again, and even in the motionless aspect of his body his distress in the subject was obvious.

Pitt and Drummond glanced at each other, but it would be

pointless and intrusive to interrupt. To offer sympathy now would be to misunderstand.

"She couldn't," Byam went on, his voice dropped very low. "She had never been denied before. Every man for whom she had had any regard, and many for whom she had not, had been clay in her hands. To her it was the uttermost rejection. We can only guess at what was in her thoughts, but it seemed to have destroyed everything she believed of herself." He hunched his shoulders a little higher, as if withdrawing into some warmer, safer place. "I cannot believe she loved me so much. I did nothing to invite it. I was foolish, a flirtation, no more than that. No grand declarations of love, no promises . . . only"—he sighed—"only a liking for her company, and an enchantment with her marvelous beauty—as any man might have felt."

This time the silence stretched for so long they could hear the sounds of footsteps across the hall and a murmur of voices as the butler spoke to one of the maids. Finally Drummond broke it.

"What happened?"

"She threw herself off the parapet," Byam replied so softly they both strained to hear him. "She died immediately." He put his hands up to his face and stood with his head bent, his body rigid and unmoving, his features hidden not only from them, but from the light.

"I'm sorry," Drummond said huskily. "Really very sorry."

Slowly Byam raised his head, but still his face was invisible to them.

"Thank you." His words caught in his throat. "It was appalling. I would have understood it if Anstiss had thrown me out and never forgiven me as long as he lived." He pulled himself straighter and reasserted his control. "I had betrayed him in the worst possible way," he went on. "Albeit through blindness and stupidity rather than any intent, but Laura was dead, and no innocence or remorse of mine could heal that." He took a deep breath and let it out with an inaudible sigh. He continued in a tone far less emotional, as if the feeling had drained out of him. "But he made the greatest effort a man can and he forgave me. He let his grief for her be sweet and untainted by rage or hatred. He chose to view it as an accident, a simple tragedy. He gave it out that she had gone onto the balcony of her room at night, and in the dark had slipped and fallen. No one questioned it, whatever they might have guessed. Laura Anstiss was deemed to have died by mischance. She was buried in the family crypt."

"And William Weems?" Drummond asked. There was no way to be tactful.

Byam turned at last and faced them, his expression bleak and the faintest shadow of a smile touching his lips.

"He came to me about two years ago and told me he was related to someone who had been a servant in the hall at the time, and knew that Lady Anstiss and I had been lovers, and that she had taken her own life when I ended the affaire." He came over towards the sofa opposite them. "I was taken aback that anyone should know anything about it, beyond what was public"—he shrugged very slightly—"that she had died tragically. I suppose my face reflected the feeling of guilt I still have, and he fastened onto it."

At last he sat down. "Of course I denied that I was her lover, and he may have believed me or not, but he affected not to." His smile became broader and more bitter. "No doubt to illustrate to me how unlikely it was that society would either. The general assumption would be that no woman as lovely and charming as Laura Anstiss would take her own life over something so trivial as the ending of a flirtation." He crossed his legs. "It must have been a great passion to affect her so." His face was filled with a dark, self-mocking humor. "It wasn't, I assure you. It was so very far from it it is ridiculous! But who would believe that now?" He looked at Drummond. "I should be ruined, and I cannot bear to think what it would do to my wife—the pitying looks, the whispers, the quiet amusement and the doors that would be so very discreetly closed. And naturally my career would be ended, and in time I should be relieved of my position." He moved one hand dismissively. "No reasons would be given, except a quiet murmur and an expectation that I should understand; but it would all be as relentless as the incoming tide, and as useless to fight against."

"But it would be his word against yours," Drummond pointed out. "And who would accept, or even listen to, such a man?"

Byam was very pale. "He had a letter, or part of a letter to be more precise. I had not seen it before, but it was from Laura to me, and very—very outspoken." He colored painfully as he said it and momentarily looked downward and away from Drummond.

"So you paid him." Drummond did not frame it as a question, the answer had already been given.

"Yes," Byam agreed. "He didn't ask a lot, twenty pounds a month."

Pitt concealed his smile. Twenty pounds a month would have beggared him, and any other policeman except those like Drummond with private means. He wondered what Drummond thought of the yawning difference between Byam's world and most men's, or if he was even aware of it.

"And do you believe Weems might have kept this letter, and record of your payments in some way traceable to you?" Drummond said with slight puzzlement.

Byam bit his lip. "I know he did. He took some pains to tell me so, as a safeguard to himself. He said he had records of every payment I had made him. Whatever I said, no one would be likely to believe it was interest upon a debt—I am not in a position to require loans from usurers. If I wished further capital I should go to a bank, like any other gentleman. I don't gamble and I have more than sufficient means to live according to my taste. No—" For the first time he looked at Pitt. "Weems made it very plain he had written out a clear record of precisely what I had paid him, the letter itself, together with all the details he knew of Laura Anstiss's death and my part in it—or what he chose to interpret as my part. That is why I come to you for your help." His eyes were very direct. "I did not kill Weems, indeed I have done him no harm whatever, nor ever threatened to. But I should be surprised if the local police do not feel compelled to investigate me for themselves, and I have no proof that I was elsewhere at the time. I don't know precisely what hour he was killed, but there are at least ninety minutes yesterday late evening when I was alone here in the library. No servant came or went." He glanced briefly at the window. "And as you may observe it would be no difficulty to climb out of this bay window into the garden, and hence the street, and take a hansom to wherever I wished."

"I see," Drummond agreed, and indeed it was perfectly obvious. The windows were wide and high, and not more than three feet above the ground. Any reasonably agile man, or woman for that matter, could have climbed out, and back in again, without difficulty, or rousing attention. It would be simple to look out far enough to make sure no one was passing outside, and the whole exercise could be accomplished in a matter of seconds.

Byam was watching them. "You see, Drummond, I am in a predicament. In the name of fellowship"—he invested the word with a fractionally heavier intonation than usual—"I ask you to come to my aid in this matter, and use your good offices to further my cause." It was a curious way of phrasing it, almost as if he were using a previously prescribed formula.

"Yes," Drummond said slowly. "Of course. I—I'll do all I can. Pitt will take over the investigation from the Clerkenwell police. That can be arranged."

Byam looked up quickly. "You know through whom?"

"Of course I do," Drummond said a trifle sharply, and Pitt had a momentary flash of being excluded from some understanding between them, as if the words had more meaning than the surface exchange.

Byam relaxed fractionally. "I am in your debt." He looked at Pitt directly again. "If there is anything further I can tell you, Inspector, please call upon me at any time. If it has to be in my office in the Treasury, I would be obliged if you exercised discretion."

"Of course," Pitt agreed. "I shall simply leave my name. Perhaps you could answer a few questions now, sir, and save the necessity of disturbing you again?"

Byam's eyes widened almost imperceptibly as if the immediacy took him aback, but he did not argue.

"If you wish."

Pitt sat forward a little. "Did you pay Weems on request, or on a regular and prearranged basis?"

"On a regular basis. Why?"

Beside Pitt, Drummond shifted position a fraction, sitting back into the cushions.

"If Weems was a blackmailer, you may not have been the only victim," Pitt pointed out courteously. "He might have used the same pattern for others as well."

A flicker of annoyance crossed Byam's face at his own stupidity.

"I see. Yes, I paid him on the first day of the month, in gold coin."

"How?"

"How?" Byam repeated with a frown. "I told you, in gold coin!"

"In person, or by messenger?" Pitt clarified.

"In person, of course. I have no wish to raise my servants' curiosity by dispatching them with a bag of gold to a usurer!"

"To Clerkenwell?"

"Yes." Byam's fine eyes widened. "To his house in Cyrus Street."

"Interesting—"

"Is it? I fail to see how."

"Weems felt no fear of you, or he would not have allowed you to know both his name and his whereabouts," Pitt explained. "He could perfectly easily have acted through an intermediary. Blackmailers are not usually so forthright."

The irritation smoothed out of Byam's expression.

"No, I suppose it is remarkable," he conceded. "I had not considered it. It does seem unnecessarily rash. Perhaps some other victim was not so restrained as I?" There was a lift of hope in his voice and he regarded Pitt with something close to appreciation.

"Was that the only time you went to Cyrus Street, sir?" Pitt pursued.

Drummond drew in his breath, but then changed his mind and said nothing.

"Certainly," Byam replied crisply. "I had no desire to see the man except when it was forced upon me."

"Did you ever have any conversation with him that you can recall?" Pitt went on, disregarding his tone and its implications. "Anything at all that might bear on where he obtained information about you, or anyone else? Any other notable people he might have had dealings with, either usurious or extortionate?"

A shadow of a smile hovered over Byam's lips, but whether at the thought or at Pitt's use of words it was impossible to tell.

"I am afraid not. I simply gave him the money and left as soon as I could. The man was a leech, despicable in every way. I refused to indulge in conversation with him." His face creased with contempt—Pitt thought not only for Weems, but for himself also. "Now I suppose it might have been an advantage if I had. I'm sorry to be of so little use."

Pitt rose to his feet. "It was hardly foreseeable," he said with equally dry humor. "Thank you, my lord."

"What are you going to do?" Byam asked, then instantly his features reflected annoyance, but it was too late to withdraw the question; his weakness was apparent.

"Go to the Clerkenwell police station," Pitt replied without looking at Drummond.

Slowly Drummond stood up also. He and Byam faced each other in silence for a moment, both seemed on the verge of speech which did not come. Perhaps the understanding was sufficient without it. Then Byam simply said thank you and held out his hand. Drummond accepted it, and with Byam giving Pitt only the acknowledgment required by civility, they took their leave. They were shown out by the same footman, who was now considerably more courteous.

In another hansom clopping along out of the quiet avenues of Belgravia towards the teeming, noisy streets of Clerkenwell, Pitt asked the blunt questions he would have to have answered if there was to be any chance of success.

"Who do you know, sir, that you can have a murder case taken away from the local Clerkenwell station without questions asked?"

Drummond looked acutely uncomfortable.

"There are things I cannot answer you, Pitt." He looked straight ahead at the blank inside wall of the cab. "You will have to accept my assurance that it can be done."

"Is that the same acquaintance who will have informed Lord Byam of Weems's death?" Pitt asked.

Drummond hesitated. "No, not the same person; but another with the same interests—which I assure you are beneficent."

"Who do I report to?"

"Me—to me."

"If this usurer was blackmailing Lord Byam, I assume there may be other men of importance he was also blackmailing."

Drummond stiffened. Apparently the thought had not occurred to him.

"I suppose so," he said quickly. "For God's sake be discreet, Pitt!"

Pitt smiled with self-mockery. "It's the most discreet job of all, isn't it—tidying up after their lordships' indiscretions?"

"That's unfair, Pitt," Drummond said quietly. "The man was a victim of circumstance. He complimented a beautiful woman, and she became infatuated with him. She must have been of a fragile and melancholy disposition to begin with, poor creature, and could not cope with a refusal. One can understand his wanting to keep the matter private, not only for himself but for Lord Anstiss's sake as well. It can benefit no one to have the whole tragedy raked over again after twenty years."

Pitt did not argue. He had considerable pity for Byam, but he was uneasy about the certainty with which Byam had called on Drummond and had manipulated the placing of a police inspector sympathetic to him to take charge of the case. It was a mere few hours since the body had been found and already Drummond had removed Pitt from his current case, called upon Byam at his home, and now they were going to Clerkenwell to override the local man and take over the case themselves.

They rode the rest of the way without resuming the conversation. Pitt could think of nothing else relevant to say. To have made polite conversation was beneath the respect they had for each other, and Drummond was apparently consumed with his own thoughts, which to judge from his face were far from comfortable.

At Clerkenwell they alighted and Drummond went in ahead of Pitt, introduced himself, and requested to see the senior officer in charge. He was conducted upstairs almost immediately, leaving Pitt to wait by the duty desk, and it was some ten or twelve minutes before he returned looking grim but less ill at ease. He met Pitt's eyes squarely.

"It's settled, Pitt. You are to take over the case. Sergeant Innes will work with you, show you what they have so far, and do any local investigations you may wish. Report your progress to me."

Pitt understood him perfectly. He also knew him well enough not to doubt his integrity. If it proved that Byam had killed his blackmailer, Drummond would be distressed and deeply embarrassed, but he would not defend him or seek to conceal it.

"Yes sir," Pitt agreed with a bare smile. "Does Sergeant Innes know I am coming?"

"He will in another five minutes," Drummond answered with a flicker of humor in his eyes. "If you wait here he will join you. Fortunately he was here at the station—or perhaps it was not fortune . . ." He left the rest unsaid. Such a thing had become possible with the invention of the telephone, a magnificent and sometimes erratic instrument which made immediate communication possible between those possessed of one, as was Byam, and presumably someone in the Clerkenwell station.

Drummond took his leave, back to Bow Street, and Pitt waited in the shabby, overused hallway until Sergeant Innes should appear, which he did in a little more than the five minutes promised. He was a small, wiry man with a very large nose and a sudden smile which showed crooked white teeth. Pitt liked him straightaway, and was acutely aware of the indignity of the position he had been put in.

"Sergeant Innes." Innes announced himself a trifle stiffly, not yet knowing what to make of Pitt, but having appreciated from his rank that it was not Pitt who had engineered this sudden overtaking of his case.

"Pitt," Pitt replied, holding out his hand. "I apologize for this— the powers that be . . ." He left it unfinished. He did not feel at liberty to tell Innes more; that was presumably the reason the local station was not permitted to conduct the affair themselves.

"Understood," Innes acknowledged briefly. "Can't think why, very ordinary squalid little affair—so far. Miserable usurer shot in his own offices." His expressive face registered disgust. "Probably some poor beggar he was squeezing dry 'oo couldn't take it anymore. Filthy occupation. Vampires!"

Pitt agreed with him heartily and was happy to say so.

"What do you have?" he went on.

"Not much. No witnesses, but then that would be too much to hope for." Innes flashed his amiable smile. "Usury is a secret sort of business anyway. 'Oo wants the world to know 'e's borrowin' money from a swine like that? You got to be pretty desperate

to go to one o' them." He started to walk towards the door and
Pitt followed. "Easiest ter see the corpse first," Innes went on.
"Got 'im in the morgue just down the road. Then we can go to
Cyrus Street, that's where 'e lived. 'Aven't really 'ad much time
to look 'round that yet. Just got started when a constable came
flyin' 'round ter tell us ter stop everythin' and come back ter the
station. Left the place locked and a man on duty, o' course."

Pitt went down the steps outside and onto the busy pavement.
The air was still warm and heavy, sharp with the smell of horse
dung. They walked side by side, Pitt's long, easy stride and Innes's
shorter, brisker march.

"Just begun to question the local people," Innes went on. "All
know nothing about it, o' course."

"Of course," Pitt agreed dryly. "I imagine no one is particularly
grieved to see him dead."

Innes grinned and glanced at Pitt with sidelong amusement.
"No one's even pretending so far. A lot of debts written off there."

"No heir?" Pitt was surprised.

"No one claimed to be so far." Innes's face darkened. His own
feelings in the matter were transparent. Pitt would not be surprised
if a few of the records of debt were kept overlong by the police in
their investigations, important evidence, not to be released too
soon. Personally if they were misplaced he would not be overduly
concerned himself. He had sharp enough memories of hunger and
cold and the gnawing anxiety of poverty from his own childhood
to understand the despair of debt and wish it on no one.

They strode along between busy women with bales of cloth,
baskets of bread and vegetables and small goods to sell. Coster-
mongers pushed barrows along the cobbles close to the curbs, crying out their wares; peddlers stood on corners and proffered
matches, bootlaces, clockwork toys and a dozen other trivial items.
Someone had a cart with cold peppermint to drink, and was doing
an excellent trade. A running patterer's singsong voice recited the
latest scandal in easy doggerel.

The morgue was grim and there was a musty carbolic smell as
soon as they were in the door. The attendant recognized Innes
immediately but looked at Pitt with some suspicion.

Innes introduced him laconically and explained his presence.

"I suppose you want to see Weems?" the attendant said with a grimace, pushing his hand over his head, and smoothing off his brow a single strand of fairish hair. "Disagreeable," he said conversationally. "Most disagreeable. Come with me, gentlemen." He turned around and led the way to a room at the back of the building, stone floored with tiled walls and two large sinks along the far end. A stone table stood in the middle with guttering leading away from it to the drain. There were gas jets on the walls, and one pendant lamp from the center of the ceiling. On the table, covered by a sheet, Pitt saw the very clear outline of a body.

Innes shivered but kept his face stoically expressionless.

"There you are," the attendant said cheerfully. "The late Mr. William Weems, as was. Of all the citizens of Clerkenwell, he'll be one of the least missed." He sniffed. "Sorry, gentlemen, p'r'aps I spoke out of turn. Shouldn't cast aspersions at the dead—not decent, is it." He sniffed again.

Pitt found the smell of death catching at his stomach, the wet stone, the carbolic, the sweet odor of blood. He wished to get it over with as quickly as possible.

He lifted the sheet off the body and looked at what remained of William Weems. He was a large man, flaccid in death now that the rigor had worn off and the muscles of his abdomen were relaxed and his limbs lay slack, but in life Pitt guessed him to have been quite imposing.

The manner of death was hideously apparent. The left half of his head had been blasted at close range by some sort of multiple missile, a gun with a very large barrel and loose bullets or even scrap metal. There was nothing left to judge what his appearance might have been, no ear or cheek or hairline, no eye. Pitt had seen many a constable sicken and faint at less. His own stomach tightened and beside him he heard Innes suck in his breath, but he forced himself to remember that death would have been instant, and what was left here on this table was simply the clay that used to be a man, nothing more; no pain, no fear inhabited it now.

He looked at the right side of the head. Here the features were intact. He could see what the large broad nose had been like, the wide mouth he could guess at, the heavy-lidded, greenish hazel eye was still open, but somehow inhuman now. It did not strike him as having been a pleasing face, although he knew it was unfair to judge in any manner of death, least of all this. He was ashamed of himself for feeling so little grief.

"A shotgun of some sort," Innes said grimly. "Or one of them old-fashioned things they load at the muzzle, with all sorts o' stuff, bits of iron fillings an' the like. Very nasty."

Pitt turned away from the body and back to Innes.

"I take it you didn't find the gun?"

"No sir. At least I don't think so. There's an old-fashioned hackbut on the wall. I suppose 'e could 'ave used that, and 'ung it back up again."

"Which means he didn't bring it with him," Pitt said doubtfully. "What does the doctor say?"

"Not a lot. 'E died some time yesterday evening, between eight an' midnight 'e reckons. As you can see, it must 'a bin straightaway. Yer don't 'ang around with a wound like that. No tellin' at this time what distance away, but can't 'a bin far, 'cos the room in't that big."

"I suppose no one heard anything?" Pitt asked ruefully.

"Not a soul." Innes smiled very slightly. "I doubt we'll get a great deal o' help from the locals. 'E weren't a popular man."

"I never knew a usurer who was." Pitt took a last look at the pallid face, then allowed the attendant to cover it with the sheet again. "I suppose they'll do a postmortem?"

"Yeah, but I dunno what for." Innes pulled a face. "Plain enough what killed 'im."

"Who found him?" Pitt asked.

"Feller what runs errands for 'im an' does some clerking." Innes wrinkled up his nose at the odor in the room. "If you don't want anything more in 'ere, can we get on to Cyrus Street, sir?"

"Of course." Pitt moved from the wet stone, carbolic and death with a sense of release. They thanked the morgue attendant and escaped out into the heat, dirt, noise, the gutters and horse manure and overspilling life of the street. He resumed the questions. "He has no housekeeper?"

"Woman what comes and cooks and cleans a bit." Innes marched sharply beside him. "She only does breakfast in the mornings. She saw the light on in the office and took it 'e was awake, so she made his meal and left it on the table without disturbing him. She just called out that it was ready, and weren't bothered when she 'eard no answer. Apparently he weren't given to pleasantries an' it didn't strike 'er as nothing wrong." He dug his hands into his pockets and skipped a step to avoid tripping over a piece of refuse. It was a brilliant day and still hot. He squinted a trifle in the sun. "O' course she fairly threw a fit when we told 'er as she'd cooked breakfast for a dead man, within yards of 'is corpse. 'Ad ter fetch 'er two glasses o' gin to bring 'er 'round."

Pitt smiled. "Had she anything interesting to say about him, in general?"

"No love lost. On the other 'and, no particular grudge either, no quarrel as far as we can learn. But then she'd not likely mention it if there was."

"Any callers of interest?" Pitt avoided a fat woman with two children in tow.

"Who knows?" Innes replied. "People don't often make a big show o' calling on a moneylender. Come in the back door, and leave the same. 'Is establishment was designed to be discreet. Part of 'is trade, as it were."

Pitt frowned. "It would be. He would discourage a good deal of his custom if he were obvious, but for precisely that reason I would have expected him to keep some sort of protection." They stopped at the curb, waited a few moments for a space in the traffic, then crossed. "After all he must have had a lot of unhappy clients," he said on the far side. "In fact a good many even desperate. Who was he receiving alone at night?"

Innes supplied the obvious answer. "Someone 'e weren't frightened of. Question is, why wasn't 'e? 'Cos 'e thought 'e were protected?" He sniffed. "Or 'e thought the person weren't dangerous? 'Cos 'e was expectin' someone else? 'Cos 'e were crossed by someone 'e knew? Gets interestin', when you think about it a bit."

Pitt would like to have agreed, but at the back of his mind was the spare, charming figure of Lord Byam. Would Weems have expected his lordship of the Treasury to commit murder over a sum of twenty pounds a month? Hardly. And if he were going to, then surely he would have at the beginning, not now, two years later?

"Yes it does," he agreed aloud. "What about this clerk and errand runner? What sort of a man is he?"

"Very ordinary." Innes shook his head. "Sort of gray little man you see ducking in and out o' alleys, hurryin' along the edge o' pavements all 'round Clerkenwell, an' can never bring ter mind again if yer try. Never know if it were the one you were lookin' for, or just someone like 'im. Name's Miller. They call 'im Windy, don't know why, unless it's because 'e's a coward." He pulled a face. "But then I'd say 'e was canny rather, more sense than ter stay and fight a battle 'e in't fitted ter win."

"Description fits half a million gray little men around London," Pitt said unenthusiastically, passing a group of women arguing loudly over a basket of fish. A brewer's dray lumbered by majestically, horses shining in the sun, harness bright, drayman immaculate and immensely proud. A coster in a striped apron and flat black hat called out his wares with no audible pause to draw breath.

They bore left from Compton Street into Cyrus Street, and within moments Innes stopped and spoke to a constable standing to attention on the pavement. He stood even more stiffly and stared straight ahead of him, his uniform spotless. His buttons gleamed and his helmet sat straight on his head as if it had been dropped on a plumb line.

Pitt was introduced.

"Yessir!" the constable said smartly. "No one come or gorn since I bin 'ere, sir. No one asked for Mr. Weems. I reckon as 'ow the word's gorn out, and no one will now. Everyone pretendin' as they never knew 'im."

"Not surprisingly," Pitt said dryly. "Murdered men are often unpopular, except with a few who love notoriety. But people 'round here won't want that kind of attention; most especially those who actually did know him. His friends won't want to own such a man for acquaintance now, and his enemies will make themselves as close to invisible as they can. As you say, the word will have gone out. We'd better go inside and have a look at the rooms where it happened."

"Right sir," Innes said, leading the way. The front of the house appeared to be an apothecary's shop such as one might drop into to purchase a headache remedy or other such nostrum, but past the rows of dusty jars and bottles there was another door, much heavier and stronger than would be usual in such a place. At present it was unlocked and swung open easily on oiled hinges, but when they were through into the carpeted passage Pitt looked back and noticed the powerful bolts. This was certainly not an entrance anyone would force without several men behind a battering ram. William Weems had been well prepared to defend himself, it would seem. So who had gained his confidence sufficiently to obtain entry, and when Weems was alone?

The office was up the stairs along a short passage and had a pleasant window overlooking Cyrus Street. It was a room perhaps ten feet by twelve and furnished with an oak desk with several drawers, a large, comfortable chair behind it, three cabinets with drawers and cupboards, and a chair for visitors. The door on the far side led presumably to the kitchen and living quarters.

Weems had apparently been sitting in the chair behind the desk when he was shot. There was a large amount of blood spattered around and already in the heat a couple of flies had settled.

On the walls were three sporting prints which might or might not have been of value, a very handsome, brightly polished copper warming pan, and the hackbut Innes had mentioned in the morgue. It was a beautiful piece of workmanship, the metal butt engraved, the flaring barrel smoothed to a satin-fine gleam. Pitt reached out and took it down very carefully, holding it in his handkerchief and from the underneath, not to smudge any marks there might be on it, any threads of fabric, smears of blood, anything at all that would be of use. He looked at it carefully, turning it over and over. It was beautifully balanced. He peered down the barrel and sniffed it. It smelled of polish. Finally he held it as if to fire it, and tightened his finger, pointing it at the floor. Nothing happened. He pulled hard.

"The firing pin has been filed down," he said at last. "Did you know that?"

"No sir. We didn't touch it." Innes looked surprised. "Then I suppose it can't've bin that what killed 'im!"

Pitt looked at it again. The blind pin was not shiny. It had not been touched with a file or rasp recently. There was a dark patina of time over it.

"Not possible," he said, shaking his head. "This is strictly ornamental now.'' He replaced it on the wall where he had found it. On the shelf below there were half a dozen little boxes, three of metal, one of soapstone, one of ebony, one of ironwood. He opened them all one by one. Three were empty, one had two small shotgun pellets in it, the other two each had a few grains of gunpowder.

"I wonder when that was last full," he said thoughtfully. "Not that it helps us a lot without a gun." He looked down and saw with surprise the excellent quality of the carpet, which was soft and dyed in rich, muted colors. He squatted down and turned over the corner and saw what he expected, dozens of tiny hand-tied knots to every inch.

"Find something?" Innes asked curiously.

"Only that he spent a lot of money on his carpets," Pitt replied, straightening up. "Unless, of course, he took it from someone in repayment of a debt."

Innes's eyebrows shot up. " 'Round 'ere? No one who borrows from the likes o' Weems 'as carpets at all, let alone ones what are worth sellin'."

"True," Pitt agreed, straightening up. "Unless he had a different class of customer, a gentleman who got in over his head gambling, perhaps, and Weems had a fancy for the carpet."

"That'd mean Weems went to 'is 'ome," Innes pointed out. "An' I can't see any gentleman bein' pleased ter entertain Weems in 'is 'ome, can you sir?"

Pitt grinned. "No I can't. You may as well know, the reason the powers that be are so concerned in this case is that our Mr. Weems indulged in a little blackmail as well. He had some very important connections, through a relative who was a servant, we are told."

"Well now." Innes looked interested, and there was a flash of satisfaction in his sharp, intelligent face. "I was wondering, but I thought as maybe you wasn't able ter say. We don't usually get cases like this taken from us. After all, who cares about one usurer more or less? But a blackmailer is different. You reckon it were someone 'e 'ad the squeeze on as shot 'im?"

"I hope not. It's going to be very embarrassing if it is," Pitt said with sudden vehemence. "But it's certainly not impossible."

"An' I suppose you can't say as who it is?"

"Not unless I have to."

"Thought so." Innes was quite resigned and there was no resentment in him. He knew he had been explained to as far as Pitt was permitted, perhaps further, and he appreciated that. "Either way, some things come ter mind," he said thoughtfully. "It were someone as 'e weren't frit of as was 'ere, an' 'e should 'a bin frit out of 'is skin of someone important 'e 'ad the black on."

Pitt grinned. "Whoever it was, he should have been frit to death!" he said wryly.

Innes flashed him a look of bright candor. " 'Alf o' me 'opes we don't catch the poor beggar. I 'ate blackmailers even more than I 'ate moneylenders. Vermin all o' them."

Pitt agreed tacitly. "Where was he?"

"In the chair be'ind the desk, like 'e were talking ter someone, or takin' money. 'E weren't expectin' it, that's fer sure. Nothin' upset, chair weren't knocked over—"

Pitt stared at the scene for several moments, trying to visualize the large, complacent Weems sitting back in his chair staring at whoever it was standing roughly where Pitt was now. He had almost certainly come prepared to kill. Hardly anyone possessed a gun, let alone carried one about with them. Perhaps the meeting had been civil to begin with, then suddenly it had changed, either a quarrel, or else simply the visitor had reached the point where he no longer needed to pretend, and he had taken the gun from its concealment and fired it. Except what could conceal a gun large enough to fire that spray of shot?

He looked around. All the drawers were closed, nothing was out of order, nothing crooked, nothing broken.

As if reading his thoughts Innes shook his head.

"If they searched they did it very careful," he observed.

"Have you looked yet?" Pitt asked.

"Not yet. We went fer witnesses first. 'Oped someone might 'ave seen someone comin' or goin', but if they did they in't sayin'."

"What about this errand runner—Miller?"

"Nothin' so far, but I'll try again."

"Better keep at it, might turn up something. Meantime we'll look. Weems's papers might be interesting, not only for what they say, but for what they don't."

"Reckon the murderer took 'is own records?" Innes said hopefully.

"Seems a likely thing to do," Pitt assented, opening the first drawer in the desk.

Innes began on the cabinet nearest him and they worked systematically for over an hour. Innes found the general accounts full of names and addresses of local people, together with neatly written records of money borrowed and repayments made, with exorbitant interest, down to the last farthing, with dates and amounts all scrupulously noted, plus balance outstanding and the date on which it was due, and the ever increasing usury.

There were also the ordinary accounts of his daily household expenses, purchases and investments, which were considerable.

It was Pitt who found the other list of names and far larger sums written beside them, this time without dates. But there were addresses and they were not in Clerkenwell or any area like it, but Mayfair, Belgravia and Hyde Park. His eye skipped over them again for the name of Sholto Byam, but he did not see it. It was a short list, too short to make such an error.

"Got something?" Innes was looking at him with interest.

"Another list," Pitt replied. "It seems our Mr. Weems had a second and quite different clientele."

"Nobs?" Innes said quickly.

"Looks like it," Pitt agreed. "I've heard some of these names, and the addresses are certainly nobs. Not likely their servants—wouldn't get the chance to spend this kind of money, for a start, and no usurer in his right mind would lend more than a few shillings to a servant."

"Interesting." Innes stopped what he was doing.

"Very." Pitt looked at the list again. "Most of the amounts had already been repaid in full. There are only three outstanding: Addison Carswell of Curzon Street, Mayfair; Samuel Urban of Whitfield Street, Bloomsbury; and Clarence Latimer of Beaufort Gardens, Knightsbridge." He stopped with a sick jolt. The name Samuel Urban was familiar. Surely it was a coincidence? The Urban he knew was an inspector of police in his own station of Bow Street! He could not possibly be in debt to a usurer like Weems. Not for the figure here, which was in excess of two years' salary.

"What is it?" Innes's face was totally innocent. Obviously the names meant nothing to him.

"One of these people is a colleague," Pitt said slowly. "In my own station."

Innes looked stricken, his sharp features touched with both confusion and pity.

"You mean one of us? Is it for much?"

"It would take me two years to earn it," Pitt replied unhappily. "And he's the same rank as I am—in uniform."

"Oh my Gawd!" Innes was obviously shaken. "What about the other two. D'yer know them?"

"No—but we'll have to look into them."

"Maybe that's why you were put in," Innes said, pulling a face. "Maybe it in't only ter protect the nobs, mebbe we got some ti-dying up of our own to do."

"Maybe." Pitt folded the list and put it in his pocket. "But that isn't all."

"D'yer find anything about the nob on 'ose account yer came?"

"Not yet," Pitt said, beginning to go through the drawer below the one he had just finished. "Let me know if you find any more names on lists other than routine household accounts."

"Right." And Innes also resumed his task.

But three hours later when every piece of paper on the premises had been examined, and the office and the bedroom, the kitchen and the bathroom facilities had been searched, even the mattress turned and the carpet lifted, they had found nothing more of interest. They finished in the kitchen, staring despondently into the dead fireplace.

"Easy to see 'ow Mrs. Cairns just made 'is breakfast in 'ere an' seein' the light through there"—Innes gestured towards the office—"took it as 'e was up, called out it was ready, and then left 'im to it. I gather she weren't overfond of 'im neither. She lives local, so I suppose she knew 'is reputation."

Pitt debated whether to see the woman himself, but decided Innes was efficient and he would not slight him by redoing his job.

"Yes," he agreed absently, staring at the wooden dresser with its racks of blue-and-white plates.

"I can't see anything but keeping our noses to the ground, and following up these lists," Innes went on, his eyes on Pitt's face.

"Nor can I, for the moment." Pitt made as if to look through the kitchen drawers one at a time, then abandoned it. He had already done it twice.

"Find any traces o' your nob?" Innes asked anxiously.

"No . . ." Pitt replied slowly. "No I didn't—and that is very strange, because he was sure I would: that is why I was sent for. Weems actually told him he had records of their dealings, for his own protection." He did not mention the letter.

"Then whoever killed Weems took them," Innes said, pushing his lips together grimly. "Looks bad for your nob, sir—I'm afraid."

"But if he took them, why did he call us?" Pitt reasoned. "That doesn't make sense."

"Mebbe 'e wasn't sure 'e 'ad 'em all," Innes suggested.

"So he called us and confessed the connection anyway?" Pitt shook his head. "He's not a fool. He'd have ridden it out and called us only if something did come up. No, he expected us to find his name here."

"Mebbe he tried ter find it an' couldn't." Innes was playing devil's advocate.

"Does the place look to you as if it has been searched?" Pitt asked.

"No," Innes conceded. "Or, if anyone took anything, they knew where ter find it. It was all as neat as yer like."

"So either there was nothing here, or the murderer knew where it was, and took it with him."

"Can't think of anything else." Innes frowned. "But it's curious, I'll give yer that—very curious."

"We've a long way to go yet." Pitt straightened up and looked towards the door. "We'd better get on with finding some of Weems's customers."

"Yes sir," Innes agreed obediently. "Poor devils."

CHAPTER
TWO

Charlotte Pitt was frantically busy. Her sister Emily, remarried less than a year after her widowhood, was now expecting a child, which was a source of great happiness both to her and to her husband, Jack. But since Jack had very recently committed himself to seeking nomination as a candidate for Parliament, her rather erratic health was something of an embarrassment. Her first pregnancy with Edward several years before had been relatively easy, but this time she was suffering moments of dizziness and nausea, and found herself unable to stand for the long hours necessary for greeting and receiving at all the sorts of functions it was required both to attend and to host, if Jack were to succeed.

Therefore Charlotte had accepted Emily's offer of a little financial assistance to go toward employing extra domestic help in her own home, several quite marvelous new gowns, and the loan of three or four pieces of Emily's jewelry, her first husband having been both titled and extremely wealthy. All of which was held by Emily to be a fair exchange for Charlotte's time, thought and endeavor to act as hostess for her, or with her, when the occasion required.

Tonight was just such an occasion. Emily was lying in her room, feeling distinctly poorly, and this was the night of the ball she had arranged in order to meet several of the most important people in Jack's campaign for selection. The seat for which he was hoping was a safe Liberal stronghold, and if he could obtain a nomination for the candidacy, when election time came he was sure to win, so the competition was strong. The Conservatives had not held that seat in decades.

This function was of great importance, therefore Emily had dispatched a footman with a letter only this afternoon, and now Charlotte was pacing the floor in the hall, her heart in her mouth with nervousness, going over arrangements for the umpteenth time. She looked yet again at the banks of flowers at the top of the stairway, in the reception rooms, in the withdrawing room and on the dining room table. The table had been a source of immense anxiety, even though it was Emily's plan and the cook's and the kitchen staff's execution, yet Charlotte still felt it was her final responsibility.

All manner of fruit was arranged in with the mound of flowers so that the center of the table was covered from end to end with its gorgeous display. Around the rest of the surface were piled all the requisite delicacies: crackers, cakes and bonbons; fruit-flavored soufflés, dazzling creams, bright jellies and foaming trifles in glass dishes; oyster patties, lobster salads, veal cakes; cold salmon, game pie, and fowls of several sorts, both boiled and roasted. These last had been carefully carved before having been brought to the table, and then tied together with white satin ribbon so they needed merely a touch of the hand to enable guests to help themselves to meat. Soup was the only dish that would be hot, and that would be served in cups for ease.

Also, naturally, there would be sherry, claret, light and sparkling wines, punch, fruit cups and gallons of champagne.

The Hungarian band was already present, partaking of a little refreshment in the servants' hall before tuning up ready for the evening. The footmen were in their livery, hair powdered immaculately, the pink-and-silver lights were on at the front of the house, and Chinese lanterns in gay colors were lit in the garden for those who wished to take a little air.

She could think of nothing more to be done, and yet she could not sit down or relax in the slightest. It was a little before ten o'clock, and she could not expect even the earliest guests, those who quite pointedly felt they had somewhere better to finish the evening, to arrive for another hour.

Jack was in his evening clothes ready to receive his guests, and had gone into his study to ponder over the information he had been given on various people's political interests, relationships and spheres of influence. There was plenty of time for Charlotte to go upstairs again and see Emily, and assure her one more time that everyone would understand her absence, and the whole evening would be an excellent success because her foresight and planning had been so thorough.

She went slowly up the great winding staircase, lifting her skirts so as not to trip on them, and along the balcony above, which was now decked with flowers. In another hour she would be standing there welcoming the guests and explaining herself, and Emily's absence. Please heaven she would remember what the footman at the door had said were their names, or they would have the tact to introduce themselves again!

Up the next flight she turned left along the landing to Emily's room. She knocked briefly and went in. Emily was lying on top of the bed in a loose, pale-blue-and-green peignoir, her fair hair over her shoulders. Her face was unusually pale and a trifle pinched around the nose and mouth. She smiled rather wanly as Charlotte came in and sat down on the bed beside her.

"Ah, my dear," Charlotte said gently. "You do look wretched. I'm so sorry."

"It'll pass," Emily said with more hope than conviction. "It wasn't nearly so bad with Edward. I felt a trifle squeamish some mornings, but it was gone by ten or eleven o'clock at the very worst. Did you feel like this with Jemima or Daniel? If you did you were very stoic. I never knew it."

"No I didn't," Charlotte admitted. "In fact for the first two or three months I felt better than ever. But you are very early yet. This might not last more than a few weeks."

"Weeks." Emily's blue eyes were full of disgust. "But I've so much to do! This is the beginning of the season and I must give balls, receptions, and attend the races at Ascot, the Henley Regatta, the Eton and Harrow cricket match, and endless luncheons, dinners and teas." She slid down in the bed a little, hunching herself. "Jack won't get the candidacy if they think his wife's an invalid. The competition is terribly hot. Fitz Fitzherbert is highly suitable, and under all that devastating charm I think he might be quite clever."

"Don't meet disaster halfway," Charlotte said, trying to comfort her. "No doubt Mr. Fitzherbert will have his problems as well, it is simply that we do not know of them. But then it is our business to see that he does not know of ours. Let us just get this evening over successfully, and by next week you may feel much better. Everything is in good order, the table looks like a Dutch still life—it seems a shame to touch it."

"What about the band?" Emily said anxiously. "Are they here? Are they properly dressed, and sober?"

"Of course they are," Charlotte assured her. "They are immaculate, all in black with lovely blue sashes. And yes, they are perfectly sober—I think. Maybe one of the fiddlers was a touch more cheerful than is warranted so far, but quite well behaved. You have no cause for concern, I promise you."

"I'm very grateful. But Charlotte, please, do be sweet to everyone." She reached out her hand and took Charlotte's. "However fatuous they are, or condescending, or whatever objectionable opinions they express? We cannot afford to offend them if Jack is to succeed. He is so new in the political arena. And some of the oddest people are highly influential."

Charlotte put her hand on her heart. "I promise I will be the essence of tact and will neither express an undignified or unasked-for opinion about anything, nor laugh at anything at all except what was unquestionably meant as a joke." She watched the tension ease out of Emily and the uncertainty change to laughter.

"I will not mention that my husband is a policeman," she went on. "I know that is quite socially disastrous, unless of course he is of such senior rank, and a gentleman born, like Micah Drummond. And since Thomas is neither of these things, and both would be necessary, I shall lie like a horse trader." Pitt's father had been a gamekeeper on a country estate. Pitt came by his beautiful diction by having been educated with the only son of the big house, to keep the boy company. He was not a gentleman by birth, sympathy or inclination.

Charlotte, who had been born to an aspiring middle-class family, considerably above those who labored for a living and yet not quite into the aristocracy, had had to learn how to cope with only one resident serving girl, and a woman who came in twice a week to do the heavy scrubbing. She had learned how to cook and how to mend clothes, to shop economically, and to manage her household with efficiency, and even some enjoyment.

Emily, on the other hand, had learned how to oversee the workings of an enormous mansion in fashionable London, and on weekends from time to time, and longer spells out of season, of Ashworth Hall in the home counties. She had always been socially ambitious and quick to learn, enjoying the color and the subtleties, the challenge of wits and the exercise of charm. By now she had built herself a considerable reputation, which had even survived her early remarrriage, and she was determined to use it to help Jack attain his newly set goal, affirmed so intensely after the revelations made during the murders at Highgate Rise.

"I shall be the soul of tact to absolutely everyone," Charlotte finished triumphantly. "Even if I burst my stays with the effort."

Emily giggled. "Be especially nice to Lord Anstiss, please? He will probably be the most important man here." Suddenly the lightness vanished and she was utterly serious. "If anyone drives you frantic, stop before you say anything and think of that poor little woman in her wretched rooms Stephen Shaw took you to, and tens of thousands like her, sick and hungry and cold because their landlords won't mend the roofs or the drains, and they cannot afford to leave because there's nowhere else to go. Then you'll be civil to the Devil himself if it will help."

"I will," Charlotte promised, leaning forward and brushing the hair off Emily's brow gently. "Believe me, I am not so self-indulgent or so undisciplined as you think."

Emily said nothing, but lowered her eyes and smiled more widely.

For another thirty minutes they talked of fashion, gossip, who might be coming this evening, whom they liked or disliked, and why. Then Charlotte tidied the bed, straightening the sheets and plumping the pillows, and assured Emily one more time of her preparations, and the tact she would exercise, regardless of temptation, and took her leave ready to await the first arrivals.

Jack met her on the stairs. He was a handsome man, not perhaps in the most traditional way, but he had remarkably fine dark gray eyes with lashes any woman would have committed crimes for, and the most utterly charming smile. Indeed in their first acquaintance both Emily and Charlotte had discounted him as a deal too smooth to be of any virtue at all. But a guarded wariness had gradually turned into respect and then affection when he had proved himself a friend of both courage and judgment in exceptionally difficult circumstances after Emily's first husband had been murdered, and Emily herself had fallen under suspicion. It had been some time before Emily had learned to love him, but now she had no doubt about it whatever, and Charlotte was happy every time she thought of them both.

"How is she?" Jack asked, glancing upwards towards Emily's room.

"She'll be all right," Charlotte said quickly. "It will pass, I promise you."

He made an attempt to look unconcerned. "Are you ready?" He glanced at her new gown, a gift from Emily for the occasion and something she would never have had the money for herself, nor indeed an event at which to wear such a thing. It was a deep Prussian blue, a shade which suited her dark auburn hair and honey-warm complexion. Naturally, since it was Emily's gift, it was up to the minute in fashion, décolleté at the front, with a paneled skirt embroidered asymmetrically, very à la mode, and scarcely any bustle at all. The best people were wearing only the very slightest padding this season, but a most elegant train.

Jack had been farsighted enough to learn something about fashion, and he fully appreciated the gown both for its social statement and for the way it flattered her. But mostly, she suspected, because he understood the way it made her feel. He too had spent a good deal of his life with insufficient money to dress or behave as he wished.

His smile broadened to a grin. There was no need for words; explanations would have been crass.

They had reached the top of the stairs when the clatter of horses outside announced the first arrivals, and a moment later the doors opened to a babble of chatter and laughter, a rustle of cloaks being removed, hard heels on the marble floor, and silk and taffeta skirts rattling against each other, and against the balustrade of the stair. The guests swept upward to be greeted, mortified that they were first, but totally unable to retreat and return at a better time. It was simply not done to be first. Then who else would mark one's arrival?

"Sir Reginald—Lady West, how delightful to see you," Charlotte said with a radiant smile. "I am Mrs. Pitt. Mrs. Radley is my sister, but most unfortunately she has been taken unwell, so it is my good fortune to stand in her place and make you welcome. Of course you are already acquainted with my brother-in-law, Mr. Jack Radley."

"How do you do, Mrs. Pitt," Lady West said a trifle coolly, taken aback at not finding whom she expected. "I hope Mrs. Radley's indisposition is nothing serious?"

"Not at all," Charlotte assured her. It would be indelicate to mention its cause, but it could be implied. "It is one of the trials women have to bear, and it is best done graciously."

"Oh—of course—I see." Lady West collected her wits and managed to force a smile. It was annoying to be caught out in slow thinking and she was irritated with herself for being stupid, and also with Charlotte for having observed it. "Please give her my very best wishes for her recovery."

"I will—most kind of you. I am sure she will be obliged." And with that the Wests moved on to greet Jack, and for him to escort them into the first room cleared for dancing. Charlotte turned to the couple immediately behind them, a dyspeptic-looking young man with ginger hair and a girl in pink, while at the foot of the stairs yet another couple were already being helped out of their cloaks and looking upward.

It was a further half hour before the first guest arrived whom Charlotte knew even by reputation other than Emily's careful schooling, and a further fifteen minutes before she saw with great pleasure the tall, erect, almost gaunt figure of Lady Vespasia Cumming-Gould. She had been Emily's first husband's great-aunt, and for many years now one of Charlotte's dearest friends. Indeed Great-Aunt Vespasia had conspired with Charlotte and Emily in helping to solve many of Pitt's cases, meddling with considerable flair in the detection of crime, and less successfully in the reform of laws regarding social conditions about which they felt most passionately.

Had it not been totally unacceptable, and therefore embarrassing to everyone, Charlotte would have raced down the stairs and taken Aunt Vespasia's cloak herself. As it was she had to be content to mutter some polite nonsense to the large woman she was at that moment greeting, and something agreeable but equally inane to her husband, who was dressed more vividly than she. There was a scarlet sash over his chest with a wonderful array of medals and orders bejeweling him. She could do no more than glance over their shoulders at Great-Aunt Vespasia climbing slowly up the curve of the staircase, her silver head high, her tiara winking in the lights, her dove-gray gown sewn with crystals like stars, and her train precisely, to the inch, the most fashionable length.

"Good evening Charlotte, my dear," she said calmly when she reached the top. "I assume you are standing in for Emily?"

"I am afraid she is not feeling well this evening." Charlotte dropped the very slightest curtsey. "She will be terribly disappointed not to have seen you, but I am delighted to be in her place."

Vespasia smiled with perfectly genuine pleasure, inclined her head in acknowledgment, spoke warmly to Jack, and then swept past to join the throng in the first reception room. As she entered there was a hush, a turning of heads and a quick murmur of appreciation. Everyone knew who she was. Fifty years ago she had been one of the great beauties of her day, and even now at eighty she had a structure of bone and a hairline across the brow that made many a younger woman envious. She was frailer than she had been even a short while ago, but she still held her head as if her tiara were a crown, and could with a glance freeze an impertinent comment on the lips of an unfortunate offender.

Charlotte felt a lift of pleasure, almost excitement, as she watched Aunt Vespasia disappear among the crowd. With her here the whole evening would have a quality of glamour and purpose far deeper than a mere social exercise. Something of importance might be begun.

A few moments later she welcomed Mr. Addison Carswell and his wife. Emily had told her he was a magistrate of considerable influence, sitting in one of the central city courts. He was not a remarkable man in appearance, of average height and slightly stocky build. His hair was receding although it was still thick from the top of his head backwards, but it was nondescript brown, and his mustache was minimal, his cheeks clean shaven. It was only when she was speaking to him in the usual polite, rather stilted phrases that she observed the strength of his features, and the intelligence in his eyes. It was a face of good balance, and without meanness.

Mrs. Carswell was a solid woman, strong and thickset, but her face was handsome in its own fashion, with straight nose, steady eye and a candor of bearing that indicated an inner calm. This social whirl might find her out of her depth. She looked the kind of woman who had no ready wit to swap comments with the ladies of high fashion, but neither would she need it for her happiness. Her values might rest largely in her home and family.

Accompanying their parents were the four Carswell daughters, each presented in turn. The eldest, Mary Ann, had come with her husband, Algernon Spencer. He was a large, rather bluff young man with too much hair for the current mode, but presentable enough otherwise. Mary Ann herself was as pleased as any girl might be who has succeeded in marrying reasonably well, and ahead of her sisters.

Miss Maude, Miss Marguerite and Miss Mabel were all fair haired, rose skinned and comely enough, if rather too like each other to be easily told apart or offer any memorable individuality. They all curtseyed gracefully, looked under their eyelashes with modest expressions of pleasure, and proceeded up the stairs to take their places, be presented to whomsoever their mother chose, or could arrange, and talk inconsequentially but with charm. They had been well schooled in their duty and knew it down to the last glance, murmur, gesture of fan and swish of skirt. No doubt within the next two seasons even the youngest of them would find a suitable husband, which was quite necessary, since two seasons was all society permitted a young woman before writing her off. Naturally they were all dressed in white, or as close to it as made little difference.

On this occasion their brother, Mr. Arthur Carswell, was not with them, having decided to go to a different function, because there would be present at that a young lady whose hand in marriage he aspired to win.

A little behind the Carswells Charlotte was delighted to see Somerset Carlisle. His curious, wry and highly individual face was full of interest, not at the social scene, in which he took no concern at all, but at the interplay of character and political ambition. He had been a member of Parliament himself for several years, to begin with conforming with his party's views, then as his passion for reform overcame his discretion, branching more and more into his own activities. Charlotte had first met him when his zeal had overridden his propriety to the extent of involving him in the events surrounding the murders in Resurrection Row some years earlier. She had liked him personally, and sympathized with his aims, even then. He had also become a fast friend, and in many instances a collaborator, with Great-Aunt Vespasia. It was Somerset Carlisle, with Aunt Vespasia, who had encouraged Jack to consider Parliament.

He reached the top of the staircase and Charlotte greeted him with delight.

"Anything I can do to help Jack," he replied with a smile. "I need an ally in the House, heaven knows!"

"What do you think are his chances?" she said more seriously, lowering her voice so those around them could not overhear.

"Well Fitzherbert is his main rival," Carlisle replied. "I don't think the others count. But Fitz is well known and well liked. He's unmarried as yet, but he's betrothed to a Miss Odelia Morden, who is very well connected." He raised his eyes momentarily, and then met hers again. It was a very expressive gesture. "Her mother is third daughter of the earl of something, I forget what, and there is plenty of money." His voice lifted cheerfully. "On the other hand, not more money than Emily, and Emily has hers now, whereas Odelia may not see a penny for years. Emily certainly has more intelligence and political savoir faire. And as we know, Emily is capable of learning and adapting to almost anything, if she has a mood to; and she can doubtless be as witty, as fashionable and as charming as anybody alive."

"I don't think Mr. Fitzherbert has arrived yet," Charlotte said, trying to recall the names of everyone she had welcomed so far. "Is he very ambitious? What are his beliefs, the issues he cares about?"

Carlisle's smile broadened. "I don't think he has anything so specific as an issue, my dear. He is not a crusader, simply a very charming fellow who has decided that Parliament offers a more interesting career than any other presently open to him." He lifted one shoulder a little. "He will fill it with all the intelligence and grace he possesses, which are considerable, but I doubt with passion, unless something occurs in his life to waken his sensibilities." His smile remained but his eyes were serious. "Don't underestimate him. That is precisely the kind of man many leaders desire— popular with the electorate, not disturbing to the prejudices or the intellect, and above all malleable."

Charlotte's spirits sank. Already she could see failure more sharply, which hurt not only for Emily's and Jack's sakes, but because she truly believed in the goals they would strive for. She had seen the fearful slums just as clearly as Jack, and cared every bit as much for their victims. She had wished as fiercely to begin some small legislative step towards crushing the profiteers who hid behind anonymous companies and ranks of rent collectors, managers and offices of lawyers with gray clothes, scratching pens and hard, blank faces.

"It also depends a great deal on individual patrons," Carlisle went on, lowering his voice still further. "Whatever the actual politicians say, if you can get Lord Anstiss on your side, you are almost assured of selection. He has a great deal more power and influence than most people realize. And of course selection for the seat is tantamount to victory. The Tories haven't won it in living memory!"

The arriving guests were beginning to crush closely behind Carlisle. She was holding up progress by indulging in overlong conversation with him. Already she had failed to perform her duty to the highest. She caught his eye and saw a quick understanding in it as he felt the pressure behind him, and he bowed very slightly and proceeded across the landing towards the first reception room and was lost in the bank of flowers, the swirl of skirts and the glitter of jewels and medals.

Charlotte had not heard about Pitt's latest case, so the names of Lord and Lady Byam meant nothing to her. But as the stair was now becoming more than a trifle cramped she did no more than smile at them dazzlingly and say how delighted she was that they had come, and inwardly note his sensitive, unusual face with its arresting eyes, and the calm inner dignity of Lady Byam, as if she knew the social stage for what it was worth, and no more. It was a quality Charlotte admired.

Odelia Morden she was also able to speak to only in the briefest manner, as she reached the top of the staircase in rather a crush of other fashionable ladies at the optimum moment that convention demanded: not early enough to insult, nor late enough to overflatter or dull her own worth. After all one did not wish to allow others to think one had nowhere else to go. It did not do for people to think too well of themselves. Mr. Morden and Lady Flavia Morden were ordinary enough in appearance, in spite of her having been born daughter of an earl, if Somerset Carlisle was correct. But Odelia had an air of distinction about her; she was unusually handsome, with fine hazel eyes, fair hair a trifle lacking in thickness, and regular features. Her smile was sufficiently individual that one remembered her without difficulty, and yet it was not forward nor insolent, nor yet lacking in candor.

Charlotte summed her up as a rival worthy of respect and certainly not to be taken lightly.

Herbert Fitzherbert came only a few moments after his betrothed. He made rather more of a stir at his entry. He was remarkably charming, seemingly effortlessly so. He had simply to smile and people found themselves warming to him. There were in his eyes both imagination and humor, as if he were willing to share some deep understanding with whoever he spoke to, and at the same time a total lack of deliberate guile. There seemed a vulnerability in him that led many a woman to imagine some secret hurt which only she could ease, and dreams that lay waiting to be realized if only opportunity offered. And yet he was not a poseur, or very little, and with his charm the temptation was great. He had enough intelligence to be able to laugh at himself now and again, and sufficient good humor not to resent it if from time to time others did also.

Charlotte could imagine there were several he irritated, probably men, as would be inevitable, but she also thought that if he took the trouble to court them they would nearly always thaw. To dislike him would appear both petty and churlish.

He was a trifle above average height, with fair hair and gray-blue eyes, but it was the innate grace with which he did everything that left the most lasting impression, along with his rueful, whimsical smile.

Even before Charlotte had finished speaking to him she considered the very real possibility that with all Emily's work, the money she had inherited and the efforts that Great-Aunt Vespasia might put forth on his behalf, Jack still would not win the selection. "Fitz" would have to make some serious mistake before his loss could be counted on. She was ashamed to find ugly hopes fluttering through her mind—perhaps he would drink too much and commit an unforgivable indiscretion, like making an indecent suggestion to an elderly duchess? But with his charm she might well enjoy it! Or perhaps he would seduce someone's daughter—a wife would matter far less, as long as she was discreet. Or he might vociferously espouse some completely unacceptable cause, such as female suffrage, or Irish Home Rule. Perhaps that was the best hope?

"Good evening, Mr. Fitzherbert," Charlotte said with a dazzling smile. She intended to be especially courteous to him, as a sort of barrier, and was annoyed to find herself liking him even before he spoke, in spite of all her mental precautions. "I am Mrs. Pitt, Mr. Radley's sister-in-law."

"Oh yes," he said with a quick understanding. "Emily said you might be here, if she were not feeling her best. It is remarkably kind of you to give up your time. At least half of us are bound to bore you to within an inch of sleep."

"I am sure the other half will more than make up for it." She wanted to be unquestionably polite, and yet keep a cool distance between them. Let him consider himself in whatever half he pleased. She would claim total innocence.

He laughed outright.

"Bravo, Mrs. Pitt," he said frankly. "I am sure I am going to like you."

To rebuff him would be appallingly rude, and quite insincere.

Despising herself for being quite genuinely outwitted, and without a shred of dislike, she thanked him.

Lord Anstiss was one of the last to arrive. He came up the stairs almost alone and stopped behind Fitzherbert. He was a man of barely average height and sturdy build not yet run to fat although he was probably in his early fifties. He was balding, with fine side whiskers, but no mustache or beard, leaving his blunt, candid features plainly visible. His appearance was commanding because of his obvious strength of will and intelligence. One had only to meet his eyes once to be aware of his personality and to sense his confidence in himself, springing from achievement. He needed no one else's praise to bolster his self-worth.

Fitzherbert collected his wits rapidly and with grace, turning on the spot to smile at Lord Anstiss and apologize for causing him to wait, and moving with alacrity across the floor and into the reception room.

Charlotte turned back to the stairhead with a butterfly of nervousness high in her stomach.

"Good evening, Lord Anstiss," she said, swallowing hard and smiling. This man mattered intensely to Emily's plans. "We are so pleased you were able to come. I am Mrs. Pitt, Mrs. Radley's sister. Unfortunately she was taken unwell, which has given me the honor of standing in her place for the evening."

"I am sure you will do it with grace and skill, Mrs. Pitt," he said courteously. "But please be so kind as to convey my sympathies to Mrs. Radley, and my hope that she will be restored to full health very soon. I trust it is nothing serious?"

Mindful that a member of Parliament needs a wife who is not delicate or liable to fail in her duty, Charlotte had already worked out what to say to him.

"I am sure she will," she said with conviction. "It is a malady which affects women only in the first month or two, but if we are to provide heirs for our husbands it seems inevitable."

"I am afraid it does," he said with a slight bow. "I am delighted it is for such a fortunate reason." He glanced at the momentarily empty staircase behind him, then offered her his arm. "May I escort you to the ballroom? I hear the sounds of music." And indeed the band had already begun the opening quadrille.

So far all was well. Everyone who was of importance had accepted her. Now she must make sure she spoke to everyone, passed some small exchange that seemed personal and yet not intrusive, offended no one, and ensured that everyone felt welcome, no one was insulted or overlooked, and that there were no social disasters, the refreshments lasted, the champagne was cold, and the music in time.

"Thank you, I should be charmed," she accepted, and sailed across the landing and into the ballroom amid the flowers on his lordship's arm. They did not join the quadrille, being a trifle late, but dallied in small talk for a while, made trivial comments and smiled at everyone. Then after a suitable pause the band struck up the lancers and she was swept onto the floor. She could only just recall what to do with her feet and the train of her gown. Then familiarity reasserted itself, the years vanished and it was as if she were a girl again being traipsed around fashionable balls in hope of finding a husband. Although to be truthful, her mother had never taken her to a function as distinguished as this. It was considerably above the Ellisons' social station. They had never aspired to the aristocracy, only to gentle birth and comfortable income.

When the music was finished she thanked his lordship and curtseyed, then excused herself. Duty called. Out of the corner of her eye she saw Jack and smiled fleetingly, before introducing herself to a group of ladies she knew were influential. She had taken great heed of Emily's detailed instructions.

Since she knew very little of fashion, it being quite beyond her budget, and to speak about it only rubbed salt in the wound, she was unable to hold a conversation of any detail. Similarly, since she knew nothing about who was courting whom, who had rebuffed whom, been admired or insulted, or what drama was currently playing at which theater, she had decided to exert her charm entirely by asking other people their opinions and listening intently to their answers. It was a ploy which sat ill with her nature, but it was forced upon her by necessity, and it worked astoundingly well.

"Indeed?" she said with wide eyes as a thin lady in blazing sapphires expounded her views on the drama currently playing at the theater in the Haymarket. "Do please tell us more. You make it sound so vivid."

The lady required no second invitation. She had disliked the play and was bursting to assure her that everyone else did also, and for the same reasons.

"I am not narrow-minded, you understand," she began vigorously. "And I hope I can appreciate literature of all sorts. But this was totally self-indulgent, every conceivable horror was there and unimaginably vile appetites. It is hardly an excuse that each sin was punished in one manner or another. We still observed things which would outrage every moral instinct."

"Good gracious!" Charlotte was amazed and fascinated. "I wonder they were able to perform it in public."

Her eyes widened. "My dear Mrs. Pitt, that is exactly what I said myself."

A young man walked past them laughing, a girl giggled and blushed on his arm.

"I am so pleased I did not take my daughter," another woman in gold said fervently, shivering a little and setting her diamonds sparkling. "And I had intended to. Good drama can be so uplifting, don't you think? And a girl has to have something intelligent to discuss. Silliness is so unattractive, don't you agree?"

"Oh most," Charlotte said sincerely. "The prettiest face in the world can become tedious quite quickly if the owner has nothing of sense to say."

"Quite," the lady with the sapphires conceded hastily. "But this, I assure you, was beyond a decent person's desire to discuss, and quite unthinkable for any young lady hoping to attract a respectable gentleman. If she discussed this it would appall any person of sensibility that she was even aware of such subjects."

Another couple swept past, the girl laughing loudly.

Great-Aunt Vespasia joined the group with a gracious inclination of her head.

"So fashionable, Mrs. Harper," the sapphire lady observed, watching the couple retreating, heads close together. "Don't you agree, Lady Cumming-Gould?"

"Up to the minute," Vespasia granted. "Lovely, until she opens her mouth."

"Oh! Is she vulgar—or foolish? I had not heard." There was implicit criticism in her tone.

"Neither, so far as I know," Vespasia replied. "But she has a laugh like a frightened horse! One can hear it two streets away on a calm night."

Someone giggled, and suppressed it hastily, unsure whether it was appropriate or not. There was a hesitant silence. Suddenly all the other sounds intruded, the slither of leather soles on the polished wooden floor, the rustle of taffeta, tulle and satin bustles and trains, the murmur of talk, the chink of glass and in the next room one of the violinists retuning his instrument.

"What is the title of the play?" Charlotte inquired innocently.

"*Titus Andronicus*, but it was said to be Shakespeare," the sapphire lady answered quickly. "So I went in the belief that it would be noble and uplifting."

"Was not the language fine?" Charlotte asked.

"My dear Mrs. Pitt, I have no idea." She bridled slightly. "But if it were, that is no excuse. Far too much is excused these days on a point of style, as if style mattered! We are losing all our values. There is scandal everywhere." She sniffed. "I feel so sorry for the Princess of Wales, poor creature. She cannot help but have heard what people are saying."

"I doubt it," Vespasia said dryly. "She is as deaf as a post, poor thing—but it may save her the malicious whisperings that would otherwise be bound to wound."

"Yes indeed," said another woman, in pink, who nodded her head and set her tiara blazing in the light. "It is fearful what people will say. What with her husband keeping mistresses quite openly for all the world to see—Lillie Langtry—I ask you! The woman is nothing better than a—" She shrugged and refused to speak the word. "And her son a complete wastrel, of which she can hardly be unaware. Do you know I even heard that the Duke of Clarence was creeping out of the palace at night and visiting women of the streets. Can you believe it?"

"I heard it was one particular woman." The sapphire lady raised her eyebrows very high and her face took on an expression of great knowledge. "And that the affaire was far beyond the mere satisfaction of one of the less forgivable appetites." She lowered her voice confidentially. "Of course it is only speculation, but some say that it had to do with those fearful murders in Whitechapel last year.

The Ripper, you know." She avoided Vespasia's eyes and her tone became critical.

"Of course I was always dubious about the value of a police force. My grandfather was irrevocably against it." She shrugged. "He said they would be expensive, intrude into a man's dignity and independence, interfere where they had no business, and do very little good. Which seems to be the case." She looked from one to another of them. "If such a thing could go on in the heart of London and six months later they have caught no one at all, it rather proves my point, does it not?"

Vespasia kicked Charlotte just as she was about to explode in defense of Pitt in particular, and the police in general.

"Your logic is impeccable," Vespasia said with a wry smile. "I should do away with doctors also. They are clearly quite useless. They could not even save the Prince Consort. In fact when I come to think of it, absolutely everyone I ever knew of died in the end."

They all turned to stare at her, none of them except Charlotte quite sure how to take this last, totally ridiculous remark.

Vespasia's face was marvelous. Not a muscle moved and there was not even a glimmer of humor in her beautiful silver-gray eyes.

Charlotte waited with her breath held. She would not spoil the delicious moment.

"Ah . . . er," the sapphire lady began, then stopped. Everyone looked at her hopefully, but she had exhausted her aplomb for the moment and fell silent.

The pink lady fidgeted, opened her mouth then changed her remark into a cough.

At last Vespasia took mercy on them.

"It is a hard world," she said sententiously. "The surgeons and physicians cannot prevent mortality, they can only ease pain and help a few accidents and diseases here and there; and the police cannot get rid of human iniquity, they can only apprehend some of the perpetrators and see they are punished, which discourages the rest." She avoided meeting Charlotte's eyes. "Even the Church has not got rid of private sin. The pity of it is I cannot think of a better idea."

"I . . . er . . . I—" Again the sapphire lady did not know what to say.

"Has anyone seen Gilbert and Sullivan's latest opera?" Charlotte came to the rescue, but did not dare look at Vespasia.

"Ah indeed, *Ruddigore*," the pink lady said gratefully. "A little sad I think, don't you? I much preferred the *Pirates of Penzance*. And I didn't understand *Princess Ida*. I am not sure whether they are for women's education or against it!"

"Women should be educated in the gentilities, nothing more," the sapphire lady said decidedly. "Academic subjects are of no use and only disturb the mind. We are not designed for such things, either by God or by nature!"

"Are they not the same?" Charlotte inquired.

"I beg your pardon?"

"God and nature," Charlotte explained.

The sapphire lady's eyebrows shot upward. "I hardly think—"

In the distance the band had begun the valse.

"If you will permit me?" Charlotte seized the opportunity to abandon the subject and move away.

But they would not permit her to escape so easily.

"Did you enjoy it, Mrs. Pitt?" the pink lady inquired with great interest.

"I beg your pardon?" Charlotte was totally confused.

"*Ruddigore!*" the lady explained patiently.

"I regret I have not seen it," Charlotte admitted. "I wonder—"

"Oh you must! I am sure—"

"Of course." Vespasia cut across and took Charlotte by the arm. "We are monopolizing you, my dear. Come with me, I shall introduce Lady Byam to you. I am sure you will find her most agreeable." And without permitting anyone to interrupt her again, she swept Charlotte away.

"You did that on purpose," Charlotte whispered fiercely.

"Of course," Vespasia agreed without a shred of remorse. "Laetitia Fox is a fool and not a particularly pleasant one. She bores me silly. But you will like Eleanor Byam, and her husband is a most important man. He has great power not only in the Treasury, but within political circles in general. His approval will help Jack. Although of course Lord Anstiss is the one whose patronage you really need."

"Tell me more about him," Charlotte requested. "I know he

is a great patron of the arts and has benefited many galleries and theaters, and that he has also given a great deal of money to charities of all natures, but what is he like as a person? What are his tastes, his likes and dislikes? What shall I speak to him of?"

"You want a great deal, my dear." Vespasia nodded courteously to people as they passed. She knew and was known by almost everyone who mattered in society, although few of them could claim more than an acquaintance with her.

Charlotte glanced at the band, who were still playing vigorously; the center of the floor was swirling with dancers.

"Regina Carswell," Vespasia said absently as they passed the Carswells engaged in conversation with a group of elderly gentlemen. "Agreeable woman, and more sense than many, but three more daughters to marry, and that is no easy task, especially when they are all much the same."

"But she has both position and money," Charlotte pointed out as they skirted around a general in scarlet and two subordinates.

"Indeed. Addison Carswell is a magistrate," Vespasia agreed. "But three daughters is still a formidable task. It is to her credit that she has kept any sense of proportion at all."

"Lord Anstiss," Charlotte prompted.

"I heard you, Charlotte. He is a man used to great power, great wealth and the respect that those things bring with them, the ability to support arts and sciences as he wishes." Vespasia accepted a glass of chilled champagne from a footman in livery. "To patronize individuals and causes," she continued, "which of course means people court his favor. All this considered, he is remarkably gracious and restrained." She nodded to an acquaintance. "There is nothing vulgar about him and he abhors ostentation, although he does enjoy good company and is not so noble as to despise admiration."

"Very good," Charlotte said softly. "Do you like him?"

"That is irrelevant," Vespasia replied.

"You don't."

"I neither like nor dislike him," Vespasia said in defense. "I know him only publicly. He has qualities I admire, and his acts I certainly approve. Personally I have spoken with him little." She sipped her champagne. "Although he has intelligence, and that always appeals. No my dear, you will have to make up your mind yourself. Just remember he has great power, never forget that, and at the moment it is Jack who matters."

"I shan't."

Vespasia smiled.

"Thank you," Charlotte said sincerely.

"Then you had better be about your duties," Vespasia prompted, and Charlotte obediently took her leave, at least temporarily. And since Emily had also stressed his importance, she felt it obligatory to make a specific effort to speak again to Lord Anstiss and assure as far as it was possible that he was in good company and aware of his welcome.

She found him with little difficulty, standing with a wineglass in one hand and talking with Lord and Lady Byam and a thin woman with flaxen fair hair and a marvelous emerald necklace. They moved aside to include Charlotte as soon as she approached them.

"An excellent affair, Mrs. Pitt," Anstiss said courteously. "Of course you know Mrs. Walters?" He inclined his head slightly, indicating the woman with the emeralds.

Charlotte had no idea who she was.

"Of course," she murmured; she would not admit to ignorance, it would be too insulting. "How charming to see you, Mrs. Walters."

"How kind," Mrs. Walters replied noncommittally. "Lord Anstiss was speaking of the opera. Do you care for music, Mrs. Pitt?"

"Indeed I do," Charlotte answered, hoping they would not ask her for a list of the performances she had seen lately. Such things were quite beyond her finances. "I enjoy all forms of music, from one person singing to please himself through to the grandest choruses."

"I had great voices in mind, rather than merely large numbers," Mrs. Walters said coolly, and it crossed Charlotte's mind that in some way this woman resented her intrusion. She wondered what the conversation had really been. She looked more closely at Mrs. Walters, and saw the fine lines of irritation in her face, as if her habitual expression was one of anticipating anger. There was a mixture of eagerness and tension in her now, and she seemed acutely aware of Lord Anstiss. Her eyes flickered to him as if she was uncertain whether to speak or not.

Charlotte smiled at her sweetly, and indeed she felt a certain sympathy.

"I was thinking of type rather than quality. Perhaps I expressed myself poorly. I apologize. Have you seen anything of great interest recently, Mrs. Walters?"

"Oh—" Mrs. Walters shrugged. "I saw *Otello* a few weeks ago. Verdi, you know? It is his latest. Have you seen it?"

"No," Charlotte admitted readily. "I have been rather preoccupied with other things. Was it excellent?"

"Oh yes. Do you not think so, Lord Anstiss?" She turned to him with a bright glance.

"Indeed." Anstiss gave a lengthy, informed and sensitive opinion of the work and of the particular performance he had seen, his face full of power and animation, his choice of words individual and obviously colored by his own intense feeling. No one interrupted him, and Charlotte listened with interest. It made her wish dearly that such events were within possibility for her. But it was never going to be more than a dream, and this was a game, a few days out of Emily's life. Charlotte should enjoy them for what they were, and do her best to acquit herself honorably.

"How well you describe it, my lord," she said with a smile. "You make me feel not only as if I had been there, but in the most excellent company."

A quick pleasure lit his face. "Thank you, Mrs. Pitt. What a charming compliment. You have made my evening doubly enjoyable in retrospect." The phrase was conventionally polite, and yet she felt had he not meant it he would have said nothing.

Mrs. Walters's face darkened. "I am sure we all find you most interesting to listen to," she said a trifle peevishly. "You must have seen something of note, Mrs. Pitt. You surely have not spent all your time pursuing your brother-in-law's career? I thought he was but very lately come to political interest."

Next to Mrs. Walters, Lord Byam disengaged himself from his group and turned towards them.

"His interest is long-standing," Charlotte contradicted. "It is his decision to stand for Parliament which is recent."

"A nice distinction," Anstiss observed with relish. "Don't you think so, Byam?"

Byam smiled, a warm, natural gesture. "I take your point, Mrs. Pitt. Still, it is a pity if it has required so much of your time you have had no opportunity to refresh yourself with theater or music."

"Oh I have, my lord." Charlotte did not wish to appear too earnest or single-minded. She racked her memory for any acceptable affair she had attended, and stretched the truth by a few years. "I did a short while ago see a delightful performance of a light opera by Messrs. Gilbert and Sullivan. Not quite Verdi, I confess, but a charming evening."

Mrs. Walters raised her eyebrows, but said nothing.

"I agree," Eleanor Byam said quickly. "We cannot be indulging in great tragedy all the time. I saw *Patience* again last month. I still found it highly entertaining, and so many tunes stayed in my mind." She glanced at her husband.

"Indeed," he agreed, but he looked not at her but at Anstiss. "Did you not find the whole plot and the humor of it delicious—knowing your opinion of the aesthetic set?"

Anstiss stared somewhere over their heads, his eyes bright with inner humor, as if he took some point deeper than the mere words. "Mr. Oscar Wilde should be flattered," he replied lightly. "His wit and his ideas have been immortalized and will be sung and whistled by half London, and done so without their knowing why."

"Particularly the song about the silver churn," Byam said quietly, smiling and looking at no one in particular. He hummed a few bars. "Magnetism is a most curious quality. Why do some have it, and some not?"

"Are you talking of metals or people?" Anstiss asked.

"Oh either," Byam answered. "The mystery is equal—to me."

"Rather an effete young man, I heard," Mrs. Walters said with a quiver in her voice. "Do you approve of him, Lord Anstiss?"

"I admire his turn of phrase, Mrs. Walters," Anstiss replied carefully. "I am not sure I would take it further than that." His tone was very slightly condescending. "I was referring to his characterization in Bunthorne. Mr. Gilbert was making satire of the aesthetic movement, of which Mr. Wilde is the leading light."

"I know that," she said crossly, and blushed.

Anstiss flashed a look at Byam, then they both looked away again, but the understanding had been there, and in Byam's face a spark of sympathy.

"Of course," Anstiss said soothingly. "I said it only to explain my own feelings. I am not personally acquainted with Mr. Wilde, or with any of his admirers, for that matter. I have read a little of his poetry, that is all."

"I prefer the classical theater." Mrs. Walters now chose to take a completely different line. "Don't you, Lady Byam? I saw Sir Henry Irving in *Hamlet* recently. That was truly inspiring."

With a quick smile at Anstiss and a glance at Eleanor Byam, Charlotte excused herself, making a remark about her duty to other guests, and retreated, leaving the field to Mrs. Walters.

Charlotte spent the next half hour exchanging polite inconsequentialities with almost everyone she had not yet spoken with, passing by the table several times to make sure it was still in good order, watching the band to ascertain they were indeed sober, about which she had some doubts, and snatching an opportunity to report to Jack on the general success of the evening.

By midnight she was again walking with Great-Aunt Vespasia in a pleasant and companionable silence. They had reached the balcony beyond the main ballroom and came upon Lord and Lady Byam standing beneath the Chinese lanterns, the soft light casting a warmth over them and making Eleanor, with her dark hair, look faintly exotic.

Greetings were formal and very polite, then conversation passed quickly through the trivial to common interests, which of course were centered on the political scene. Not unnaturally the matter of future elections arose. Neither Jack nor Herbert Fitzherbert were mentioned, but a great deal of subtle reflections were made and more than once Charlotte caught Eleanor's eye and they smiled at each other.

"Of course the matter is very complex," Byam said quite seriously, but without the pomposity that Charlotte found most trying in some people who held high office. "One can seldom make a financial decision that affects only one group of people or one interest. I think some of our would-be reformers do not appreciate that. Money represents wealth, it is not wealth itself."

"I don't understand you," Eleanor said with admirable candor. "I thought money was perhaps the most obvious form of wealth."

"Money is merely paper, my dear," Byam explained with a small smile. "Or at best gold, a comparatively useless commodity. You cannot eat it, or clothe yourself in it, nor will it serve any other of life's requirements. It is pleasing to the eye, and it does not corrupt with time, as do lesser metals; but it is less useful than steel, and immeasurably less useful than coal, timber, cotton, grain, wool or meat."

"I do not take your point." Eleanor was not yet satisfied.

At that moment they were joined by a young man with hooded, brilliant eyes, a strong nose and the most remarkably beautiful, curling, deep auburn hair, which was ill cut at present, and far too long. He plunged in to answer the question without hesitation, and without waiting to be introduced.

"Money is a convenience by which civilized man has agreed to make bartering immeasurably easier, but it is a mechanism." He held up long, sensitive hands. "And if our agreement fails because one party possesses all the goods that are worth bartering, then the means itself is useless. A loaf of bread is always a loaf of bread. It will feed a man for so many days. But a piece of paper is worth whatever we agree it is worth, no more, no less. When the agreement fails, we have financial anarchy." He looked from one to another of them. "That is what happens when we lend money to people at exorbitant rates, and pay them too little for their goods or their labor, so they can never earn sufficient to repay us. The fact that we begin with the advantage enables us to set the prices we will pay, and keep the debtor always in our power."

"You sound passionate about it, Mr. . . ." Vespasia said with interest; indeed her hesitation because she was unaware of his name did not carry the criticism of his manners that Charlotte would have expected.

"Peter Valerius." He introduced himself with only the faintest blush for having intruded in such a fashion. "Forgive me. Yes I am."

Charlotte, as hostess for the evening, introduced the others, remembering to speak of Vespasia first, as the socially senior member, and herself last. She could not recall meeting Mr. Valerius as he came in, but she could scarcely ask him now if he had been invited.

"I think usury, whether local in one man to another, or international in one nation to another, is one of the vilest practices of humanity." He turned to Charlotte. "I hope trade and banking practices will be subjects to which Mr. Radley will turn his attention?"

"I am sure he will," Charlotte said quickly. "I shall draw his attention to it myself. He is highly sensitive to social wrongs—"

"It will not win him his party's approval," Valerius warned her, seeming hardly aware of Lord Byam's presence almost at his elbow. "He will win himself few friends, and certainly no chance of promotion to office."

"I don't think he is aiming or hoping for high office," she said candidly. "It would be more than good enough to influence those who do."

He smiled suddenly and vividly. In his intense face the gesture was both charming and startling.

"And you will no doubt learn Mr. Fitzherbert's views in the matter," Byam said wryly.

"But of course," Valerius agreed with wide eyes. "Is this not what these very delightful social gatherings are for? To learn who believes what, and who is prepared to fight, how hard, and at what risk?"

"Very blunt," Byam said ruefully. "I see why you do not run for office yourself, Mr. Valerius."

Valerius colored very slightly, but he was not deterred. However before he could pursue the subject any further they were joined by a duchess like a galleon under full sail, followed by her three daughters.

"My dear Lady Byam," she said in a penetrating contralto. "How perfectly delightful to see you. Is this not a magnificent ball?" She lowered her voice only fractionally in what was apparently meant as a confidence. "And I really do believe this is Mrs. Radley's own house! At least Lady Bigelow swears it is. So many ladies hire other people's houses these days, their own not being suitably impressive, one never knows." She opened her pale eyes wide. "How can one possibly assess someone if one does not even know if the furniture belongs to them? The whole of society is coming to pieces." She leaned forward. "I must learn more about this Jack Radley. Who is he, do you know? I must admit I know nothing about him whatever." She seemed oblivious of the rest of them, and Charlotte caught a gleam of amusement in Lord Byam's eyes, but no malice.

Eleanor drew in her breath to reply, half turning toward Charlotte as if to introduce her, but the duchess plunged on.

"He isn't radical, is he?" She stared fiercely. "I can't abide radicals—so unreliable. What does Lord Anstiss think? Perhaps I shall give a ball myself. I shall invite Mr. Radley, and of course Mr. Fitzherbert, and see for myself. Shall you be at Henley this year?"

"Oh indeed," Eleanor replied. "I love watching the boats, and if the weather is agreeable it is a delightful way to spend a summer day. Shall you, your grace?"

"But of course. I have three daughters still to marry, and as we all know, regattas can be splendid for that." She nodded meaningfully. "Lord Randolph Churchill proposed to Miss Jerome after only four days' acquaintance at the Cowes regatta."

"I heard the Duke and Duchess of Marlborough were very much against it," Eleanor replied. "Although of course that was some time ago now. And it did not prevent the marriage."

"Well she was an American," the duchess pointed out reasonably. "And not everyone is prepared to marry an American, no matter how beautiful she is or how much he may need the money. I am not at all sure I should. But I shall certainly be at Henley, you may depend upon it."

She glanced around for the first time to make sure her daughters were still with her. On assuring herself they were, she resumed the conversation. "And that is one place one may be reasonably certain one will not run into the fearful Mrs. Langtry. All over London ladies are obliged to invite the wretched creature, or the Prince of Wales and the whole Marlborough House set will not come. It is too bad."

"I would rather forgo the privilege than be obliged to invite someone I did not care for," Eleanor said candidly.

"Well of course one would," the duchess agreed tartly. "But we cannot all afford to. Your position is assured, and you have no daughters to marry. I cannot indulge myself so. The duke, may the Lord bless him, has neither wit nor influence to obtain a position in the government, and I am obliged to society for all my entertainment." She screwed up her face in an expression of intensity. "Have you any acquaintance with Mr. Oscar Wilde and that very eccentric set? I hear they are quite marvelously amusing, and of course pretend to be very wicked."

She lifted her shoulders. "Young Fitzherbert told me it is all a pose. He associated with them, before he agreed to stand for Parliament, but he had to give it up. There is a fine marriage proposed. Her mother is delighted." Her voice cooled and her face lost its enthusiasm. "Quite a feather in her cap. Though I admit Odelia—if that is her name—is a handsome enough girl and knows precisely what to do, what to say, and how to dress; always an advantage. Don't you think so, Mrs. . . . ." She turned to Charlotte, her wide blue eyes full of inquiry.

"Mrs. Pitt," Charlotte supplied. "Mrs. Radley is my sister." She thought she had better explain herself before anything further was said which might prove embarrassing. "Indeed, there is always an advantage in being well taught, and biddable."

The duchess looked at her with acute perception.

"Pray do not humor me, Mrs. Pitt. I fear I have overstated my case. It is good in brides; it becomes a bore in a married woman." She snorted very slightly. "No one ever had any pleasure out of life being biddable. I think I shall inquire more into Mr. Oscar Wilde. If I am forced to entertain the disreputable, I had rather it were a man, and a wit, than a harlot any day." Her eyebrows shot up. "What on earth use have I for yet another beautiful woman of amenable virtue? I am pleased to have met you, Mrs. Pitt. You must call upon me some time. Lady Byam. Come Annabel, Amelia, Jane. For goodness sake, child, stop gazing at that fatuous young man. He is nobody at all. Jane! Do you hear me?" And without even seeing Peter Valerius she swept away again as if all sails were set and the wind behind her.

Charlotte looked at Eleanor and saw in her face humor, exasperation and a relish in the wide eccentricities of people. No words whatever were necessary, or would have been appropriate.

With a smile Charlotte excused herself and went to ascertain that the guests were still enjoying themselves and that the band was still more or less in tune, the refreshments had not yet run out, and no scandal was brewing amid the flowers or in the shaded corners where young couples were sitting in the long pauses between dances.

It was half an hour later and nearly one o'clock when she came across Herbert Fitzherbert and his fiancée, Odelia Morden, in one of those softly lit spaces provided for just such a purpose. Odelia was sitting in a corner chair half shaded by a huge potted palm, its exotic leaves throwing a dark pattern over her creamy shoulders and the pale billows of her gown, satin glimmering as if moonlit, petticoats like foam around her. It crossed Charlotte's mind to wonder if she had arranged herself so artistically on purpose, or by happy chance. Perhaps it was one of the arts the duchess had referred to.

There was a look of immeasurable satisfaction on Odelia's face as she regarded Fitzherbert sitting forward on a stool a yard away from her feet, his elbows on his knees and his attention upon her. Possibly he was the more graceful of the two of them, because his pose was effortless.

Charlotte hesitated before intruding, they were so obviously absorbed in each other, but she had to remind herself of her duty to Emily. In the distance she could hear the band begin the Highland Schottishe. She wished she were free to dance, and someone would ask her, but the role she had been invited here to play was quite different.

"Good evening, Miss Morden," she said cheerfully. "I am so pleased you were able to come. I have been looking forward to meeting you. Mr. Fitzherbert."

Fitzherbert rose immediately and bowed, and as a younger, unmarried woman Odelia rose also, but far more slowly, and her smile was polite but cool. If Fitz had not recalled that Charlotte was Jack Radley's sister-in-law, Odelia certainly had, and she was ambitious.

"Good evening, Mrs. Pitt. It was most kind of Mrs. Radley to invite us. It is a charming event, and I hope we shall meet at many more, most particularly if poor Mrs. Radley's health does not improve. She has my deepest sympathy. It is a most unfortunate time to be unwell."

It was a series of remarks with many edges, and Charlotte was aware of all of them. She looked Odelia straight in the eye and joined battle.

"Of course it is," she said with a radiant smile. "But the bounties of nature are frequently heralded by a certain discomfort, as I hope you will be blessed to discover for yourself, eventually. And perhaps it is more fortunate to be unwell now than later on when running for Parliament. Election times are so short, and one cannot so easily explain to the general public as one can to friends." Again she smiled with absolute directness, and no candor at all. "And Emily is fortunate, she takes a confinement very well."

"How agreeable for her," Odelia murmured. "But the timing!"

"Mrs. Gladstone had eight children," Charlotte said sweetly. "And cared for them all herself, refusing even to have a wet nurse. She taught them all their lessons and heard their prayers at night, and did endless charitable work as well. It does not seem to have hampered her husband from being the best prime minister this century."

"Good gracious!" Odelia's eyes opened wide. "Does Mrs. Radley fancy to be a prime minister's wife?"

Charlotte ignored the sarcasm as completely as if she had failed to perceive it.

"I have not asked her, but it seems a noble ambition. Do you not?" She turned and smiled briefly and with some sympathy at Fitz. There was a spark of humor in his eyes.

"I wish to be Fitz's wife," Odelia said sweetly. "And to do that to the best of my ability. Of course if he is successful to that degree, I shall aim to do everything possible to excel equally, and not quite as eccentrically as Mrs. Gladstone. I hear her entertaining was most erratic, and offended many."

Charlotte was caught off guard. She knew nothing about it.

"Then it would seem the offense was of no importance," she replied hastily. "I have heard nothing but admiration for her, and

Mr. Gladstone must surely be the most politically successful man in the last half century."

Odelia changed her point of attack.

"I do admire your gown, Mrs. Pitt; such a—a robust shade! So fashionable. I shall not forget it."

Charlotte translated in her own mind, knowing precisely what Odelia meant. "Let me warn you, Mrs. Pitt, the color is too loud, verging on the vulgar, and it is so up to the minute that next month it will be out of date, and I, for one, will be acutely aware if I ever see you in it again—and will probably say so at the most inconvenient moment."

"Why thank you, Miss Morden," Charlotte said with an even wider smile. "Your own gown is most delicately suitable, both to the occasion and to yourself." To be translated: "Your gown is insipid and entirely forgettable. If you wear it on every other occasion this entire season no one will notice, or care."

Odelia's face froze.

"Most kind," she muttered between her teeth.

"Not at all." Charlotte nodded to Fitzherbert, and excused herself, sweeping back into the ballroom to accept an invitation to dance the Highland Reel with Peter Valerius.

At half past one, after the last cotillion, the guests adjourned to take supper, and Charlotte was completely occupied with making sure that the maids were on their toes; that the footmen waited upon everyone; and that there were none but the most civilized of unpleasantnesses.

By half past two the party was still in full swing, and at three people were still dancing, a certain sign that the whole venture was a success.

The first high wing of false dawn was glimmering faintly in the sky above the garden, the ferns and the Chinese lanterns, when Charlotte observed the encounter which gave her the most food for thought of the entire evening. She was leaving the room beyond the ballroom and walking towards the balcony and the garden for a breath of air. She was beginning to feel tired and her attention was less sharp than it had been. She passed a bower of white flowers and hesitated a moment to enjoy the cool perfume of them, when her eyes were caught by a gleam of light on a white shirt front and the scarlet splash of a sash of some order, the sparkle of the star.

She hesitated in case she should intrude on someone; such meetings were often more in the nature of assignations between young couples otherwise unable ever to be alone together.

Then she saw that the second person was not a woman but a man. It took her a moment to focus her gaze and recognize Lord Byam. He was standing well beyond the first man and staring out at the garden, the dark web of the trees across the eastern sky, the fancy lanterns still lit and far above them the faint wing of the reflected light over the horizon where in a short while the true dawn would come. She moved a step forward soundlessly.

The other man half turned. It was Lord Anstiss. His face was set in a most curious expression: his lips smiled as if there were some pleasure involved, and yet his eyes stared into the darkness wide and bright. From the very slight flaring of his nostrils Charlotte could not avoid the sensation that he was angry. His hand rested on the balustrade of the balcony, a short, broad-palmed hand with spatulate, artistic fingers. It was perfectly relaxed, even caressing the marble as if the polished texture of the stone satisfied him. There was no tension in it at all; it was a hand ready to caress, not to strike.

Byam was facing sideways, but his eyes were on the press of guests beyond Charlotte moving towards the head of the staircase on the way down to the waiting carriages. His expression was one of deep thought, a little wistful, but there seemed both eagerness and pain in him, and his face was curiously vulnerable.

"Too early to tell," Anstiss said quietly. "Radley's a bit of a wild card, but I like the look of him. A man who knows people, I think."

"And Fitz?" Byam asked, still looking past Anstiss towards the stair head.

"Lightweight," Anstiss replied. "No staying power. Too easily molded, I think. What I might make of him, another might as easily unmake. By the way, what about Mrs. Radley? Is she delicate?"

"Don't think so," Byam said lightly. "Expecting a child, that's all. Used to be Lady Ashworth. Always in society then."

"Sounds acceptable. Who is this Mrs. Pitt, for heaven's sake?"

"Her sister, I gather." Still Byam was facing the open door and the stair beyond. "It hardly matters, she'll be gone soon enough. Just standing in for these few weeks. Seems agreeable, and she's certainly handsome, and quick witted."

Anstiss pulled a face of distaste. "Hope she doesn't have social ambitions. God preserve me from ambitious women."

"No idea." Byam moved in the direction of the far doorway. "I must go—considerable amount to do tomorrow—"

"Of course," Anstiss agreed with a shadow of amusement in his voice. "Good night."

"Good night," Byam replied, and then without turning back he disappeared between the banks of flowers towards the stair head.

Anstiss turned to the false dawn again, now a white fin above the treetops.

CHAPTER

THREE

Charlotte naturally slept at Ashworth House for what little remained of the night, so Pitt had not seen her when he left for the
Clerkenwell police station the following morning. Nor, of course,
had he mentioned the murder of William Weems to her. Not that
he would have. Apart from the connection with Lord Byam, which
was highly confidential, it was a singularly uninteresting case.
Charlotte cared why people did things, not how. The fact that the
hackbut did not work, or that no other weapon had been found,
would be incidental to her. She might well wonder how a person,
especially of Lord Byam's standing, could wander around unnoticed
with a gun large enough to cause such destruction to Weems's
head, but it would be quickly forgotten, because she would not find
Weems sympathetic, and his debtors would engage her feelings only
too much.

As well as an occasional laundress and a woman who came in
twice a week to do the heavy work, the Pitts had a maid, Gracie,
who lived in the house, and she cared for the children. Jemima
was now a bright and extremely talkative seven-year-old of an endlessly inquiring mind and rather disturbing logic. Her brother Daniel, two years younger, was less voluble and far more patient, but
very nearly as determined in his own way.

Gracie made breakfast for Pitt, busying herself discreetly about
the kitchen, which seemed oddly empty without Charlotte, even
though everything else was there as usual. The cooking range was

blacked and cleaned and stoked, but in this summer weather damped down to do no more than boil a kettle and heat one pan to fry Pitt's eggs. Promotion to handling the more sensitive cases had brought its rewards, a new winter coat for Charlotte, new boots for the children, eggs every day if they wished them, and mutton for dinner two or three times a week, fires stoked higher in the winter, and a small raise for Gracie, with which she was delighted, not only for the money but as a matter of pride. She regarded herself as a cut above other housemaids in the area because she worked for such interesting people, and from time to time had a hand in affairs of mighty importance. Only a few months ago she had herself actually gone with Charlotte in pursuit of a murderer and seen some sights she could never forget for their pathos and their fear. Other girls scrubbed and swept and dusted and carried coal buckets and ran errands. She did all of these, but she also had adventures. That made her the equal of any woman in the land, and she never forgot it.

She placed Pitt's breakfast before him, without meeting his eyes. She was acutely conscious that she was standing in for her mistress, and she did not want to spoil it by presuming.

He thanked her, began to eat, and thanked her again. She really was quite a good cook and she had obviously tried very hard. The kitchen was warm in the sun, the light reflected off the china on the dresser and winked on the polished surfaces of the pans. The room smelled of bread, hot coals and clean linen.

When he had finished he rose, thanked Gracie again, and went out into the passage and to the front door. He put his boots on and collected his jacket. A button came off in his hand as he fastened it. He put it in his pocket along with a small penknife, a ball of string, a piece of sealing wax, several coins, two handkerchiefs and a box of matches, and went outside into the sun.

At the Clerkenwell station he was met by Innes, looking bright and very keen, which surprised him since he knew of nothing to pursue today but the people whose names appeared on Weems's list of debtors. Perhaps Innes thought he was going to work on the men like the magistrate Addison Carswell, or Mr. Latimer, whoever he was, and the policeman Samuel Urban. He could not have looked forward with anything but dread to investigating Urban, but the other two might be more interesting. If that were so, Pitt would have to disabuse him very quickly. Handling such delicate areas was presumably also why Drummond had taken Pitt from his fraud case and put him onto this. There were not only Lord Byam's feelings to be considered, but other people's, especially if a member of the force was involved.

However before Pitt could approach the subject Innes made it unnecessary.

"Mornin' sir," he said, straightening to attention, his eyes wide, his face keen. "Doctor sent a message for us to come to the morgue. 'E's found something as 'e's never seen in 'is life before. Says it makes this a poetic kind of a murder."

"Poetic," Pitt said incredulously. "A grubby little usurer has his head shot off in Clerkenwell, and he thinks it's poetic! Probably some poor debtor driven to despair couldn't take it any more and his mind snapped, nothing more to lose. I don't think I could face a doctor who sees poetry in that."

Innes's face fell.

"Oh I'm coming," Pitt assured him quickly. "Then we'll have to start going through the list and finding these poor devils. At least we can weed out those who can prove they were elsewhere." As he was speaking he turned around and went out into the street again, Innes matching him pace for pace, stretching his legs to keep up.

"Would you take family's word for it, sir?" he said doubtfully. "They'd stick together, natural. Wife's word's not much good. Any woman worth anythin'd say 'er man were at 'ome. An' that's where 'e's most likely to be at that time o' night. Unless 'e 'as night work."

"Well that'd be something," Pitt conceded. He knew he was going to hate this. It was painful enough to see the despair of poverty, the thin faces, the cramped, ill-drained houses, the undersized, sickly children, without having to pry into their fears and embarrassment, and maybe leave them terrified of a yet worse evil. "We'll exclude some of them."

"What about the big debtors, sir?" Innes asked, skipping off the pavement onto the roadway, dodging a dray cart and making a leap back onto the curb at the far side. "Are you goin' ter see them?"

Pitt ducked under the huge dray horse's head as it shied upward, and made a dive at the curb himself.

"Yes, when we've got a start on the others," he replied, out of breath.

Innes grinned. "I guess as you in't lookin' forward to that much, askin' nobs if they're in debt ter a back street usurer, an' please sir did yer shoot 'is 'ead orf?"

Pitt smiled in spite of himself. "No," he said wryly. "I'm still hoping it won't be necessary."

Innes was saved from replying by the fact that they had reached the steps of the morgue. He fell behind Pitt and followed him up and inside. Again the smell of carbolic, wet stone and death met them, and involuntarily they both tightened their muscles and flared their nostrils very slightly, as if somehow one could close one's nose against it, stop it from reaching the back of the throat.

The doctor was in a small room off the main hall, sitting behind a wooden table which was covered with odd sheets of paper.

"Ah!" he said as soon as he saw them. "You on the Clerkenwell shooting? Got something for you. Very rummy, this corpse of yours. Most poetic thing I ever saw, I swear."

Innes pulled a face.

"Shot," the doctor said unnecessarily. He was wearing a scruffy coat splashed with blood and acid, and his shirt was obviously laundered, but no one had bothered trying to remove the deep ingrained stains from it. Apparently he had recently left some more grisly work for this meeting. He was sitting facing them, a goose-quill pen in his hand.

"I know." Pitt was confused. "We know he was shot. What we don't know is with what gun. The only gun in his office was a hackbut, and it was broken."

"Ah!" The doctor was increasingly pleased with himself. "What kind of bullets though—you don't know that, now do you, eh?"

"We didn't see any," Pitt conceded. "Whatever it was made a terrible mess of him. But it was pretty close range. The hackbut could have done it, only the pin was filed down."

"Wouldn't have recognized it if you had," the doctor said, now positively oozing satisfaction. "Wouldn't have thought a thing of it. Most natural event in the world."

"Would you be good enough to explain yourself?" Pitt said very levelly, sounding each word. "What have you got?"

"Oh—" The doctor caught his exaggerated patience and realized he had tempted them long enough. "This!" He put his hand in his pocket and pulled out his handkerchief, and very carefully unfolded it to show a bright gold guinea.

For a moment Pitt did not understand.

"So you have a gold guinea—"

"I found it in your Mr. Weems's brain," the doctor said with relish. "Got another, pretty bent. That one must have hit a lot of bone. Gold isn't very hard, you know. But this one's in good shape. Queen Victoria, 1876, thirteen years old." He pulled a face. "Your usurer, gentleman, was shot by a gun loaded with gold coin. Someone has a nice sense of irony."

The room they were in was bare and functional. Their voices echoed slightly.

"Poetry," Pitt agreed with a humor that had a dark chill to it, a crawling on the skin, and a clamminess.

"Shot with 'is own money?" Innes said with amazement. "Oh that's black, that's very black."

"Wouldn't have thought any of those poor beggars would have that much imagination," the doctor said with a shrug. "But there it is. Straight out of his brain—with a pair of forceps. Swear to it on the Bible."

Pitt imagined it with a shiver: the quiet room above Cyrus Street, the lamps burning, gas hissing gently in the brackets, the sound of hooves from the street below, Weems sitting at his desk implacable, yielding nothing, the shadowy figure with a huge barreled weapon loading it with gold—and the explosion of the shot, the side of Weems's head blown apart.

"What happened to the other pieces?" he asked. "You aren't saying two gold coins did all that damage, are you?"

"No—not possible," the doctor agreed. "Must have been four or five at least. I can only think the man, whoever he was, picked up those that weren't embedded too deep in flesh—if you can imagine that. Cold-blooded devil.''

Innes shuddered, and swore under his breath.

"But the gun," Pitt persisted, forcing the picture out of his mind. "It would take a wide-barreled gun, a big gun, to shoot gold pieces like that."

"Well it couldn't 'ave bin the 'ackbut,'' Innes reasoned. "There was no way the devil 'imself could've fired that. 'E must 'ave brought it with 'im—and taken it away again. Although 'ow no one noticed a feller carryin' a great thing like that I don't know." He pushed out his lip. "O' course maybe they did notice it, and no one's sayin'. Could be a sort o' silent conspiracy. No one loves a usurer, especially not Weems. 'E were 'ard, very 'ard.''

"Even if the entire neighborhood was against him," Pitt agreed, "that doesn't account for why he himself sat there while this maniac scooped up the gold, filled the pan with powder, put the coin into the barrel, rammed it, leveled it and fired. Why did Weems remain sitting in his seat staring at him all the time?"

"I don't know," Innes said candidly. "It don't make sense."

"Only the facts." The doctor shrugged expansively. "I just find the facts for you, gentlemen. You have to put them together. I can tell you he was shot with a terrible blast, close to his head, not more than four or five feet away—but maybe you know that from the size of the room anyway. And I picked two gold guinea pieces out of his brains—or what was left of them."

"Thank you," Pitt answered. "If there's anything else please let us know immediately."

"Can't imagine what else there could be. But of course I'll tell you."

"I'm obliged. Good day." And Pitt turned around and left, Innes close behind him.

Out in the street in the sun Innes sniffed hard and shook his head. "What now, sir? The list?"

"Yes," Pitt said grimly. "I'm afraid so—poor devils."

And it was even harder and more painful than he had foreseen. They spent the next three days going from one sparse uncarpeted worn-out house to another where frightened women answered the door, children clinging to their skirts, pale faced and barefooted.

"Yes?" the first woman said nervously. She was frightened of him because she was frightened of everyone who came to the door.

"Mrs. Colley?" he asked quietly, aware of the passersby, already curious, turning to stare.

She hesitated, then saw no way of escape, and she accepted defeat.

"Yes." Her voice was flat and without hope. She still stood on the step, apparently it was better to her in spite of her neighbors' stares. To allow him inside would leave her even more vulnerable, and her desperate poverty more exposed.

He did not know how to tell her who he was without frightening her even more.

"I'm Inspector Pitt, from Bow Street. This is Sergeant Innes—"

"I 'aven't done nuffink!" Her voice shook. "Wot's 'appened? W'y are you 'ere?"

The quickest answer was the least cruel.

"Someone your husband knows has been killed. You may be able to help us learn something about it . . ."

"I dunno nuffink." Her white face and dull eyes held no guilt, no duplicity, only resignation to misery.

A rag and bone man pushed his cart past, his face turned towards her with interest.

"Is your husband in work, Mrs. Colley?" Pitt went on.

Her chin came up. "Yes 'e is. At Billingsgate, at the fish market. 'E don't know nuffink about anyone bein' dead."

Innes glared at the rag and bone man, who increased his pace and disappeared around the corner into an alley.

"What did he do on Tuesday, Mrs. Colley?" Pitt pursued. "All day, please?"

Haltingly she told him, the child at her knees catching the fear in her voice and in her body and beginning to cry.

"Thank you," he said quietly. "If that's true then there's no need to concern yourself. I shall not be back." He wished he could tell her that Weems was dead, and perhaps her debts would be forgotten, but that would be precipitate, and only raise hopes that might not be realized.

The next small, weary woman was different only in trivial ways; her eyes were brown, her hair grayer, her dress the same colorless cloth, washed and rewashed, patched in places, so thin it hung lank about her body. There was a dark bruise on her cheek. She did not know where her husband had been. His pleasures were few, and she thought he had been down the road at the Goat and Compasses public house. He had come home drunk and slept the night on the kitchen floor where he had fallen when he came home around midnight.

And so it went on, the cycle of wretchedness, born in poverty where there was little food, crowded houses with no drains and no water except from a standpipe down the street, sickness, no education and so the meanest work, and more poverty. And for many the only escape was in alcohol, where present pain was drowned into oblivion. And in drunkenness came violence, loss of work, the pawnshop or moneylender, and another slow step downward.

Pitt hated the men like Weems not because they could have changed it—no one knew how to do that—but because they made a profit out of it. He was going to find it very difficult to care who had killed him. Perhaps a few of his victims would find their cancerous debts wiped clean. There would be no one to claim them, to watch the interest accrue and collect someone's last few pence every week to pay off a burden that never decreased.

There was nothing to report to Micah Drummond, so Pitt went home to Charlotte and his clean, warm house where everything smelled sweet and he had no fear of the knock on the door. She would tell him all about the ball at Emily's, the clothes, the food, the chatter. He could watch her face and hear the excitement in her voice, and imagine her playing the society hostess for one night and getting more pleasure out of it than all the duchesses put together, because it was a game, a fancy dress parade. She could come home to sanity at the end, to her children, comfort that had some sort of proportion with the lot of others, the ordinary, sane things like baking bread, mending the children's clothes, taking the dead heads off the roses, sitting by the open window in the evening and watching the moths in the summer garden.

The following day he and Innes resumed working their way through the list, this time with the genteel poor, those who struggled to maintain the appearance of respectability and would rather sit in the cold all winter than forgo having a maid because quality always had a maid; people who would eat bread and gravy when they were alone, so that when callers came they could present better fare. These were people who had only one outfit of clothes that were not threadbare, out of fashion, boots that leaked and no coat, but they walked to church every Sunday with heads high and polite smiles and nods to neighbors, and made fantastic excuses why they did not accept invitations, because they could not return the hospitality. He ached for them also, and knew why the doors were answered with fear, and why he was offered tea which was served with shaking hands. He felt a hard, compulsive satisfaction when they could prove where they were when William Weems was shot. It was one advantage the poor had over Lord Byam; privacy was a luxury they tasted very seldom indeed. Almost all of them were crowded with others at that time in the evening, and all night. Few had any space alone, even to wash or to sleep. Many of the very poor shared a single room and they would not do more than dream of a time when they could do otherwise. One loan piled upon another, and the interest swallowed all they had, the capital was never paid off. Debt was a way of life.

Pitt heartily wished whoever had murdered Weems had destroyed all his records. Pitt hated him for that omission far more than for having blown the man's brains out with half a dozen of his own gold coins.

On the fifth day Pitt took a hansom back to Bow Street to tell Micah Drummond that he had learned nothing so far either to implicate Lord Byam or to exonerate him. It was a little after five in the afternoon and the sun was still high and warm. The trees in the square were in full leaf, and music floated across from the band in Lincoln Inn Fields as he peered out of his cab. Children in bright clothes played with hoops and sticks painted like horses' heads, and a solemn man with his sleeves rolled up flew a red kite for a small boy whose upturned face was full of wonder. A courting couple strolled by arm in arm, the girl giggling with pleasure, the man swaggering very slightly as if he had something worth showing off to the world. A nursemaid passed going in the opposite direction, wheeling a perambulator, her head high, her starched apron dazzling white in the sun. Two old gentlemen sat on a wooden seat in the sun, looking faintly dusty in the bright light, their faces benign.

By the time Pitt reached Bow Street he had almost forgotten the all-pervading want he had seen all day, tasting it in the air as if it were a kind of grit.

He paid the cabby and went up the steps of the police station. He was barely inside when he heard a commotion outside. The door flew open again and a uniformed constable came in backwards, stumbling as he tried to restrain a portly gentleman with bristling whiskers and a scarlet face, who was obviously in a monumental rage and determined that no one should put a hand on him. He flung his body about like a fish on the end of a line, and the constable, with both his youth and length of reach on his side, was fast losing the battle.

Pitt went to his assistance and between them they overcame the man when he realized the futility of fighting against such odds. Quite suddenly they all stopped, the constable with his jacket pulled crooked, two buttons missing, and his helmet over one ear. Pitt had a pocket torn and dust over his trousers where the man had scraped his boots in his efforts to get free. He himself was in worse condition yet; his fine head of hair was on end, his jacket was hitched up under his armpits and wildly crooked, his shirt was torn, his collar had sprung loose from its studs and his tie looked in danger of strangling him. His trousers were twisted around his body and torn open at the top button at his waist.

"Are you all right, Constable?" Pitt asked as soberly as the ridiculousness of the situation allowed.

The constable pulled his uniform back to position with one hand, keeping the other firmly on his prisoner.

"Yes, thank you sir. I'm obliged to you."

"How dare you," the prisoner demanded furiously. "I don't think you know who I am, sir. I am Horatio Osmar!" This last was addressed to Pitt, whom he had realized to be the senior officer and thus worthy of his attention.

It was a name Pitt recognized although it took him a moment to place it. Horatio Osmar had been a junior minister in the government until about two years before when he had retired.

"Indeed sir?" Pitt said with some surprise, looking over Osmar's head at the discomfited constable.

"I am prepared to accept an apology and let the matter go," Osmar said stiffly, adjusting his jacket to cover the disarray of clothes at his waist. His hands hesitated a moment as if to do up his trousers, then changed his mind. His face was still very red from his exertion.

"I can't do that, sir," the constable said before Pitt had time to ask him. "I've got to charge you."

"That's preposterous," Osmar exploded, yanking his arm away from the constable and glaring at Pitt. "You look like a reasonable fellow. For God's sake explain to this—this overzealous young person who I am."

Pitt looked at the constable, who was now pink faced and unhappy, but standing stiffly to attention, his eyes unwavering.

"What is the charge, Constable?"

"Behavior likely to cause an affront to public decency, sir."

"Balderdash," Osmar said loudly. "Complete balderdash. Nothing of the sort!"

"Are you quite sure, Constable?" Pitt said dubiously.

"Yes sir. Constable Crombie has the young lady."

"What young lady?"

"The young lady with whom Mr. Osmar was—was sitting in the park, sir." The constable looked straight ahead of him, his eyes unhappy, his face hot.

"That's it," Osmar shouted. "Sitting!" He was quivering with indignation. "It is not an offense, sir, for a gentleman and a young lady to sit together on a seat in the park and enjoy a summer day." He yanked his jacket straighter. "It is an outrage when they are disturbed and insulted in their pleasure by two young jackanapes policemen."

"Two?" Pitt raised his eyebrows.

"Indeed. Two sir! The other one arrested my friend, Miss Giles. What a fearful experience for a young lady of gentle birth." The man's face was highly expressive with round eyes and shapeless nose. "I am mortified it should happen to her in my company, where she must surely have considered herself safe from such assault. I shall not forgive it!"

"Where is Miss—Miss Giles, Constable?" Pitt said with some concern. This looked like being a serious mistake, and one which could become very ugly indeed if Horatio Osmar chose to press it.

"Right be'ind me, sir." The constable kept his eyes on Pitt's and in spite of his embarrassment, there was no flinching in him.

At that moment the door opened again and the second constable came in with a young woman held firmly by both hands. She was very handsome in a bold and buxom fashion. Her fair brown hair was falling forward uncoiled out if its pins and her dress was crooked and open at the top. It was not possible to tell if this had happened in her struggle with the constable, or whether he had found her in this disarray.

"Constable Crombie, I presume?" Pitt said dryly.

"Yes sir." The constable was out of breath and out of countenance. He was not accustomed to having to struggle with young women of any birth or gentility, even of the most general sort, and the episode embarrassed him. It showed in his earnest young face.

"Is the lady under arrest?" Pitt asked.

"Yes sir. She was in the park with that gentleman." He indicated Horatio Osmar, who was glaring ferociously at them and about to burst into indignant speech again. "They were be'aving in a manner likely to offend any decent people," the constable went on suddenly. "Doin' things best done in their own bedrooms, sir, or in their own sitting rooms at worst."

"How dare you." Osmar could contain himself no longer. "That's a scandalous slander, sir." He struggled to free himself and failed. "We were nothing of the kind. You insult Miss Giles, and I will not stand for it—be warned!"

"We saw what we saw, sir," the constable said stolidly.

"You saw what you imagine you saw, sir." Osmar's voice was raised very considerably and by now the nearer occupants of the station were also aware of the commotion. One of the inner doors opened and a uniformed inspector came out into the room. He was a tall man, almost as tall as Pitt, fair haired with a strong, blunt face.

"What's the problem, Constable?" He addressed Crombie directly, not immediately realizing that Pitt, not in uniform, was also an officer.

Crombie was visibly relieved.

"Oh Mr. Urban, sir; I'm glad as you're 'ere. Allardyce and me arrested this lady and gentleman for improper be'avior in the park. They was bein' indecently familiar with each other on one o' the park benches, sir; disarrangin' each other's clothes, and 'ands where they shouldn't 'a bin, 'cept in private."

"That is untrue," Osmar said angrily. "Quite untrue. You are apparently unaware who I am, sir." He jerked his jacket down with both hands, now suddenly free. "I am Horatio Osmar, late a minister in Her Majesty's government."

Urban's eyes opened only a fraction wider; the remainder of his expression did not change at all.

"Indeed sir. And the lady?"

The young woman opened her mouth to speak, but Osmar answered before she could.

"Miss Beulah Giles, a totally respectable young acquaintance of mine. A lady of irreproachable reputation and unquestioned virtue."

Urban looked at Pitt. "And you, sir?"

"Thomas Pitt, inspector of detectives; but this case is nothing to do with me. I came to report an entirely different matter to Mr. Drummond."

This time Urban's expression did change. Politeness turned into undisguised interest. "So you're Thomas Pitt. I've only just moved to Bow Street, but I've heard of you. Samuel Urban—" He held out his hand.

Pitt took it and was held in a firm, warm grip.

"I'll leave you to sort this out," he said with a smile. "It looks like a difficult affair." And with that he turned and went past the duty desk and up the stairs to tell Drummond that he had still learned nothing to implicate, nor to clear, Lord Sholto Byam. It was not until he was at the top of the stairs that he stopped, almost tripping over the step, a cold chill inside him. Samuel Urban. That was the name on Weems's list for a huge amount of money.

He went on along the wide corridor towards Drummond's room.

———

Horatio Osmar and Beulah Giles were kept in police cells overnight and the next day taken before the police court. Micah Drummond did not attend, but he told Urban that he wished to be kept informed at all points. It was not a light thing to charge an ex-minister of the government with indecent behavior in a public place.

It was nearly noon when Urban knocked on his door.

"Come in," he said quickly, looking up from his desk. He half hoped it would be Pitt to say he had learned something in the Weems case, but perhaps that was too optimistic.

When Urban came in it was a different anxiety that touched him, but he could not blame the man. It was in a way unfortunate the two constables had been at that precise spot at that time. But given that they were, he would not have had them ignore the matter simply because the man was a public figure.

"Well?" he asked.

Urban stood to attention, not obviously, but there was both formality and respect in his attitude.

"Mr. Osmar was charged, sir, and pleaded not guilty, with some heat and indignation."

Drummond smiled ruefully. "I should have been amazed had he not."

"I thought a night in the cells might have cooled his temper a trifle," Urban said regretfully. "And perhaps made him consider a plea of guilty would cause less publicity than fighting it." He was standing in a broad splash of sunlight on the bright carpet and the radiance of it picked out the freckles on his skin and cast the shadow of his eyelashes on his cheek. "Miss Giles said very little. Seems to take her cue from him, which I suppose is natural."

"Any newspapermen here?" Drummond asked.

"Not that I know, but I expect they'll get hold of it pretty quickly."

"Not if Osmar's lucky. They may have looked through the docket of crimes and found nothing worth their time. After all a trivial indecency is hardly worthy of comment in ordinary circumstances."

Urban pulled his mobile face into an expression of rueful contempt. "No sir, but Osmar hasn't that much sense, it seems. He insisted on putting a personal call through to the home secretary."

"What?" Drummond nearly dropped his pen in disbelief. He stared at Urban. "What do you mean, a call? He found a messenger?"

"No sir." Urban's eyes were bright with humor. "He used one of those new telephone instruments. That caused a stir in itself."

"And he got through?" Drummond was not only amazed but beginning to feel some alarm. The story was getting uglier by the minute.

Urban ironed all the amusement out of his face. "Yes sir, apparently he did. Although I'm not sure what difference it made to anything, except that it delayed proceedings for quite a while, and thus also his getting bail. Which considering the nature of the charge was bound to be granted."

"And the girl, Miss—?"

"Miss Giles. She got bail also, both on their own recognizance." He shrugged. "All of which we could have taken for granted, except his choosing to contact the home secretary. Maybe if we'd charged him with theft he'd have called the prime minister—and if it had been assault he'd have called the Queen."

"Don't," Drummond said grimly. "The man's a menace. What on earth's going to happen when he comes to trial?"

"Heaven knows," Urban confessed. "Perhaps he'll have taken decent advice by then and have decided to keep quiet. Oh—we returned his case to him."

"His case?" Drummond had no idea what Urban was talking about.

Urban relaxed a little, putting one hand in his pocket.

"Yes sir. A man came to the station about half an hour after Crombie and Allardyce arrested Mr. Osmar, and said he had been in the park at the time, and Osmar had left a small attaché case on the seat where he and Miss Giles had been . . . sitting. He picked it up and brought it along. Apparently he had some appointment which he had to keep, someone he was waiting for, and he half expected the constables to come back for it anyway. But when no one did, and he had met his friend, he brought it to the station. At least Osmar cannot accuse us of having caused him to lose it."

"He got it back again?"

"Yes sir. He had it in his hand when he left the police court."

"Well that's something, I suppose." Drummond sighed. "What a mess. Why couldn't the old fool behave himself on a public bench?"

Urban smiled, a bright, easy gesture full of humor.

"Heat of the moment? Spring in the air?"

"It's summer," Drummond said dryly.

"Perhaps we're lucky. He might have been worse in spring."

"Get out!"

Urban grinned.

Drummond put the pen down and stood up. "Keep an eye on it, Urban," he said seriously. "I've got more to worry about with real cases. I've got a very ugly murder we've been called in to help with."

Urban looked puzzled. "Called in, sir?"

"Not on our patch. I'm going now to see someone touched by it." He crossed over to the stand by the door and took his hat and put it on. It was far too warm for a coat above his ordinary jacket, but he straightened his tie automatically and eased his shoulders and set his lapels a little more evenly.

Urban did not appear to notice anything unusual. Gentlemen like Micah Drummond might be expected to dress immaculately wherever they were going, not in deference to whom they visited, but because it was in their own nature.

Outside Drummond hailed a hansom and set out for Belgravia.

He sat back in the smooth upright interior and thought about Lord Byam, and the obligation which had drawn him into this affair. For some ten years now he had been one of an exclusive group known as the Inner Circle, a brotherhood whose membership was unknown except to each other, and even then only to the closest few to each man, and it was sworn with profound oaths to remain so. In secret they did many good works, helped those in misfortune, fought to right certain injustices, and gave generously to many charities.

They had also covenanted to assist each other, when called upon and identified with the signs of the Circle, and to do so without questioning the matter or counting the personal cost.

Sholto Byam had appealed to him under such a covenant. As a fellow member Drummond had no option but to do all he could, and without telling Pitt anything of the brotherhood in any way, even by implication. He could explain nothing. It was a situation which embarrassed him unaccountably. London was full of societies of one sort or another, some of them charitable, many of them secret. He had thought little of it at the time he joined. It was something that many of his peers had done, and it seemed both a wise and an admirable step, for friendship and for his career. It had never caused him unease until now.

It was not that he feared Byam was guilty, or that had he been he would do anything whatever to protect him from the consequences of his act. It was simply that he could not explain his behavior to Pitt, nor tell him why he was so easily able to have him put in charge of a case which rightly belonged in Clerkenwell. There were other members of the Inner Circle he could appeal to, men in positions to have a case investigated here, or there, by whomsoever they chose, and he had but to identify himself as a brother and it was done, without explanation asked or given.

Now he would do all that was required by honor to help Byam, and do it with the necessary grace.

He arrived at Belgrave Square, alighted, and paid the cabby. As the horse drew away, he straightened his tie one more time. He walked up the steps under the portico and reached out his hand to pull the bell. But the footman on duty was alert, and the door opened in front of him.

"Good morning, Mr. Drummond," the footman said courteously, remembering his master's eagerness to see this gentleman on his previous call. "I regret to say, sir, that Lord Byam is away from home at the moment, but if you care to see Lady Byam, I shall inform her you are here."

Drummond felt dismay, and a stirring of confusion half mixed with pleasure. His immediate thought was that Lady Byam might be able to give him some insight into her husband's personality, his habits and perhaps some fact he had overlooked or forgotten which might point towards his innocence. His memory brought back the grace with which she had moved, the gentleness of her smile when he had come that first night he had been sent for.

"Thank you," he accepted. "That would be excellent."

"If you will wait in the morning room, sir." The footman led the way and opened the door for Drummond, showing him into a room furnished in cool greens and filled with sunlight. There was a large fireplace of polished marble; Drummond guessed it to be an Adam design from the previous century, simple and unadulterated of line. The pictures on the walls to either side were seascapes, and when he turned around, behind him were Dutch pastoral scenes with cows. He had never realized before how pleasing to the mind were the awkward, gentle angles of a cow's body. It was uniquely restful.

The long green velvet curtains were splayed out on the floor and swagged with braided sashes, the only thing in the room which jarred on him. He had no idea why, but he disliked the display of overlength curtains, even though he knew it was customary in houses of wealth. It was a conventional sign of plenty, that one had enough velvet to waste.

There was a large cut-glass bowl of roses on the low mahogany table between the chairs.

He walked over to the window and stood in the sun waiting for the footman to return.

However when the door opened it was Lady Byam herself who came in, closing it behind her, making it apparent she intended to speak with him in this room rather than conducting him elsewhere. She was taller than he had remembered, and in this sharp, hard light he could see she was also older, perhaps within a few years of his own age. Her skin was pale and clear and there was light color in her cheeks, and he could see a few very fine lines about her eyes. It made her seem more approachable, more vulnerable, and more capable of laughter.

"Good morning, Mr. Drummond," she said with a faint smile. "I am afraid Lord Byam is out at the minute, but I expect he will return soon. May I offer you some refreshment until then?"

He had no need of either food or drink, but he heard himself accepting without hesitation.

She reached for the bell cord and pulled it. The footman appeared almost immediately and she sent him for tea and savories.

"Forgive me, Mr. Drummond," she said as soon as the footman

was gone. "But I cannot help but ask you if you have any information regarding the death of Mr. Weems?"

He noticed that in spite of the blackness of her hair, her eyes were not brown but dark gray.

"Very little, ma'am," he answered apologetically. "But I thought Lord Byam would wish to hear how we have progressed, regardless that it is so slightly, and all of it merely a matter of elimination."

"Elimination?" Her cool, level voice lifted with a moment of hope. "You mean reason why it was not my husband?"

He wished he could have told her it was. "No, I am afraid not. I mean people whom we had reason to suspect, people who had borrowed money from Weems, but whom we find can account for their whereabouts at the time of his death."

"Is that how you do it?" Her brow was furrowed; there was anxiety in her eyes and something he thought was disappointment.

"No," he said quickly. "No—it is merely a way of ruling out certain possibilities so we do not waste time pursuing them. When someone like Weems is killed it is difficult to know where to begin, he had so many potential enemies. Anyone who owed him money is at least a possibility." He found himself talking too quickly, saying too much. He was aware of doing it and yet his tongue went on. "We have to establish who had a reason for wishing him dead and then who had an opportunity to commit the crime, and would have the means at their disposal. There will not be many who had all three. When we have thus narrowed it down we will try to establish from the evidence which of those people, assuming there are more than one, actually is guilty." He looked at her to see if she understood not only his bare words, but all the meaning behind them; if it was of any reassurance to her that they knew their profession.

He was rewarded to see her doubt lessen, and her shoulders relax a trifle under the soft fabric of her gown, which was dark green like the room, reminding him of deep shade under trees in summer. But the anxiety was still there.

"It sounds extremely difficult, Mr. Drummond. Surely people must lie to you? Not only whoever is guilty, but other people as well?" Her brows furrowed. "Even if we have no part in it, and no knowledge of the murder, most of us have things we would rather were not known, albeit petty sins and uglinesses by comparison. How do you know what to believe?''

Before he could answer, the footman returned with tea and the requested small savories. Eleanor thanked him absently and he withdrew. She invited Drummond to partake of the food, and poured tea for him and herself.

The savories were delicious, tiny delicate pastries, merely a mouthful, and small crisp fingers of toast spread with pâté or cheeses. The tea was hot and clean in the mouth. He sat opposite her, trying to balance himself and eat at the same time, feeling clumsy compared with her grace.

"It is difficult," he said, taking up the conversation as if there had been no interruption. "And of course from time to time we make mistakes, and have to begin again. But Inspector Pitt is an excellent man and not easily confused."

She smiled fully for the first time. "Such a curious man," she said, looking down at the roses in their exquisite bowl. "At first I wondered who in heaven's name you had brought." She smiled apologetically. "His pockets must have been stuffed with papers, his jacket hung at such an odd angle, and I cannot believe he has seen a good barber in months. Then I looked at his face more closely. He has the clearest eyes I have ever seen. Have you noticed?"

Drummond was taken aback, unsure how to answer.

She smiled at herself.

"No, of course you haven't," she answered her own question. "It is not a thing a man would remark. I should feel ashamed if your Mr. Pitt caught me in an untruth. And I don't find it hard to believe he would know. I hope he has a similar effect on other people he questions—" She stopped as she saw the doubt in his face. "You think I am fanciful? Perhaps. Or maybe I hope too much—"

"Oh no!" he said quickly, leaning forward without realizing it until he found he had nowhere to place the cup still in his hand. He put it down on the table self-consciously. "Pitt is extremely good at his job, I assure you. I would not have assigned him to this case did I not have full confidence in him. He has solved some remarkably difficult murders in the past. And he is a man of both compassion and discretion. He will not seek his own fame, or to cause hurt by scandal."

"He sounds a paragon," she said quietly, looking not at Drummond but at her plate.

He was aware of having overpainted it.

"Not at all. He is perfectly human," he said rather too quickly. "Frequently insubordinate, he detests being patronized and is the scruffiest man I know. But he is a man of both integrity and imagination, and he will find out who murdered Weems if anyone can."

For the first time she looked directly at him with a candid smile full of warmth. "You like him, don't you?"

"Yes I do," he confessed. And it was a confession. A woman of Lady Byam's social position would not expect a gentleman like Drummond to have personal feelings for a subordinate such as Pitt.

She said nothing in reply to that, but he had a sharp awareness that she was pleased, although he was uncertain as to why: whether it was simply that if Pitt was liked it made the whole unpleasantness a little more bearable, and she might also trust him not to be clumsy; or whether it had anything to do with her approval of him.

That was a rather ridiculous thought, and he dismissed it hastily. He drew in his breath to speak, but at the same moment she pushed the serving plate a fraction forward.

"Please take another savory, Mr. Drummond?" she offered. She seemed to search for something to say, and found it in a triviality, her voice losing the low-pitched melody it had had before. "I was at a ball the evening before last, given by Mr. and Mrs. Radley. She used to be Lady Ashworth, and has recently remarried. Her husband wishes to stand for Parliament and this was in the nature of introducing his campaign. But Mrs. Radley herself was unwell, and her sister, a Mrs. Pitt, was standing in her place for the evening. You know for a moment I could not think where I had heard the name recently." Her voice was growing higher as if it were tight in her throat. "I wonder what those people would have thought had they known that today I should be sitting in my own home discussing a police investigation and hoping to clear my husband of suspicion of the murder of a usurer. I wonder how many of them would have spoken to me so civilly and been happy to court my company."

A multitude of answers rose to his lips, the instinct to tell her who Charlotte was, which he dismissed reluctantly. It would be unfair to Charlotte, and possibly close an avenue of acquiring knowledge. Charlotte had certainly been acute enough in her judgment in the past. He wanted to assure Eleanor Byam that any friend who abandoned her because of such a thing was not worthy of her association, let alone her affection. Then he realized that she knew it as well as he, but she still needed the comfort of being accepted. She was afraid of scandal, of the unpleasantness of being cut, of the cruel whispers, the speculations, the unjust thoughts. Courage did not prevent the hurt, only helped one to endure it with dignity. Even the knowledge that those one had thought friends were shallow and cruel was no balm for the disillusion. She would prefer they were not put to the test. She did not want to see their faults.

"Pitt is discreet," he said seriously. "He is pursuing the notion that many people borrowed money from Weems, and it is probably a debtor grown desperate who killed him."

Her face was instantly touched with pity, and self-mockery.

"I wish it were not necessary to learn who is guilty in order to prove that it was not Sholto," she said earnestly. "I expect it is inexcusable of me, but I cannot entirely blame someone in desperate financial straits, if Weems threatened to foreclose, and they had nowhere else to turn." She bit her lip. "I know murder is no answer to anything, but I cannot help imagining the poor creature's feelings."

"So will Pitt," Drummond said before he thought, and because he felt somewhat the same himself. If ever a victim was unmissed it was William Weems.

She looked up at him again and saw his own reaction mirrored in his eyes.

He found himself blushing.

She looked away. "Sholto is taking it very well," she said, forcing a lightness into her voice. "If he is afraid, he masks it with a confidence that in time you will be able to learn who is responsible. The whole tragedy of Lady Anstiss's death was so long ago, it is ridiculous it should shadow our lives today. What a grubby thing it is to be so greedy!"

He pulled a wry face at such an understatement.

"Did you know her?"

"No, not at all. It was some years before Sholto and I met." She looked across at the window and the leaves moving in the wind.and the sun. "I believe she was very beautiful, not just the usual regularity of feature and clarity of complexion which one sees very often, but a vulnerable, passionate and haunting beauty that one could not forget. I have seen a painting of her in Lord Anstiss's home, and I admit I could not put it from my mind myself." She turned to him with puzzlement in her gray eyes. "Not because of her tragic death, simply because her face was so individual, so full of intensity, so very unlike the traditional English lady I had expected." She blinked. "When we speak of vulnerability I had thought to see a fragile face with fair hair, very young, very soft. She was not like that at all. She was dark, with a proud nose, high cheekbones and such a marvelous mouth. I admit, I find it dreadful to think someone who looked so alive should have taken her own life. But I had no difficulty believing she would have loved fiercely enough to die for it."

"I'm sorry," he said awkwardly, acutely aware it was Eleanor's husband for whom Laura Anstiss had felt such a passion. He admired her deeply that she could speak of it with gentleness, and without a shadow of resentment. She must be very sure that Sholto Byam now loved her, whatever his foolishness, his error of judgment or his embarrassment in the past.

She looked down at the carpet and the patterns of sunlight creeping slowly across the floor.

"I have always admired Lord Anstiss for holding no grudge against Sholto." Her voice was very quiet and low. "It would have been so easy to descend into bitterness and blame, and no one could have held him unjust for it or failed to understand. And yet after the first shock and bewilderment, it seems he never did. He allowed his grief to be untainted by hatred. I suppose he knew how dreadfully Sholto felt, and that he would have gone to any lengths to have undone his thoughtlessness." She sighed. "But of course it was too late when he realized how violently she felt." She bit her lip and looked up at him. "It seems Laura had never been refused anything before. No man had failed to fall under her spell, and it seemed to her as if all her power was stripped from her. She was confused and terribly hurt. Suddenly she doubted everything."

She stopped for a moment, but he said nothing.

"It must be strange to be so lovely no one can help gazing at you," she went on, as much to herself as to him. "I had never thought before what a doubtful blessing it is. Perhaps everyone is so spellbound by your face they fail to see the person behind it, and realize you have dreams and fears just like everyone, and that you can be every bit as lonely, as unsure of yourself, of your worth or of anyone else's love for you." Her voice sank even lower. "Poor Laura."

"And poor Lord Anstiss." Drummond meant it profoundly. "He must be a man of very great spirit to have overcome anger and bitterness and kept his friendship for Lord Byam intact. It is a quality I admire above almost any other, such a generosity of spirit, and an ability to forgive."

"I too," she agreed quickly, lifting her eyes again and staring at him with intense emotion. "It is beauty far greater than that of face or form, don't you think? It is one of the qualities that brings a sweetness to everything it touches, in men or women. As long as there are such people, we can bear the men like Weems, and whichever poor soul was driven to shoot him."

He was about to answer when he heard the sound of footsteps in the hall and low voices, then the door opened and Byam came in. At first he looked vigorous and in good heart, but when he crossed the bar of sunlight from the window Drummond could see the faint lines of tiredness around his eyes, and there was a tension in him, almost disguised but not quite. He showed no surprise at seeing Drummond; obviously the footman had forewarned him in the hallway.

Drummond rose to his feet.

"Good morning, my lord. I came to acquaint you with the progress we have made so far, and what we intend doing next."

He nodded. "Morning, Drummond. Good of you. I appreciate it. Good morning, Eleanor, my dear." He touched her shoulder lightly, a mere brush of the fingertips. The delicacy of the gesture, and the fact that he removed his hand, she took as a dismissal, subtle and gentle, but allowing her to know he wished to speak to Drummond alone. Possibly he believed the detail of the matter offensive to her, and unnecessary for her to hear.

She rose to her feet and with her back to her husband, but close to him, she faced Drummond.

"If you will excuse me, Mr. Drummond, I have domestic responsibilities to attend. We have guests to dine this evening, and I must go over the menu with Cook."

"Of course." He bowed very slightly. "I appreciate your generosity in remaining with me and giving me so much of your time."

She smiled at him politely. It was a formal speech he had made, precisely what he would have said to anyone in the circumstances; she could not know how honestly he meant it.

"Good day, Mr. Drummond."

"Good day, Lady Byam."

And she turned and walked out of the room, closing the door softly behind her.

Byam glanced at the empty tray, and refrained from offering any further refreshment. Drummond could see the anxiety in the tightness of his movements, the lack of ease and the way he stood, and he did not oblige him to ask what news he had come to bring.

"I am afraid most of our progress so far is merely a matter of excluding some of the more obvious possibilities," he said without preamble.

Byam's eyes widened a fraction; it was far less than a question, he simply waited for Drummond to continue.

"There were two lists of debtors in Weems's office," Drummond went on. "A long one, of very ordinary unfortunates who had borrowed fairly small sums at regular intervals and were paying back similarly. Most of the poor devils will never repay all the capital at his rate of usury, but be scraping the bottom for the rest of their lives. It is a despicable way to profit from other people's wretchedness!" As soon as the words were said he realized they were out of place. He should not have allowed his own feelings to intrude.

But Byam's face twisted in sympathy and harsh humor.

"He was a despicable man," he said in a hard voice. "Blackmail is not an attractive manner in which to acquire money either. If my own life were not at stake I should not give you the slightest encouragement to find out who killed Mr. Weems, I assure you. But since it is, I am obliged to pursue the matter with all the vigor I have."

It was an invitation, even a request, to continue more relevantly. Drummond took it.

"So far we have eliminated a great number on account of their having been in company at the time Weems was shot—"

Byam pulled a rueful face.

"I wish I could say as much. Unfortunately even my servants did not disturb me that evening."

Drummond smiled back at him. "That is a small advantage to poverty; they live in such cramped quarters allowing of almost no privacy at all, they have a number of witnesses to swear they were here or there, well observed, at the time. Many of them share one room with an entire family, or were working, or in a public house."

Byam's face quickened with hope. "But not all?"

"No, not all," Drummond agreed. "Pitt and his men are pursuing those who were alone, or only with their wives, whose testimony cannot be relied upon. It would be most natural for a wife to say her husband was with her, as soon as she understood the meaning of the questions." Drummond shifted his position a fraction. "And of course word of Weems's murder spread very quickly. Some who lived outside the Clerkenwell area had not heard. But the very fact that the police are inquiring is a warning to them that something serious is amiss. They have the arts of survival."

"Not very promising." Byam attempted to sound lighthearted, but there was a catch in his voice; the smoothness of it was gone, the timbre thin, and the knuckles of his hands on the chair back were white.

"There is another list," Drummond said quickly. "Of people who have borrowed considerably more heavily."

"Why did you not try them first?" Byam asked, not abruptly, but with obvious failure to understand what seemed to him so plain a point.

"Because they are gentlemen," Drummond replied, and phrased

that way he disliked the sound of it himself. "Because they were borrowing equally according to their means," he added. "Perhaps less. And probably they have a better likelihood of coming by the extra to repay, should their ordinary income not stretch to it. They would have possessions to sell, if that were a last resort."

"Perhaps he was blackmailing them also," Byam suggested.

"We had thought of that." Drummond nodded fractionally. "Pitt will investigate that also, but it must be done with discretion, and some care, simply in order to learn the truth. Men do not usually admit easily to such things." He met Byam's wide, dark eyes and saw the flicker of humor in them, self-mocking. "And other secrets may not be as merely tragic as yours. They may be something for which one would have to prosecute."

"I suppose that is true," Byam conceded. Suddenly he became aware that Drummond was still standing. "I'm sorry! Please sit—I cannot, I simply find it too difficult to relax myself. Does it discomfit you?"

"Not at all," Drummond lied. As a matter of courtesy he could not admit that it did. Accordingly he resumed the seat he had occupied while talking to Eleanor, and stared up at Byam still standing behind the other chair, his fingers grasping its back.

"What surprised me," Drummond went on, "is that whoever murdered Weems did not take his list of names. It would seem such an obvious thing to do."

Byam hesitated, looked down, and then up again facing Drummond.

"What did you do with his record of my payments to him? Does your man Pitt have it?" He swallowed painfully. "And the letter?"

"We didn't find either of them," Drummond replied, watching him closely.

Byam's eyes darkened; it was almost imperceptible, a tightening of the muscles of the face, a stiffening of the body under the fine wool of his coat. It was too quick and too subtle to be assumed. It was fear, mastered almost as soon as it was there.

"Did he search properly?" Byam demanded. His voice was very slightly altered in pitch, just a fraction higher, as if his throat was tight. "Where else would Weems keep such things? Isn't that where he lived? You said you found his other records there."

"Yes we did," Drummond agreed. "And that is where he lived. I can only presume the murderer either took them or destroyed them, although we found no evidence of anything having been burned or torn up. Or else Weems lied to you, and there never was any account of your dealings. Why should he keep a record of such things? It was not a debt."

"Presumably to safeguard himself from my taking any action against him," Byam said sharply. "He was not a fool. He must have been threatened with retaliation before." He closed his eyes and leaned forward a little, dropping his head. "Dear God. If whoever murdered him took it, what will they do with it?" His hands curled on the back of the chair, his fingers white with the pressure he was exerting in his grip. His voice was husky with strain. "And the letter?"

"If it was a desperate man, like yourself," Drummond said quietly, "he will most likely destroy them both, along with the evidence that implicates him. We found no evidence of other blackmail, just simple debts—"

"Unless the second list was blackmail," Byam said, looking up at him, his face pale. "You said they were men of means. Why should such people borrow from a petty usurer like Weems? If I wanted extra money I wouldn't go to the back streets of Clerkenwell, I'd go to a bank, or at worst I'd sell one of the pictures or something of that sort."

"I don't know," Drummond confessed, feeling inadequate, angry with himself for such a futile answer. "Perhaps they had no possessions to sell, they may be in trust, or possibly they did not wish their families to be aware of their difficulties. Men need money for many things, not all of them they wish to have known."

Byam's mouth tightened; again the bleak humor was there.

"Well, falling into the hands of a usurer is no way out. Every week just digs you in the deeper. Anyone but a fool knows that."

"It is possible he bought someone else's debts," Drummond said slowly.

Byam laughed, a low, gentle sound utterly without pleasure.

"You are trying to comfort me, but you are reaching for straws. It must have been whoever killed him who took both the list and Laura's letter to me, and I can only pray it was because all Weems's records were together and he had no time or inclination to look through them and find his own, and that he will not use it for gain."

"If he does, he will betray himself as having killed Weems," Drummond reasoned. "That would be a very dangerous thing to do."

Byam took a deep breath and let it out in a sigh.

"Please God," he said quietly.

"At least it tends to vindicate you," Drummond pointed out, seeing something to encourage him. "Had you known the evidence implicating you had been taken away, or destroyed, you would not have called me and told me of your involvement. You had no need to say anything at all."

Byam smiled thinly. "Something to cling to," he agreed. "Do you think your man Pitt will see it that way?"

"Pitt is a better detective than I am," Drummond said frankly. "He will think of anything I do, and more."

"But what can he do?" Byam's face furrowed. "He can't arrest a man simply because he cannot prove he was elsewhere. Did you find the gun?"

"No—but we found the shot."

"Not a great achievement," Byam said dryly. "Presumably it was still in Weems's body. How does that help?"

"It was gold," Drummond answered, watching Byam's face.

"It was what?" Byam was incredulous. "You mean golden bullets? A nice touch, but who on earth would be bothered to do that, let alone have the gold to use? That doesn't make sense!"

"Not gold bullets," Drummond explained. "Gold coin. It may have been Weems's own money. The trouble is there was no gun in the room capable of firing it. There was a hackbut on the wall, a beautiful thing, a collector's piece, which is presumably why he had it, but the firing pin had been filed down. There was no way anyone fired it in years."

"Then he brought his own gun," Byam reasoned. "And took it with him when he left, along with whatever papers he wanted.

Perhaps he brought his own ammunition, then preferred the gold, as a touch of irony.''

Drummond raised his eyebrows. "And Weems sat in his chair and watched him load, take aim and fire?"

Byam sighed and turned away, walking slowly to the window. "You are right. It makes no sense."

"Can you tell me anything about Weems?" Drummond asked quietly. "You went to his office several times, you said. Did anyone else call while you were there? Did he say anything about anyone else, mention any other debtors, or victims of blackmail?" He put his hands in his pockets and stood looking at Byam's back, his hunched shoulders. "What kind of a man was he? Was he cruel, did he enjoy the power he had over you? Was he afraid? Careful? Did he take any precautions against visitors?"

Byam bent his head in thought for several moments, then finally spoke in a quiet, concentrated voice.

"He made no mention of anyone else that I can recall, certainly not that he blackmailed anyone other than me. Of course I never went during his ordinary hours of business, so it is hardly surprising I saw no one. I insisted on its being organized that way. It would defeat my purpose in paying him for silence if I ran the risk of meeting anyone else there."

He shrugged. "What kind of man was he? Greedy. Above all else he was greedy. He liked the power money gave him, but I felt it was only to get more money." He turned around and looked at Drummond again. "I didn't notice that he was overtly cruel. He did not blackmail for the pleasure it gave him to torment, at least I got no impression that he did. He wanted the money. I can picture quite clearly how his eyes lit up when he saw money on the table in front of him. He had rather a pallid skin, and greenish brown eyes." He smiled sourly. "He put me in mind of a frog that has been kept in the dark. And to answer your other questions, I never saw him afraid. I cannot tell what he thought, but he did not behave as if he had the slightest fear. He acted as though he thought money gave him a kind of invulnerability."

He walked over towards the fireplace and turned again. "I'm glad he was proved so dramatically wrong. I would like to have seen the expression on his face when he saw that gun pointing at him and looked at the eyes of the man who held it, and knew he was going to shoot." He regarded Drummond steadily. "Does that sound offensively vindictive? I'm sorry. The man has cost me dearly in peace of mind. And I imagine will continue to do so for some time to come."

"I'll do everything I can," Drummond promised. He could think of nothing else to ask and he had discharged his commitment both to a man he was feeling increasing sympathy for and to a brother in the Inner Circle.

Byam smiled bleakly.

"I'm sure you will, and I do not wish to sound either ungrateful for your discretion or unbelieving of your man's abilities. It is hard when you cannot see a solution yourself to realize that someone else whom you do not know can solve it for you. I am not used to feeling so helpless. I am obliged to you, Drummond."

"We'll find him," Drummond said rashly, perhaps Eleanor Byam more in his mind than her husband. "Pitt won't rest until he finds the truth—I promise you that."

Byam smiled and offered his hand.

Drummond took it, held it a moment, then walked to the door.

CHAPTER
FOUR

Since the first list had yielded nothing, Pitt was faced with the necessity of pursuing the names on Weems's second list. He wanted to put off as long as possible the burden of investigating his fellow police officer, therefore he began with Addison Carswell. He already had his address so beginning was not difficult; it was merely a matter of choosing which aspect of his life to examine first.

The sensible place seemed to be his home. One may learn a great deal about a man by seeing how he lives, what his domestic tastes are, how much money he appears to have at his disposal, and upon what he chooses to spend it. Perhaps even more may be learned about his financial circumstances by meeting his wife and estimating his family responsibilities.

Accordingly Pitt set off for Mayfair. The hansom sped through warm, busy streets, passing broughams, landaus and carriages with ladies about errands. It was far too early for morning calls, which anyway were paid in the afternoon; this was the hour for visiting dressmakers and the like. There were delivery carts with all manner of goods, other hansoms with gentlemen beginning the business day, and here and there the occasional public omnibus, packed with men, women and children sitting upright or squeezed together, scrupulously ignoring each other and waiting for their own stop at which to dismount.

At Curzon Street, Pitt paid the cabby and alighted. It was a gracious way, and looking up and down it, he judged it to have been expensive and discreet for most of its history. If Addison Carswell was in financial difficulty he would find it a serious drain on his resources to maintain a residence here for long.

He went to the front door, hesitated a moment, rearranging in his mind what he planned to say, then pulled the bell, a fine brass affair with engraved numbers beneath it.

The door was opened by a parlormaid in a dark dress and crisp, lace-edged cap and apron. She was a handsome girl, tall and with a clear, country complexion, shining hair—everything a parlormaid should be. Addison Carswell would seem to pay attention to appearances—or perhaps it was Mrs. Carswell who cared. Very often it was women to whom such things mattered most.

"Yes sir?" she said with well-concealed surprise. Whoever she had expected, it was not Pitt.

He smiled with as much charm as he could, which was considerable, more than he was aware.

"Good morning. Mrs. Carswell is not expecting me, but I have a rather delicate errand with which she may be able to assist me. I would be most obliged if you would ask her if she would receive me." With a feeling of considerable satisfaction he pulled his card out of his inner pocket and presented it to her. It stated his name but not his police rank. It was an extravagance he had indulged in a few years ago, and it still gave him inordinate pleasure.

The parlormaid looked at it doubtfully, but in spite of his less than elegant appearance, his voice was beautiful, well modulated, and his diction excellent. She made a rapid judgment of her own, and smiled back.

"Certainly sir. If you will wait in the morning room I will inform Mrs. Carswell you are here."

"Thank you." Pitt had no time to look around the entrance hallway, but when he was left in the morning room he spent the ten minutes she kept him waiting in close scrutiny of everything in the room. This was his primary purpose in coming, and if she refused to see him, might well be all he would achieve.

The furniture was very traditional, showing far more comfort than imagination in its style. It was mostly of heavy oak, over-ornamented for Pitt's taste, but of good quality. Nothing was scratched or marred as if it had been carelessly used, or cheaply purchased. The sofa and chairs had been recently upholstered, there were no worn patches, and the antimacassars were embroidered and without blemish.

The photographs on the mantel were framed in silver, polished and gleaming. He looked at them closely. The largest in the center was a family group: a man in formal pose, stiff collar and fixed expression; a handsome woman beside him, full bosomed, smooth throated, richly gowned; and around and behind them a young man, whose features closely resembled the woman, and three girls, all fair haired and wide-eyed, who seemed so alike it was difficult to tell them apart. A fourth girl with darker hair sat on the ground in front, making a charming and almost symmetrical picture. It was stiff in composition, and yet the naturalness of the resemblance and the affection between them gave it a warmth that no photographer could destroy.

The other frames held portraits of the same people individually, several taken some years earlier at different stages of youth. There was also a rather awkward picture of a nervous older couple, afraid of the camera and holding the pose so carefully their lips were pressed together and their eyes staring. Perhaps they were the parents of either Mr. or Mrs. Carswell.

He walked over to the window and looked into the sunlit garden full of flowers, early roses and late lupins making splashes and spires of pink. The curtains were respectably heavy, and draped across the floor at the bottom. He had learned to know that for the display of wealth it was intended. He smiled to himself, and turned back to the room to look at the pictures on the walls.

Here he was surprised to see they were of excellent quality. His work with art theft and fraud had taught him a great deal about paintings and their value, and he recognized a number of artists with ease. He especially liked watercolors for their delicacy and subtle use of light, and he knew as soon as he saw these that they were recent artists and of high quality. Someone in the Carswell house either had excellent taste or was prepared to spend liberally, even on so little used a room as this; or else Mr. Carswell chose to spend his money on art, and was very well advised in the matter.

It would be very interesting to see what he had chosen for the more frequently used rooms, such as the withdrawing room.

He was still looking at a soft landscape, a view of a shaded walk under trees, when Regina Carswell came in. She was obviously the woman at the center of the large photograph, dark haired and broad browed. There were several lines in her face, but they were all comfortable and gave her expression an air of calm.

"Mr. Pitt? My parlormaid tells me you believe I may be of assistance to you. Pray, in what way?"

"Good morning, Mrs. Carswell. It is very gracious of you to give up your time," he said quickly. "I hope I do not inconvenience you. I am from the metropolitan police. I am inquiring into several recent art thefts, perpetrated in a particularly ingenious manner. The thieves present themselves as gentlemen who are lovers of fine paintings and are here on behalf of certain small museums, both in England and abroad." He saw the polite interest in her face, and continued. "They say they have heard you have some excellent and little-known works and they would be interested in borrowing them for exhibition, for which of course they would reimburse you accordingly. It would only be for a matter of two or three months, then your paintings would be returned to you—"

"That doesn't sound dishonest to me," she said frankly.

He smiled. "It is not, to this point," he agreed. "Except that there is no museum. They take the paintings—and in three months' time return to you not your own painting, but an excellent forgery. Unless you examine it closely you would not know. And since it is in your frame, and you believe them to be reputable people, there is no reason why you should look at it more than cursorily, as you replace it on the wall."

Her face pinched very slightly.

"We have had no such gentlemen here, Mr. Pitt. I'm sorry I cannot be of any assistance to you at all."

It was what he had expected. "At least, Mrs. Carswell, be prepared," he said easily. "And if anyone does call with such an offer, refuse it, and inform me at the Bow Street police station, at your earliest opportunity." He glanced at the walls. "I see in the room here you have some delightful work which such thieves would love to obtain. I hope your locks on the windows and doors are all in good condition? Perhaps I might look at them and advise you?"

"If you wish, but I assure you my husband is most careful about such things. He is a magistrate, you know, and quite aware of both the nature and the frequency of crime.''

"Indeed, ma'am. If you would prefer . . .'' He left it hanging in the air, hoping she would not accept his withdrawal. He needed to see as much of the house as possible.

"Not at all,'' she said graciously. "I shall have Gibson show you all the downstairs doors and windows.'' And so saying she rang the bell to summon the butler. When he came, a small man with abundant whiskers, she explained to him Pitt's office and his purpose.

"Certainly, ma'am.'' He turned to Pitt. "If you will come this way, sir,'' he said with chill civility. He did not approve of police persons inside the house, and he wished Pitt to realize he was doing this under sufferance.

Pitt thanked Mrs. Carswell again, and followed Gibson's retreating figure to examine the security of the house.

As he had supposed, the window latches and door locks were all in excellent repair, and he was assured they were checked every night before the last servant retired. Not that he would have expected Gibson to admit to less. What was far more interesting to him was the furnishing and the decor.

The withdrawing room was large, but lacked a look of spaciousness because the walls were covered in patterned paper, and the furniture was of the most modern design, clean lined, but engraved and inlaid so the impression was still of complicated surfaces. The curtains were heavy velvet, tied back with gilded, embossed and fringed sashes.

Pitt felt overpowered with opulence, and yet he knew it was no more than he would have found in most homes of men similarly situated both as to wealth and social rank. He had seen many such fireplaces with marble pilasters up the sides and ornate carving over the top, other gilt and ormolu clocks, other surfaces covered with china. In this case it was a top-heavy, elaborately scrolled Minton potpourri vase of neo-rococo design: blue, gold and white with lush flowers. He thought it hideous, but knew it was well thought of by many, and certainly valuable.

More to his taste in its simple lines was a Bohemian-red etched glass goblet, a souvenir of the Great Exhibition of 1851. Another memento was a painted and gilded lacquer box with pictures of the Crystal Palace.

He inspected the windows to satisfy the story he had told, watched by Gibson, as was his job. At least the man seemed sensible to the fact that callers such as Pitt could be just as dishonest as the thieves they were detailed to prevent. He watched Pitt with eyes like a hunting cat, not missing a gesture. Pitt smiled to himself and inwardly praised the man.

The dining room was equally splendid, and the porcelain in evidence was of excellent quality. There was a certain amount of Chinoiserie, as was popular, but these examples were blue and white and one at least, Pitt thought, was quite old—either Ming or a very good copy. Certainly if Addison Carswell wished to sell something and raise a little money, he could have found many times the amount Weems's books had him owing.

The ladies' sitting room, known as the boudoir, was quite different, perhaps decorated according to Mrs. Carswell's taste rather than her parents-in-law, from whom she had possibly inherited the house. Here were pre-Raphaelite paintings, all brooding and passionate faces, clean lines of design and dark, burning colors. Figures of legend and dream were depicted in noble poses. All sorts of ancient stories were brought to memory and their effect was curiously pleasing. The furniture was William Morris, simple lines and excellent workmanship; perhaps some were even genuine rather than imitations.

Here there were more pictures of the daughters, the three fair-haired girls in carefully decorous poses, features stylized to show large eyes and small, delicate mouths, the passion carefully ironed out—or perhaps it had never been there, but Pitt doubted that. Few young women were as childishly pure as this artist had drawn. These were pictures designed to portray them as the marriage market wished them to be seen.

A fourth girl, dark haired, looked much more natural. There was a streak of individuality in her face as if the artist had not felt the pressure to convey a message. Pitt looked down and saw she had a wedding ring on her slender hand. He smiled to himself, and moved on to the next room.

The remainder of the house was as he would have expected,

well furnished in traditional style, unimaginative, comfortable, full of ornaments, paintings, tapestries and mementos of this and past generations, small signs of family life, pride in the only son, gifts from parents, old samplers stitched by the daughters as young girls, a variety of books.

By the time he had seen the kitchen as well, and the servants' quarters that were on the ground floor, Pitt had a very clear idea of a close, busy, rather bourgeois family, undisturbed by scandal. The tragedies and triumphs were largely of a domestic sort: the dinner party that succeeds; the invitations extended and accepted; the suitor who calls, or does not call; the dress which is a disaster; the awaited letter which never arrives.

From the servants he picked up small remarks about callers when he asked about outsiders with entry to the house. He was told of dressmakers, milliners, women friends coming to tea or leaving cards. And of course the family entertained. There were parties of many sorts. Right now there were invitations to a ball in return to one they had only recently given.

Pitt left Addison Carswell's house feeling really very little wiser with regard to the death of William Weems. He had a strong sense of an agreeable upper-middle-class family: affectionate, pleasantly domestic, no more obtuse than was normal in wishing their daughters to marry well both socially and financially. That much he had gathered quite easily. He smiled and thought how much more Charlotte would have read into it, the subtleties and refinements he could only guess at vaguely. But none of this led him any further towards knowing if Carswell was in heavy debt to Weems, or whether the issue might be one of blackmail, as it was with Byam. The household was not on the surface any more extravagant than he would have expected for a man in Carswell's position. And it was always possible Mrs. Carswell had a little money of her own to contribute, which might account for the very excellent pictures.

He walked along Curzon Street in the sun, his hands in his pockets, his mind deep in thought, scarcely noticing the carriages with their liveried footmen passing him by. He could go to Carswell's associates and ask them certain trivial questions, on some pretext or other, but even so, what would the answers tell him? That he played cards, perhaps? If he did, what of it? They would not admit if he had lost heavily lately. That was the sort of thing one gentleman did not reveal about another.

He turned the corner into South Audley Street then left along Great Stanhope Street into Park Lane.

Was Carswell worried or anxious lately? If he had confided in anyone, the confidant would not betray him by repeating the matter, least of all to a stranger he would recognize instantly as not one of their own, even if Pitt did not identify himself as a policeman. And worry indicated nothing. It could be about any number of things that had nothing whatever to do with William Weems. It could be a matter of health, or a Carswell daughter being courted by someone unsuitable, or, perhaps as bad, being courted by no one at all. It could be a complicated case he had been required to judge, a decision he was unhappy over, a friend in difficulties, or simply indigestion.

Beautiful carriages were passing him, their passengers ladies taking the air, faces sheltered from the sun by huge hats, nodding to friends on the footpath. Beyond them the trees in Hyde Park barely moved in the breeze.

Had Carswell developed erratic habits of late? If he had any ability at all he would conceal such a thing.

It was time he met Carswell himself, and asked him outright if he were in debt to Weems, and gave the man an opportunity to prove he had been elsewhere at the time of Weems's death, and eliminate himself from inquiry.

Pitt hailed a cab and asked the driver to take him to the police court in Bow Street, where Carswell would be sitting. It took him half an hour traveling east through heavy traffic and by the time he arrived and paid the driver he was impatient. But one could not simply walk in and see an official of the court. The place was grim, busy and extremely formal, everyone consumed in their own importance, hurrying along corridors with sheaves of paper.

Pitt attempted to straighten his tie, and loosened it, ending up with it worse than before. He pulled his jacket down a little and moved some of the extraneous articles from one pocket to the other, trying to attain a little more balance. Then he presented himself to the clerk of the court and requested to see Mr. Addison Carswell when he had the opportunity between cases.

He filled in the waiting time by overhearing as much as possible of snatches of conversation between police on duty and witnesses waiting to give evidence. He hoped to gather some other opinions of Carswell, and was surprisingly successful.

"Yer got a fair chance," one sharp-faced little man observed, sucking at his teeth with a hissing sound. " 'E in't too bad, Carswell. 'E in't vindictive, like."

"All beaks is vindictive," his friend replied gloomily. " 'E in't never goin' ter believe I got it fair and square. 'E's goin' ter say I nicked it. I can see it comin'."

"Well keep yer yap shut an' 'e won't know," the other said sharply. "Don' offer 'im nuffin' 'as 'e don' ask yer."

"I should 'a paid old Skinjiggs ter give me summat—"

"No yer shouldn't. I tol' jer, there's some as yer can be friends wiv an' they take it badly, an' Carswell in't one of 'em. Jus' keep yer lip buttoned an' don' say nuffin' as yer don' 'ave ter."

Then the conversation degenerated into speculation as to what sentence their mutual friend would receive. They had no doubt he would be found guilty.

Further along a pale young woman in gray was being comforted by her lawyer, a sandy little man with a white wig on a trifle crooked over his right ear and an earnest expression of entreaty.

"Please, Mrs. Wilby, don't agitate yourself so. Mr. Carswell is extremely consistent. He does not give exemplary sentences. He is a very predictable judge. I have never known him to step outside the average."

She sniffed and dabbed her nose with a scrap of handkerchief, and continued staring at the floor.

Were they simply the words of a nervous young man trying to comfort his client, or was Carswell really a man whose career showed no erratic decisions, no questionable behavior?

Pitt approached another lawyer who seemed to be standing around in hope of finding a little business, and asked him a few pertinent questions, as if he had a friend presently awaiting trial.

"Excuse me," he began tentatively.

The lawyer looked at him dubiously. "Yes?"

"I have a friend up on a charge before Mr. Carswell," Pitt said, watching the man's face in case his expression betrayed more than his words. "I wonder, can you tell me what sort of chance he has?"

The lawyer pulled a face. "Depends what he's up for. But he's a pretty fair chap on the whole, no better than most, no worse. He has his dislikes—is your friend a pimp, by any chance?"

"Why?" Pitt tried to look anxious.

"Hates pimps," the lawyer said expressively. "And pornographers—and anyone who abuses women. Has a soft spot for women, it seems."

"Thieving," Pitt amended quickly.

"He'll be all right. Inclined to be lenient to a bit of simple thieving. Unless, of course, he was violent? No? Or robbed the old or the very poor? No—then don't worry. He'll be fine."

"Thank you sir," Pitt said enthusiastically, finding himself wishing more and more strongly that he would find Addison Carswell was not guilty of having murdered Weems.

Eventually the clerk came scurrying along to him, the tails of his gown flying, his face furrowed with agitation.

"Mr. Pitt, Mr. Carswell will see you now. I do hope you won't keep him long, we have a great deal to get through and it would really be most inconvenient if he were to be delayed. You assured me it was urgent police business, and I have taken you at your word, sir." His wispy eyebrows rose and he desired to reconsider that he had understood correctly and it truly justified his extraordinary intrusion.

"Indeed it is," Pitt said, hiding a slight smile and reminding himself of Weems's disfigured corpse in the mortuary, to force his priorities back to where his brain told him they should be. "You may be easy in your mind that I am not wasting Mr. Carswell's time."

"Ah—indeed. Then will you come this way, quickly now." And so saying he turned and walked away so rapidly it was all but a trot.

Pitt strode after him and only two minutes later was shown into the chambers where Addison Carswell took short respites between one batch of cases and another. He had no time to look at it beyond noticing the walls were lined with bookshelves, presumably law tomes by their leather covers and great size. The single window overlooked a quiet courtyard and he could see the sunlight on an old stone wall at the far side. A single large desk was empty but for a silver salver with a bottle of Madeira and two glasses.

Carswell was standing with his back to the bookshelves. He was imposing now in his robes of office and with the weight of his calling so sharp in his mind. In the courtroom only a few yards away his power over his fellow beings was enormous. But stripped of these things Pitt judged he would be a very ordinary man, like thousands of others in London. He was well-to-do but not beyond the reach of anxiety; comfortable in his home and family of conforming disposition in both religion and political views; socially popular, accepted, but not a leader, still aspiring to climb considerably higher. In fact he was a man of very ordinary ambition and perhaps a few private dreams a little more individual, which would probably always remain just that: private—and only dreams.

"Yes, Mr. . . . Mr. Pitt?" Carswell said curiously. "What can I do for you, sir? I have but little time, as I am sure you realize."

"Yes sir," Pitt said immediately. "Therefore I shall not waste it with a lengthy preamble. May I be blunt?"

Carswell winced very slightly. "I suppose it would be an advantage."

"Thank you. Can you tell me where you were between eight o'clock in the evening and midnight of Tuesday last week?"

Carswell thought for a moment, then a faint pink tinge appeared in his cheeks. "Is there some reason why I should, sir?"

"It would help to clear up a matter in which certain parties may be lying," Pitt said, evading the issue.

Carswell bit his lip. "I was in a hansom cab, traveling from one place to another. The places need not concern you. I witnessed nothing out of the ordinary."

"Where did you pass, sir?"

"That is a private matter."

"Are you acquainted with a Mr. William Weems?" Pitt watched Carswell's face closely for the smallest change of color or expression, and saw nothing but an attempt at recollection.

"Not that I think of," Carswell said after a moment. "Was he concerned in a case I tried?"

"I don't believe so." Pitt had no idea whether he was completely unaware of Weems's identity, either as a usurer or the victim of a recent murder, or whether he was a superlative liar. "He lived in Clerkenwell."

"I do not have occasion to visit Clerkenwell, Mr. Pitt." Carswell frowned. "If you forgive me, sir, you seem to be somewhat less direct than you intimated to me. I do not know Mr. Weems. Who or what is he, and why did you suppose I might know him?"

"He was a usurer, sir, who had your name on his book as having owed him a considerable amount."

Carswell's amazement might have been comic in any other circumstances.

"Owed him money? That is preposterous! I owe no one money, Mr. Pitt. But were I to be in financial difficulties I should not go to a usurer in Clerkenwell, but to my bankers to tide me over until circumstances improved." He frowned as the absurdity of the thought became even more apparent to him. "But anyway, should that occur, and I assure you it has not, I have many personal possessions which I would dispose of, and I would do, before falling into the clutches of such a person. I have had far too much experience of tragic cases of men in debt to usury through my court to allow myself into such a desperate pass."

It did not seem to occur to him that Pitt would doubt him. Perhaps it was too easily proved for him to imagine anyone would tell anything but the truth. Of course he did not know that Pitt had been to his home and knew for himself that he had much he could have realized money on, had he the need, but his very lack of pressing the point made Pitt think it the more likely he felt no guilt in the matter. Even now he stared wide-eyed and amused more than angry at the suggestion, and there was no fear in him, no tension in his body, no shadow in his eyes.

"He must have had my name for some other reason," Carswell went on with a shrug of his shoulders. "My calling means that my name is known to various people of unsavory character and dubious occupation. Perhaps one of his clients passed through my court?"

"Very possible," Pitt agreed. "But his book stated quite specifically that you owed him a large amount of money. The sum was written out, and the date at which you borrowed it, at what rate of interest, and when the loan was due. It was not simply a casual reference."

Carswell drew his brows down. "How very peculiar. I assure you, Mr. Pitt, it is quite untrue. I have never borrowed money in my life." His otherwise pleasant voice grew a trifle sharper. "I have never required to. My situation is more than comfortable, which I could prove to you, had I the mind to, but I prefer to keep my financial affairs confidential, and I see no reason why I should break that custom because you have come across a moneylender with a malicious sense of amusement."

He leaned back a little and looked very directly at Pitt.

"Go back and tell Mr. Weems that I do not appreciate having my name taken lightly, and that he would be well advised to be truthful in future, or it will go ill with him. One can be prosecuted for willfully making mischief with another man's reputation."

"You have never met Mr. Weems?"

"I have not, sir." His tone grew sharper; his patience was thinning and he no longer felt anxious. "I thought I had made that plain! Now if that is all you have to say, I would ask you to allow me the remainder of my respite from court in peace so I may collect my thoughts and take some refreshment."

Pitt looked at him carefully, but he could see nothing in Carswell's face whatever but the good-natured irritation any man might feel at such a liberty both with his name and his time.

"Mr. Weems is dead," he said quietly. "He was murdered a week ago."

"Oh." Carswell was obviously taken aback, but still there seemed no fear in him. "I'm sorry. I did not mean to speak lightly of any man in his extremity. But I am afraid I still cannot help you. I do not know him. Nor can I think of any reason why he should have my name in his papers. It seems to me extremely mischievous." He frowned, a flicker of anxiety returning to his face. "Is there some conspiracy, Mr. Pitt? You mentioned that people may be lying. You asked me where I was, and now you say this man Weems has been murdered. Did your suspect claim to have been in my company at the time?"

Pitt smiled, a small, rather bleak gesture. "I too would prefer to reserve some of my information, sir," he said as courteously as was possible with such a statement. "Thank you for sparing me your time in the middle of the day. I will find my own way out. Good day, Mr. Carswell."

"Good day," Carswell replied from behind, his voice subdued and thoughtful.

There was little purpose in seeking information from Carswell's friends or colleagues. They would only infer that the police had been inquiring about him, and he would realize he was suspected of Weems's murder. He was far too used to criminal procedure to imagine Pitt would waste his time otherwise. It would put him on his guard without offering any benefit, and the chance that any friend would betray anything of import was so remote as not to be worth pursuing.

All that was left now was the tedious and wearing task of following him for as many days as were necessary, either to establish that he had a pattern of spending, a debt that would tend to confirm his borrowing from Weems, or some secret that would make blackmail possible; or else find nothing, which would mean that he was aware of his danger and clever enough to conceal his weaknesses, or there were none, and Pitt would have to look further to find out why his name was on Weems's list.

It was a morning and evening job through the week. Carswell was safe enough in the court through the days, except perhaps at midday when he might well take his luncheon out. Pitt could hardly stand around inside the court building to see who visited him, as he had done himself, through the day. He did not wish Carswell to be aware he was being observed—apart from warning him, it would make keeping him in sight so much more difficult.

Pitt hated having his hours and his whereabouts dictated in such a way; it was an oddly irritating limitation he had left behind with his first promotion. The freedom to act for himself without forever reporting and accounting to someone else was one of the things he liked best about being a detective rather than a uniformed officer. He smiled at his own frailty that such a small thing should feel so cramping, and resented it just as much.

But Carswell, Urban and Latimer were the best suspects, unless it was Byam after all, which was a thought he would avoid as long as possible. And he was deeply reluctant to find it was one of the ordinary borrowers, the small men and women driven to despair by cold, hunger and worry. If it was one of them he would feel an icy finger of temptation to call the case unsolved, and he did not want to face the moral dilemma of that. He might find his judgment confounded by emotions of pity and anger against the endless grind that allowed one man to bleed another into hopelessness and rob him of the dignity of a choice that was better than death by cold and hunger not only for himself but for his children—this terrible violence. If you drive a man to choose between death of his body or corruption of his soul, how much are you also to blame if his choice is the wrong one?

Such were Pitt's thoughts as he stood, hands in his pockets, head down, as he waited for Carswell to leave the court at the end of the day. It was harder following people in the summer. The evenings were light until ten or later, the weather was warm, so there was no excuse for pulled-down hats, turned-up collars, and no shadows to sink back into. Not often was there fog to blanket one, and little rain to hurry through with head down. And his height was against him; he stood half a head above the crowd. If Carswell once realized he was there, he would recognize him and pick him out easily enough again.

When Carswell emerged he had little difficulty in following him to Curzon Street, where he waited until well after the dinner hour, when he decided he was probably going to remain there all night. He gratefully gave up and, shivering a little from the long standing still, he turned and strode off to the main thoroughfare where he could find a hansom to take him back to Bloomsbury and his own home.

It was only when he was lying in bed listening to Charlotte's quiet breathing and feeling her warmth beside him that he realized with a start of guilt that there was no real reason why Carswell could not have gone out again once his family was asleep. If he had any nefarious purpose to fulfill, it might very well be accomplished in the night, the one time he could best count on a measure of privacy, and not feel any call to explain his whereabouts. Perhaps that was when he had visited Weems—not in the evening but the middle of the night, the short summer night which would only amount to five or six hours of darkness.

It was too late now. But tomorrow he would have to go to Clerkenwell police station and request at least one other man to help him. Carswell must be watched all the time, day and night.

He turned and put his arms around Charlotte, touching her hair soft over her shoulder, heavy and warm, smelling faintly of the lavender water she liked. He smiled and put his guilt behind him. She stirred slightly and moved a little closer.

Innes continued to investigate the borrowers on Weems's first list, and in the small room in the Clerkenwell station he told Pitt of seven who were in deep distress with nothing else to pawn, no food and owing rent, no clothes but those they stood in, hollow eyes filled one moment with resignation, the next with a sudden flame of anger and the will to fight. None of these few could find anyone to swear as to their presence somewhere else when Weems was killed. Innes told Pitt their names with a deep unhappiness. He made little effort to hide his own wish that it should be one of the "nobs" who was guilty. He stood in the Clerkenwell station in the room they had lent Pitt, his thin body stiff, his shoulders squared, looking at Pitt a little defiantly.

It would have been clumsy to express understanding in words. The feeling was both too profound and too delicate: a mixture of pity; guilt for not suffering with them, for seeing what should have been private; and fear that in the end they would have to arrest one of them and take him to be tried and hanged, exactly as if they had understood nothing.

"Then we'd better follow Mr. Carswell very thoroughly," Pitt said with no particular expression in his voice, and looking a little beyond Innes's stiff face. "We'll need another man. Can you see to that?"

"Why would a magistrate borrer money from a swine like Weems, sir?" Innes said without relaxing in the slightest. "It don't make no sense."

"He probably didn't," Pitt agreed. "I expect it was blackmail."

"Is that wot 'appened to your nob?" Innes asked baldly, his stare unwaveringly in front of him.

"Yes," Pitt admitted equally baldly. "But there's no crime involved, only a misjudgment of character. A woman became infatuated with him and took her own life. It would be a scandal, and unpleasant for his family."

" 'Ardly compares wiv what I've seen." Innes was still grudging. He stood stiffly beside the table. Pitt was leaning on the only chair.

"No—which is why I don't think he killed Weems. He didn't have enough to lose. But maybe Carswell did."

"I'll see ter gettin' 'im followed." Innes relaxed a little at last. "What times do yer want ter do it yerself, sir? Or would yer like two men so they can do it all?"

"One will do," Pitt conceded. "I'll do it during the day. I've nothing better to do."

Innes forgot himself for a moment.

"What about the nob o' yours, sir? Even though 'e's not afraid o' scandal, if 'e were prepared to pay, maybe 'e got tired of it, and decided to get rid o' Weems. 'Specially if Weems got greedier and upped 'is price?"

"I have thought of that," Pitt said very levelly, his voice not exactly cold, but very precise. "I will pursue it if I exhaust the other possibilities."

Innes opened his mouth, about to apologize, then some element of pride intruded—or perhaps it was a sense of dignity and a desire to maintain a certain relationship—and he remained silent.

"Then we'll look at the other debtors on the second list," Pitt went on. "Mr. Urban and Mr. Latimer."

"I could start on them right away, sir," Innes offered.

"No," Pitt said rather too quickly, then seeing Innes's face, felt obliged to explain. "We'll leave them till we have to—Urban at least. He's a colleague."

"Whose colleague?" Innes did not yet understand.

"Ours, Innes," Pitt said flatly. "He is police."

Innes's face would have been comical were the situation not

so painful. All the ugly possibilities flickered through his mind and across his wildly expressive face, debt, gambling, blackmail and corruption.

"Ah," he said at last. "I see. Yes sir. Let's dispose o' Mr. Carswell first then. I'll see to it that 'e's followed all night, every night, sir." And with that he turned on his heel and went out, leaving Pitt alone in the small, cramped room.

During the next four days Pitt followed Addison Carswell from the Bow Street court to his home; to Kensington, Chelsea and Belgravia to dine with acquaintances; to his club, where he had to remain outside, unable to learn if he gambled, won or lost, whom he owed or with whom he spoke. It was almost a waste of time, since all he could learn of use was closed to him, but he had not yet any grounds to go in and demand information with any authority.

He followed Carswell to his tailor, who seemed to receive him without the rather stiff, hostile familiarity tailors employed if they were owed money. Indeed the man was all smiles when he came to the door to bid Carswell good-day.

It was not until the fifth day, when Pitt was losing heart, that Carswell finally went somewhere of interest. Shopping of itself held no particular meaning, nor even what he purchased. A pretty hat and a lace parasol, all wrapped in tissue and pink boxes, were not remarkable purchases for a man with a wife and four daughters, three of them unmarried. It was the fact that when he emerged from the shop, Pitt close behind him, he hurried along the footpath, head down, occasionally glancing sideways. Once when he saw ahead of him someone he seemed to know, he pulled his hat forward and leaped over the gutter to dart across the street in front of a brougham, almost under the horse's hooves, startling the animal and causing the driver to jerk on the reins and swear violently, then draw up his vehicle, shaking with fear that he had so nearly killed a man.

Pitt had lost sight of Carswell and felt a twinge of uncertainty. The sweat broke out on his skin as he struggled to find a space between the broughams, barouches, landaus, phaetons and victorias to go over himself. He danced on the curb in impatience as a brewer's dray went past him, with huge bay horses, flanks gleaming, manes braided and ribboned, hard followed by a hansom, then a clarence. At last he ran out into the street, defying an open landau with two women taking the air, raced in front of a barouche going the other way, and reached the opposite side amid a group of fashionable idlers. Carswell was nowhere in sight. He brushed past three men talking, calling out apologies, and ran along the path, only catching up with Carswell as he was about to climb into a cab.

Pitt hailed a hansom immediately behind.

"Follow that cab that just pulled out!" he ordered.

"What?" The cabby was suspicious, turning on his box to stare at him.

"I'm a policeman," Pitt said urgently. "A detective. Follow that cab!"

"A detective?" The man's face brightened with sudden interest.

"Get on with it!" Pitt said exasperatedly. "You'll lose him."

"No I won't!" The cabby caught the spirit of it. "I can follow anybody anywhere in London." And with enthusiasm and some skill he urged his horse and turned into the traffic, butting ahead of a victoria and across the path of a berline. They were going westward towards Curzon Street, but south, which made Pitt at last feel that he was about to discover something of Carswell that was not utterly predictable and totally innocent.

He sat upright in the cab, wishing he could see forward as well as sideways as they went over the river at Westminster Bridge, then turned south into Lambeth.

They traveled up Westminster Bridge Road and Pitt could see couples out walking, the women in pastels and flowers and laces in the late afternoon sunshine. One or two carried parasols, more for elegance than to protect them from the soft light, and the heat was gone. He wondered who Carswell's gifts were for. The married daughter in the pictures in Curzon Street? She might live south of the river. But it seemed more likely Carswell would visit her later, with his wife and in his own carriage, not alone in a hired vehicle.

They turned into Kennington Road. It was full of people taking the evening air, open carriages, street peddlers with all manner of food: pies, eels, peppermint water, fruit sherbets, cordials, sand-

wiches. Girls offered bunches of flowers, matches, packets of lavender, little dolls. An organ grinder played hurdy-gurdy music and
in the summer street it sounded unexpectedly pleasing, all its
harshness and tawdriness sweetened by the open air, the clopping
of horses' feet and the hiss of wheels.

Pitt's cab stopped and the driver leaned out.

"Yer fare's got out, sir," he said quietly. " 'E went inter the
coffee'ouse on yer left."

"Thank you." Pitt climbed out and paid him. "Thank you very
much."

"Who is 'e?" the cabby asked. "Is 'e a murderer?"

"I don't know," Pitt said honestly.

The other cab had moved away so presumably Carswell intended remaining where he was for some time. "Thank you, that's
all," Pitt said, dismissing the cabby, to his acute disappointment.
He moved away reluctantly, still giving the occasional glance backwards over his shoulder to see what was happening.

Pitt smiled to himself and pulled his coat even further open
and took his tie off altogether, then followed Carswell into the
coffeehouse.

Inside was warm, stuffy and full of chatter, clinking glass and
rustling skirts, and the smell of coffee beans, pastry and sugar. On
the walls were colorful theater posters, and now and again someone
roared with laughter.

In a corner over to the right Addison Carswell was being
greeted by a slender, pretty girl with a mass of soft honey-brown
hair which was piled on her head in the very latest fashion, the
short ends curling onto her neck as only nature can and no art has
learned to imitate. In spite of her youth her features were strong
and her face full of vitality, her eyes wide and clear. Pitt judged
her to be in her early twenties.

Carswell was looking at her with a smile he could not mask
and an anticipation in his eyes as he gave her the hatbox and the
parcel containing the parasol. She opened them with quick fingers,
tearing at the paper, every few moments glancing up at him, then
down again. When she finally took off the last pieces and let them
flutter to the ground she held up the parasol with unfeigned delight,
and then the hat.

Carswell put out his hand and touched her wrist, restraining her before she could swing the hat up and try it on. She smiled, blushing as if she suddenly remembered her foolishness, and put her hand down again.

Carswell's face reflected an extraordinary tenderness, an emotion so transparently genuine it startled Pitt and made him uncomfortably aware of being not merely a detective, but at this moment a voyeur.

He watched them for another thirty minutes. They sat at the table, the hatbox and the parasol at the girl's feet, leaning forward speaking to each other one minute earnestly, the next lightly and with laughter, but it was not loud, neither did the girl have any of the mannerisms of flirting. Rather it seemed an affection of two people who have known each other some time and shared many experiences which have given them a treasury of understanding from which to draw.

When Carswell arose and left after having bade the girl farewell, Pitt did not follow him, but turned his face away just in case Carswell should glance his way. But as it happened he looked neither to right nor left, but with a smile on his face and a spring in his step, he went out into Kennington Road. Pitt paid his bill and went out onto the pavement. He watched Carswell march away down towards Westminster Bridge where he might find a hansom, and presumably return home to Curzon Street and his wife. Perhaps before then he would have taken the jauntiness out of his stride and the dreaming from his face.

A few moments later when the girl left also, Pitt was waiting for her. She did not look for a cab, but walked along the pavement carrying the hatbox and the parasol, holding them close to her, also. Her step too was quick and light, almost as if she would have skipped, had it not been absurd and likely to draw attention to herself.

She crossed the road a hundred yards further along, passing the organ grinder and giving him a coin. He spoke to her cheerfully, touching his hat as if perhaps he knew her, and redoubled his efforts at the music. She turned off at St. Albans Street and a short way along, at number 16, stopped, fished from her reticule a latchkey, and went in.

Pitt stood on the pavement staring. It was a very ordinary house, small, narrow fronted, without a garden, but at least on the outside, eminently respectable, even if there was no servant to answer the door. It was the sort of house lived in by a petty clerk, a small trader or a teller in a bank, or perhaps the mistress of a man of means just sufficient to keep two establishments.

Then why did Carswell meet her in a coffeehouse, where they could do no more than talk and perhaps hold hands?

The obvious answer was that she did not live alone. Either she was married, although there had been no ring on her hand, or she shared her home with a parent or a brother or sister.

He turned away and retraced his steps to Kennington Road. It was not difficult to invent some trivial story, and learn from the shopkeeper on the corner that since poor Mrs. Hilliard became an invalid, number 16 was occupied by Miss Theophania Hilliard and her brother, Mr. James, and a very nice couple they were, always polite and paid all their bills on time. Never any trouble to anyone.

Pitt thanked him and left with an intense feeling of depression. He also walked down towards the bridge where he could find a cab which would take him home. But even when one passed him he felt an urge to continue on foot; he wanted to use the energy, as if the anger and disappointment inside him could be burned away in physical effort. There was everything here for tragedy: a middle-aged man of public respectability, a wife and daughters at home, who chose to buy expensive and highly feminine gifts and cross the river alone to give them to a young and pretty girl for whom he very obviously had intense feelings. In many ways it would have been less serious had it simply been a visit to a brothel; such things were more readily understood, and hardly worth blackmailing any-one over, certainly not worth committing murder to hide.

But Theophania Hilliard was not a casual appetite, and the hat and parasol did not seem to be bribes for favors past or future, rather gifts for someone towards whom he felt the most profound emotions. But had they been those of a nature he could acknowl-edge, why had he come furtively, going to such lengths to avoid being seen by anyone he knew? He had risked being killed, in careering across the road as he had, just to avoid being seen by an acquaintance. And why a coffee shop on the Kennington Road, if it were acceptable to her brother? Presumably he also objected to the liaison, or else he was entirely ignorant of it.

How much was this relationship costing Carswell? Did he bring her gifts often, or was this an isolated time? She had not seemed particularly surprised, at least looking back on it Pitt thought not. Had he brought such things for Charlotte she would have shown more amazement, more—he visualized her face if he were able to spend money on such pretty luxuries. She would have cried out, tried them on immediately, paraded up and down in them and twirled around for him to admire, her eyes would have danced, her voice would have been high, lifted with excitement. He wished with a sharp, almost hurting intensity that he could do such a thing for her, something extravagant and totally unnecessary, just beautiful, feminine, endlessly flattering. There must be a way he could save enough, something he could do without, or put off paying for.

It was so painfully easy to understand Addison Carswell—especially the first time, and this was assuredly not the first. Theophania Hilliard was accustomed to receiving pretty things from him—but once begun how could he stop, whatever it cost?

Was that it? Was he borrowing to finance his desire to please her? He would not readily admit it.

Or was it far uglier than that? Had Weems been blackmailing him too? And had he been driven beyond the point of reluctant compliance and into violent escape from a pressure he could no longer bear? Was it Carswell's innate sense of justice which had loaded some gun with gold coins and shot away half Weems's head?

Had he been with Theophania Hilliard that night which he refused to account for—or had he been in Clerkenwell, in Cyrus Street?

The next morning Pitt went to the police court early, intending to speak to Carswell at the first break from duty. It was a confrontation he was dreading, but it was unavoidable. The man must be given the opportunity to reconsider his silence and explain where he was the night Weems was murdered, and his relationship with

Theophania Hilliard. It was just conceivable there was an innocent answer to it—not innocent of all culpability, but innocent of murder.

The first case to be heard was a clerk who had embezzled a few shillings from his employers. He might, as the defense claimed, simply have been careless with figures, and have miscalculated the funds. It was just possible, although Pitt thought, looking at the man's pale intelligent face, he was more probably struggling to pay a bill and had taken his first step into crime. Or as the prosecutor maintained, he might have been testing the water preparing for a career of theft. Carswell inclined towards the last view, and sentenced him to a short term of imprisonment. Having found him guilty there was little alternative open to him and Pitt thought it was probably an accurate judgment, and not overharsh.

The second case came to him as a surprise. The accused's name was familiar even before his portly figure and angry face appeared in the dock. Horatio Osmar. Beside him, buxom, fair hair gleaming, but very scrubbed and demure, was Miss Beulah Giles, also accused.

The clerk of the court read out the charges, to wit that they had both been behaving in an unseemly manner likely to offend against public decency, and the time and place of the offense added to make the issue perfectly plain. Somehow such details made it sound even more down-to-earth, and indescribably small and grubby.

Horatio Osmar stood very stiff, balancing on the balls of his feet. His coat was immaculate, if a trifle lopsided at one shoulder, as if he had struggled with his escort and snatched himself away from a restraining grip. His face was overpink, his shapeless nose shone and his whiskers bristled, his eyes glared at everyone who chanced to catch his glance.

Miss Giles stood motionless with eyes downcast, and her dress, on this very different occasion from the one when Pitt had first seen her, was buttoned right up to her throat, and of a sober shade of blue-gray, with a touch of teal in it so at moments one was not sure whether it was entirely blue, or perhaps green. It could not have been gentler or more designed to make one think well of her.

The lawyer stood respectfully to plead for them, in both cases, not guilty.

Pitt leaned forward, startled even more. The man was a Queen's Counsel, one of that highly select group of lawyers who had taken silk and now dealt only in the most prestigious cases. What on earth was a Q.C. doing in a magistrate's court arguing a case of indecent behavior in a public park? It was natural Osmar should want to be found not guilty, but the facts were overwhelmingly against him, and to have such eminent counsel would only draw the press's attention to an incident which might otherwise have gone unreported.

The prosecution began by calling a very self-conscious P.C. Crombie, who took the witness stand and swore to his name and occupation, and that together with P.C. Allardyce he had been on duty in the park at the relevant time and place.

"And what did you see, Constable Crombie?" the prosecution asked, raising bushy eyebrows in inquiry.

P.C. Crombie stood to attention.

"I saw the accused sitting on the bench together with their arms 'round each other, sir."

"And what were they doing, Constable?"

Osmar snorted so fiercely it was audible in the body of the court.

P.C. Crombie swallowed. " 'Ard to say exact, sir. They looked like they was struggling over something, not fighting, like, just rocking back and forth—" He stopped, the color rising up his face with embarrassment.

"And what did you do, Constable?" the prosecution persisted, his face lugubrious as if his interest were barely engaged.

"P.C. Allardyce and me went up to them, sir," Crombie answered. "And as we got close the gentleman rose to 'is feet and started to rearrange 'is clothes—sir—"

Again Osmar grunted loudly and Carswell glared at him. There was a murmur around the room among the few spectators.

"Rearrange?" the prosecutor asked. "You must be more specific, Constable."

P.C. Crombie's face was scarlet. He looked straight ahead of him at some point in the woodwork on the far wall.

" 'Is trousers was undone, sir, and 'is shirt was 'anging out at the front. 'E tucked it in and did up 'is buttons, sir."

"And the young lady, Constable?" The prosecutor was merciless, his beautifully modulated voice cutting the silence like a silver knife.

P.C. Crombie closed his eyes.

"She was doin' up 'er blouse, sir, at the—" He raised his hands and held them roughly where his bosom would have been, had he one. He was a young man, and not married.

"Are you saying she was in a state of indecency, Constable?"

The Q.C. rose to his feet and there was a sharp rustle of interest around the room. Osmar smiled.

"My lord, the prosecution is leading the witness," the Q.C. said with injured gentility. "He did not say Miss Giles was indecently dressed, merely that she was fastening her blouse."

"I apologize to my learned friend," the prosecution said with a touch of sarcasm. "Constable, how would you describe the state of dress of Miss Giles?"

"Well sir—" Crombie glanced at Carswell, uncertain now how to proceed in what he was permitted to say. His face was burning red.

Osmar shifted in the dock, his face shining with satisfaction.

The prosecution smiled drily.

"Constable, did her state of dress embarrass you?"

"Yes sir! That it did!"

Beulah Giles hid a smirk less than satisfactorily.

The Q.C. was on his feet again. "My lord, that is surely irrelevant?"

"No it is not," the prosecution insisted, still smiling. "P.C. Crombie is part of the general public, and his reaction may be an acceptable indication of what other passersby might have felt when they saw this spectacle of a man and woman in such a degree of intimacy on a park bench for all to see."

"My lord, that has yet to be proved!" The Q.C. simulated outrage. "It may be argued that P.C. Crombie's susceptibilities are the sole issue here. It was he who arrested my client, and therefore he has something of an interest in the outcome of this case. He cannot be considered an unbiased witness. The prosecution's argument is circular."

Now the spectators in the room were agog, every face staring, bright with attention.

Carswell looked at the prosecution.

"Is this all you have, Mr. Clyde? If so, it seems very thin."

"No sir, there is also P.C. Allardyce."

"Then you had better call him."

Accordingly P.C. Crombie was excused and P.C. Allardyce was called. He was an older man by some three or four years, and married. He was less easily embarrassed, and as soon as he spoke the Q.C. realized it. He did not challenge his evidence but let it remain. He made no counterclaim when Allardyce described the struggle Horatio Osmar had made upon his arrest, his less than gentlemanly language and his arrival purple faced and furious at the police station, nor Miss Giles's similar state of dishabille.

He began his defense by calling Horatio Osmar himself to testify. He yanked his clothes straighter, stretched his neck as if to settle his collar, then faced Carswell directly for a moment before turning to the prosecution and waiting with polite inquiry for him to begin.

"Would you give us your account of this deplorable affair, please, Mr. Osmar," the Q.C. asked courteously.

Pitt watched with interest to see how Osmar would dress it in some form of respectability. The whole thing had been a miserable and excruciatingly silly affair, but for his dignity Osmar could not admit it here. How much easier if he had simply pleaded guilty and accepted a fine. Carswell would surely not have given him more than a caution, and a sum to pay he would easily afford. Whoever had advised him to employ a Queen's Counsel was either extremely foolish, or was secretly desiring his downfall.

Osmar put his shoulders back and stared defiantly at the spectators in the room, and they fell silent, not entirely out of respect, Pitt thought, but more largely so as not to miss anything.

Osmar's whiskers bristled and he cleared his throat importantly and sniffed. Then he began. "Certainly sir, I shall do that. I was taking the air in the park when I encountered Miss Giles, a young lady of my acquaintance. I greeted her and asked after her health, which she informed me was excellent."

The prosecution began to fidget and Carswell glared at him.

"Please continue, Mr. Osmar," he directed with a tight smile.

"Thank you, sir. I shall." He too glared at the prosecution, then straightened his tie ostentatiously.

There was a movement around the court and someone laughed.

Osmar began again. "I also asked after her family, as was only civil, and she began to tell me of their condition. I suggested that we might take a seat, which was nearby, rather than stand in the middle of the path. She accepted that it was a good idea so we adjourned to the bench upon which we were seated when the two constables saw us."

"And were you struggling with Miss Giles, sir?"

"Certainly not!" Osmar sniffed and his expression registered his contempt for the idea. "I had asked after a nephew of hers, and she showed me a picture of the child which was in a locket around her neck. She had to fumble a moment to open the catch, it was very small and not easy to find." He glanced around at the crowd. "I assisted her with it as it was quite naturally not in a position in which she could see it."

Pitt's opinion of Osmar's invention went up, and of his veracity went down. He looked at Carswell to see how he took this vivid piece of fabrication, and was startled to see an expression of total sobriety on his face.

"An innocent enough pastime," Carswell said with raised eyebrows and a look of irritation at the prosecution.

The prosecution looked puzzled, caught off guard, but it was not prudent for him to speak now and he knew it. He sat back in his seat, biting his lip.

"And was your dress in disarray, sir?" the Q.C. asked Osmar.

"Of course not!" Osmar said sententiously. "I am not a tidy man, as you may observe—" There was a titter around the room. "I had been searching my pockets for a note which I had mislaid," Osmar went on. "I am afraid I was somewhat hasty in my efforts, and may well have looked in disarray when I was accosted by the constables, but I was untidy, not more—and that is not yet a crime against anything but good taste."

The prosecution pulled a face of disbelief, the Q.C. smiled and Beulah Giles kept her face in a sober expression with obvious difficulty. For the first time Carswell looked faintly uncomfortable.

"And did you explain this to the constables, Mr. Osmar?" the Q.C. inquired, his eyes wide, his voice eminently reasonable.

"I attempted to." Osmar looked hurt. "I told them who I was, sir." At this his shoulders straightened even further back and his chin lifted. "I am not unknown in certain circles—I have a reputation, and many years of honorable service to my Queen and country."

"Indeed," the Q.C. said hastily. "But the constables would not listen to you?"

"Not a word," Osmar said with an acute sense of injury. "They were very rough with me, which is objectionable enough, but what I cannot forgive is the appalling way in which they treated Miss Giles, a young woman of respectable family and unspotted reputation."

Someone in the crowd shifted noisily. Beulah Giles colored and Osmar's face darkened.

"Forgive me, Mr. Osmar," the Q.C. said with a very slight smile. "But we have only your word for this—this order of things—so different from the account given to us by Constables Crombie and Allardyce."

"Ha!" Osmar's voice quivered and his cheeks puffed out. "That is not true, sir; not true at all. There was another witness—a man who was only a short distance away. He saw it all, because he observed that in my distress when I was arrested, I left behind the attaché case which I had with me. He picked it up and at a later hour he went to the police station and turned it in, so that I might reclaim it."

There was an audible sucking in of breath around the room.

"He was close enough to observe this?" The Q.C. feigned amazement. "And why did the police not call him as a witness here, now?"

Osmar assumed an expression of injured innocence, his little eyes wide open.

"I can give no answer to that, sir, which is not critical. It would be better that they answered for themselves."

"If they can." The Q.C.'s voice was now unctuous. He turned to Carswell. "My lord, I respectfully submit that the police have been negligent in their duty; they have not called a witness to the event who could perhaps have cleared my client. Now he cannot be called because there is no record of his name or whereabouts. Therefore I request that the case be dismissed and my client leave without a stain on his character."

Constable Crombie swiveled to stare in consternation at Constable Allardyce, and the prosecution half rose from his seat, but Carswell stopped them all with an imperious gesture.

"Your request is granted, Mr. Greer. The case is dismissed." And he banged his gavel on its rest to indicate the end of the matter.

Pitt was dumbfounded. They had not even called Beulah Giles. There had been no opportunity to question her, and she must surely be the best witness of all. It was an extraordinary procedure, and Osmar had got away with it. Certainly it was a trivial offense, causing embarrassment at the most. No one was injured or robbed, and in the circumstances very probably no one had even been discomfited, as there appeared to have been no other passersby at the time. But that was not the issue. The police had been made to look foolish and ineffectual, and Osmar had defied the law.

And perhaps most serious of all as far as Pitt was concerned, Carswell had behaved unaccountably. Only the crowd was satisfied, and that not because they were partisan in the case, simply that they had been thoroughly and unexpectedly entertained.

On the way out Pitt passed the two constables looking confused and angry. He caught Crombie's eye and the unspoken message of understanding flashed between them. Neither knew the reason for such acts, but both shared the emotions.

The Q.C. strode along the passage, gown tails flapping, features composed in lines of deep thought. He no longer had the oozing satisfaction he had had in the courtroom. Either his own feelings were mixed, or else his attention was already upon the next case. Horatio Osmar was nowhere to be seen, nor the handsome Miss Giles.

Pitt had another half hour to wait around the corridors before Carswell retired to his chambers and Pitt was able to see him.

"Yes Mr. Pitt?" he said, looking up from his desk, his face furrowed with mild irritation. Obviously he had considered the matter concluded at their last interview, and had no wish to have to turn his mind to it now. "I am afraid I must ask you to be brief," he went on. "I have many other affairs that require my time."

"Then I will proceed immediately," Pitt said very quietly. He hated this, but it was inescapable. "Are you sure you would not care to tell me where you were on the night William Weems was murdered?"

Carswell's face darkened, and his voice had an edge to it. "I am quite sure. I do not require to account for myself, sir. I did not know the man or have any dealings with him whatever. I have no idea who killed him, nor, beyond my civic duty, do I care. Now if that is all, please attend to your calling, and leave me to mine."

"Weems was also a blackmailer." Pitt stood perfectly still.

"Indeed? How unpleasant." A look of distaste crossed Carswell's face, but there was no start of anxiety or sudden fear. "I grieve for his death still less," he said tersely. "But I did not know him, sir. I have already said so, and do not intend to waste my valuable time repeating it to you. You may believe me or not, as you choose, but since it is the truth, you will not find proof of anything different. Now if you please, prosecute your inquiries somewhere else!"

"Are you quite sure you do not care to tell me where you were that night?"

Carswell half rose from his seat, his face deep pink.

"I do not, sir! Now do you leave like a gentleman, or do I summon the ushers and remove you like a felon?"

Pitt sighed and took a deep breath. He did not dislike Carswell, and he hated having to do this to him.

"Perhaps Miss Hilliard was acquainted with him, and gave your name as collateral for a loan?" he suggested quietly and very levelly. "Neither she nor her brother are in such fortunate circumstances—"

Carswell's face went white as the blood fled from it, and then blushed scarlet again, and his legs seemed to fold under him. He collapsed back into his chair and stared helplessly, unable to clear his thoughts or muster any argument to deny.

"Did Miss Hilliard know Weems?" Pitt repeated, not because he thought Theophania Hilliard guilty of murder for an instant, but he did not want to prejudice Carswell's answers by suggesting them in the form of his questions.

"No! No—" Carswell's voice sank again. "No, of course not. It is—" He took a deep, shuddering breath and let it go. "It is I— it—" He looked up at Pitt, his eyes anguished. "I did not kill Weems." He pushed the words between his teeth. "I had no occasion to. Before God, I swear to you, I never knew the man, and I was not there that night!"

"What is your relationship with Miss Hilliard, sir?"

Carswell seemed to hunch inside himself, almost to grow smaller in his chair.

"She is—she is—my mistress." It was so hard for him to say it came out in a whisper.

Was there any point in asking if Weems was blackmailing him? The cause for it was only too obvious. And what would a denial be worth? It would surely be instinctive, a man protecting himself, denying guilt automatically.

"And Weems knew?"

Carswell's face tightened.

"I am saying nothing more, except that I did not kill him. And if you have any humanity in you, any justice at all, you will not involve Miss Hilliard. She knows nothing whatever of any part of it—please—" The word was almost strangled in his throat. It was a measure of his distress that he could bring himself to speak it at all. His hands were clenched on the desk top and his body looked hunched and beaten.

"Miss Hilliard is under no suspicion," Pitt said before he considered the wisdom of telling him. "It is not a crime a woman might have committed, nor is there anything to connect Miss Hilliard with Weems." Then to salvage something of his advantage. "It was your name we found on his books."

Carswell sat back in his chair, pale, tired, his body slowly relaxing into limpness. He opened his mouth to say something, perhaps even thanks, then changed his mind and closed it again.

Pitt inclined his head in a small bow, and excused himself. There was nothing more to say and it was a pointless cruelty to stand and watch the man's embarrassment. He would learn nothing new from it. He would like to have asked him why on earth he had ruled as he had on the case of Horatio Osmar, but that was a privileged decision which Pitt had no authority to investigate. There were no grounds to suppose it was corrupt, only eccentric and inexplicable.

"What?" Micah Drummond was incredulous. "Carswell dismissed it?"

"Yes sir," Pitt agreed, standing in Drummond's office in the sun. "He threw it out. Allardyce and Crombie could hardly believe it."

"Did you say Horatio Osmar?" Drummond said more thoughtfully. "Wasn't he a junior minister in the government a few years ago?"

"I believe so, but does that make it any better?" Pitt was ready to be angry at the abuse of privilege.

Drummond smiled with a small lift of his shoulders.

"None at all, but it may explain Carswell's behavior—"

"Not to me," Pitt said hotly. "If that is the sort of justice he dispenses then he is not the man I thought him, nor is he fit to sit on the bench."

Drummond's eyes widened. "A forceful opinion, Pitt."

Pitt felt his face color. He admired Drummond and was suddenly aware he had exceeded his position and breached the social gap which lay between them in criticizing a man out of his own class, and in Drummond's.

"I apologize," he said huskily. "I should not have expressed it."

Drummond's face relaxed into genuine humor.

"I like your choice of words, Pitt, there is a nice difference between that and saying that you were mistaken in your estimate." He moved from behind the desk. "I am inclined to agree with you, if that were the case, but I meant that Carswell and Osmar may have associates in common who may well have—" He hesitated, again uncomfortable, seeking to explain something which seemed to embarrass him. Pitt was suddenly reminded of the emotion he had felt riding beside him through the darkness in the hansom to see Lord Byam the first time.

Pitt waited. The silence lay in the bright air. Outside someone dropped a wooden crate on the pavement, and in the distance a coster cried his wares, the sound coming clearly through the open window.

"—have reminded him of friendship," Drummond finished, "of obligation."

"I see," Pitt said quietly, although he did not. It was a cloudy mass of possibilities, none of them hard-edged, all confused in the darkness of social pressures, debts of money, favor, the whisper of corruption, however politely phrased, and behind it all blackmail, and the ugly body of William Weems.

Drummond pushed his hand into his pocket and looked miserable.

"I suppose this mistress business is an excellent motive for murder, poor devil," he said resignedly. "What about the other names on Weems's list? Have you looked at them yet?"

"No sir." Pitt felt his heart sink. "One of them is on the force—"

Drummond's face paled. "Oh God! Are you sure?"

"I suppose there is a remote hope it is someone else by the same name," Pitt said without any hope at all.

Drummond stared at the floor. "Well I suppose you'd better do it. What about the gun?" He looked up. "Have you found that yet? You said the one there—what was it?"

"A hackbut," Pitt replied. "Ornamental, on the wall."

"You said it wasn't in working order?"

"It isn't. It wouldn't have killed him, but it must have been something like it, muzzle loaded and with a wide barrel, to accommodate the coins."

Drummond winced. "I suppose you've got the local police looking for it? Yes, of course. Sorry. Well you'd better learn what you can about the others on the list. It gets uglier as it goes on."

"Yes," Pitt agreed. "I'm afraid it does."

CHAPTER

FIVE

Charlotte sat at the dinner table at the Hotel Metropole opposite Emily and felt an immense satisfaction. Tonight was going to be marvelous. She had on her very best gown, a gift from Emily and Jack for her help over the last two weeks, and she was quite sure she looked splendid. She had paraded before the mirror enchanted by the grand lady she saw reflected in it, a magical change from the woman she ordinarily saw. This creature was perfectly corsetted to the ultimate shape, her shoulders were creamy white above the Venetian red of the satin fabric, cut in a style up to the very minute, with the new, slender skirt, and hardly any bustle. It was so new it was almost ahead of the mode. Her hair was piled up in a shining crown, and her face was radiant with the contemplation of the evening. They were dining in the most elegant of places, then going to the opera, to *Lohengrin*, no less, the greatest draw of the season. Personally she would have preferred something Italian, but this was the "in" thing this year, and who would quarrel with that on such a night? After all, it was still part of Jack's campaign, and as such a duty.

Emily was dressed in her favorite delicate water green. She was feeling a great deal better and looked as lovely as an early flower with her fair hair and alabaster skin. Certainly she could have done with a trifle more color, but an attempt to lend it artificially had looked so awful they had both laughed heartily, and Emily had scrubbed it off. The Ashworth diamonds at her ears and around her neck would lend all the sparkle her uncertain health might lack, and she was determined to enjoy herself.

Jack sat next to her, looking at her every few minutes in concern. But far more extraordinary than that, Pitt was present, dressed after considerable argument, and a mighty victory for Charlotte, in a borrowed dinner suit which really fitted remarkably well. Charlotte thought privately this was due to some clever and exceedingly tactful planning on Jack's part. Pitt was sitting a trifle uncomfortably, now and again running his hand around inside his collar, and stretching his arms as if his cuffs were riding up, but he was smiling, and even when no one was looking at him, still appeared remarkably pleased with himself.

That might have been due at least in part to another occupant of the table—not Lord Anstiss, sitting playing with his fork and a mouthful of smoked salmon, his concentration on his plate, his face wreathed in mild anticipation, but Great-Aunt Vespasia, her hair pale silver, wound on her head like a coronet, the light shining through it, her eyes bright with humor, a tiny smile on her lips as she looked at Charlotte, then at Pitt. In fact as she watched Pitt ease his shoulders again in his jacket her smile widened and the affection in it was plain, as most definitely was the amusement.

The waiters came and served the next course, and Lord Anstiss resumed his extraordinary tale of courtly romance about Edward Heneage Dering who in 1859 had fallen in love with Rebecca Dulcibella Orpen.

He had gone to her aunt, Lady Chatterton, a woman quite naturally old enough to be his mother, and somehow so mishandled his request for Rebecca's hand that the aunt had assumed the offer intended for herself, and accepted it forthwith. He had been too much the gentleman to disabuse her of her illusion.

"In 1865 all three were received into the Catholic church," he went on with a wry smile. "And two years after that Rebecca Orpen married a friend of Dering's named Marmion Edward Ferrars, also a Catholic."

Charlotte was fascinated. Had she known him better she would have challenged the truth of this odd story, as it was she had to content herself with a hasty glance at Aunt Vespasia, who nodded imperceptibly.

Anstiss saw the look, but his face registered only amusement.

"Indeed," he said with relish, "they all four settled in Ferrars's home at Baddesley Clinton, a marvelously isolated house in Warwickshire, with a moat."

Pitt coughed but Anstiss took no exception to it as a comment. In fact their incredulity seemed to be precisely the reaction he desired. He looked to Vespasia for confirmation, which she readily gave.

"Ferrars had no money to speak of." Anstiss picked delicately at his food. "And Dering had a great deal, so he paid off the mortgage, restored the local church and they all four settled down together to devote their lives to good works—and philosophy and sitting reading Tennyson together in the evenings. Dering wrote bad novels; Ferrars, who believed, quite correctly, that he resembled Charles I, dressed and cut his beard accordingly; Rebecca painted rather good watercolor portraits of them all.

"Lady Chatterton—she still called herself that—died in 'seventy-six. Marmion Ferrars died in 'eighty-four, and the year after Dering at last married Rebecca, where they still live—one presumes happily ever after."

"Absolutely marvelous," Emily said with delight. "And you swear it is true."

"In every particular," he said, meeting her eyes with unfeigned amusement. "There have been a great many people devoted to the romantic ideal, artists, poets, painters and dreamers. We are only now being taken over by the aesthete movement, which I suppose is a natural progression from extreme innocence to ostentatious 'experience.' "

They continued speaking until the waiter brought the final course, then a trifle more hastily than would ordinarily have been the case, and still smiling, they repaired to their respective carriages and set out for Covent Garden and the opera.

"Of course all the world and his wife will be there," Emily warned as they sat almost stationary, moving forward barely a step or two at a time in the press of traffic. "It is necessary to come this early if one hopes to arrive at a civilized time and not inconvenience everyone and make a spectacle of oneself by taking one's seat after the music has begun. And of course that is hopelessly vulgar, because it is the cheapest way of making everyone look at you." She settled a little more comfortably. "Never mind. It is an excellent opportunity to catch up on events. I have not seen you for simply ages, Thomas." She smiled with vivid humor which she did not bother to suppress. "You hardly look like yourself. It is most difficult to tell how you are."

"I am sitting very carefully so as not to rumple my shirt, crease my jacket or lose my cuffs up my arms," he replied with a grin. "But I am greatly obliged—and looking forward to the evening."

"And are you pursuing some interesting case?" she went on. "I gather not, because Charlotte has said nothing about it. I doubt even Lord Anstiss's tales could hold her interest against a really good case—or mine either."

"The murder of a usurer," he replied with a wry expression. "And I don't yet know whether it is going to be 'good' or not."

"A usurer?" Her voice reflected her disappointment. The carriage moved another twenty yards forward and stopped again. Somewhere ahead of them a footman shouted angrily, but it made no difference; they stayed precisely where they were. "That does not sound very promising."

"I know they provide a service of sorts." Jack pulled a face. "But I loathe them—most of them bleed their clients dry. I'm sorry, but I have some sympathy with whoever killed him."

"He was also a blackmailer," Pitt added.

"A lot of sympathy," Jack amended.

"I too," Pitt confessed. "But he blackmailed some interesting people—or it appears from his books that he did."

"Oh?" Emily sat up a little straighter, her attention sparked. "Such as whom?"

Pitt looked at her without apology. "That is presently confidential, and the matter is one of indiscretion in one case, and poor judgment of character in another, which led to a tragedy, but there is no crime involved in either. There are others I have yet to investigate."

Emily was quick and subtle to read his face in the light from the neighboring carriage lamps.

"And you are hating it. Are they people you admire?"

He shrugged ruefully. He had forgotten how very astute she was, not quite as brave as Charlotte or as passionate, but a better judge of others, and a far better actress when it came to presenting exactly the right expression and gesture to govern a situation. Emily was supremely practical.

"People I know," he replied. "It will feel like a kind of betrayal, and I do not want to know their weaknesses, even if they turn out to be innocent of murder."

Emily flashed him a quick smile of understanding.

"Of course not."

Pitt fidgeted with his collar yet again. "Since I have nothing to contribute, let us speak of your affairs. Tell me something of Lord Anstiss. I hear he is a great patron of the arts and a political and social benefactor. He is certainly very entertaining. Is there no Lady Anstiss?"

"She died many years ago," Emily answered. Then she leaned forward confidentially. "I believe it was very tragic."

At that moment their carriage moved several steps forward, stopped abruptly, rocking a little on its springs, then went another fifty yards before stopping again.

"Oh?" Pitt did not attempt to keep the interest out of his voice.

It was all the invitation Emily required.

"She died by accident. It was dreadful; she went out onto her balcony at night, and slipped over the edge. She must have been leaning out, although one cannot imagine for what reason." She shivered a little at the thought. "There was speculation that she might have had a good deal too much wine at dinner. It is not easy to fall over the edge of a balcony if one is stone cold sober."

"What was she like?" Pitt asked, screwing up his face. "What kind of woman?"

"Beautiful," Emily answered without hesitation. "The most beautiful woman in London, so they said, perhaps in England."

"Her nature?" Pitt pressed. "Was she spoiled? Many great beauties are."

Charlotte hid her smile, but did not interrupt.

The carriage jerked and moved forward yet again.

"Really the traffic is getting so bad," Jack said sharply. "I wonder if it can go on like this much longer, or we shall all be reduced to walking!"

"People have been saying that for years," Emily replied soothingly. "But we still manage." She turned back to Pitt. "I suppose she may well have been spoiled, but I haven't heard it. No, that's not true: Lord Anstiss himself did say something that was not quite that, but one has to make allowances for his own emotions, and his grief. He did say all manner of people loved her and she had a charm that made everyone her slave. I think it was his own way of admitting that no one ever denied her anything, which is the same as being spoiled, isn't it?"

"It sounds like it," Pitt agreed.

"Except Great-Aunt Vespasia," Emily went on. "She said she only met her a few times, but she liked her, and Aunt Vespasia loathes spoiled people." She grinned broadly. "And from a woman who was one of the greatest beauties herself, and ruled London society with a glance of steel in her day, it is an opinion that merits much respect."

The carriage moved forward again, this time considerably, and Jack leaned out of the window.

"I think we are nearly there," he said with satisfaction.

And indeed within a few minutes they were alighting. Emily on Jack's arm, Charlotte on Pitt's, they mounted the steps and went into the foyer, which was glittering with lights, swirling with satins, laces and velvets, and patched and dotted with the slender black of men's dress jackets and white gleam of shirt fronts, the blaze of jewels at throats and ears and in hair. Everywhere the babble of sound rose and mounted in pitch.

Charlotte felt a thrill of excitement. She gazed around at the beautifully decorated walls, the sweeping stairs, the chandeliers; in fact she leaned so far backwards staring up that it was well she was on Pitt's arm or she might have overbalanced. It was all so vivid, so pulsing with life and anticipation. Everyone was talking, moving; the air was filled with the rustle of skirts and chatter of voices.

She leaned closer to Pitt and squeezed his arm, and he tightened his hold. There was no need for words, and for once she could think of none that would fill the occasion.

As they were moving up the stairs towards their box she glanced down and saw quite clearly Lord Byam's dark head. It was quite distinctive in its smooth, handsome shape, and in the sprinkling of silver at the temples. He carried it at an angle not quite like anyone else, and when he glanced around to acknowledge an acquaintance she saw his marvelous eyes. Next to him Eleanor Byam was elegant, but without the remarkable individuality he possessed. She seemed somehow more subdued and not quite as effortlessly graceful. Neither of them looked up, nor in all likelihood would they have remembered her if they had.

At the top of the stairs she turned for one last look down at the foyer and saw a man's head. He had thick hair, too long, like Pitt's, but as richly toned as dying leaves, and she wondered if it were the odd young man who at Emily's ball had seemed so obsessed with the injustices he saw, or thought he saw, in international finance.

Upstairs they had no difficulty in getting to Emily's box. She had kept it ever since her marriage to George Ashworth, and still retained it now both for necessary entertainments, such as this, and for pleasure, because she genuinely liked the music as well as the occasion.

Vespasia and Lord Anstiss were there ahead of them. Anstiss rose as they came in and held Emily's chair for her to seat herself at the front where she could see most easily. Charlotte was offered the chair in the center with Aunt Vespasia to her right. As soon as the gentlemen were seated also, Vespasia handed Charlotte her opera glasses to indulge in the beginning of the evening's entertainment, which was to gaze at the occupants of the other boxes, observe who they were, who they were with, how they looked, what they wore, and above all who called upon them and how they deported themselves.

It was several minutes before she recognized anyone she knew. This was not to be wondered at since she had very seldom been to the opera before. It had not been an occasion her mother had considered likely to produce results in attracting a suitor fitting its expense. However, Pitt had taken her once or twice as a great treat to see Gilbert and Sullivan at the Savoy Theatre, but that was not quite the same.

"Who have you seen?" Vespasia said softly.

"Mr. Fitzherbert and Miss Morden," Charlotte replied in a whisper. "He really is extraordinarily handsome."

"Indeed," Vespasia said dryly. "A deal too much so. And what of Miss Morden?"

"She looks very well too," Charlotte said with less pleasure. "And I think she is aware of it, from the way she is sitting with her face in the light and a satisfied smile on it."

"Do you think so?"

"That is the way I sit when I think I am at my best," Charlotte admitted with candor. "I dislike women as ostentatiously pleased with themselves as she seems. She has the world on a string, and she contemplates it with some satisfaction."

"Perhaps," Vespasia agreed dubiously. "But not everyone who wears a brave face feels as certain underneath. I am surprised that you do not know that. Many a gay laugh hides loneliness or fear of all manner of things. A wild night does not mean a happy morrow." Her voice softened. "I think perhaps, my dear, it is you, with Thomas to love you, who has grown a trifle complacent."

Charlotte sat rigid, keeping the glasses to her eyes to hide her face, and hoped no one else saw the slow, hot color burn up her cheeks. Suddenly and quite overwhelmingly she knew Vespasia was right. She had grown very used to happiness, very certain of the things that mattered most. Involuntarily she turned around and looked at Pitt watching Jack and Lord Anstiss talking to each other. He smiled at her and pulled a face.

She turned back, crowded with emotion, and stared across at the box where Herbert Fitzherbert was looking down at the stage, and half behind him, Odelia Morden was smiling vacantly into the air, her thoughts obviously miles from the glittering crowd and the rising buzz of excitement.

Charlotte moved the glasses further around the arc of the balcony and saw Micah Drummond, his eyes on the vast, closed curtain, and three boxes beyond him Eleanor Byam, sitting forward, her hands on the velvet-padded edge of the box, fingers gripping tightly. For a moment she seemed to be looking at Drummond, then she saw someone she knew and raised her hand in a small, rather stiff salute. Beside her Lord Byam's face was in the shadows and his expression hidden.

There was a sudden hush, the house lights dimmed and a spotlight blossomed on the stage. The prima donna appeared in front of the curtain, and the orchestra, which had been tuning their instruments under the hum of conversation, began to play the national anthem. At one stroke the chatter died. The prima donna's glorious voice broke into the words, "God save our gracious Queen," and as a single person every man and woman stood.

The evening had commenced.

The curtain rose on a magnificent scene, brilliantly lit, static, and the slow, magical story unfolded.

Charlotte found it strangely cold. The music was huge, full of great chords, grand passages, and sweeping gestures, but it had none of the personal passion she had expected from her small knowledge of the Italian operas, and she found her attention wandering. She borrowed Vespasia's glasses again, and when she hoped no one would notice, she swung them around to watch the occupants of the other boxes.

The slow drama played itself out on the stage in a glory of sound and lights, and in the dim, plush-lined balconies other comedies and tragedies took place of which Charlotte saw snatches and was fascinated. An elderly general, gorgeous in stars and medals, snoozed gently, his white mustache fluttering as he breathed, while his wife smiled and nodded imperceptibly at a young lieutenant in a box opposite. Two women, sisters from their likeness to each other, giggled behind their fans and flirted with a portly middle-aged gentleman who admired them extravagantly. Two duchesses sat together, diamonds blazing, and gossiped about everyone in sight. They could have had no idea whether the work on the stage was *Lohengrin* or *The Mikado*.

In the first interval the lights went up and they all arose to take whatever respite they most wished. Jack and Anstiss excused themselves and retired to the smoking room, naturally peopled only by men, where they could discuss politics. Emily granted her permission graciously only because she knew that this was the principal purpose of the whole evening. The visit to the opera was merely a civilized way of achieving it.

Pitt, a trifle self-consciously, escorted Aunt Vespasia, Emily and Charlotte to the foyer, where he bought them refreshments of cool lemonade in tall glasses, and they swapped greetings, gossip, and trivial conversation with passersby. It was a glorious, gay, noisy, brilliant throng of people, swishing skirts, clinking glasses, blazing jewelry and eager faces. Charlotte found it immensely exciting and could hardly keep her eyes on one person more than a moment or two, because there were so many things to see.

However she did observe Herbert Fitzherbert, so close he almost bumped her elbow, although quite unaware of her. He was speaking to Odelia Morden, their heads together, laughing at some small, private joke, or perhaps no joke at all, simply that they were happy and felt themselves in love.

Suddenly Odelia gave a little start and turned sharply to see a young man accidentally step on the edge of her gown, and blush in embarrassment.

"Oh—I am sorry, ma'am!" he exclaimed in confusion. "I do beg your pardon!"

Odelia stared at him in horror, still uncertain how damaged her gown might be, and not at all sure if the stitches might have been ripped at the waist, leaving her in danger of becoming something of a spectacle should it tear any further.

The young man colored furiously. "I—I am most profoundly sorry, ma'am! If there is any way . . ." He tailed off, becoming aware there was nothing whatever he could do and all his protestations were quite pointless.

His companion, a remarkably pretty girl with a mass of soft, honey-brown hair in natural curls and a peculiarly vivid face, looked more practically at the damage, then smiled at Odelia.

"It is only two or three stitches at the hem," she reassured. "It will cause you no embarrassment, and I am sure your maid will be able to repair it. But we do apologize. My brother was bumped against by a gentleman a little too happy for the occasion, and I am afraid he lost his balance." Her smile was bright and friendly, but there was nothing abashed in it, nor was she going to accept blame for what was not her fault.

Charlotte resisted the pressure to move with the crowd and

stayed behind the potted palm where she could both hear and see unobserved. Pitt and Aunt Vespasia carried on.

Odelia breathed out, still uncertain how to react, whether to accept the situation with a gracious wave of her hand, dismissing the whole matter, or whether to remain injured and keep in them a sense of discomfort. She glanced at Fitz.

Fitzherbert looked at the girl, at her bright, frank face, and bowed.

"Herbert Fitzherbert, ma'am." He turned to Odelia. "And may I present Miss Odelia Morden." He touched her arm proprietorially. "We are delighted to make your acquaintance, and a small piece of fabric is a trivial price to pay. Please think no more of it."

The girl smiled and dropped a tiny curtsey.

"Theophania Hilliard, but if you should ever think of me by name, I should greatly prefer it to be Fanny, which is what my friends call me. And this is my brother, James."

"Fanny!" James said quickly. "We have already intruded more than enough on Mr. Fitzherbert and Miss Morden! They are very unlikely to wish to know us any better, in case we ruin their entire wardrobe!"

"You don't make a habit of it, do you?" Fitz asked with humor. "If you do, I have several acquaintances I should like you to meet. I think it could be most entertaining . . ."

Charlotte moved even closer to the palm and tucked her skirts out of the way.

A flash of irritation crossed Odelia's face. She looked at Fanny. "He is joking," she said a little stiffly. "I am afraid his sense of humor is not of the most readily understood. I am sure you do not customarily stand . . ." She tailed off, realizing that she had put herself in a position where to continue would be unnecessarily discourteous.

Fanny smiled at her very briefly, then her eyes moved back to Fitz.

"There is no need to explain," she said gaily. "I understand perfectly. Such exchanges are like bubbles, very pretty, and fly only if you do not touch them."

"Perfect!" Fitz said with obvious pleasure. "You have a gift for the exact expression, Miss Hilliard. Tell me, are you enjoying the opera?"

"If you mean the music," she replied, wrinkling her nose, "not a great deal. There is nothing in it I shall remember, and certainly nothing I shall hum in the street. But the spectacle is wonderful. And the story is certainly romantic enough. It starts all sorts of dreams in my head, and makes me want to go and read the great poems about heroes, like El Cid, and Roland and Charlemagne and the battle at Roncesvalles, and of course King Arthur." Her eyes were brilliant and she closed them for a moment as if the knights in splendor were riding across her vision as she spoke.

"How charming," Odelia said dryly. "How delightful to be so . . . young . . . and have such a touching imagination."

Fanny opened her eyes wide. "I suppose it passes as one gets older?" Then as Odelia's face went white she realized just what an unfortunate thing she had said, blushed deep pink and burst into giggles, putting her hand to her mouth. "Oh I'm so sorry! I'm just as bad tripping over my tongue as James was over your dress. I thought you meant I was being a little naive—and I don't suppose you meant that at all."

Charlotte drew in her breath, but did not move.

Odelia was perfectly caught.

"Of course not," she lied quickly. "It is an excellent quality." She could think of nothing else to add and fell into an uncomfortable silence.

Fitz was biting his lip with ill-hidden pleasure in the sheer humor of the situation.

"We perhaps should get tripped over less if we were less often in the way?" he said lightly. "But I hope we are in your way again some time soon, Miss Hilliard. In fact I shall engage to make sure we are. I trust you will enjoy the remainder of the evening."

"Thank you, Mr. Fitzherbert," she said with bright eyes. "If everyone else is as charming as you are, I am sure we shall. Good evening, Miss Morden. It was a great pleasure to meet you."

"Delighted," James said, still uncomfortable and avoiding Odelia's glance. Then taking his sister's arm he almost pushed her away and they were lost in the crowd.

"Really!" Odelia said between her teeth. "The clumsy oaf! He has torn my gown, you know! And she is as awkward with her tongue as he is with his feet. She will be a disaster in society. She is far too brash."

"I thought she commanded the situation very well," he said without a trace of ill-humor. "There is a fearful crush in here, and anyone might lose their balance and tread on someone else without meaning to, or being able to help it." He looked at her wryly. "Anyway, you can never predict what society will do. It takes a fancy to some of the oddest people—far odder than she is."

"You have too little discrimination, Fitz," she said proprietorially, linking her arm in his and moving a little closer to him. "You will have to learn to distinguish between the people one should know socially and those one should simply be civil to because one does not wish to be seen being less than civil."

"It sounds like a bore to me," he said, wrinkling his nose. "I don't think I care to have my acquaintances dictated by such criteria."

Odelia's answer to that was lost as they moved away, and Charlotte was left wishing Fitz were not Jack's rival for the nomination, because she found him most agreeable. On the other hand, Odelia Morden did not appeal to her nearly so much. She hoped that Emily would be more than a match for her, but she was not at all sure; Miss Morden had a touch of steel under that complacent, pretty face.

During the second act Charlotte again found her attention wandering, and with Vespasia's glasses she was able to see very clearly at least those who sat forward in the boxes where the light caught their faces.

She was examining, as discreetly as she could, the people sitting in the tier above hers, and on the far side, when she saw the curtains at the back of one of the boxes open and the distinctive figure of Micah Drummond come in. She remembered him with personal gratitude for the understanding he had displayed towards her at the dreadful culmination of the murders on Westminster Bridge, when it would have been natural for him to have been furious with her. Instead he had been so gentle she felt her own faults without the instinctive defense which an angrier, less sensitive man would certainly have produced in her. But she had hurt so deeply, and felt so overwhelmingly frightened and guilty.

Now she moved the little wheel on the glasses to focus them more clearly, and looked at the tense, self-conscious expression on his face as he spoke to the occupants of the box. All she could see of them was the back of the woman's head, her beautiful black hair wound in the currently fashionable Greek style, and laced with pearls. Her shoulders were very white and she sat upright. Micah Drummond bowed to her and raised her hand to his lips. He did it so gently it seemed to Charlotte to be more than just the usual formality but rather a gesture that was meant for itself. It gave her a little shiver of empathy with the woman, whoever she was, as if she too had sat in that dark box and felt his lips brush her skin.

The man in the box moved forward a step and his face was no longer in complete shadow, but in a half-barred light so at least his profile was visible. Charlotte knew him: the straight, jutting nose, a little short, was familiar, and the clean angle of his head, hair perfectly straight and smooth. But she could not think who he was.

Drummond turned to the man, his brows furrowing with anxiety, and began to speak. It was listened to earnestly, the man leaning a little towards him.

Charlotte moved on and saw Odelia Morden and Fitz sitting close together, his face toward the stage, hers towards him.

She looked back again at the drama as the music rose to a long sustained climax and there was a rush of applause.

When she turned back at the box where Micah Drummond had been he was no longer there, and the man appeared to be staring towards Charlotte, which made her acutely embarrassed. He seemed so close, as if he would see her as clearly as she saw him. He had no glasses, but hers magnified him alarmingly and she felt caught in a gross act of intrusion. There was a curious expression on his face, beyond her ability to interpret. Only his mouth was in the full light. He looked melancholy, vulnerable, and yet there was a driving intensity in the feeling, nothing passive about it except the openness to hurt, almost an anticipation of pain.

The woman in the box turned towards the stage and leaned over the balcony rail. Now that she was in profile in the light

Charlotte could see it was Eleanor Byam, and knew in that same moment that of course the man was Lord Byam. Now that she was aware who it was, the curve of his head was perfectly easily discernible, the hollows of his fine eyes.

He too moved forward a bit and Charlotte realized with a blush of relief, and as if a guilt had been removed, that it was not she he was looking at, but someone beyond her and a trifle to her left. She returned the glasses to Vespasia with a whisper of thanks, and thus was able to look to her left with good excuse. The only person there was Lord Anstiss, and he was watching the singers on the brilliantly lit stage as though oblivious of everything and everyone else, the other members of the audience.

The second interval was less diverting but Charlotte was still full of the exhilaration of the occasion and all the glamour and laughter and swirl of silks. She felt as if she walked on air and she wanted to see and hear and remember it all so she would recall everything years from now when she was back in her own home on the ordinary days that would come so soon, full of comfortable, repetitive chores. And she would have to tell Gracie as much as she could. She would want to know every detail.

Pitt stood with his back against a pillar; this time he had fewer duties of courtesy towards the women. Jack was escorting Emily, Lord Anstiss had offered to fetch refreshment for Vespasia, which she had accepted, and Charlotte was too interested in looking and listening to care about such things.

"Enjoying yourself?" Pitt asked quietly, putting his arm around her shoulders and leaning a little closer so he could be heard above the buzz and clatter.

She looked at him wordlessly; the bubble of happiness inside her was too large to need description, and nothing could do it justice anyway. They stood together watching the people pass by in twos and threes, in groups, and here and there one alone. It was halfway through the apportioned time when she saw the tall, lean figure of one such man, his face intent in thought, apparently not seeing the crowd as individuals but merely as a bright mass, like a field of flowers. After a moment or two Charlotte recognized Peter Valerius, the young man at Emily's ball who had been so passionate about finances and the rates of interest charged and the restrictions

attached where certain businesses were involved in colonial countries, dependent upon the rich nations of Europe, and on Britain
in particular. It was a subject in which she had no interest whatever, but his face had such a power of feeling in it she had found
herself drawn to him, in spite of her complete lack of intellectual
engagement. He seemed to be alone, and she wondered why he
was here at such a social event, in so many ways superficial.

A few moments after he passed, going back towards the stairs
up to the boxes, she saw Lord and Lady Byam. They were walking
close to each other, side by side, but she was not on his arm, and
she held herself very erect. He seemed a little abstracted, his mind
elsewhere. He turned as something caught the edge of his vision,
and saw Pitt, a little taller than the average and outlined against
the pink stone of the pillar. A flicker of recognition crossed his
face, then puzzlement, a small furrow between his brows as he struggled to place him in his mind.

It was all over in a few moments. Byam passed and his attention
was taken by someone else. Pitt smiled with a dark, wry amusement.

"That's Lord Byam," Charlotte whispered. "Do you know
him?"

Pitt's smile became softer, reflective. He came to some decision
within himself. He turned to face her and exclude the party of
laughing people behind him.

"Yes. Yes I do. The usurer whose murder I am investigating
was blackmailing Byam over Lady Anstiss's death."

"What?" she gasped, looking at him in amazement. "Laura
Anstiss. But what had he to do with that? It was an accident,
wasn't it?"

"No," he said very quietly. "She fell passionately in love with
Byam, who was Anstiss's closest friend, and when he did not return
it, she took her own life. They covered it up to make it look like
an accident, to protect her—and of course the family reputation."

"Oh." She was stunned. Thoughts whirled around in her mind,
passion and tragedy, a beautiful woman lonely, rejected and in
despair. She could hardly imagine Anstiss's grief, his sense of betrayal by a man he had believed his friend. Byam's guilt. All that
was twenty years ago, Vespasia had said. But what did they feel

now? What had the years healed? Was that the strange emotion she had seen in Byam's face as he looked out of the shadows of his box across at Anstiss?

The bell rang for them to return to their seats, and Charlotte took Pitt's arm and sailed, head high, back up the stairs, jostling with the crowd, the chatter and laughter, the rustle of taffeta and scrape of heels. Fortunately he was looking where they were going, so it was unnecessary for her to.

The last act was the dramatic and musical climax and Charlotte gave it her attention, at least outwardly. Inwardly her mind was still thinking of the sharper, more immediate drama in the faces of Byam and of Fitz, and in the bright eyes of Fanny Hilliard.

After the final curtain, when the applause had died away, they joined the queue to leave, going very slowly down the stairs, pretending indifference to the crush and the waiting. There was no point in pushing their way through; they might so easily become separated, and then their carriage would not be there yet anyway.

It was nearly an hour later that they were sitting at a small, elegant supper table swapping gossip. Anstiss and Jack were talking quietly, sipping champagne, and Emily was telling Pitt all she could remember about Eleanor Byam.

"Did you enjoy the opera?" Vespasia asked Charlotte, looking at her flushed face and smiling.

"Yes," Charlotte replied more or less honestly. Then she was compelled to add, "But I am not sure that I understood the story, and I don't think I shall remember any of the music. I shall remember the way it looked, though. It was splendid, wasn't it!"

"The best I've seen, I think," Vespasia agreed, the smile still hovering about her lips.

Charlotte frowned. "Doesn't opera ever have songs you can remember, like the music halls?"

Vespasia's silver eyebrows rose. "My dear girl, I have no idea."

Charlotte was disappointed. "But you come to the opera often, don't you?"

Vespasia's lips quivered. "Certainly. It is the music halls I do not frequent."

"Ah!" Charlotte was filled with confusion. "I'm sorry."

Vespasia started to laugh. "I have heard that Vesta Tilley has a song or two that are memorable." And very quietly, in a sweet contralto, she began a racy, lilting song. She stopped after about eight bars. "I'm sorry I don't know any more. Isn't it a shame?"

Charlotte began to laugh as well, and found the hilarity bubbling up inside her till she could not stop.

It was nearly two in the morning and they were all tired, beginning to yawn, the women to become aware of tight shoes and even tighter stays, when Lord and Lady Byam came towards them, passing close by the table in order to leave. Beside Jack, Lord Anstiss was facing towards them and it was unavoidable they should acknowledge each other.

"Good evening." Byam spoke first, being the one who had entered the circle. His face had a curious expression, his wide eyes were restless. Had it not seemed ridiculous Charlotte would have said he was seeking something, some answering emotion which he did not find, and the lack of it did not surprise him, and yet it still hurt. Or perhaps it was not ridiculous, if what Pitt had said was true and the old tragedy of Laura Anstiss had involved Byam. Anstiss was still alone; he had never remarried. Perhaps under his wit and outward composure the wound was still new. He had loved Laura, and even now no other woman could take her place. It was guilt and hope for forgiveness she had seen in Byam's eyes, and in Anstiss's face a continued courtesy, the outward show of a decent man trying to do what he believed was Christian.

Byam had stopped by their table.

Anstiss leaned back a trifle in his chair and looked up at him. "Good evening, Byam," he said agreeably, but without warmth. He smiled very slightly. "Good evening, Lady Byam. How pleasant to see you. Did you enjoy the opera?"

She smiled back at him, though with a shadow in her eyes, an uncertainty beneath the social ease which was inbred in years of polite trivia. "It was delightful," she replied meaninglessly. One did not own to any other feeling, unless one wished to enter into a discussion. "It was most beautifully staged, don't you think?"

"The best I can recall," he agreed, equally as a matter of form. His eyes moved to Byam with an unflinching gaze. Had he been a less exquisitely civilized man Charlotte would have thought it almost aggressive.

Byam moved as if to continue his journey towards the door, then glanced back at Anstiss, who was still staring at him.

Eleanor Byam stood with a frown puckering her face, for once not sure what to say, or even whether to speak or not.

Beneath the superficial inquiries and answers Charlotte could feel a tension so powerful it was like a heat in the room. She glanced at Emily, then at Pitt, and saw Pitt's face intent in concentration. Jack was lost, uncertain whether to intrude or not. Charlotte could bear it no longer.

"Is Wagnerian opera always like this?" she said, rushing into the silence, not caring how much ignorance she betrayed. "*Lohengrin* is the first I have seen. It all seems a trifle unreal to me."

The moment was broken. Eleanor let out her breath in an inaudible sigh. Byam relaxed his tight shoulders.

Anstiss turned to Charlotte with a charming smile, his back to Byam. "My dear, most of it is far more unreal than anything you have seen tonight, believe me. This was eminently worldly and sensible compared with the *Ring* cycle, which concerns gods and goddesses, monsters, giants and dwarfs and all manner of unlikely events, not to say impossible ones." His eyes were brilliant with wit and imagination. "I think you might greatly prefer the Italian operas, if you like your stories of ordinary men and women, and situations with which one can readily identify." He saw that that might sound a little patronizing and went on to soften the effect. "I admit I do. I can take only a very small amount of mythology at this level. I prefer my fantasy to have an element of humor, like Messrs. Gilbert and Sullivan, even an element of the delightful absurd, rather than the German angst. There is a touch of sophistication combined with innocence in their conception that I find pleases me."

"You are too English," Byam said from behind him. "Wagner would say your imagination is pedestrian. We make fun of the grand design because we do not understand it, and cannot sustain an intellectual passion because at that level we are still children."

Anstiss swung back to him. "Would he?" he said coldly. "Where did you hear that?"

"I did not hear it," Byam replied with a touch of asperity. "I deduced it. Now if you will excuse me, it has been a superb evening, but it is now extremely late and I am quite ready to find my carriage and go home.''

"Of course." Anstiss was smiling again. "Such a comparison of philosophy will keep until another time. We must not keep you. Good night, Lady Byam."

Byam hesitated as if for a moment he would have pursued the discussion.

"Good night, my lord," Eleanor said with an unsuccessful attempt to keep the relief out of her voice, and taking Byam's arm she turned him away and together they went out between the other tables towards the door, without glancing backwards.

Charlotte looked at Pitt, but he was staring into some place in the distance, his brows puckered and his eyes dark with thought.

"How much was said that had nothing to do with what was meant?" Vespasia said so softly under her breath that Charlotte only just caught the words.

"What do you mean?" she whispered back.

"I have no idea," Vespasia answered. "Or at least very little. But I would swear that the whole conversation was merely a vehicle for a sea of feelings that were quite unrelated to Mr. Wagner or his operas. Perhaps that is so with a great deal of conversations, all the 'good evening's and 'how are you's. We are simply measuring each other. It gives one an excuse to stare, to meet each other's eyes in a way that would be quite unacceptable were we standing there in silence."

Before Charlotte could think of a reply, which would certainly have been an agreement, they were approached by a considerable group of people who were also wending their way towards the door. Charlotte recognized the man immediately, although it was a moment before she could recall his name. Then it came to her just as the group was passing the next table. It was Addison Carswell, whom she had met at Emily's ball, and with him were his wife, the woman she had admired for her good sense, and the three fair unmarried daughters, all dressed in shades from pink through to the richest burgundy. They reminded Charlotte of a drift of magnificent hollyhocks in bloom all toning with one another. They were a striking sight, more effective together than any one of them would have been alone. Charlotte respected Mrs. Carswell's strategy.

Carswell glanced sideways at their table, as one does when not occupied in speaking. His eyes passed over Jack and Emily with a cursory smile and nod, and acknowledged Vespasia, without knowing who she was, simply that her bearing commanded it. Then his eye fell on Pitt and a tightness came over his features, a stiffness to his body so that quite suddenly his clothes looked uncomfortable and he seemed far more tired than he had the moment before, as if all the evening's events had caught up with him and exhausted him in that instant. The recognition was quite plain, but he made not the slightest movement to speak or acknowledge Pitt.

Charlotte realized with a shiver of amazement that whatever the circumstances in which he knew Pitt, it must be professional, and that he was distressed by it. And also, from the fact he gave no overt sign now, that his wife was unaware of it.

However Regina Carswell had recognized Charlotte and out of good manners she stopped to speak.

"Good evening, Mrs. Pitt, how very pleasant to see you again. I hope you are well?"

"Very well, thank you, Mrs. Carswell," Charlotte replied. "How kind of you to stop." She turned to Vespasia. "Aunt Vespasia, may I present Mrs. Addison Carswell? I am not sure if you are already acquainted." And she introduced them all around the circle, introducing Pitt to Mr. Carswell. They spoke to each other stiffly and without a flicker of anything to signify they had ever met before.

The group was still exchanging stilted pleasantries, words fumbling on their tongues, minds too tired to think easily of the necessary trivialities to cover the discomfort underneath, when they were made aware by the arrival of Herbert Fitzherbert with Odelia on his arm that they were blocking the aisle. She looked perfectly composed again, her face glowing with a calm radiance, every hair in place in spite of the lateness of the hour.

"I'm so sorry!" Carswell collected himself and grasped the opportunity to escape. "We are in your way, sir," he said with alacrity. "I do apologize. If you will excuse us?" He bowed perfunctorily to Vespasia, and made as if to leave.

"Not at all," Fitzherbert said quickly, oblivious of the panic in Carswell's face. "My dear sir, we have no desire to spoil your party. It would be unforgivable." He smiled devastatingly at Vespasia, then glanced at Jack and Emily. "Good to see you, Radley, Mrs. Radley. What a splendid evening, is it not? Ah, Mrs. Pitt. You look extremely well, if I am not impertinent to say so." He knew perfectly well he was not.

Charlotte would like to have rebuffed him, or at least taken some of the satisfaction from his face, but his charm was so spontaneous she did not know how without being churlish, which would entirely defeat her purpose. And perhaps she was being unfair to Jack. He was perfectly capable of measuring up to Herbert Fitzherbert. And if he were not, perhaps he should not win the selection anyway.

"Thank you," she said with a sweet smile. "I have enjoyed myself so much it would be hard not to feel well. Good evening, Miss Morden. How pleasant to see you again."

Odelia smiled a trifle fixedly, and formal introductions were made. Carswell had missed his opportunity to leave without making his departure abrupt to the point of discourtesy. He mumbled something polite, and conversation about the evening was resumed.

He thought a second chance had offered itself when they became aware yet again that they were occupying all the space between the tables and others wished to pass. But when he turned to apologize and offer to leave, his whole body stiffened and the blood rose in a pink tide up his face, then fled, leaving him ashen. Beside him stood young Theophania Hilliard and her brother. Her eager face also looked pale, but it might have been tiredness. It was, after all, well past two in the morning.

"I—er—" Carswell stammered. He seemed to shrink within himself. "I—I'm so sorry, Miss—er—"

"Not at all," Fanny said huskily. "We have no wish to intrude." She swallowed hard. "It was uncivil of us. We shall leave by another route—please—"

"I—er—most—" Carswell breathed deeply.

"Wouldn't think of it," Fitz said cheerfully. "Miss Fanny Hilliard, are you acquainted with Mr. Addison Carswell, and Mrs.

Carswell? And the Misses Carswell?" And completely unaware of any discomfort, Fitz proceeded to introduce them all. Carswell cast one look at Pitt for only the smallest part of a second, then away again. Had Charlotte not been watching him she would have missed the anguish and the mute appeal, so instantly did it vanish again.

Pitt looked at him blankly, and silently. Whatever he felt, he gave no sign.

Gradually Carswell regained some control of himself. The color came back faintly to his cheeks.

"I am delighted to meet you, Miss—er, Hilliard," he said hoarsely. "Forgive me for leaving so hastily, but we were about to depart, and it is very late. Good night to you."

"Good night, sir," Fanny said with downcast eyes. "Good night, Mrs. Carswell." Her eyes flicked up and she looked at Regina with interest.

Regina was too tired to notice.

"Good night, Miss Hilliard. Come Mabel." She raised her voice fractionally to her daughter, who was falling into conversation with Odelia. "Come, my dear. It is past time we were at home."

"Yes Mama," Mabel said obediently, and with a little shrug of her shoulders, excused herself and trooped off behind her sisters.

"It is certainly time we too were leaving," Charlotte said quickly, looking at Emily. "Perhaps we might find a hansom, since it would be foolish to take you so far out of your way when we are going to Bloomsbury and you to Mayfair. I am sure it is time you were in bed."

Indeed Emily had begun to flag a little, and Jack was concerned for her, by the look upon his face, and his arm around her shoulder.

"I shall take you home in my carriage," Vespasia announced, rising to her feet. "It is not so very far, and I sleep longer than I need to anyway."

"I would not hear of it," Pitt said firmly. "It has been a marvelous night, and I will not spoil my enjoyment of it by taking you out of your way and keeping you up an extra half hour at the very least. We shall find a hansom."

Vespasia drew herself up with great dignity and stared at Pitt with a mixture of affection and outrage.

"I am not some little old lady whom you need to assist across the street, Thomas! I am perfectly capable of organizing my carriage to do as I please." There was a tiny smile at the corner of his lips and both Charlotte and Pitt knew precisely why she was taking them home. "And I may lie in bed in the morning for as long as I desire—until luncheon, if it takes my fancy—which is a deal more than you may say. I shall take you home to Bloomsbury, and then go to my own house thereafter." She fixed Charlotte with a fine, silvery-gray eye, and with a small smile Pitt did as he was told.

They bade good-night to Emily and Jack, thanking them yet again for their generosity, and had the doorman call Vespasia's carriage. When they were inside, the doors closed, and had begun the journey, Vespasia looked across at Pitt, who as the gentleman was naturally sitting with his back to the driver.

"Well Thomas," she said quietly. "Is this case something you are not free to discuss?"

"It is . . . confidential," he answered carefully. There was no smile on his face, but his eyes were very bright in the light from the coach lamps. He and Vespasia understood each other perfectly, neither the humor nor the knowledge of pity needed to be expressed.

"It may be simply a matter of debt and despair," he went on. "Or it may be blackmail. I don't know yet—but it is certainly murder."

"Of course," she agreed with a sigh. "They would hardly use you for anything less."

His answer was lost in the sound of carriage wheels, but apparently Vespasia did not require to hear it.

"Who has been murdered?" Her voice brooked no evasion.

"A particularly disagreeable usurer," he replied.

Charlotte settled further down into the seat, putting her cloak around her, and listened, hoping to learn some new scraps.

"Who do usurers blackmail, for heaven's sake?" Vespasia said with disgust. "I cannot imagine their even having the acquaintance of anyone to interest you. It is hardly a political matter—or is it?"

He smiled, his teeth white in a sudden flash of light from the lamps of a passing brougham.

"It may well be."

"Indeed? Well if I may be of assistance to you, I trust you will let me know." It was said as a polite offer, but there was something of the imperiousness of an order in it also.

"Of course I will," he agreed sincerely. "I would be both ungrateful and unwise not to."

Vespasia snorted delicately, and said nothing.

The following day Pitt left early and Charlotte was busy trying to catch up with some of the domestic chores she should have done the day before, had she not been trying to dress at Emily's and preparing for the opera. She had done a large laundry of different items which all required special care, instructing Gracie in the finer arts of preserving colors, textures and shape, all the while retelling the events of the evening before, the opera, the clothes, the people, and something of Pitt's present case.

She washed a lilac dress which needed a pinch of soda in the rinse, exactly the right amount was necessary or it faded the color, and a green cloth gown for which she used two tablespoons of vinegar in a quart of rinse. She had been keeping her best floral dress and two of Jemima's to wash until she had time to make the recommended mixture she had recently heard of: new ivy leaves added to a quart of bran and a quarter of a pound of yellow household soap.

Gracie observed her as carefully as the continuing story of the evening would allow.

And then there was the starching to do, or more correctly the stiffening. Fine muslin was treated with isinglass, of which she had three half sheets. She broke them up carefully and dissolved the pieces in water, and dipped the lawns and muslins and hung them up to dry, before ironing them. The chintzes would have to wait for another day. She was certainly not boiling rice water as well.

When all the laundry was finished, in the middle of the afternoon, she set about cleaning the smoothing irons by melting fresh mutton suet and spreading it over the still-warm irons, then dusting them with unslaked lime tied in muslin. For some time now they had had a woman come in to take the household linen, and return it two days later clean and ironed.

By evening she was exhausted, and thoroughly complacent with virtue.

The following day she was sitting at the kitchen table trying to decide whether to have a little fish roe on toast for luncheon, or a boiled egg, when Gracie came tripping down the hall to say that Mrs. Radley was here. Emily herself followed hard on her heels in a swirl of floral muslin and lace, with an exquisite parasol decorated with blush-pink roses.

"I'm going to the Royal Academy exhibition," she announced, sitting down on one of the other chairs and leaning her elbows on the scrubbed wooden table. "I really don't want to go alone, and Jack is off to see someone about factories and new housing. Please come with me? It will be entertaining if we go together, and a terrible bore alone. Do come."

Charlotte wrestled with temptation for a moment or two, then with additional encouragement from Gracie, gave in to it. She ran upstairs and changed as quickly as she could into a spotted muslin gown trimmed with green, took up the best hat she had, decorated with silk roses Emily had brought back with her from her honeymoon, and came downstairs again. She was not quite as immaculate as if dressed by a ladies' maid, but nonetheless very handsome.

The Royal Academy exhibition was every bit as formal and hidebound as Emily had said. Elegant ladies with sweeping hats and flowered parasols moved from one painting to another, looking at them through lorgnettes, standing back and looking again and then passing their instant opinions. Gowns were gorgeous, etiquette absolutely precise and the social hierarchy unyielding.

"Oh, I don't care for that. Much too modern. I don't know what the world is coming to."

"Quite vulgar, my dear. And talking of vulgarity, did you see Martha Wolcott at the theater last evening? What an extraordinary shade to wear. So unflattering!"

"Of course she's fifty if she's a day."

"Really? I would have sworn she said she was thirty-nine."

"I don't doubt she did. She's been saying that for as long as I've known her. Presumably in the beginning it was quite true, but that was a dozen years ago. Well I declare, did you ever see anything like that? Whatever do you suppose it means?"

"I'm sure I have not the faintest notion!"

Charlotte and Emily overheard many such snatches of conversations as they passed between the crowds, speaking to someone here, passing a compliment there, exchanging small politenesses, but above all being seen.

They were at least halfway around the exhibition, and they felt compelled to see all of it, when they ran into Fitz and Odelia looking charming, courteous, and most of the time interested.

Emily made a little growling noise in the back of her throat.

"There are times when I loathe that man," she whispered, forcing a brilliant smile to her face as Odelia caught her eye. "And her," she added, inclining her head graciously. "She is so terribly certain of everything."

"*Complacent* is the word," Charlotte elaborated, smiling and nodding also. "The way she condescended to Miss Hilliard the evening at the opera, I was longing to be thoroughly rude."

Emily's eyebrows shot up. "And you weren't? My dear, I am sensible of your sisterly loyalty. I shall tell Jack; he will be overcome."

"You will spoil it if you tell him I only overheard the conversation, so I was not in a position to say anything at all."

"You always ruin a good story by being overliteral, Charlotte. Is that Miss Hilliard over there? I was so tired by suppertime I don't remember what she looked like."

"Yes it is. I liked her spirit. She gave as good as she got, I thought, and she was at a definite disadvantage."

"Good. They are about to encounter Fitz and Odelia again. This time I shall be there—and you hold your tongue." And so saying she hastened towards Fitz and Odelia as if their simple smile of acknowledgment had been an urgent invitation.

They arrived precisely as James and Fanny Hilliard stepped back from a picture the better to consider it, and were so close Emily could very easily bump into James and apologize with devastating sweetness. A moment later they were all exchanging greetings.

"How charming you look, Miss Hilliard." Odelia smiled. "Such a lovely hat. I meant to compliment you on it last time, and somehow it slipped my mind."

Fanny colored faintly, quite aware that the meaning of the remark was not that it was especially handsome, but that she had worn the same hat on the previous occasion also.

"Thank you," she said simply. "How kind of you to say so."

"Such an attractive quality, don't you agree?" Emily said quickly, turning to Odelia. "I admire it above all others!"

"Remembering hats?" Odelia's eyebrows shot up incredulously. "Really, Mrs. Radley. I cannot think why?"

"Kindness," Emily corrected. "I admire kindness, Miss Morden. The ability not to take advantage, to find generous pleasure in someone else's success, even when you are not finding particular success yourself. That takes a truly fine spirit, don't you think?"

"I was not aware that I was being particularly kind." Odelia frowned, a spark of suspicion in her eyes.

Emily's hand flew to her mouth in a delicate gesture of embarrassment.

"Oh—your own hat is charming. I simply meant your generosity in admiring Miss Hilliard's hat with such candor."

Charlotte stifled a giggle with difficulty, and avoided meeting anyone's eyes.

Both James Hilliard and Fitz looked a trifle puzzled.

"Are you enjoying the exhibition?" Fitz asked quickly. "Have you seen anything you would buy?"

"I like the roses over there," Charlotte answered instantly, struggling for anything that would fill the silence. "And I thought some of the portraits were very fine, although I am not sure who they are."

"The woman in the white gown with the lace is Lillie Langtry," Fitz said with a broad smile.

"Oh is it?" Charlotte was interested in spite of herself, and the pucker of disapproval between Odelia's brows did nothing to discourage her. "If it is a good likeness, then she is very lovely. Have you met her?"

"One meets everyone sooner or later. Society is very small, you know."

"Do you not find that, Mrs. Pitt?" Odelia asked with a spark of interest.

There was no purpose in lying; she would only be caught in it and look even more foolish. And she did not hunger for social rank enough to pretend to it.

"I did before I was married," she said with a candid stare. "But since then I have spent far more time at home with my family. I only departed from it this season to be what help I can to Emily, in the circumstances."

"Very generous of you," Odelia said politely, having established a certain superiority. She linked her arm in Fitz's and leaned a fraction closer to him. "I am sure she will feel greatly eased in her mind for your company. It is something of a disadvantage that the selection of a candidate should occur just now, however I am sure it will not influence a decision." She lifted one slender shoulder slightly. "You have met many of the most important people. I saw you with Lord Anstiss at the opera. Such a fine man. Most of us will never know how much he gives away to all manner of deserving causes. Some of the artists here are only able to exhibit at all because of his patronage, you know."

And the conversation moved to the much safer subject of Lord Anstiss's benefactions in many fields, Fanny and James Hilliard joining in where a pleasant but uninformed opinion was acceptable.

Charlotte glanced at Emily and saw with a flash of understanding that she was equally bored. Fitz caught the look.

"Who cares?" he agreed with a laugh. He turned to Fanny, and her face flooded with relief and humor. "Let's talk of something more fun," he said quickly. "What is the latest scandal? There must be something entertaining?"

"I don't know of anything," Odelia said with regret. "It is all a matter of who may marry whom, and unless you know them it is all very tedious, and probably quite predictable anyway."

They moved a few steps to the next picture without looking at it.

"There is the matter of Mr. Horatio Osmar," James said tentatively. "That seems to have elements of the ludicrous about it."

"Horatio Osmar?" Fitz seized on it. "Isn't he a minister in the government? Do tell us: what has he done? Or, to be more accurate, what do they say he has done?"

"He used to be a junior minister of sorts," James corrected.

"Oh dear—I should know that, shouldn't I?" Fitz said ruefully. "What about him? Is it money?"

"Nothing so dry." James smiled. It was a gentle, diffident and very warm expression which lit his face, giving him a charm he had lacked before. "He was arrested for indecent behavior with a young woman—on a park bench!"

They all burst into laughter, making several heads turn and causing a few elderly ladies to frown and mutter to themselves on the indelicacy of the young, and their increasing lack of decorum. One lady dressed in gray with a stuffed bird on her hat glared fiercely, and held her head so high the bird wobbled violently and appeared as if it were attempting to fly, and she was obliged to reach up with her hand to make sure it did not overbalance.

"Very out of date," Fanny whispered a trifle too loudly.

"What is?" Charlotte asked.

"Stuffed animals on your clothes," Fanny replied. "Don't you remember—it was all the rage a couple of years ago. My mother's cousin had a hat with flowers with all the beetles and spiders in them."

"You are twitting us!" Fitz said with wide eyes.

"Not at all! And I have a friend whose aunt had a gown with stuffed mice on the hem and up the outer fold of the skirt."

"Ugh!" He was staring at her with delight. "Really?"

"I swear it."

"How disgusting!"

"Worse than that. We have a domestic cat—" She was giggling as she said it. "She was an excellent mouser. It was a disaster."

"A mouser," Fitz said quickly. "Oh do tell us."

Odelia pulled a face of distaste but Fanny was looking at Fitz and was totally unaware of her.

"Aunt Dorabella had been asked to favor us with a song, which she did with some enthusiasm. It was the Kashmiri Love Song, you know?"

"Pale hands I love," Fitz said quickly.

"Yes, that's right. Well she swept across the space we had

cleared for her, swirling her skirts behind her, raising her hands to illustrate the song—and Pansy, the cat, shot out from under the drapes 'round the piano legs and bolted up Dorabella's skirt after the mouse. Dorabella hit a high note very much higher than she had intended—and louder—"

Fitz was having trouble keeping his composure, and Charlotte and Emily were not even trying.

"Pansy took fright and ran down again," Fanny went on, "with the mouse between her teeth, and a sizable piece of the skirt with it. Dorabella tripped over the rest and fell against the pianist, who shrieked and overbalanced off the stool."

Fanny shrugged her shoulders and dissolved into giggles. "We disgraced ourselves so utterly," she finished, "that my friend was cut out of Uncle Arthur's will. I've never laughed so hard in my life. I was so sorry, but if it had been my fortune at stake, I could not have helped myself. Fortunately, it would have been only two rather ordinary chairs—and Uncle Arthur lived to be ninety-three anyway! Of course I apologized profoundly, but Aunt Dorabella did not believe a word, and neither of them ever forgave us."

"How marvelous," Fitz said sincerely. "I'm sure it was worth it." He looked around to each of them. "Is there a great deal more you wish to see here?"

"Not I." Emily shook her head, still smiling, but Charlotte had a good idea she had had enough of standing for a while anyway.

"Nor I," she agreed quickly.

"Then let us find some refreshment," Fitz suggested. "Come, James, I shall take you all to tea, and you shall tell us what befell poor Mr. Osmar." And he offered his arm to Fanny, who accepted it with a quick smile. James escorted Odelia, and Charlotte and Emily were left to bring up the rear.

They took both carriages, and met up again inside the hotel, where they were served a most delicious tea in a large, softly lit room with the most flattering pinks and apricots. They began with thinly sliced cucumber sandwiches on brown bread, cream cheese beaten with a few chopped chives, then smoked salmon mousse. There were white bread sandwiches with smoked ham, egg mayonnaise with mustard and cress, and finely grated cheese. When these had blunted the edge of appetite, they were served scones so fresh they were still warm, with plenty of jam and cream, then lastly cakes and exquisite French pastries, choux and puff pastries filled with whipped cream, lacelike icing and thin slices of fruit.

During all this James Hilliard entertained them with the story of Horatio Osmar, his trial and unaccountable acquittal, without mentioning the name of the magistrate, which apparently he did not know.

"What did the young woman say?" Charlotte asked.

"Nothing," James replied, setting his cup down on its saucer. "She was not asked."

"But that's absurd!" Charlotte protested.

"The whole thing is absurd," he answered. "And now I hear they are talking of police perjury—"

"Oh! Which station did you say it was?"

"Bow Street."

She drew in a deep breath. Under the table Emily reached out and touched her. There was nothing she could say. She forced herself to smile.

"Oh dear. How unfortunate," she said meaninglessly, aware how inadequate it sounded.

Emily folded her napkin and laid it on the table.

"It has been the most charming afternoon," she said with a smile at each of them. "It is time we excused ourselves and went home to change for the evening."

"Of course." Both Fitz and James Hilliard rose to their feet. Good-byes were said and Emily and Charlotte departed to their carriage.

Charlotte reached her own home at nearly six o'clock and swept in to find Gracie preparing dinner and giving Jemima and Daniel their supper at the same time. She looked tired and harassed, her hair falling out of her cap, her sleeves rolled up, her face flushed.

Charlotte was smitten with instant guilt, aware how long she had been away, and that she had neglected her duties. It did not help at all when Pitt came home shortly afterwards and, on seeing the state of the kitchen, Charlotte's gloriously piled hair and flushed face, and Gracie looking weary and untidy, he lost his temper.

"What the devil is going on?" he demanded, staring at Gracie then at Charlotte. "Where have you been?"

There was no point in lying. He would find out, and she was no good at it anyway, not to him.

"At the Royal Academy exhibition—"

His face was bleak, the warmth and tenderness vanished. His eyebrows rose.

"Indeed? And for what purpose did you go there?"

For a wild moment she thought of saying "To look at the pictures," then saw his eyes and knew it was not the moment for levity.

"Just to accompany Emily," she said very quietly.

"And left Gracie here to do your work!" he snapped. "I don't admire your selfishness, Charlotte."

It was the most cutting thing he could have said, and she had no answer to it. The only way she could defend her dignity was to force herself into sufficient anger to stop herself from crying.

Supper was eaten in miserable silence. Gracie had gone upstairs, sniffing with unhappiness at the unusual conflict in what she regarded as her own home, and in a curious sense, her family.

Afterwards, Charlotte sat in her chair in the parlor opposite Pitt and pretended to be sewing, but she had no pleasure in it, and accomplished nothing. She knew she had been selfish, thinking only of the glamour and the excitement, not of her children and house, where she should have been, or at the very least of her responsibility.

Pitt sat quietly reading a newspaper, without once looking over it at her.

At bedtime she went upstairs alone, more crushingly miserable than she could remember being for a year or more.

She took off her dress and hung it up, then extricated the pins from her hair and let it fall over her shoulders without the usual sensual pleasure, knowing that Pitt loved it. Strange how all the warmth and light could go out of everything just because she felt such a gulf between them. Odelia Morden's face kept coming back into her mind as she climbed into bed, feeling the sheets chill on her skin. She could see her so clearly, the look of sudden, wounded surprise as she saw Fitz's eyes on Fanny Hilliard, heard them laugh together, and realized that something was slipping away from her and she was powerless to cling onto it. There was a warmth between Fitz and Fanny Hilliard, an ease of understanding, laughter at the same things. Odelia would never be part of it. Today Charlotte had seen the first wing of loneliness touch her, and a premonition of loss. Whatever happened in the future, Odelia had become aware that something precious was beyond her reach.

And Charlotte had thought her so complacent. She was just at the beginning of pain.

Aunt Vespasia had said it was Charlotte who was too satisfied, not nurturing what was precious.

Pitt came to bed in the dark, lying next to her but apart, his back towards her.

She had no idea whether he was asleep or not, or what he was thinking. Did he really feel she was totally selfish? Surely he knew her better than that—after all these years. Could he not understand how much the opera had meant to her, and that she had gone to the exhibition only to keep Emily company?

No. He knew how it had thrilled her. She had seen that in his face. And he knew how long she had waited—until Emily took them.

Emily took them—not Pitt.

She reached out her hand and touched him.

"I'm sorry," she said quietly. "I should have thought—and I didn't."

For seconds nothing happened. She began to think he was asleep. Then slowly he moved over and touched her fingertips, saying nothing.

Tears of relief filled her eyes and she wriggled down to be comfortable, and at last composed herself to go to sleep.

CHAPTER

SIX

Pitt left the house the following day still feeling depressed in spirit. He and Charlotte had been civil over the breakfast table, but the old warmth was not there. The episode of the exhibition could not easily be repaired. Some of the sweetness had gone out of his life lately, the lift in his spirits as he turned towards home at the end of the day, no matter how ragged or disappointing it had been. It was not that Charlotte was not always there. That he understood and accepted. She had often spent time with Emily, or even very occasionally with her mother. And goodness knows he had long ago stopped fighting against her joining in his cases because it was unseemly, or even dangerous. In fact he was proud of her abilities to judge people he would never know except from an outside view.

It was not that. As he trudged along the dusty pavement towards the main street where he could get an omnibus, he was honest enough to admit it was because she was stepping into Emily's world, and enjoying it. And it had been her world until she married him. It would have remained hers, had she chosen someone suited to her own social position, and her family's expectations.

That was it. He felt guilty—and shut out. He had been invited to the opera as well, of course. Emily would never have excluded him. And he had enjoyed it—at least some of it. He did not care for the music a great deal. But then neither had most of the people who were there. It was a social event for them, not an artistic one. Everyone knew everyone else, if not in person then by repute.

The omnibus drew to a halt and he stepped on, choosing to climb the open spiral steps at the back up onto the top deck. There were plenty of seats available and he sat alone, still deep in thought.

He had looked at Charlotte more than at the stage. He had never seen her more beautiful, her hair shining and coiled, dressed by Emily's maid, her face flushed with excitement, her eyes bright. She had loved it. That was what hurt. He would love to have been the one who took her. But all he could ever manage would be once, and it would be a great occasion. Now she had already been, and if Emily chose, would go again, as often as she wished. The top of the omnibus was open and the sun was warm on his face.

He wanted Jack Radley to succeed in Parliament, not only for Jack's own sake, because he liked him, and for Emily, but for the good he might do. But it was not the same as when Charlotte and Emily were meddling in one of his cases and he felt as if he had a part in it. There was no way he could help Jack. In fact his relationship would more likely be a hindrance, were it known.

That was it, not very attractive, not easy to admit, but he was jealous.

The omnibus halted again for a few moments, then jerked forward as the horses began up a slight gradient, pulling hard.

On the other hand, he was justified in being angry. Charlotte had no business to go off in the afternoon simply to look at an exhibition of pictures, leaving poor Gracie to do the housework and prepare the dinner.

Which did nothing to make him feel better. Being justified was a cold thing.

He arrived at the Clerkenwell police station in a poor mood and went straight through to the small back office. Innes's sharp, intelligent face was little cheer. This case was every bit as unpleasant and intractable as he had feared at the outset. There were too many elements in it that worried him. How had Byam heard of the murder so quickly? What was there in it that distressed Micah Drummond, and yet he could not speak of it and kept on through his embarrassment and obvious discomfort? Why had William Weems sat behind his desk and allowed someone to bring in a gun?

A gun capable of firing the gold pieces would have to be a muzzle loader. Who walks through the streets carrying such a thing? It argued a very careful premeditation. Where were the incriminating papers and the letter Byam had said were there? If Byam was guilty, and he had removed them, why had he bothered to call Drummond and admit any connection at all? And what about Addison Carswell?

"Mornin' sir," Innes said cheerfully. "Lovely day again."

"Yes," Pitt agreed dourly. "Going to be hot."

"Got anything further?" Innes was relentlessly optimistic, although his quick eyes had taken in Pitt's expression. "Any of them other people look hopeful? We got nothing 'ere, an' I can't 'elp wonderin' 'ow any o' these people would get 'old o' the kind o' gun that killed the poor devil." He shrugged and put his hands in his pockets, a comfortable and informal gesture.

"I wish we could find that, Mr. Pitt," he said with a frown. "I'd feel a lot closer if we could. I bin 'round all the cabbies, like you said, but no one remembers a fare carryin' anything like a gun big enough ter blow Weems's 'ead off." He screwed up his face. "You sure it couldn't 'a bin the one wot was already there on the wall? They couldn't 'a used it then taken the pin down after, to confuse us, like?"

"No," Pitt said grimly. "It was filed down and there was a patina of use on the metal. You don't fake that in a few minutes. And who would think to bring a file—or hang around with that corpse to use it?"

Innes shrugged. "Yer right. It don't make no sense. An' there weren't 'anging space fer another gun, nor there weren't one moved on the wall, I looked fer that."

"Did we ask the cleaning woman—what's her name?"

"Mrs. Cairns."

"Did we ask her if she'd seen another gun any time?"

"Yes—she said she 'adn't seen nothing—but I don't know whether to believe 'er or not. She'd no love fer 'im, as she don't want ter get involved with any part of it."

"You think she'd lie?" Pitt sat on the windowsill, this time leaving the chair for Innes, if he wished.

"I think she'd deliberately forget," Innes said judiciously. "The local opinion is pretty well on the side of 'oever done it. 'E weren't liked, weren't Mr. Weems."

"What a surprise," Pitt said sarcastically. "Still, I think I'll go and take another look at his rooms. Are all the papers still there?"

"Yes sir. Place is locked. I'll get the key. Mind, I'm beginning ter think it were one o' your nobs. Sorry sir, but I do."

"So do I," Pitt admitted. "But I'm often surprised." He stood up again. "Come on—get that key and we'll look again."

Half an hour later they were methodically sorting through sheets of paper and putting them from one pile to another, uncertain what they were looking for. They found the close office with its stale air, and their knowledge of what was done there, heavily oppressive, even to the rise of nausea if they stopped to imagine that night, the despair, the violence and the sudden horror of blood, an act irretrievable, and the fear afterwards.

"Got it!" Innes said suddenly in triumph, his voice ringing out in the heavy silence. " 'Ere!" He held up a sheet of paper with a name in capitals on the top, and figures and dates and amounts all down it, finishing at the bottom with a line of handwriting.

"What?" Pitt said, puzzled as to what it could be and afraid to hope.

" 'Ere!" Innes was not to be dampened in his victory. "Look!" He thrust the paper forward. "Walter 'Opcroft, paid 'is last installment of interest in 'is debt with a blunderbuss—same day as Weems was shot!" His voice rose with conviction. "It must 'a bin 'ere in the office when 'is murderer came! 'E just took advantage of it! Stands ter reason." His face was beaming.

Pitt straightened up from the drawers where he had been sifting through papers yet again. "And what?" He frowned. "He and Weems had a quarrel and he saw the blunderbuss, went to the powder boxes, tipped the powder into the breach, picked up the gold coins from the desk, or wherever they were, loaded them, and then shot half Weems's head off? What was Weems doing?"

Innes stood motionless.

"Well at least we know w'ere the gun came from," he said defensively.

Pitt sighed. "We do," he agreed. "Well done. Now we have to work out how in heaven's name he managed to load it and fire it without Weems stopping him. What happened here, Innes? Can you think of anything—anything at all—that would explain it?"

"No sir," Innes said, pulling a face. "Maybe when we know who it is, we'll understand." He looked hopeful.

"Maybe," Pitt agreed. "I was rather looking for it to be the other way, knowing what happened would lead us to who it is."

Innes took a deep breath. "I don't like to 'ave ter say this, sir, but could this nob o' yours 'ave come 'ere, for whatever reason, an' 'ad a quarrel with Weems, an' 'is bein' a nob, Weems don't think 'e'd turn nasty, so 'e didn't believe it when it 'appened. P'r'aps the nob—sorry sir—but not knowin' 'is name I 'ave ter call 'im something, p'r'aps 'e admired the gun, casual like, and Weems, since 'e 'ad the upper 'and, jus' sat there an let 'im go on!"

Innes drew a deep breath. "An' o' course Weems knew 'e 'adn't any shot for it, an' 'e wouldn't think o' gold coin as bein' ammunition. An' the nob—sorry sir—'e quietly loads it, talking agreeable like, an' keepin' the gold coins in 'is pocket w'ere Weems don't know about them—until the last moment when 'e shoved them down the barrel and lifted it up. And Weems were so surprised 'e didn't believe it, till the gentleman fired, an' it were too late!" He stood expectantly, waiting for Pitt's comment.

"Doesn't sound very probable," Pitt said slowly. "But it's better than anything else we've got so far. Pity we didn't know Weems—only got other people's ideas of him to know whether he was as complacent as that, or sure of having the whip hand."

"From what I 'ear, 'e was," Innes said with disgust. " 'Ad a lot o' power 'round 'ere—and liked the taste of it."

Pitt pushed his hands into his pockets.

"Who did you get that from?" Pitt asked, realizing how little he had pressed Innes for the sources of his knowledge about the dead man. Perhaps he had been remiss. It was just conceivable the murder had been personal after all, and nothing to do with debt or blackmail, although it was so remote a possibility he did not believe it for a moment.

"We 'ad the errand chappie, Windy Miller, in again," Innes replied, still holding the sheet of paper in his hand. "Nasty little beggar, but 'e certainly knew Weems pretty well. Got 'im summed up ter rights. Read 'im like a book, an' 'ated 'im according." Innes pushed out his lip. "Thought we might 'ave 'ad summink there, but 'e's got twenty witnesses'll swear 'e was in the Dog an' Duck 'alf the night playin' dominoes, and drunk under the table the other 'alf. Besides, 'e 'ad a good job wi' Weems, and not like ter get another easy."

Pitt sat down on the edge of the table.

"And he couldn't tell you anything useful? Didn't Weems have any female attachments, even just . . ." He hesitated, not sure how to phrase what he meant.

"No," Innes answered for him with a wry grin. "Seems 'e 'adn't no use fer women. Nor nobody else," he added hastily. "Some people's like that—not many, mind, but Weems were one of 'em. Liked money, an' the power it give 'im. Windy said 'e'd always bin like that. 'Is pa were a gambler, rich one day and dirt poor the next. Died in debtors' prison somewhere. Never knew 'is ma."

"What did the housekeeper say about him?"

"Nothin' much," Innes said with a shrug. "Nasty piece o' work."

"Mrs. Cairns?"

"No—although she's no jewel, but I meant Weems. Watched every farthing, she says, wouldn't give nobody an inch. She didn't say it in them words, but I gather as 'e 'ad no sense o' 'umor neither. Liked 'is food and spent money on it, but that's about all. Oh—'e liked ter be warm. Didn't mind spendin' money on keepin' the fire in 'is own room. Rest o' the 'ouse was like an icebox in winter, she said, but always a good fire in 'is office."

"Anyone have a good word for him?" Pitt said dryly.

"Tradesmen," Innes replied with a meaningful look. " 'E paid 'is bills in time, and to the penny."

"Bravo." Pitt was sarcastic. "No one else?"

"Not a soul."

Pitt looked around the room. "So what happened to this blunderbuss? I suppose the murderer took it away with him. It certainly wasn't here when you found Weems."

"I'm sure o' that," Innes said decisively.

"You'd better start a search specifically for a blunderbuss," Pitt instructed. "But don't waste much time on it. It could be anywhere, and it wouldn't give us much idea who used it, even if we did by some miracle come up with it. I've got some other ideas to follow up—and some more people on his list."

"Nobs?"

"Yes. So far we've got to who could have done it, and certainly had cause, and so far as I can see, opportunity. And now it seems pretty well anyone who came that night had the means, since it was sitting here in the office."

"Nasty one, sir," Innes agreed.

"Yes." Pitt knew that Innes hoped it was a "nob," not one of his own people, some Clerkenwell debtor pressed beyond his bearing. Pitt was inclined to agree, except he did not wish it to be Carswell. He could imagine his desperation vividly; it made him real, and painfully immediate. But why on earth had Carswell dismissed the case of Horatio Osmar without even hearing Beulah Giles's evidence? It made no sense.

And it would be almost worse if it were Urban. He could imagine the scandal, and the injury to the already unpopular police force, still suffering from the ignominy of not having caught the Whitechapel murderer known as Jack the Ripper only last autumn. He must find the last name—Clarence Latimer. It was his only escape from tragedy.

Or was it Byam after all? That thought was no better. And Drummond would take it very hard.

And that was another problem that needed to be faced. Why had Micah Drummond interfered in the case at all? Why had he been so quick to defend Byam?

Innes was busy tidying up, closing drawers to leave the place as they found it.

Pitt would have staked his career that Drummond was utterly honest and would not have altered the course of an investigation on a friend's behalf, however close. And it had not seemed that Byam was more than an acquaintance anyway.

There was no point in asking him, trying to press. His attitude had already made it plain he did not feel free to discuss it. It must be some debt of honor; that was all that would hold a man like Drummond so obviously against his wishes. He was suffering—Pitt had known that from the beginning. He hated doing it, and yet he felt unavoidably compelled.

Why? For what?

"I'm going back to Bow Street," Pitt said aloud. "I've got to look into the other people on the list. Do what you can about the blunderbuss, and anything else you can think of. Have you found all the debtors on the first list?"

"Almost sir. Poor bastards!"

"Then you'd better finish it. Sorry."

"Yes sir." Innes smiled lopsidedly. "Not that it's any worse than what you've got ter do."

Pitt looked at him with a sudden warmth.

"No," he agreed. "No it isn't."

But when he arrived at Bow Street the immediate problem of asking Urban about Weems was temporarily put out of his mind by the news given him by the desk sergeant.

"No sir, I think Mr. Urban is busy with the solicitors, Mr. Pitt. Can't interrupt 'im now."

"Solicitors?" Pitt was taken aback. Knowing his own errand, views of prosecution flashed into his mind and he felt a chill of both apprehension and pity.

"Yes sir." The desk sergeant's pink face was full of confusion. " 'E's got a very important gennelman in there now." His voice dropped to a whisper. "From Parkins, Parkins and Gorman."

Pitt had heard the name and knew it to be one of the foremost firms of solicitors in London. They were certainly not the people an ordinary man would employ to organize a defense, it would be completely beyond his means. Pitt's mind raced, trying to think of any reason for Urban's seeking legal advice of such an order, before any investigation had begun, let alone charges brought.

"Do you know why?" he asked the desk sergeant, then immediately wished he had not.

The sergeant looked embarrassed.

"No sir. I 'eard tell as it were to do with perjury, and summink about someone in this station 'avin' lied. I know Mr. Urban were very angry."

Pitt turned towards the corridor that led to Urban's office.

"You can't go in there, sir!" the sergeant said hastily, moving from one foot to the other, not sure how he was going to stop Pitt, who was both senior to him and larger.

Pitt smiled sourly and sighed. "Let me know when Mr. Urban is free, will you? I need to see him, to do with an investigation."

"Yessir."

Pitt turned away and was about to leave, frustrated because he wanted to get the matter over with, when a slim dapper man in pin-striped trousers and a frock coat came out of the corridor. He nodded briefly to the desk sergeant, who leaped to attention, then with a flicker of irritation relaxed again. The man went out of the door into the street without looking behind him.

"You can go in and see Mr. Urban now, Mr. Pitt, sir," the sergeant said quickly.

"Thank you," Pitt acknowledged and moved smartly to Urban's office door. He knocked and as soon as he heard the least sound inside, pushed it open and went in. The room was very like his own, similarly furnished but much tidier.

Urban was standing by his window with his back to the door, his hands in his pockets and his feet apart. He was a tall man, slender and fair haired and dressed in the police uniform of a senior inspector. He turned slowly as he heard the latch on the door.

"Hello, Pitt." His voice was light and pleasing with a slight south country accent. "What are you doing here? Can we help with something?"

Pitt was surprised that Urban knew him so quickly. He would not have recognized Urban had he walked into Pitt's office unannounced. He looked at Urban's face for anxiety, even fear, and saw only a slowly clearing anger, now being overtaken by curiosity.

"No," he said uncertainly. "I don't think so." Then realizing that that made no sense he hurried on. "Am I interrupting you?"

Urban laughed abruptly. "The solicitor? No. He's gone. This is as good a time as any. What is it?"

There was no alternative but to go ahead with what he had planned to say before the desk sergeant had told him about the solicitor being there.

"Do you know William Weems, of Cyrus Street, Clerkenwell?"

"The usurer that was murdered?" Urban's fair eyebrows rose. Obviously the question was one that he had not expected, but it seemed to cause him no alarm. "No. Know of him of course. Caused something of a stir, his death. Releases a lot of debts, it would seem. No heir so far. Why?"

Urban was not the sort of man upon whom to try trickery, and Pitt found himself oddly ashamed that he had thought of it.

"He had two lists of debtors," he replied. "One the usual you would expect, ordinary people in financial difficulties. The second was very much smaller, only three names were indicated as still being in debt." He watched Urban's face and saw nothing in it but mild interest. There was no start of surprise, no anxiety, only the still-clinging remnants of anger.

"Oh? Someone I know, I presume, or you wouldn't be here."

Pitt bit his lip. "Yes—your own name is there."

Urban was obviously astounded. He stared in complete disbelief. His wide blue eyes searched Pitt's face as if he expected to find some horrid joke. Then gradually he grasped that Pitt was serious and the statement required a response.

"I don't owe him any money," he said slowly. "Or anyone else." Then there was a flicker, a shadow in his clear eyes, and Pitt knew he was suddenly less than honest, in thought if not in word. A chill touched him inside. He tried to keep the knowledge of it from his expression.

"But you have encountered him?" he said with conviction.

"I've never met him," Urban denied. He had chosen his words carefully, but his face was open and he met Pitt's gaze easily. "Cyrus Street is out of my area—yours too, for that matter." His eyebrows rose. "Why are you concerned anyway?"

Pitt told all the truth that he could. "Because of the people who may be involved."

"Not on my account. Who else is on the list?" Urban asked, pointing to the chair near Pitt, and sitting down in his own chair behind the desk.

Pitt smiled ruefully. "Confidential," he apologized.

"But important people," Urban pressed. "Weems was killed several days ago now. I'm not the first you've come to see—and you've been handling the political cases this last year or so. There's someone of considerable influence involved in this." He was watching Pitt's face and he knew he was right. It was beyond Pitt's ability, or his desire, to conceal it.

"It was a large amount of money," Pitt said instead.

"What? That Weems has me down for?" Urban looked puzzled. "But it's irrelevant—I didn't owe him anything. I never had anything to do with him." He took in a breath as if to add something, then changed his mind.

"Why was the solicitor here?" Pitt asked abruptly.

"What?" Urban's mouth tightened in irritation again. "Oh—that damned Osmar!" He shook his head. "They not only threw the case out of the magistrate's court, you know, now the wretched man is charging that Crombie and Allardyce committed perjury in saying he behaved indecently in the park, and he wants them prosecuted for it. Can you credit it? I had the best solicitor I could find to see if we can reopen the case and try him again."

"Osmar?"

"Yes. Why not? Parkins thinks there's a good chance."

Pitt smiled. "Good. At least save Crombie and Allardyce from charges."

"I intend to. And I'd like to know why the magistrate threw it out." This time it was Urban who saw the momentary evasion in Pitt's eyes. He hesitated on the edge of asking him, then some professional instinct asserted itself and he remained silent.

"You have no idea why?" Pitt asked.

"None at all," Urban replied, and Pitt knew he was lying.

"Thank you for your time," he said. "I'll have to go back to the list and see what else I can find."

"Sorry I can't help you," Urban apologized again, and smiled courteously as Pitt took his leave.

Investigating Urban proved to be both as difficult and as distasteful as Pitt had expected. He began by going to Urban's home. This time he took the public omnibus, as the route took him to within five hundred yards of the street, and he was in no particular hurry. Indeed the hot, noisy ride on the bus, sitting squashed between a thin woman in blue with a cold in her head and a large man smelling of beer, gave him an opportunity to let his thoughts roam. Not that it accomplished anything. He had liked Urban and the thought of prying into his private life was increasingly unpleasant. And because he was intelligent and forewarned, this would prove very difficult to accomplish without his becoming aware of it.

By asking him openly about Weems he had forewarned him that Pitt knew he was connected with the case. He was still feeling angry and miserable about Charlotte, furious with her for behaving as if she were a lady with leisure and money to do as she pleased, and for not making better use of her time than entertaining herself. And he was miserable because that was what she had been born to expect, and she was so easily and naturally enjoying the chance that Emily had given her and Pitt never could. And it hurt that she should still find these things so important. He had enjoyed the spectacle of the occasion himself. People had always interested him, people of every sort, and he had been enthralled watching the faces, and observing the ritual games they played with one another, and the passions behind the masks.

But this investigation he was carrying out alone. For once Charlotte knew almost nothing about it, and her concern was not engaged. It was a curiously lonely thing and he missed her sharing it, even if she did not know the people and could contribute nothing but her interest.

What should he learn about Urban? His reputation among his fellows? His home, his life, the money he spent? His professional integrity? He was lying about something, even if only by omission. Could he possibly know why Addison Carswell had dismissed the case against Osmar? Carswell's name was on Weems's list as well—but what had Osmar to do with it? And if it was blackmail, why was Byam's name not there?

He got off the omnibus and walked the last distance along the narrow pavement in the heat, passing women with children, old men gossiping, a tradesman sweeping his shop's front step, a rag and bone man shouting in a singsong voice, and a housemaid in a crisp cap arguing with a butcher's boy standing in the areaway wiping his hands on his blue-and-white apron. It was not far from where he lived himself, and not unlike his street. He pushed the thought of Charlotte out of his mind; that was another hurt, for another time.

Urban's house was quite small and ordinary from the outside, exactly like its neighbors. The front step was scrubbed clean, the door recently painted, the garden was small and neat with a few roses around and a pocket handkerchief lawn. He had already debated with himself what he was going to say. There was little point in duplicity. It would be too easily discovered, and then would create an ill feeling that would be hard, if not impossible, to repair. And if Urban was innocent, that would be an impediment to future work.

The door was opened by a small woman in a gray stuff dress and a plain white apron. Her thick reddish hair was tied back in a knot and there was a white cap balanced precariously, and crookedly, on top of her head. She reminded him of the woman who came to do the heavy scrubbing for Charlotte, and whom Gracie bossed around mercilessly, now that she considered herself a senior servant.

"Yes?" the woman said impatiently. Obviously he had interrupted her in her work and she did not appreciate it.

"Good morning," he said quickly. "I am conducting a police investigation and I need to examine some papers of Inspector Urban's. My name is Pitt. May I come in?"

She looked doubtful. " 'Ow do I know you're tellin' me the truth? You could be anyone."

"I could," he agreed, and produced his police identification.

She looked at the card carefully. Her eyes did not move along the line, and Pitt guessed she could not read. She looked up at him again, studying his face, and he waited for her to make her judgment.

"All right," she said at last. "If it's police yer'd better come in. But 'e in't done nuffink wrong."

"It's information I need," he said, somewhat begging the question, and followed her into the narrow hallway where she opened one of the doors into the front parlor. "That's where 'e keeps 'is papers," she said stiffly. "Anyfink yer wantin'll be in there. If it in't, then it in't 'ere at all." It was a definite statement he was not going to be allowed anywhere else.

"Thank you," he accepted. She remained standing rooted to the spot, her eyes hard and bright. Obviously she was not going to leave him alone, policeman or not. He smiled to himself, then began to look around. It was not a large room, and the space was further crowded by at least a dozen paintings on the walls. They were not at all what he would have expected, family portraits, sentimental pastoral scenes or sporting prints. Rather they were very modern impressions of sunlit landscapes: bars of light, blurs of water lilies all blues and greens with flashes of pink; a dazzle of shades and points of vivid color which conjured peasant women lying under the trees by the side of a cornfield. They were highly individual experiments in art, the selection of a man who had very definite opinions and was prepared to spend a good deal of money investing in what he believed to be good. There was no need to look any further for the part of Urban's life-style that would run him into debt. It was here on his walls for any caller to observe.

He stayed a few minutes longer, examining the pictures more closely, seeing the brushwork, the imagination and the skill that had gone into them. Then he went over to the desk and opened it in order to satisfy the waiting housekeeper that he was indeed looking for information of a sort she could understand. He shuffled through a couple of papers, read one, and closed the drawer. Then he swung around to face her. She looked faintly surprised that he should be finished so soon.

"You all done then?" she said with a frown.

"Yes thank you. It was only a small thing, and easily found."

"Oh—well then you'd best be gone. I got work to do. Mr. Urban's not the only gennelman as I see after. Mind my step as you go out. Don't go dragging your feet over it. I just done that, I did."

Pitt stepped over it carefully and went on down the path and out of the gate. The beauty of the pictures, the courage to back such individual and daring taste should have pleased him. Ordinarily it would have; but this time, knowing Urban's salary, and that he was lying over something, he found it deeply depressing. Was Urban so wooed by loveliness, so caught by the collector's fever, that he had borrowed from Weems, and then realized he could never hope to repay? Or was there something even uglier:

had he obtained the money in some other way, dishonest, even corrupt, and Weems had learned of it and blackmailed him?

Pitt lengthened his stride along the hot, dusty street, passing an errand boy whistling between his teeth, swinging a bag, then two old women standing in the middle of the footpath, heads together, gossiping. At the end of the street he came into the main thoroughfare and stood waiting for the omnibus, his mind moving from one unhappy thought to another.

He knew what he must do next, and he chose a series of omnibuses because he was in no hurry to get there. Before coming to Bow Street, Urban had worked in Rotherhithe, south of the river. Now Pitt must go to his old station and ask his colleagues about him, what manner of man he was, and try to read between the loyalty of their answers the truth of what they knew, or suspected. He would have to look through his previous cases, such as were distinctly his. It was not so clear-cut with uniformed men. And lastly he would have to find the people on the edge of the criminal underworld who had most dealings with the police and ask them, learn what Urban's reputation had been, see if he could find there the ends of the threads which would lead him to the money that had bought those wild and lovely pictures.

He stopped and had a brief luncheon at a public house, but his thoughts were too much engrossed in Urban to enjoy it. By two o'clock he was in the Rotherhithe police station, explaining his inquiries to the superintendent, a large man with a lugubrious smile and a hot untidy office full of piles of paper. In a patch of sun on the floor a small ginger-and-white kitten lay stretched out asleep on a cushion, every now and then its body twitching in some ecstatic dream.

The superintendent's eyes followed Pitt's.

"Found 'im in the alley," he said with a smile. "Poor little beggar was starvin' an' sickly. Don't think 'e'd 'ave lasted more'n another day or two. 'Ad ter take 'im in. Need a mouser anyway. Can't 'ave the station overrun wi' the little beggars. 'E'll be good fer that when 'e's a bit bigger. Thinks about it already, by the looks of 'im."

The kitten gave another twitch and made a little sound in its sleep.

"What can I do for yer?" the superintendent said in a businesslike manner, pushing a pile of papers off a chair to make a place for Pitt to sit down. The cushion remained for the kitten. Pitt had no objection.

"Samuel Urban," Pitt replied, looking at the little animal.

"Engagin' little beggar, in't 'e?" the superintendent said mildly. "What did you think of him?"

"Sam Urban? Liked 'im. Good policeman." His face puckered with anxiety. "Not in trouble, is 'e?"

"Don't know," Pitt admitted, looking at the kitten stretching out and curling its claws into the cushion, pulling the threads.

"Hector!" the superintendent said amiably. "Don't do that." The kitten disregarded him totally and kept on kneading the cushion. "Taken from 'is mother too early, poor little devil," the superintendent continued. "Suckles on my shirts till I'm wet through. What's 'e supposed to 'ave done, Urban, or shouldn't I ask?"

"Borrowed money from a usurer, maybe," Pitt replied.

The superintendent pushed out his lip. "Not like 'im," he said thoughtfully. "Always careful with 'is money, that I know of. Never threw it around. In fact I sometimes wondered what 'e did wif it. Never drank nor spent it on women, like some. Didn't gamble, so far as I 'eard. What's 'e got in debt for? Inherited an 'ouse from 'is uncle, so it in't that. In fact that's why 'e moved to Bow Street—'ouse is in Bloomsbury. Are you sure about this debt?"

"No," Pitt admitted. "His name was on the usurer's books for a very considerable sum. Urban denies it."

"I don't like the way you say 'was.' You mean the usurer is dead?"

"Yes." There was no use trying to deceive the big, good-natured man. He might take in stray kittens, but he was far from naive when it came to judging men. Pitt had seen the clear, clever eyes under the lazy stare.

"Murdered?"

"Yes. I'm following up all the debtors—or those that the lists say are debtors. So far all of them on the first list admit to owing very small amounts. Those on the second list deny it. But he was known to be a blackmailer . . ." He left the question open, an unfinished sentence.

"And you think he may have been blackmailing Urban?"

"I don't know—but I need to."

The kitten stretched, rolled over and curled up in a ball, purring gently.

"Can't 'elp you," the superintendent said with a little shake of his head. " 'E weren't always a popular man. Too free with 'is opinions, even when they wasn't asked for, an' got some airy-fairy tastes what in't always appreciated by all. But that's by the way. It's no crime."

"May I see the records of his main cases, and speak to a few of his colleagues?"

"O' course. But I know what goes on in my station. You won't find anything."

And so it proved. Pitt spoke to several of the men who had worked with Urban in the six years he had been in Rotherhithe, and found a variety of opinions from affection to outright dislike, but none of them saw in him either dishonesty or any failure of prosecution that was not easily accounted for by the circumstances. Some considered him arrogant and were not afraid to say so, but gave not the slightest indication they thought him corrupt.

Pitt left in the warm, still early evening and came back over the river north again on the long journey home. He felt tired and discouraged, and underneath was a growing unease. The Rotherhithe station had offered nothing about Urban that suggested he was dishonest. Everything Pitt learned created the outline of a diligent, ambitious, somewhat eccentric man respected by his colleagues but not often liked, a man whom no one knew closely, and whom a few conservative, small-visioned men were tacitly pleased to see apparently in trouble.

And Pitt was sure in his own mind that Urban was concealing something to do with Weems's death, and it was something Pitt had said which had made the connection in his mind. But was it the questions about Weems and his debtors, or could it be as it appeared, the extraordinary case of Horatio Osmar and his unaccountable release by Carswell?

He was obliged to travel on several omnibuses, changing at intervals as each one turned from his route back to Bloomsbury. At one change he saw a tired, grubby-faced little girl selling violets, and on impulse he stopped and bought four bunches, dark purple, nestling in their leaves, damp and sweet smelling.

He strode along his own street rapidly, but with an unfamiliar mixture of emotions. It was habit steeped in years that his home was the sweetest place he knew. All warmth and certainty was there, love that did not depend upon gifts or obedience, did not matter whether he was clever, amusing or elegant. It was the place where he gave the best of himself, and yet was not afraid he would be rejected for the worst; where he strove to be wise, to blend honesty with kindness, to make patience natural, to protect without domineering.

Nothing had changed in the deep core of it, but perhaps his perception had deluded him into believing Charlotte was happier than was true. Some of the bright peace of it was dulled.

He opened the door and as soon as he was inside took off his boots and hung up his jacket on the coat hook. Then he went with a nervousness that startled him, stocking footed, along to the kitchen.

It was bright and sweet smelling as always, clean linen on the airing rack suspended from the ceiling, wooden table scrubbed bone pale, blue-and-white china on the dresser and the faint aroma of fresh bread in the air. Jemima was sitting at the table solemnly buttering bread for Daniel. He was watching her and holding on to the jar of raspberry jam, prepared to give it to her only when she had met his exacting standards and there was butter right to every corner.

Charlotte was dressed in floral muslin with a long lace-edged apron on, her sleeves rolled up and her hands in the sink preparing fresh vegetables. There was a pile of shelled peas in a dish on the table near Jemima, and a little heap of empty pods on a newspaper ready to be thrown out.

Charlotte smiled at him, took out the last of the carrots and dried her hands.

"Hello Papa," Jemima said cheerfully without stopping her task.

"Hello Papa," Daniel echoed, still holding on to the jam jar.

Pitt touched them both gently but his eyes never left Charlotte. He held up the violets.

"They're not an apology," he said guardedly.

She looked totally innocent, mystified. "For what?" she asked with wide eyes, then betrayed herself by a quiver of laughter at the corners of her mouth. She buried her nose in their damp fragrance and breathed in with a sigh. "Thank you. They smell wonderful."

He passed her the small blue-and-white cup she usually put short-stemmed flowers in.

"Thank you," she repeated, and filled the cup with water, all the time meeting his eyes. She put the cup in the middle of the table and Jemima immediately smelled the flowers too, holding them up to her nose and breathing in, eyes closed, with exactly the same expression.

"Let me!" Daniel reached for it and reluctantly she passed it over. He breathed in, then breathed in again, not sure what he was doing it for. Then he set the cup down, satisfied, and took up the jam jar again, and Jemima resumed her buttering.

Supper was conducted with the greatest good manners, but not with heads bent and eyes downcast as the previous evening, and intense concentration on the most trivial occupations as if it mattered enormously that every last pea should be chased into a corner and speared with the fork, every crumb of bread picked up. Now the food was barely glanced at. It could have been anything, and all the care that went into preparing it was wasted, but their eyes met and though nothing was said, everything was understood.

Pitt continued to investigate Urban without success for another two days, going through the cases on which he had worked in Bow Street and finding nothing untoward, no pattern that spoke of anything other than hard work and intelligence, sometimes intuition beyond the normal skills, but no questionable judgments, no hint of dishonesty. He kept his private life very much to himself, he mixed little with his colleagues, which earned him their respect but not their affection. No one knew what he did with his spare time and amiable inquiries had met with equally amiable rebuffs.

Finally Pitt decided to confront Urban with the frank question as to where he was on the night of Weems's death. That at least would give him the opportunity to prove himself elsewhere, and make further pursuit unnecessary, at least as far as the murder was concerned. There was still the question of debt, and in Pitt's own mind, the conviction that Urban was lying about something.

He arrived at Bow Street station later in the morning than usual to find an atmosphere of uncharacteristic tension. The desk sergeant looked harassed, his face was pink and he kept moving papers from one place to another without adding anything to them, or apparently reading them. His top tunic button was undone but still he looked as if the neck were too tight. Two constables glanced at each other nervously and shifted from one foot to another, until the sergeant barked at them to get out and find something to do. An errand boy came in with a newspaper and as soon as he was paid, fled out past Pitt, bumping into him and forgetting to apologize.

"What is it?" Pitt said curiously. "What's happened?"

"Questions in the 'Ouse," the desk sergeant replied with a tight lip. " 'E's 'oppin' mad."

"Who's hopping mad?" Pitt asked, still with more curiosity than apprehension. "What's happened, Dilkes?"

"Mr. Urban called the solicitors to bring up the case against Mr. Osmar again, and 'e got wind of it and complained to 'is friends in the 'Ouse o' Commons." Awe mixed with disgust in his face. "Now they're askin' questions about it, and some of 'em is sayin' as Crombie and Allardyce lied 'emselves sick in court, an' the police is corrupt." He shook his head and his voice became anxious. "There's some awful things being said, Mr. Pitt. There's enough folk undecided as to if we're a good thing or not as it is. An' then all that bad business in Whitechapel last autumn, an' we never got the madman what done it, an' folks sayin' as if we were any good we'd 'ave got 'im. An' all the trouble over the commissioner too. An' now this. We don't need trouble like this, Mr. Pitt." He screwed up his face. "What I don't understand is how it all came up over summat so, beggin' yer pardon, damn silly."

"Neither do I," Pitt agreed.

"So 'e was 'avin' a bit o' 'anky-panky in the park. 'E should 'a known better than to do it in public, like. But 'e's a gennleman, and gennlemen is like that. Who cares, if 'e'd just said yes, 'e was a bit naughty, sorry, an' it won't 'appen again, me lud. Only now we got questions asked in the 'ouses o' Parliament, an' next thing the 'ome secretary 'isself will want ter know wot we bin doing."

"I don't understand it myself," Pitt agreed. But he was thinking more of Addison Carswell, and becoming uncomfortably aware of the general feeling against the police, especially as the desk sergeant had said, since the riots in Trafalgar Square known as Bloody Sunday, and then last autumn the failure to catch the Whitechapel murderer, followed almost immediately by the hasty resignation of the commissioner of police after a very short term of office and amid some unpleasantness. The thought kept intruding into his mind that Carswell and Urban were both on Weems's list for very good reasons, which only too probably spoke of blackmail. And he still had to find Latimer, the third name.

"Is Mr. Urban in?" he asked aloud.

"Yessir, but—"

Before the desk sergeant could add his caveat, Pitt thanked him and strode along the passage to Urban's door and knocked.

"Come!" Urban said absently.

Pitt went in and found him sitting behind his desk staring at the polished and empty surface. He was surprised to see Pitt.

"Hello. Got your murderer yet?"

"No," Pitt said, disconcerted that with his very first words Urban had made it impossible for him to be subtle or indirect. "No I haven't."

"Well what can I do for you?" Urban's face was totally innocent. He regarded Pitt out of clear blue eyes, waiting for an answer.

Pitt had no alternative but to be completely frank, or else retreat altogether, and the whole exercise would become pointless if he were to do that.

"Where were you on Tuesday two weeks ago?" he asked. "Late evening."

"Me?" If Urban were feigning amazement he was doing it supremely well. "You think I killed your usurer?"

Pitt sat down in the chair. "No," he said honestly. "But your name was on his list, and the only way I can eliminate you is by your proving you were somewhere else."

Urban smiled. It was charming and candid and there was a flicker of humor in the depths of his eyes.

"I can't tell you," he said quietly. "Or to be more accurate, I don't wish to. But I was not in Cyrus Street, and I did not kill your usurer—or anyone else."

Pitt smiled back.

"I'm afraid your word is not proof."

"No, I know it isn't. But I'm sorry, that's all you're getting. I assume you've tried the other people on this list? How many are there?"

"Three—and I've one man left."

"Who were the other two?"

Pitt thought for a moment, turning over the possibilities in his mind. Why did Urban want to know? Was he being helpful, seeking some common denominator, or an excuse, someone else to lay the blame on? Urban had to know that he would rather be suspected than admit to it.

"I prefer to keep that confidential for a little longer," Pitt replied, equally calmly and with the same frank smile.

"Was Addison Carswell one of them?" Urban asked, and then his wide mouth curled in a faint touch of humor when he saw Pitt's face, the start of surprise before he formed a denial.

"Yes," Pitt conceded. There was no point in pretending any more. Urban had seen it in his eyes and a lie would not be believed.

"Mm," Urban grunted thoughtfully. He seemed not to find it necessary to ask who the third was, and that in itself had meaning. "You know that damned Osmar has put his friends up to raising questions in the House?" he said with anger and incredulity in his voice.

"Yes, Dilkes told me. What are you going to do?"

"Me?" Urban leaned back in his chair. "Carry on with the prosecution, of course. The law for ex-government ministers is the same as for anyone else. You don't play silly beggars on the seats of public parks. If you must make an ass of yourself with a young woman, you do it in private where you don't offend old ladies and frighten the horses."

Pitt's smile widened.

"Good luck," he said dryly, and excused himself. He wondered how Urban knew the first name on Weems's list had been Addison Carswell. From what reasoning did he deduce that?

He could not possibly follow Urban himself; they knew each other far too well by sight. Reluctantly he would have to hand it over to Innes.

He went home earlier than usual. There was not much more he could do unless he began to investigate Latimer, and that could wait until tomorrow. He felt no guilt at putting off what would almost certainly be another extremely distasteful task, and after his discoveries about Carswell and Urban, he dreaded what he would find.

The following day Pitt took over Innes's duties pursuing the investigations of the people on Weems's first list, the long catechism of misery, ill education, illiteracy, humble employment, sickness, debt, drunkenness and violence, more debt, falling out of work, small loans, larger loans, and finally despair. Innes had already found all of them and questioned them. Most of them had been where they could easily be vouched for: in public houses, brawling in the streets or alleys, some even in police charge. The more respectable—men quietly despairing—had been at home sitting silent and hungry, worrying about the next day's food, the next week's rent, and what their neighbors would think, what else there was left to pawn.

It was bitterly miserable and all the pity in the world would change none of it. He was pleased to get home again in the heavy, sultry evening and find Charlotte had been visited by Emily and was full of colorful and superficial gossip.

"Yes, tell me," he urged when she brushed it all aside and dismissed it as too trivial to bother him with. "I should like to hear."

"Thomas." She looked at him with wide, laughing eyes. "Don't be so terribly agreeable. It's unnatural and it makes me feel nervous, as if we were not quite at ease with each other."

He laughed and leaned back in his chair, putting his feet up on the small stuffed pouffe, something which he did regularly, and which always annoyed her because his heels scuffed it.

"I would love to hear something totally inconsequential," he said honestly. "About people who are always well fed, well clothed, and have nothing more serious to worry about than what he said to her, and she said to him, and what someone else wore and whether it was fashionable or not, and if the shade became them."

Perhaps she understood. For a moment there was a softness in her face, then she grinned and settled herself back, arranging her skirts to be comfortable.

"Emily was telling me about some of the latest debutantes being presented to the Queen, or perhaps it was the Princess of Wales," she began in rather the same voice she used when telling Jemima or Daniel a particularly good story. "Apparently it is a fearful crush, and after hours and hours of standing around waiting, one finally gets to the royal presence. One is so busy keeping one's headdress straight—all those feathers, you know—and not falling over one's skirt, or seeming too bold with raised eyes, that one does not even see the Queen." She tucked her feet up beside her. "Only a small, fat hand which one kisses. It could have belonged to anyone—the cook, for all we know. It isn't the doing of it at all, it is the having done it, which matters."

"I thought that was the case with most of society's events," he said, recrossing his legs.

"Oh no. The opera, as you know, is beautiful, the Henley regatta is fun—so I am told—and Emily says that Ascot is terrific. The fashions are simply marvelous—and it is always wonderfully full of gossip. It matters so much who is seen with whom."

"What about the horses?"

She looked up, surprised. "Oh I've no idea about them. But Emily did tell me that Mr. Fitzherbert was there, with Miss Morden, of course. And they met up with Miss Hilliard and her brother again."

Pitt frowned. "Fanny Hilliard?"

"Yes—you remember! Very pretty girl, about twenty-four or twenty-five I should say. You must remember," she said impatiently. "She spoke to us at the opera, and then again at the supper table afterwards. Fitzherbert seemed rather taken with her!"

"Yes," he said slowly. A picture of Fanny in the coffee shop took shape in his mind, her eager face soft and full of affection as she took the hat and the parasol from Carswell.

"Well," Charlotte went on quickly, "she seems to be equally attracted to him." There was a mixture of pleasure and a sharp, sensitive regret in her face. One moment her words were rapid as if the excitement of love were echoed in her with pleasure, and the next it disappeared as she understood the cold shock of loss. "Of course he is betrothed to Odelia Morden, and I had thought they looked so set together, in such a comfortable relationship that nothing could intrude into it, or at least not seriously."

He looked at her face, the slight puckering of her brow and the gravity in her eyes. He knew it disturbed her, but not whether it was for the people concerned, or just the reminder of the frailty of happiness, how easily what you assumed safe can slip from your grasp.

"Are you sure it is not just a handsome man who cannot resist a flirtation?" he asked.

She thought for a moment, considering it.

"No," she said at last. "No, I don't think so. One . . ." She sought very carefully for the exact meaning she wanted. "One can tell the difference between fun and a feeling that threatens to hurt because it is not just"—she hunched her shoulders and slid a trifle further down in the sofa—"not just laughter and a little entertainment that one can forget when it is past, and go back to everything else and it will all be just the same. I don't think Fitz can go back and feel exactly as he used to about Odelia."

"Are you being romantic?" Pitt asked without criticism. "Is Fitzherbert a man to fall in love beyond what is pleasant and will serve his ends? After all, he has to marry someone if he is to succeed in his career. He hasn't the political brilliance to climb very far if he lacks the social requirements."

"I'm not saying he will forgo marrying Odelia," she denied. "Simply that there is something there which will not leave him without scars when he and Fanny separate and go their different ways. And Odelia won't forget. I've seen it in her face."

He smiled and said nothing, but it did cross his mind to wonder what Emily thought of it, and indeed if she had had any hand in it. If Fitzherbert jilted his fiancée it would affect Jack not at all unfavorably. He forbore from saying it.

Charlotte took a deep breath.

"And Jack has struck up quite a friendship with Lord Anstiss," she continued. "He is a most remarkable man, you know." She recalled his comments about her social ambitions with a tolerant irony. It was no more than she expected. "I don't think I have listened to anyone more interesting in such a wide variety of subjects. He has so many tales about people, and he recounts them with such a dry, clever wit. And Emily says nothing seems to bore him. Sometimes one might forget how important he is, until one looks at his face for a moment in repose. There is a great deal of power in him, you know."

He listened in silence, watching her face, the animation, the play of light and shadow over her features and the intense vividness of her interest.

"He was telling Emily about the pre-Raphaelites and the beautiful pictures they have painted creating a whole new idealism, and about William Morris and his furniture. She said he was so interesting he made it all seem urgent and important, not just a collection of facts. And also she met that odd young man, Peter Valerius, who is so consumed with interest in international finance in Africa—of all the tedious subjects so utterly the opposite of Lord Anstiss who is absolutely never a bore."

She continued about other people Emily had told her of, what they wore and to whom they spoke, but he did not listen with any great attention. Rather he allowed it to wash over him in a pleasant blur of sound. He was far more pleased just to see her face full of life and know that she was telling him not because it was important to her either, but because she was sharing it with him and that mattered intensely.

It was only another day before Innes reported on the unenviable task of following Urban. As a precaution he did not come to Bow Street, but sent a message that he had turned up something which he felt Pitt ought to know.

Accordingly Pitt left Bow Street, where he had been reporting to Drummond and sifting yet again through Urban's records, and tracing the will of the uncle who had left him the house in Bloomsbury to see if there were also pictures in the legacy. If there were, or if there had been money, it would at least excuse Urban's indulgence in such things. It took him some time to learn the uncle's name and trace his will through probate. When he did he found it was quite simple. The house went to "my dear sister's only son, Samuel Urban." It included the contents thereof, which were duly listed. There were no modern pictures, indeed there were no pictures at all.

Pitt was immensely relieved to have an excuse to leave the task and at least for the length of the journey involve himself in some physical action, even if it was only a hansom ride to Clerkenwell. He felt the urgency of Innes's message would allow that indulgence instead of the longer, more circuitous omnibus ride.

He was inside the hansom and bowling along High Holborn when he remembered that Innes had been following Urban, and his discovery was far more likely to concern him than one of the people on the first list. Those were being traced entirely from Clerkenwell, since they were almost all local inhabitants. Although even if Innes had found Weems's murderer there and had him in custody with irrefutable evidence, that would give Pitt no pleasure. He dreaded seeing the defeat and the guilt in the face of whatever wretched person had finally turned out of his despair into violence, and precipitated himself into even deeper disaster. Cursing or silent, fighting or crushed, underneath it he would be deathly afraid, knowing Newgate and the hangman awaited him.

Pitt realized grimly that he did not really want to find out who had murdered William Weems. And yet the case could not go unresolved from choice. Murder in theory was always wrong, and society, if it was to survive, must find the offender and punish him. It was just that in practice so often it was immeasurably more complex, and the victim was sometimes as much of an offender, in more hidden ways. It was a complicated tragedy with intertwined offenses and sufferings; one could not simply punish one participant and call the matter justly settled.

He was lost in tangled thoughts and memories when the cabby drew up at the Clerkenwell station and announced his arrival.

Pitt climbed out, paid him, and went in to find Innes.

As soon as he saw Innes's face he knew the news was disturbing. Innes's thin features were twisted in unhappiness and there were dark circles under his eyes as if he had been up too long and slept badly.

"Mornin', Mr. Pitt," he said glumly, rising to his feet. "You'd better come out." And without explaining himself any further he pushed past an overweight sergeant and a constable chewing on a peppermint stick, and led the way out again into the street.

Pitt followed close behind him and then fell into step on the pavement where there was room to walk side by side. He did not ask. The sun was bright again the morning after the previous night's rain and everything looked cleaner and there was a crispness in the air.

"I followed 'im," Innes said, looking down at the stones beneath his feet as if he must watch his step in case he tripped, although the way was perfectly smooth.

Pitt said nothing.

"If Weems were blackmailing 'im, I know what it were for," Innes went on after another few yards. He ran his tongue over his lips and swallowed hard. Still he did not look at Pitt. " 'E spent the evenin' at a music 'all in Stepney."

"That's not an offense," Pitt said, knowing there must be more. An evening at a music hall was a perfectly acceptable type of relaxation for a busy man. There were tens of thousands in the city who spent their time so. His remark was pointless; it was only a rather futile way of putting off the moment when Innes would tell him the real discovery. He could almost hear the words before they were spoken. There would be a woman, pretty, probably buxom, perhaps a singer, no doubt wooed by many, and Urban, like countless men before him, had got into debt trying to outdo his rivals.

"Get on with it," Pitt said abruptly, stepping off the pavement for a couple of yards to avoid a peddler.

" 'E worked there," Innes answered equally abruptly, catching up with him.

"What?" Pitt could scarcely believe him. "In the halls? Urban! I can't see him as a turn on the boards. He's too—too sober. He likes fine paintings—probably classical music, given the chance."

"No sir—not on the stage. As a bouncer, throwin' out them as gives trouble."

"Urban!"

"Yessir." Still Innes stared down at his pacing feet on the pavement, face straight ahead. "Quite good at it, 'e is. Big feller, and got the kind of air of authority as people don't argue wiv. I saw 'im break up a nasty quarrel between a couple o' gents what 'ad 'ad a bit too much, and 'e did it quick and quiet like, and only them closest 'ad any idea it'd been nasty.'' He moved aside to allow a woman with three children in tow to pass. "Paid 'im quite nice fer it, the management," he continued when she was gone. " 'E could 'a saved quite a bit over the years if 'e's bin doin' it long. Wouldn't 'a needed Weems's money to do quite nice fer 'isself. But o' course if Weems knew, 'e'd 'ave 'ad a nice 'old over 'im. Rozzers moonlighting. Thrown off the force. An' I don't suppose Mr. Urban wants to do bouncin' for a livin'.''

"No," Pitt said slowly. A small part of him was relieved because it was so much less pathetic than making a fool of himself over a woman he would never have married anyway. But it was far more serious. As Innes said, he would have been dismissed from the force. The mounting sense of relief was darkened over and with thoughts much uglier and more painful. If Weems knew of it, then it was motive for murder.

They walked side by side in silence for several more minutes, going nowhere, simply moving because it was easier, and stopping meant coming to some conclusion.

"You'll take care of it, sir?" Innes said at last as they came to the crossroad with the main thoroughfare. They were obliged to wait several minutes for the traffic to ease.

"Yes," Pitt answered, without any inner decision. Of course he must face Urban with it, but if in some way Urban could prove he had not killed Weems, if he had been in Stepney that night and had witnesses, then would Pitt still report his moonlighting? It was a decision he did not have to make today. If Urban was guilty of murder it would hardly matter.

Innes began across the road, dashing in and out of manure; there was no crossing sweeper. Pitt followed him, narrowly missed by a berline driven by a gentleman in a high temper.

"Mr. Pitt—" Innes began when they were over the street and on the far pavement.

"Yes?" Pitt knew he was going to ask if he had to report Urban.

"Ah—" Innes changed his mind. It was a question to which he did not really want to know the answer; he preferred to hope.

Pitt did not bother to pursue it. They both understood the justice, and the account.

Pitt found Urban in his office, and was angry because he liked the man, angry with the frailty that had made him sacrifice so much for a few pictures, no matter how lovely.

"What is it now?" Urban's face was shadowed. He knew Pitt would not have returned yet again unless there was some unavoidable need, and perhaps he saw the emotions in Pitt's all too readable face.

"Weems," Pitt replied. "Still Weems. Are you sure you don't want to tell me where you were the night he died?"

"It wouldn't make any difference," Urban answered slowly. "I can't prove it, and you can't accept my word without proof. But I didn't kill him. I didn't even know him."

"If you were in Stepney you could prove it," Pitt said quietly. "The management must keep records."

Urban's cheeks paled, but his eyes remained on Pitt's face.

"You followed me? I didn't see you, and I was prepared. I thought you might."

"No," Pitt said, biting his lip. "I had someone else do it. I'd have been a fool to try myself. Of course you'd have seen me. Is that where you were?"

"No." Urban smiled, a sad, self-mocking expression. "I wish now I had been. I went to another hall, where I thought I might get a better rate, but I didn't give my name. I didn't want word out. I might lose what I had."

"Why?" Pitt said harshly. "You're paid enough here. Are a few paintings worth it—really?"

Urban shrugged. "I thought so at the time. Now perhaps not."

He faced Pitt squarely, his eyes full of something that was half a question, half an apology. "Tomorrow I don't suppose I'll think so at all. I like being a policeman. But I did not kill Weems—I'd never heard of him until you came in here and told me about my name being on his list. Perhaps he intended blackmailing me, and was killed before he could—" He stopped, and once again Pitt had the powerful impression he was lying by omission.

"For God's sake tell me!" Pitt said furiously, his voice husky. "It's more than your career in jeopardy, man. It's your life! You had the motive to kill Weems, you had the opportunity, and so far as we know, you had as much chance of the means as anyone. What is it? What is it you are hiding? You know something. Has it to do with Osmar and why Carswell let him off?"

"Osmar," Urban said slowly, his smile becoming softer as if in some way at last he had given in. "I suppose I have nothing left to lose now, except my neck." He moved his head jerkily as he spoke as if freeing it from some grip. "The Circle may do me a great deal of harm, but it won't be as bad as the hangman . . ."

"Circle?" Pitt had no idea what he was talking about. "What circle?"

Urban sat down behind his desk and echoing his movement Pitt sat down also.

"The Inner Circle," Urban said very quietly, his voice barely more than a whisper as if he was afraid even here of being over-heard. "It is a secret society for mutual benefit, charitable work, and the righting of injustices."

"Whose injustices?" Pitt asked quickly. "Who decides what is just or unjust?"

Urban's face registered the difference with a flash of irony.

"They do, of course."

"If its aims are so fine, why is it secret?"

Urban sighed. "Some things are hard to accomplish, and those who resent it can be very obstructive, at times very powerful. Secrecy gives you some safety from them."

"I see. But what has this to do with you and Weems—and Osmar?" Pitt asked.

"I am a member of the Inner Circle," Urban explained. "I joined some time ago, when I was a young and rising man in Rotherhithe. An officer in power then thought I was a promising man, just the sort who would one day be a fine member of the Circle, a brother." He looked self-conscious. "I was a lot younger then. He flattered me, told me all the good works and the power I might have to help people. Not the superintendent they have now. He wouldn't have anything to do with it."

He leaned still further forward. "I joined. To begin with it was all very simple stuff, a little gift to a good cause and a few hours of my time, nothing remarkable.''

Pitt remained silent.

"It was several years before I came up against anything that worried me," Urban continued, "and even then nothing was said. I simply declined certain tasks I was asked to do. Six months ago the first real discipline came. I was asked to favor a man in a case. He was not accused, simply a witness, but he did not wish to testify, and I was supposed to overlook it, in the name of brotherhood. I refused. I had heard of other members of the Circle being disciplined for such acts, finding themselves suddenly unwelcome where they used to be respected, or unaccountably blackballed from clubs, when no charge had been made and no known offenses committed, criminal or social.''

"The Inner Circle disciplining its errant members," Pitt said slowly.

"I think so. There wasn't anything you could call proof, but the people concerned usually understood. And what may be more to the point, other members hovering on the brink of disobedience decided against it.''

"Effective," Pitt said. A mass of thoughts whirled in his mind, possibilities connecting Weems and Addison Carswell, and Horatio Osmar, explaining the dismissal of charges—brothers of the Inner Circle. And Urban—and presumably Latimer too? A web of tacit understandings, favors, obligations, unspoken threats, and for rebels a swift and effective discipline: a warning to others.

Was that why Micah Drummond had been so willing to help Lord Byam, and why it made him so profoundly uncomfortable, and yet unable to explain? And of course that was why Byam had been told of Weems's death in the first place, and why the Clerkenwell station had handed over the case when they were asked: all in the name of the Inner Circle, a secret brotherhood of power—used for what?

Micah Drummond!

How strong were the bonds of this brotherhood? Stronger than duty? Where did brotherhood end and corruption begin?

"And you defied them?" he said, looking at Urban again.

"I misbehaved," Urban admitted. "I think my name on Weems's list is a warning to others. But I can't prove that."

"Then the question is, " Pitt said slowly, "did Weems's murderer leave the second list there for us to find, and so embarrass you, and Carswell . . ." He deliberately left off Latimer's name. "Or was it there anyway, a precaution to be used at another time, and Weems's murder unforeseen?"

"I don't know," Urban admitted. "I don't even know beyond question that Carswell is a brother, but it would explain his dismissing the charge against Osmar. I know Osmar is. And Carswell's name was also on your list."

Pitt said nothing. His mind had grasped what Urban had said, and he knew it was very possibly true, but crowding it out and hurting far more was the memory of Micah Drummond's face as he told him of Weems's murder, and how they were going to help Byam. There were all sorts of questions springing from that. Was that why Micah Drummond agreed, and had the power to do it so easily? Why was Byam's name not there? Could he have left the second list, and then been caught by his own trap when someone else, some desperate debtor, had come later and murdered Weems? Was that why he was so afraid, not that his name was there, but that he had been there himself, and was afraid he had been seen?

That made no sense. Why leave the list, unless he knew Weems would be murdered and the police find it?

But ugliest of all was the question of Micah Drummond's part. What was his role in the Inner Circle? Was he being disciplined in some way? Was he obedient, pliant to their will? Or worse, was he the discipliner, the one who placed the threats, and the punishment? Could he have been there after Weems's death and before Pitt went and found the lists?

Or for that matter, had Byam heard from the Clerkenwell station of Weems's murder even before Drummond? Had he been to Cyrus Street and placed the second list?

Or was it someone in the Clerkenwell station whom he had not even considered yet—the unknown person who had first told Byam?

It was a secret society—who knew who its members were, or

their real purpose? Did even its own members know? How many were innocent pawns of a few?

And how many of its tentacles grasped, twisted and corrupted the police?

"No," he said aloud, breaking the long silence. "I don't know either."

CHAPTER

SEVEN

Micah Drummond found himself thinking of the Byam case more and more often, at times even when he would normally have left police matters far behind him and begun to enjoy the very considerable pleasures of life. He smiled to himself wryly now. In his mind it was the Byam case, but to Pitt it would almost certainly be the Weems case. After all it was Weems who was dead. Byam was only a possible suspect, Drummond profoundly hoped an "impossible" one. That thought had troubled him like an unacknowledged darkness at the edge of his mind, something he refused to look at but could forget only for short, deliberately engineered moments, always ending when its shadow crossed his thoughts again.

Pitt had told him about the blunderbuss. That meant that in theory at least the means were there for anyone, even the poorest debtor from Clerkenwell. But did Weems leave gold coins lying around in such circumstances? Possibly. Maybe that kind of cruelty would appeal to him—have a desperate person, unable to make his repayments, into the office and face him across a pile of gold coins, then demand of him his last pence. Not only colorfully sadistic, but also surely dangerous? In his years of usury had not Weems learned to be a good enough judge of character to avoid such a thing?

Come to think, why had he received a debtor alone in his office after dark? That could hardly be his practice. But had Pitt asked?

He would have been concentrating on finding who killed him, not on exonerating Byam.

Drummond stopped with a start of guilt. That was what he was doing: trying to exonerate Byam. He had given little thought to finding Weems's murderer if it was someone else—once Byam was cleared. He felt the heat creep up his face at the consciousness of how his judgment had lapsed, his priorities become unbalanced.

It was a summer evening, still broad daylight, and he was at home. It was not the large house in Kensington he had kept when his wife was alive and his daughters were growing up; he had sold that when the loneliness in it became overbearing and the upkeep quite unnecessary. Now he had a spacious flat off Piccadilly. He no longer had any need to keep a carriage. He could always obtain a hansom if he needed one, and one manservant and a woman to do the domestic chores and cook were all that was necessary to see to his comfort. If they employed anyone else from time to time he was only peripherally aware of it. The expense was negligible, and he trusted their judgment.

This room still contained many of his old possessions: the embroidered fire screen with peacocks on it that his mother had given him the first year after he was married; the blue Meissen plates his wife had loved; the hideous brown elephant she had inherited, and they had both laughed over. And he had kept the Chippendale chairs, even though there were too many of them for this room. He had given several of the pictures to his daughters, but there was still the Landseer and the small Bonnington seascape. He would never willingly part with them.

Now he stood in his large bay window looking towards Green Park and tried to disentangle his thoughts.

What about the other names on the list, the second list? From what Pitt had said, Addison Carswell was almost certainly being blackmailed. And he could not, or would not, account for his time the night Weems was killed. Was the wretched man really so besotted with the Hilliard girl he would rather risk everything he possessed—not just his home and his family, but his very life—by murdering Weems, rather than simply give her up? Thousands of men all over London had mistresses, all over England, for that matter. If one was discreet, it mattered little.

What could Weems have done, at the very worst? Told Mrs. Carswell? What of it? If she did not know, or guess, and if this was the first time he had strayed, she might well be distressed. But if you keep a mistress, a wife's distress is not an agony to you—certainly not worth risking the hangman's rope for. His daughters? Grieved, angry perhaps; but they were old enough to have some awareness of the ways of the world, and hardly in a position to do anything worse than cool their affection for him, treat him to some isolation in his own house. That could certainly be unpleasant, but again, the smallest triviality compared with the unpleasantness of murder and its consequences. And as a magistrate, he would be acutely aware of just how fearful those consequences were. He, more than most, would know what a spell in Coldbath Fields or Newgate could do to a man, let alone the rope.

And what had happened to Byam's letter, and Weems's record of his payments to him? Byam had been so sure they were there, he had actually called Drummond and confessed his connection with Weems, the blackmail and the death of Laura Anstiss and thus his motive for killing him. Without them he would never have been connected with it at all.

His thoughts were interrupted by the manservant standing in the doorway, coughing discreetly.

"Yes, Goodall, what is it?"

Goodall's thin face was very nearly expressionless.

"There is a Lady Byam to see you, sir."

It was ridiculous. Drummond felt his breath catch in his throat and the color rush to his face.

"Lady Byam?" he repeated pointlessly.

"Yes sir." Goodall's eyebrows rose so minutely it might have been Drummond's imagination.

"Ask her to come in." Drummond swallowed and turned away. What had happened? Why had Eleanor Byam come here to see him, to his house, and in the evening, though it was still daylight, and would be for another two hours. It was an extraordinary thing to do. Something must be wrong.

Goodall opened the door again and Drummond swung around to see Eleanor just inside the room. She was wearing a dark dress of some color between navy and gray, or perhaps it was green. It looked like the sky a little after dusk, and there was a soft bloom to her skin, reminding him that for all the cool colors of her clothes she would be warm to the touch, and very alive.

Of all the idiotic and wildly inappropriate thoughts! The heat he could feel in his face must make him look as if he were running a fever.

"Good evening, Lady Byam," he said hastily, moving forward to greet her.

Goodall closed the door and they were alone.

"Good evening, Mr. Drummond," she replied a little hesitantly. "It is very kind of you to see me without notice like this, and at such an hour." She touched her lips with her tongue, as though her mouth were dry and speech difficult for her. Obviously she too was aware that this was a circumstance requiring some explanation. Women of respectability, let alone quality, did not come alone to visit the houses of single gentlemen, uninvited and at such a time of day. She took a deep breath. He could see the rise of her breast and the tiny pulse beating in her throat. "I came because I felt I must talk to you about the case," she hurried on, still standing just inside the door, the colors of the carpet between them bright with the low evening sunlight. "I know you promised to tell my husband if there were any new events that touched on us—but I find waiting more than I can bear." She stopped abruptly and for the first time met his eyes.

Her words were ordinary; the apology he would have expected, the reasons could be understood by anyone, but far more powerful than that he could see the fear in her. Her body was stiff under the soft muslin gown and the shawl around her shoulders, a matter of decorum rather than necessity in this warm evening.

He forgot himself for a moment in his desire to make her feel at ease.

"I understand," he said quickly. "It is most natural." He felt nothing ridiculous in saying this, although in all his years in the police force no other woman had called upon him in his house because she could not contain her anxiety. But then he had never been involved in a case like this. "Please don't feel the need to apologize. I wish there had been more I could have told you so this would not have been necessary." Then he heard his words in his own ears and was afraid she might think he meant to make her visit avoidable. He fumbled but could think of no way of undoing it without being overfulsome, and that might be worse. He would appear such a fool.

She swallowed and looked even more uncomfortable, aware that she was intruding in his home with a matter which was strictly professional. They had no acquaintance other than his attempt to help her husband, for reasons of which she knew nothing. The Inner Circle permitted no women—nor indeed did any secret society of which he had ever heard. Such organizations were a totally masculine preserve.

She opened her mouth to make some apology, and looked as if she was even considering retreating.

"Please," he said hastily. "Please allow me to take your shawl." He stepped forward and held his hand ready, thinking that to reach for it would be precipitate.

She took it off slowly and handed it to him, a tiny smile on her lips. "You are very generous. I should not have intruded into your time this way, but I wanted to speak to you so much, and not at the police station . . ."

For a ridiculous instant his heart leaped. Then he told himself furiously that her eagerness was born solely of her fear—fear for her husband—and was in no way personal.

"What may I do to help you?" he said more stiffly than he had intended, placing the shawl clumsily over the back of the sofa.

She looked down at the floor, still standing, just a few feet from him. He was aware of the very faint perfume of some flower he could not identify, and he knew it was she, her hair and her skin.

"Inspector Pitt is doing all he can," he began tentatively. "And he is making progress. He has discovered strong evidence against several other suspects."

She looked up quickly and met his eyes.

"It seems terrible to say that I am glad, doesn't it? Some other poor woman somewhere may be just as afraid as I am, only for her it will end in tragedy."

Without thinking he reached out his hand and touched her arm.

"You cannot change it for her," he said gently. "You have no cause to feel oppressed by a grief that you did not create and cannot help."

"I—" She stopped, her face deeply troubled.

He became aware of his hand still on her arm and removed it quickly. Was that what she had been going to say? That he had trespassed; he was taking advantage of her anxiety to be more familiar than he would have had this been her house, and he the supplicant?

They both began to speak at once, he simply to say her name. He stopped abruptly.

"I'm sorry—"

She smiled fleetingly and then was desperately serious again.

"I know that you told Sholto you will do everything you can, and to begin with that seemed to ease my mind so much that it was almost as if the matter were already over. But now he is so worried he is ill with it." Her lips tightened for a moment. "He tries to conceal it from me, so as not to frighten me, but I hear him up during the night, pacing the floor, and for long hours the light is on in his study." She looked at him with a flash of humor so bleak he longed to be able to comfort her. He tried to think of something to say, but there was nothing.

"You will think I intrude into my husband's affairs," she went on quickly, looking downward, abashed. "But I don't. I was simply concerned in case he was ill. I went downstairs to see if there were anything I could do to help . . ." She stopped and raised her eyes slowly, her voice very soft. "I found him in his study, not working as I had thought, but pacing the floor back and forth." She bit her lip. "He was angry when he saw me in the doorway, and he denied there was anything wrong. But I know him, Mr. Drummond. He will work late, if there is occasion to. I have seen him stay up till one or two in the morning often. But never before in the eighteen years we have been married has he gone to bed, and then risen at three o'clock to go down and pace the floor of the study, with no papers out, no books, just his thoughts, and all the lights blazing."

"It would seem there is something that concerns him profoundly," he said with a chill of fear inside him. He had refused to consider that Byam might actually be guilty. Maybe he was wrong. Perhaps Byam calling him before he was even suspected was a double bluff. Perhaps the letter and the note that Weems was supposed to have kept were only his excuse to call Drummond, and there was something far more damaging yet to come.

He was torn with a dreadful mixture of emotions: dread of discovering irrefutably that it was Byam who had murdered Weems, and sickness inside at having to tell Eleanor—she would feel so betrayed. He was the person she had come to for help. Embarrassment: how could he explain all this to Pitt? He would leave him in a wretched position. And a sudden ease of a gripping weight inside him: if Byam was guilty, then Eleanor would be free.

That was a shameful thought, and the blood burned hot up his face, hot right up to his hair. Free for what? If Byam was hanged she would be a widow. That would not necessarily stop her loving him, and it certainly would not free her from terrible, overwhelming grief.

He did not even think of fear for himself, or his own involvement with the Inner Circle.

"Please—don't let us stand here," he said quietly. "Sit, and let us talk of it and learn if there is anything we can do that will resolve this problem."

She accepted and sank into the chair gratefully. He sat opposite on one of the Chippendales, perched forward on the edge and still staring at her.

"I presume you have asked him what it is that troubles him?"

"Of course, but he will not tell me. He said he simply found it hard to sleep, and came downstairs because he did not wish to disturb me."

"And is it not possible that that is the truth?"

Her smile was faint and a little twisted. "No. Sholto is not normally troubled by sleeplessness, and if he were he would have found a book from the library and taken it to bed with him, not paced up and down the study. And he looked ashen." Her eyes met Drummond's. "No one looks as he did merely because they cannot sleep. His face was haggard—as though he had seen the worst thing he feared."

He spoke quickly; a question to reach for the last hope, not a dismissal of her fears.

"You are sure it was not the lamplight playing tricks on the features of a man overtired, and perhaps woken from an ill dream?"

"Yes—I am quite sure." Her voice was very low; there was certainty in it, and pain. "Something terrible has happened, and I do not know what, except it seems inevitable to me that it must have to do with the death of the usurer. Surely if it were anything else he would have told me. He is not ill. We have no family matters, no relatives who might cause us distress." Her eyes shadowed. "We never had children." She was speaking more and more rapidly as the tension mounted in her. "My parents are dead and so are his. My brother is quite well, Sholto's brother is in India but we have had no correspondence from him in the last two weeks. I did think to ask the butler if there had been any overseas letters that perhaps I had not seen, but he said there had not."

"What about his work at the Treasury?" Drummond suggested it without belief, but he had to exhaust every possibility.

"I can think of nothing that would cause him the dread which I saw in him that night, and the constant fear I can feel at the edge of his mind even through the day." She was sitting awkwardly on the edge of the chair, her fingers clenched together. "He is nervous, ill at ease. He cannot concentrate on the things which used to give him such pleasure: music, theater, books. He declined an invitation to dine with friends we have known and respected for years."

"Could it be some friend in trouble?" He knew it was not even as he said it, but still the words spilled out, seeking any solution but the obvious.

"No." She did not bother to elaborate her answer. It was as if she understood that they were simply making questions to put off the moment. "No," she said again more softly, but still looking down. "I know him well enough. It is not the way in which he would behave for such a concern." She bit her lip. "He is not a cold man. I do not mean that he is indifferent to the suffering or distress of friends, but that he is a man of decision. Such a happening would not affect him to such . . ." She lifted her shoulders very slightly. She was slenderer than he had realized, more fragile. "To such horror and inability to act. You did not see his face."

"Then we must presume that something has happened that he

knows of—and we do not," he admitted finally. "Or at least he believes that it has. But he will not tell you what it is?" That was only half a question; she had already made the answer plain.

"No."

"Are you sure you still want to know?"

She closed her eyes. "I'm frightened. I think I can guess what it may be—the least awful guess . . ."

"What?"

"That someone else has found the letter and the notes that Weems made of Sholto's payments to him, and the reason. I suppose whoever killed him. Unless someone also was there after he was dead, and before the police found his body. And that person is now trying to blackmail Sholto himself." She looked up at him suddenly, her eyes full of pain and fear.

He ached to be able to offer her some comfort, anything to take the cutting edge from her distress, or at the very least let her feel that she was not alone. Loneliness lent sharpness to all pains, as he knew only too well. But he knew of no practical comfort, nothing to ease the truth of what she said, and personal comfort would be so appallingly misplaced it would only add a fearful embarrassment to increase her misery, which was the last thing he wished.

"That at least would be proof that he was entirely innocent," he said, clutching at a shred of hope. "If the worst happens and Pitt cannot find the murderer, then Lord Byam will have to tell what he knows, tell of the further blackmail, and expose the man." He leaned a little forward. "After all," he said earnestly, "the most he can do is make public the old matter of Laura Anstiss's death, which would be most unpleasant, and there are some who may feel he was to blame, but may well also have great sympathy with him. And surely he is keeping the matter silent almost as much for Lord Anstiss's sake as his own. It would be extremely distasteful for him also."

"I think that troubles Sholto as much as any scandal attaching to himself," she admitted. A curious look crossed her face, of confusion and distress, and then it was gone. "He admires Frederick so much. They have been friends since their youth, you know. There is something uniquely precious about an old friendship. One has shared so much, seen the passage of time, how it has marked and changed us, the hopes realized and the hopes dashed, the work to fulfill the dreams, and the dreams that are crumbled and kept secret." She smiled. "One has laughed at the same things, and developed such an understanding because at times there is no need to speak. The knowledge is there simply because sharing has been so long a habit. One knows the best and the worst, and there is no need to explain."

He felt a gulf between them with a pain so sharp it stopped him from laughing at himself for the idiocy of it. He was shut out. He had a past she knew nothing of: all his life, everything that had brought him to this day, the values, the loves and the griefs, Catriona's death, his daughters, everything that mattered. To her he was simply a policeman.

And she had a life he could only imagine. All he knew was this desperate woman whose only concern was to help her husband.

"No," he said abruptly, and heard his own words pour out while all the time his cooler brain was telling him to hold his tongue. "No—I think it is the quality of friendship which matters, not its length. One can have an acquaintance with people all one's life, and never share a minute's total understanding, or meet a stranger and feel with her some tremendous experience so deep you can never afterwards tell anyone else exactly how it was, and yet find, the moment your eyes meet, that she knows it as you do."

She looked at him with surprise and then increasing wonder as the totally contradicting idea became clearer in her mind and she considered it. For seconds they stared at each other, the street outside forgotten, Weems and his murder, even Byam's involvement with it. There was only the few square yards of the room in the amber sunlight through the big windows, the sofa and the chair they sat on, and the bright pattern on the carpet between them.

He saw her face as indelibly as if it were painted on his eyelids, the fine brow, the steady dark gray eyes with their shadowing lashes, the tiny lines woven by the years, the light on her hair, the softness of her lips.

"Perhaps you are right," she said at last. "Maybe I have mistaken familiarity for understanding, and they are not the same."

Now he was confused. He did not know what else to add. He had almost forgotten why they had spoken of friendship at all. It was something to do with Byam—yes—Byam and Anstiss. The pain of exposing Anstiss's grief that Laura's death had been suicide, because she loved another man.

"It is very horrible," he said aloud. "I expect he would hesitate, whoever it was—an old friend or not. The friendship would simply make it the more painful to himself, it would not alter the other person's grief."

"Frederick?" She smiled very slightly and turned away. "No, of course not. Sometimes I think Sholto is overly protective of him—of his interests, I mean. He still feels this gnawing guilt for Laura's death, and it colors his behavior, I am sure." She smiled, but it was a sad, worried little gesture, without happiness. "Debts of honor can do strange things to people, can't they? Especially if they can never be repaid."

He said nothing, seeing from her expression that she had not completed her thought.

"I wonder at times," she started again, "if perhaps Frederick is aware of it. He can be so funny, such an excellent companion, and then quite without warning he will say something thoroughly cruel, and I can see that Sholto is deeply hurt. Then it is all over again and they are the best of friends." She shrugged, as if pushing the thought away as foolishness. "Then again, it is probably just that Frederick is less subtle with words. When people are close, sooner or later they will hurt each other, don't you think? Simply because we use so many words, so easily, I suppose it is inevitable we should be clumsy, or take a meaning where it was not intended. I do it myself, and then wish I could have bitten my tongue out before being so stupid . . ."

She stopped, seemed to brace herself, and then began again, not looking at him but at the window and the deepening light on the trees rustling in the sunset wind. "If it is hurting Frederick that fills him with such horror, I can understand it very easily. But perhaps he will have no alternative, in the end, but to expose Weems's murderer and risk his telling everything, at his trial, if not before. I—" She hunched her shoulders and tightened her hands, her fingers knotted in the soft fabric of her skirt.

Instinctively he leaned even closer to her, then stopped. He had no idea whether she was aware of him or not.

"I wonder whether he knows who it is?" she went on, her voice very low and a thrill of horror in it. "And if it is not a stranger, not some poor debtor from Clerkenwell, but a man he has some acquaintance with, even some sympathy for—and that is why he is so reluctant to expose him? That would explain a great deal."

She shivered. "It would be easier then to understand why he is in such an agony of mind. Poor Sholto. What a fearful decision to have to make." She turned back to Drummond, her eyes wide. "And if Weems would blackmail Sholto, then he would as easily blackmail someone else, wouldn't he?"

"We believe he has," he agreed quietly, Addison Carswell in his mind, and a new shadow of pity. What a miserable and futile waste of life and all its wealth. Over what? An infatuation with a pretty face, a young body and a few hours of an appetite and a dream that could never last.

She saw the distress in his face and her expression changed from hope to sorrow.

"You know who it is?" she said in little more than a whisper.

"I know who it may be—"

In the beginning she had said "the least awful possibility." Neither of them spoke the most awful—that Byam had killed Weems and his fear was dreadfully and sickeningly for himself. He would not say it now.

It was getting late. The quality of the light was beginning to change, deepening in color, and already the shadows were across the floor and creeping up the brilliance of the far wall, lighting the peacock fire screen. He did not want her to leave, and yet he was afraid if he offered her refreshment she would realize the hour and excuse herself. But what else could he ask her?

"Mr. Drummond—" She turned around towards him, rearranging her skirt.

"I have not offered you anything by way of refreshment," he said quickly, his voice louder than he had intended.

"Oh please do not put yourself to inconvenience. It is most kind of you to have spared me your time, and at this hour. You must be tired."

"Please! Allow me to repair my oversight."

"It is not necessary, I assure you. You have been most patient."

He stood up and reached for the bell and rang it furiously.

"I have been very remiss. I would like some refreshment myself, and it is far too early for dinner. Please permit me to redeem myself."

"No redemption is required," she said with a smile. "But if it would make you feel more comfortable, then I will be glad to take a little tea."

"Excellent!" His spirits soared and he rang the bell again and immediately Goodall appeared, his face politely inquiring.

"Tea," Drummond said quickly. "And something . . ."

"Yes sir." Goodall withdrew, his face expressionless.

Drummond sat opposite her again, wondering what to discuss. The formal part of her visit seemed to have exhausted itself and he had no desire at all to pursue the subject. He wanted to know more about her, but it seemed too crass simply to ask. He had not felt so awkward with anyone since before he had been married, when he was a young man raw to the army, and not even having thought of the police force for a career. He could remember balls and soirees then when he had felt this tongue-tied and desperate for something casual and charming to say.

Before the silence grew oppressive she rescued him. No doubt it was easy for her, with a relationship which hardly mattered.

"This is a most pleasing room, Mr. Drummond. Have you always lived here?"

"No—no, I lived in Kensington before my wife died."

"I'm sorry," she said quickly. "I expect you miss her very much."

"It is some years now, but yes, there are times when it seems very silent, and I imagine what it would be like if she were here," he replied truthfully. "She was . . ." He looked at her and saw only interest in her face. He had thought he would not wish to tell her of Catriona, that it would be somehow disloyal, but now that it came to the moment it was not. In fact it seemed a very natural thing to do.

"She was so vivid. She looked at me so directly." He smiled at the remembrance. "Her father used to criticize her for it and say it was unbecoming in a woman, but I found it honest, as if she were interested in everything and would not stoop to pretending she was not. She liked bright colors, all sorts of reds and glowing blues." Involuntarily his eyes went to the peacock screen. "I recall once, years ago, she went to dinner in a gown of such a fierce flame color that she was noticed immediately one entered the room." His smile broadened. It was all so much easier than he had expected, so much more natural. "Looking back it was rather ostentatious, which was not what she meant at all. She simply loved the color and it made her feel happy to look at it. We laughed about it afterwards. Catriona laughed very easily, she enjoyed so many things."

"It is a rare gift," Eleanor said warmly. "And a very precious one. Too much happiness is lost because we spend our time regretting the past and seeking for the future and miss what we are given for the moment at hand. The gift to be happy is a blessing to all around. Do you have a picture of her?"

"She disliked the camera. She felt it caught only the outer person, and she did not care for the way she looked . . ."

Surprise flickered across Eleanor's face.

"The person you describe sounds so lovely I had imagined her beautiful."

"Catriona?" He was a little surprised. "When you knew her, she was. She had lovely eyes, very dark and wide, and shining hair; but she was a very big woman. After our daughters were born she seemed to become bigger, and never lost it again. I think she was more aware of it than anyone else. I certainly was not."

"Then it hardly matters, does it?" Eleanor said, dismissing it. "Catriona. That is an unusual name. Was she Scottish?"

"Yes—as my father was, although I was born here in England."

Goodall returned with a tray of tea and sandwiches and their conversation was interrupted while it was set down. Goodall poured and passed the cups and the plates, then withdrew again.

"We have talked enough about me," Drummond said, dismissing himself as a further topic. He was keen to hear something of her, even if it proved to be oddly painful: a whole world in which she knew and cared for other people and into which he could never intrude once this wretched case was over. "Please tell me of yourself."

He half expected her to make the usual demur that modesty dictated. It was an automatic reaction of women, required by society, to be self-effacing, and he was delighted when she began a trifle awkwardly, but without excuse, as though she wished him to know.

She sipped her tea then set the cup down and began.

"My father was a man of letters, a student, but I barely remember him." Her lips curled with a faint smile, but of far-off memories, not self-pity. "He died when I was nine, and I am afraid I can bring back to mind only the faintest recollections of him. He always seemed to have a book open in his hand, and he was very absent-minded. I recall him as thin and dark, and he spoke very softly. But I am not sure if that is true memory, or the mind of my adult knowledge painting it for me from a late picture my mother had."

Drummond thought of the privation of a new widow with a child to raise. His tea sat forgotten.

"What happened to you?" he asked with concern. "Had your mother family?"

"Oh yes. My grandfather was an archdeacon and he had a very good living. We went to live with him, my mother, my brother, my sister and myself. It was a large country house outside Bath, and very agreeable, with a garden full of flowers and an orchard where I remember playing." Again she sipped her tea and took one of the small sandwiches. "My grandmother was rather strict, but she indulged us when she chose. I was a touch afraid of her, because I never learned precisely what pleased her and what did not, so I could never judge what her temper would be. I think now, looking back, that perhaps it had nothing to do with me at all." She smiled and met his eye with sudden clarity. "I think children imagine themselves far more important than they are, and take the blame for a great deal that has no connection with them at all. Don't you?"

It had never occurred to him. His own daughters were grown up and married, and he could not remember ever having spoken with them of such things. "I am sure you are right," he lied without a flicker. "You seem to remember it very clearly."

"I do, it was a happy time. I think I knew that even then."
She smiled as she thought of it, and he could see in her eyes that
her thoughts were far away. "I think that was one of the things I
liked best about Sholto when I first met him," she said quite naturally, as if Drummond were an old friend and easy to talk to.

At last Drummond picked up his cup, as much to avoid staring
as from any taste for it.

"He saw the beauty of land," she continued. "The sunlight in
the silent orchard, dappling all the tree trunks, the boughs of blos-
som so low they tangled in the long grass. Grandpapa was always
telling the gardener to tend the vegetables so the poor man never
got time to prune the trees. We had far too many apples and plums,
but they were never very large. Geoffrey hated the place. He said
it was a waste."

"Who was Geoffrey?" he asked.

"I was betrothed to him when I was twenty-one. He was a
dragoon. I thought he was so dashing." She laughed a little at
herself. "Though looking back, I think he was probably pompous
and very self-important. But it was a long time ago."

"And you left him for Lord Byam?" He should not have asked—
it was indelicate—but he realized it only after the words were out.

"Oh no!" she said quickly. "Grandpapa heard that Geoffrey
had been paying attention to a young lady of"—she colored—"of
questionable reputation, and Grandpapa said I could not possibly
marry him. He broke off the engagement. I heard later that Geoffrey married a viscount's daughter." She laughed as she said it, and
he knew it had long ago ceased to hurt.

"Then Mama died and I found myself running the household
and caring for Grandpapa," she went on. "He was a bishop by
then. My sister died in childbirth and my brother lost a leg in the
Indian mutiny in 'fifty-eight. It was shortly after that when I met
Sholto, and we became betrothed very quickly. Grandpapa liked
him, which made it all so much easier. And Sholto's conduct was
irreproachable and his reputation spotless. Grandpapa inquired into
it exhaustively. I was mortified, but poor Sholto bore it all with
excellent temper. I could have loved him for that alone. But he
was also possessed of a greater sense of humor, and that made him
so agreeable to be with. People who can laugh at themselves are

seldom insufferable, don't you think? I have often considered if a sense of humor is not closely allied to a sense of proportion in things. Have you?"

"You are right," he agreed quickly. "It is when one's sense of proportion is offended that one can see the absurd. And when it is not ugly it is funny, but either way, we know that it cannot be overlooked. One can never be intimidated in the same way by what one perceives as ridiculous, so perhaps it has a kind of relationship to courage as well."

"Courage?" Her eyebrows rose. "I had not thought of that. And speaking of courage, Mr. Drummond, I am most grateful for your kindness to us, and your endless patience. Now I must not exhaust it by overstaying. It is growing dusk and I must return home before I cause comment by the uniformed. It would be an ill way to repay your generosity."

"Please do not worry," he said urgently. "I will do everything I can . . ."

"I know."

"And—and Pitt is an excellent man, even brilliant at times."

She smiled, a wide, generous gesture as if for a moment all her fears had been lifted, although he knew it could not be so.

"Thank you. I know it is in the best possible hands." She rose to her feet and he stood quickly, reaching for her shawl to wrap around her shoulders. She accepted it graciously. Then after a second's hesitation, she went to the door and he stepped ahead to open it for her. She gave him her hand for an instant, then withdrew it. After only the briefest words, she was gone, and he was left in the hall doorway, with Goodall looking as surprised as his position and training would allow.

"A very distinguished lady," Drummond said unnecessarily.

"Indeed sir," Goodall said without expression.

"I'll take dinner late this evening," Drummond said sharply, irritated with Goodall and with himself.

"Very good, sir."

In the morning Drummond set out for Bow Street with an unaccountable feeling of good cheer which he did not examine, for fear it would prove foolish if he discovered its reason and the little singing bubble of well-being inside him would burst. He strode along in the sun, swinging his cane, his hat at a rather more jaunty angle than customarily. He disregarded the newsboy shouting out the latest scandal in order to sell his papers, and the two dray drivers swearing at each other as they maneuvered their great horses, one around a corner, the other backing into a yard to unload. Even the barrel organist's hurdy-gurdy sounded tuneful in the open air.

He caught a hansom in Piccadilly and dismounted at Bow Street. His good humor was met with a poor reward when he saw the desk sergeant's face. He knew he was late, but that was his prerogative, and should not cause any comment, let alone alarm. His first thought was that something ugly had broken in the Weems case.

"What is it?" he asked sharply.

"Mr. Urban wants ter see yer, sir," the sergeant replied. "I don' rightly know what for."

"Is Mr. Pitt in?"

"No sir, not that I knows of. If you want 'im we can send a message. I spec's 'e's 'round Clerkenwell way. Far as I know 'e's workin' out o' there lately."

"No—no, I don't want him. I just wondered. You'd better send Mr. Urban up."

"Yessir, right away sir."

Drummond had barely sat behind his desk when there was a sharp knock on the door, and as soon as he spoke, Urban came in. He looked pale and angry, more tense than Drummond could remember seeing him in the short time since he moved from Rotherhithe.

"What is it?"

Urban stood stiffly, his face strained, his hair untidy as if he had recently pushed his fingers through it.

"I've just been informed, sir, that the director of public prosecutions has written to the commissioner of police to inquire if Constables Crombie and Allardyce were committing perjury when they gave testimony against Mr. Horatio Osmar in the matter of his being accused of public indecency—sir!"

"What?" Drummond was stunned. He had been half expecting something unpleasant on the Weems case, some other public figure involved, or worse still, another member of the police. This was totally unforeseen, and ridiculous. "That's absurd!"

"Yes sir, I know." Urban's expression did not change. "There was no explanation, simply a formal letter; the director of public prosecutions seems to be taking it all quite seriously. We have to make a proper response, sir, a formal answer, and then I presume there will be an investigation and possibly charges."

Drummond put his hands up to his face. "If this wasn't happening I would find difficulty believing it. What on earth is the man dreaming of?" He looked up at Urban. "I suppose you are quite sure? There's no possibility Crombie and Allardyce were mistaken, saw something a bit odd and leaped to a conclusion without grounds?"

"No sir," Urban replied without hesitation. "I asked them that. They are quite sure he had his trousers undone and she had her blouse open at the front and they were struggling around with each other in a way likely to cause offense to anyone passing. Whatever they were actually doing, there is no doubt what it looked like to an average person close enough to see them at all."

"What a damned nuisance no one thought to ask the fellow who brought in the case. He might have corroborated it."

"Or not," Urban pointed out.

"Well if he hadn't we'd have dropped the charges in the first place," Drummond said testily. "All right. I'll deal with it. You were involved from the beginning, you'd better leave it alone now. I'll see they send someone from another station."

"Yes sir." Urban still sounded angry, but he accepted the inevitable.

"Damn!" Drummond said softly when he had gone. Why were they wasting good men's time on such idiotic things when there were real and dreadful crimes to solve, and even rising violence to try to prevent. Although thank heaven there had been nothing this year to equal the horror and subsequent panic of the Trafalgar Square riots two years ago which had come to be known as Bloody Sunday. But the ugly rumors of anarchists and other fomenters of treason were still there just under the surface.

Drummond tried to think of anything he knew about Horatio Osmar. There was little enough, an undistinguished government career. His name had seldom been mentioned in connection with any major legislation, and even when it had it was only as a supporter or opponent, never as having innovated anything. He was a rather self-important little *bon viveur*.

What on earth made him think he could get away with it? Why was he now having questions asked in the House, and the Home Secretary upsetting the director of public prosecutions and the police commissioner and trying to raise a scandal about police perjury? Why did anyone take any notice of him? Many people protested innocence; it was instinctive. Others were not able to pursue it this far. Why Osmar?

What would Eleanor Byam think if she knew he was spending his time not pursuing the murderer of William Weems as he had promised her, but trying to find out beyond doubt whether two of his young constables had witnessed an ex–junior minister behaving indecently on a park bench, or if they had perhaps overreacted to a rather silly scene of scuffling around trying to open a locket around a young woman's neck?

Byam had brought Drummond in to help him in case he were accused of murder. Osmar had brought the D.P.P. in for a case of public indecency. But had it been done in the same fashion, in the name of the same brotherhood? It was a thought which brought a chill to his body and a rising feeling that was not unlike sickness. What was he, or any of them, being used for? He had assumed that Osmar was guilty. He had equally assumed that Byam was not. In his own mind Osmar's use of influence was corrupt. He had considered himself to be helping a brother in extreme difficulty.

But what else did the Inner Circle do? These were only two very dissimilar instances. What were all the others? Who judged what was corrupt and what was honorable? And who was at the heart of it?

A little before three in the afternoon there was another knock on his door. As soon as he spoke, it opened to admit a youngish man, perhaps in his late thirties, handsome in a most unusual fashion. His face in repose might have been considered very ordinary, nose much too bony and prominent, eyes wide set and very fine, thick hair waving back from a good brow, cheeks very lean. It was his mouth which was remarkable, delicate lipped, sensuous, and when he smiled possessed of extraordinary, illuminating charm. It was a face about which Drummond instinctively had profound reservations, and yet he wanted to like it. It should have been a strong face, with those remarkable bones, and yet there was something in the balance of it that made him doubt.

"Superintendent Latimer," the man introduced himself. "I have been sent over from the Yard to look into this miserable matter of the two constables who say they saw Horatio Osmar misbehaving on a park bench."

"Latimer?" Drummond said with a chill passing through him like a sudden shiver. "Clarence Latimer?"

The man's face remained perfectly bright. "Yes. Do you know me?"

Drummond swallowed and forced himself to smile. "Heard your name." He shrugged. He was stung by the man's imputation that the constables' word was doubtful, but he kept his voice level.

"If they say they saw him, then I accept that they did," he said with only a hint of sharpness. "They are both reliable men who have never previously overstated their case."

"Oh personally I don't doubt it," Latimer agreed easily. "But officially I have to look into it. I'll begin by speaking to them. Are they around the station, or should I send to have them come in?"

"No need." Drummond's mind was still racing with thoughts to tell Pitt. It was his worst fear about the list realized. "We were expecting you. They are on duties around the station, and you can see them as you wish. I'll be surprised if they tell you anything beyond what they have said all along."

"So shall I, but I have to ask." Latimer shrugged. "Never know, they might come up with some detail that pushes it a little one way, or the other. Then I'll find this wretched girl, what's her name?"

"Beulah Giles."

"Right. May I send someone to bring her here?"

"Certainly."

"Good. From what I've heard, nobody has really questioned her so far. Is that really so?"

Drummond kept his mind on the subject with difficulty. "Yes. The magistrate threw the case out before she was called to the stand."

"Well, well. Pity. She might have cleared up the whole matter."

"Quite. That is very possibly why she was not called," Drummond said acidly.

Latimer flashed him a broad, beautiful smile. "No doubt." And he excused himself and left.

Drummond took a piece of paper and wrote a brief note to Pitt with Clarence Latimer's name, rank and whereabouts. He left it sealed, with the desk sergeant, to be given to Pitt the first moment he set foot in the station.

At four o'clock the hansom arrived carrying Miss Beulah Giles, this afternoon dressed in a cotton print gown considerably lower at the bosom than the one she wore on her visit to the courtroom. By then, the Bow Street station was more than fully occupied with three recently arrested street robbers, with violence, a pickpocket caught in the act with his accomplice, and a man who had been charged with setting up an illegal cock fight. There was no room in which Latimer could interview Miss Giles, and he declined to keep her waiting for an indefinite period until there should be a suitable space. He considered the best alternative was to get back into another hansom and take her to Scotland Yard where his own office would be available, and he could be assured of quiet and suitable surroundings. At the time no one thought anything further about the matter.

When Pitt arrived at Bow Street after having spent a miserable morning at Clerkenwell, he was immediately handed Drummond's note. He read it with a sinking in the bottom of his stomach, but no surprise. He knew there was a Latimer at the Yard, he had not known his given name. Now he had no alternative but to begin his investigation of him.

As with the others, he started with his home. He already knew from the list where he lived; the difficulty was to think of an acceptable excuse for calling. Latimer was his senior. If he was clumsy or offensive he could very well find himself in a very unpleasant situation. Duplicity would inevitably be discovered unless he were extremely fortunate, and could find evidence to clear Latimer almost straightaway. The only alternative he could think of was to tell a great deal of the truth, simply to twist his own part in it a little.

Accordingly he arrived at Beaufort Gardens in Knightsbridge. It was a discreet residential area, quiet in the patchy afternoon sun, parlormaids in stuff dresses and crisp aprons making ready to receive callers, children out walking with nursemaids, little girls very pretty and sedate in white, lace-trimmed pinafores over their dresses, little boys in sailor suits, hopping up and down, itching to be allowed to run.

A fishmonger's boy pushed a cart along the roadway, whistling cheerfully. A postman came past with the third delivery of mail. Pitt crossed the street just before an open landau came around the corner, its mistress on her way to pay a visit to some even more elegant address. The coachman and footmen wore livery of frock coats, striped waistcoats, shining top hats with black leather cockades, and brilliantly polished boots. A spotted Dalmation dog trotted in step behind, its brass collar and insignia shining in the sun.

Pitt smiled briefly, but without pleasure.

Superintendent Latimer was doing very well for himself to live in such an area. There was the possibility, of course, that he had either inherited money or married a woman of substantial means. Both were circumstances Pitt would have to inquire into. Preliminary questions in Bow Street had elicited nothing, but he had not expected they might since Latimer was based at the Yard.

He rang the front doorbell at number 43, and after a moment the door was opened by a housemaid in a smart uniform. At least, Pitt judged her to be a housemaid; he noticed a feather duster tucked discreetly behind the hall table, as if she had put it down so she might change roles to answer the door. It was a small thing, but a sign that Mrs. Latimer cared very much about appearances. She lived in a street where most people could afford a separate parlormaid, and she could not.

"Yes sir?" the maid said politely. She looked no more than seventeen or eighteen, but of course she had probably been in service for four or five years and was well used to her job.

"Good morning," Pitt replied in a businesslike manner. "My name is Pitt. I apologize for disturbing Mrs. Latimer so early, but certain matters have arisen which it is necessary I discuss with her. Will you be kind enough to inform her that I am here?" He produced his card, on which he had added by hand his police rank.

The girl colored in annoyance at herself for not having remembered to bring the silver tray on which visitors could place their cards, but she had been caught by surprise. She had not been expecting social calls for at least another thirty minutes. There were exact times for the well-bred to do such things, and Mrs. Latimer's acquaintances knew what to do, and what not to do. She took the card in her hand.

"Yes sir. If you'll wait here I'll ask if Mrs. Latimer will see you," she said with disapproval.

"Of course," he agreed. Either there was no morning room, or else it was not available.

She scurried away and he looked around the hall. Architecturally it was spacious, but it was filled by its furniture and pictures, a stag's head on the wall, a stuffed stoat in a glass case on a table to the right, and two stuffed birds in another case to the left, a large hat and umbrella stand and a magnificent carved table with a mirror behind it. The carpets were also excellent and in very fine condition. They could not have been more than a year or two old. They were all signs of affluence.

Was the rest of the house so richly furnished? Or was this the part which visitors saw, and had been dressed accordingly, at the expense of the private rooms? He knew from long experience that hallways and reception rooms were indications of aspiration, of how people wished to be perceived, not of reality.

Mrs. Latimer came down the staircase and he was aware of her long before she had reached the bottom. She was a remarkably striking woman, slender, of average height but with hair so very fair it seemed almost luminous as it caught the light from the chandeliers. Her skin was unusually pale, and as flawless as a child's. Indeed her wide eyes and light brows gave her face a look of innocence astounding in a grown woman, and Pitt found his planned words fleeing from him as too brusque and worldly for this ethereal creature.

She came down the last steps and stopped some distance from him. She was dressed in a muslin gown of lilacs and blues on white. It was extremely elegant, but he found it jarring on his taste because it seemed so impractical, so designed merely to be gazed at rather than for any physical or purposeful use, as if the being within it were not entirely human. He preferred a woman more immediately flesh and blood, like himself.

"Good morning, Mrs. Latimer. I apologize for disturbing you so early, and without seeking your permission first," he began with the prepared apology, having nothing else thought of. "But the matter about which I come is urgent, and must be handled with discretion."

"Indeed?" she said with polite interest. He thought her voice deliberately softer in pitch than nature had intended it. There was a brightness in her eyes and he tried to assess whether it was a flash of hard intelligence or simply the light from the chandeliers, and could not decide.

"Please come into the withdrawing room and tell me of it," she offered. "My maid said you are of the police, is that correct?"

"Yes ma'am, from Bow Street."

"I cannot think why you come to us." She led the way, walking gracefully and with complete assurance. If she had the slightest apprehension or uncertainty she hid it superbly. "We are hardly in your area, and my husband, as you will no doubt be aware, is a superintendent in Scotland Yard."

"Yes ma'am, I am aware; and it is not to do with any crime in your area that I have come."

She opened the double doors into the withdrawing room and swept in, her skirts wide behind her, leaving him to follow. The room was as impressive as the hallway: opulent curtains draped well over the floor around Georgian windows looking onto a small, tree-filled garden, its size disguised by the abundance of leaves so the light and shadows were constantly dancing. She allowed him a moment to appreciate the rest of the room, then she invited him to be seated. The furniture was a little ostentatious for his taste, but extremely comfortable. The carpets had no worn patches that he could see, nor indeed did any of the fabric covering the chairs, nor the embroidered antimacassars on their backs. Again there were dried flower ornaments, glass cases with stuffed birds and silver-framed photographs. The pictures on the walls were large and ornately gilded, but a glance told him they were of little intrinsic value as works of art.

She seemed quite happy that he should be so interested in her home, no doubt admiring it, and she made no move to hurry him.

He felt compelled to say something civil; he had stared long enough to make some remark necessary.

"A very handsome room, Mrs. Latimer."

She smiled, taking it for admiration not untouched by envy. She knew from his card that his rank was merely inspector.

"Thank you, Mr. Pitt. Now what is this matter in which you believe I may help you?"

She was being more businesslike than he had expected. The childlike air would seem to be part a trick of coloring, part an art she wished to enhance, but in no way making an indecisive or timorous nature.

He began the story he had prepared. "A most unpleasant person has endeavored to impugn the reputations of several men of importance in London." That was certainly true, whether it had been Weems or not.

Her gaze remained wide and uncommunicative. It did not touch her yet, and she was unconcerned with others.

"He has suggested financial matters of a dubious nature," he continued. "Debt, usury, and a certain degree of dishonesty."

"How unpleasant," she conceded. "Can you not charge him with slander and silence him? It is a criminal offense to speak ill of people in the way you suggest."

"Unfortunately he is beyond our reach." Pitt hid the smile that came naturally to his lips.

"If he has slandered people of importance, Mr. Pitt, he is not beyond the law, whoever he is," she said with slightly condescending patience.

"He is dead, ma'am," Pitt answered with satisfaction. "Therefore he cannot be made either to explain his charges or to deny them and make apology."

Her fair face registered confusion.

"Is that not surely the most effective silencer of all?"

"Most certainly. But the charges have been made, and unless they are proved groundless the smear remains. As discreetly as possible, and without spreading them by the very act of proving them wrong, I must find a way to show that they are groundless and malicious."

Her blue eyes opened very wide. "But why, if he is dead?"

"Because others know of the charges, and the rumors and whispers may still spread. I am sure you see how damaging that would be—to the innocent."

"I suppose so. Although I cannot imagine why you come to me. I shall certainly not repeat malicious gossip, even assuming I had heard it."

"One of the names mentioned by this man is that of your husband." He watched her closely to see even the faintest, most concealed of responses.

There was nothing whatever visible in her face but incomprehension.

"My husband's? Are you quite sure?"

"There can be no doubt," he replied. "The address is given as well."

"But my husband is a member of the police—you know that." She looked at him as if she doubted his intelligence.

"Not everyone believes the police to be beyond temptation or weakness, Mrs. Latimer. It is against those people we must guard. Which is what I am attempting to do. Does your husband have private income, an inheritance, perhaps?"

"No." Her face pinched with distaste at the question. "Senior officers earn a considerable amount, Mr. Pitt. Perhaps you are not aware . . ." She trailed off; the intrusion of such questions offended her, and confused her. She did not deal in financial matters; it was not a woman's place.

Pitt had originally intended asking her if she knew of Latimer's ever having borrowed money, even for a short time to meet some unexpected expense, but looking at her smooth, humorless face he abandoned the idea. Had he been Latimer he would not have told her of anything so mundane or displeasing as financial difficulty, he would simply have handled the matter himself in whatever way he thought best, and presented her with the result. He had seen the glint of purpose in her eye. He doubted she was a stupid woman, for all the carefully cultivated extreme femininity. She was probably capable of intense determination, and acute social judgment; but she seemed to be without any breadth of imagination. The very predictability of the room evidenced that, as did her responses to his statements now.

"I am aware, ma'am," he answered her half question. "But this man has left written claims that Superintendent Latimer borrowed considerable amounts of money from him. It is my task to disprove that."

She blinked. "What is wrong with borrowing money, if you repay it?"

"Nothing. It only becomes wrong if you cannot repay—which is what this man has suggested, among other things."

"What things, Mr. Pitt?"

She had surprised him. He had not expected her to pursue that, only to deny debt. He had been right; it was a flash of steel under all the fair hair and pink-and-white skin.

"Blackmail, Mrs. Latimer."

That jolted her. She had not flinched with distaste in the outward show she had given earlier, but now her eyes widened a little, and beneath the mannerisms her concentration sharpened.

"Indeed. I think perhaps you had better speak to my husband about this. It appears to involve crime as well as malicious charges."

"The crime is also being investigated," he assured her. "It is the charges I am personally concerned with disproving. The reputation of the police force has suffered very gravely in the last year. It is most important we protect it now. I would greatly appreciate your assistance."

"I don't see what I can do."

"May I speak with your servants?" He wanted to see the rest of the house. It would give him the best opportunity he could desire to estimate their financial standing.

"If you believe it will help," she conceded reluctantly. "Although I cannot imagine how it could."

"Thank you, that is most generous of you." He rose to his feet and she did also, reaching for the bell.

When the parlormaid arrived she gave the necessary instructions and bade him good-day.

He spent a further hour asking all the servants pointless questions about callers, which enabled him to see most of the rest of the house. His ugliest fears were realized. The money had been spent on the front rooms. All the more private areas where no visitor would pass were furnished in castoffs, wood was scratched or blemished, carpets were faded in the sun, worn where feet had passed over them in constant tread, fringes on lamps and chairs were patched and missing tassels, the wallpaper was faded where the light fell on it, curtains were barely to the floor, and unlined. The domestic staff was only the barest number necessary to run such an establishment. When dinner parties were given, as they were quite often, then extra servants were hired in for that occasion, as were the required plates, glasses and silver.

He left late in the afternoon with a heavy feeling of depression. Mrs. Latimer was apparently a woman with considerable social ambition and a driving will to achieve, indeed he was obliged to leave through the servants' entrance to avoid the guests arriving at the front.

Latimer might well have felt the same ambition, but whatever his own desires he appeared determined to drive himself to the limit, and perhaps beyond. It would be very easy to believe he had borrowed from Weems in order to throw the extra party, feed his guests with the best, serve the best wines and impress all the right people. But how had he expected to repay? His salary was set.

Pitt had taken the very obvious step of learning a superintendent's salary. He could imagine no way in which it could have maintained the establishment in Beaufort Gardens, even with the stringent economies practiced in the kitchens, the family bedrooms and the servants' quarters. Thinking of it in the hansom on the way back to Bow Street he felt oppressed by the anxiety of it, the constant worry, the fear of the letter, the knock on the door, the feeling that everything was temporary, nothing safe, robbing one pocket to pay another, always juggling, thinking, deceiving, covering one lie with a second, spoken or implied.

There was little point in speaking to Latimer directly. If it were untrue he could not prove it; if it were true he would deny it. Neither would mean anything. Proof was all that would stand. He might not have killed Weems, but that was only part of the question, and now not the part that troubled Pitt the most. Whatever the truth of Weems's murder, he needed to know where Latimer had hoped to acquire the money to repay the loans. He needed to know it was an honest way, although he could think of none.

He would have to have Micah Drummond's authorization to inquire into Latimer's cases. They were not in Bow Street but in Scotland Yard, and it would need a very strong explanation before an officer from another station would be permitted to examine them.

It took him many days of close, unhappy reading in a little room off a long corridor, sitting on a hard-backed chair in front of a wooden table piled with papers. He followed case after case of human violence, greed and deceit. Latimer had worked on a wide variety of evils, from murder and arson through to organized fraud and large-scale embezzlement. It was an unhappy catalogue of behavior, probably much the same as would have been found in the records of any other officer of similar rank in a city the size of London, the largest city in the world, the hub of an empire that circled the earth, the financial capital, the industrial and commercial heart, the busiest port, the center for transport and communication, as well as the social pinnacle.

He put aside all those where Latimer had worked closely with other officers and the results were precisely what anyone with experience would have expected. He also took out those where the trail of evidence was obvious and had culminated in arrest and conviction of a known felon.

He read and reread any that ended in an acquittal, but found little that was unusual, and nothing that was unaccountable.

Lastly, tired, eyes aching and fed up with spending his days inside poring over papers instead of out dealing with people, he turned to the cases unsolved. There were three murders over the last five years, and he read them carefully. From the evidence, the statements recorded, he would have done precisely what Latimer had done. His spirits lifted a little. Perhaps after all he was going to find it was simply a case of a man in love with a beautiful and socially ambitious wife who had overextended his means to satisfy her.

But there was no reason to suppose Carswell had borrowed money, and every reason to believe he was being blackmailed. There was sufficient reason to believe that Latimer also was blackmailed. Lord Byam had admitted it from the first. Was Latimer, the third name on the list, really only an innocent observer?

Was he a member of the secret brotherhood, the Inner Circle? He was just the sort of man who would join: young, ambitious, desirous of social status and preferment. Pitt would need not proof that he was, but proof that he was not before he would alter his belief.

He went outside in the hot, close midday to find himself some luncheon. In a noisy public house with a thick sandwich and a glass of cider he sat and watched the faces of the men coming and going, recognizing each other, exchanging whispers and nods, doing quick, secretive business, making acquaintances.

Was it any use trying his underworld sources? If Latimer were assisting the Inner Circle, they would not be the petty thieves and forgers, the pickpockets, fences and pimps of the criminal world, but the practitioners of fraud in business, the corrupt lawyers, the men who gave and took bribes, the financial deceivers and embezzlers of thousands.

He looked at the narrow, foxy face of the man at the table next to his. He was dirty and his teeth were stained, his hands cracked and nails black. He very possibly stole to make his life a little more comfortable. He would almost certainly not be above taking advantage of those weaker or slower-witted than himself, and might well have abused his wife, if he had one, or his children.

Still Pitt found him less of an offense against his code than the rich men who stole indirectly from strangers in order to become richer still, and who corrupted others to escape the consequences.

He returned to Scotland Yard and his poky little room with

the pile of papers, and resumed his study, concentrating on the crimes that involved men he thought likely to be members of the Inner Circle, or to be of interest to its members.

Here at last he found what he had dreaded: lines of inquiry dropped for no accountable reason, prosecutions not proceeded with even though they might well have succeeded, curious omissions of diligence for a man otherwise exacting in his standards. Any individual one might have been explained easily enough as simple misjudgment. Latimer was no more infallible than any other man and it would be unreasonable to expect him to be right every time. He, like anyone else, could guess wrongly, be overtired, miss a connection, a link in the chain of evidence, leap to a wrong conclusion, have his prejudices and his blind sides. But taken all together they formed a very faint pattern, and the more he looked at them the more definite the pattern became. There was no way he could find out; the society was secret and the punishment for betraying a brother was severe. So Urban had said, and if he was right, Weems's list proved it. But Pitt believed all the unaccountable omissions and strange misjudgments were with cases where the interests of the Inner Circle were concerned, and Latimer had been an instrument to their ends.

Had there been one he had refused to hide, one crime that had offended him more than he could bear, and he had at last refused? And the brotherhood had punished him by putting his name on Weems's list, so he would eventually be discovered, and ruined? It was a heavy price to pay, and he would then be of no further use to them. Pitt shivered, cold in the stuffy room. But the other brothers would know, the waverers would be brought up sharply against the reality of what it meant to betray the Inner Circle, and every other brother would be strengthened in his loyalty.

What about Micah Drummond? His name had not appeared on the list. Did that mean he had never defied them, never refused their orders? Certainly he had responded quickly enough to help Sholto Byam, and the case was murder.

The thought was so intensely ugly Pitt found himself feeling sick. He liked Drummond as much as any man he knew, and a week ago he would have staked his own career that Drummond was utterly honest.

Perhaps Latimer's juniors felt like that about him too.

He tidied up the piles of papers and left the office, locking the door behind him and returning the key to the sergeant who had given it to him.

"You all right, sir?" the man asked tentatively, his face screwed up in concern. "Yer don't look all that sharp, if yer don't mind me sayin' so, sir."

"Probably need a little air," Pitt lied automatically. He needed to protect his information; he could trust no one. "Hate all that reading."

"Find what you wanted, sir?"

"No—no, I didn't. It seems it was a wrong trail. Have to try somewhere else."

"S'ppose there's no shortcut to bein' a detective, sir," the sergeant said philosophically. "Used ter think it was what I wanted, now I'm not so sure. Mebbe find out a lot o' things I'd a bin 'appier not knowin'."

"Yes," Pitt agreed, then changed his mind. "Or find out nothing at all."

"Bad day, sir? Mebbe termorrer'll be better."

"Maybe." Pitt forced a smile at the man, and thanked him again before leaving and going out into the rapidly cooling evening air. It smelled like rain. The faint wind was easterly, off the Channel, and it carried the sounds of the river up from the Pool of London and the docks. It would still be light for several hours yet, and on the Embankment there were carriages clipping along as people took the air. A pleasure boat with bright little flags fluttering made its way upstream, towards Windsor or Richmond. He could hear the laughter drifting across the water. Somewhere out of sight, also towards Westminster Bridge, a hurdy-gurdy played a popular tune and a cart was propped up on the opposite side of the Embankment, selling winkles and eel pies.

It was six o'clock, and he was ready to go home and forget Weems and his list, and all the misery and corruption it had shown him. He would have supper in his own kitchen, with Charlotte, then go outside and do a little work in the garden, perhaps cut the grass and tidy up some of the bigger weeds which Charlotte did not get to.

He would make a decision what to tell Drummond tomorrow. Perhaps in the morning it would seem clearer.

It did not really rain, just a light drizzle, so fine it lay on top of the grass, barely bending the petals of the flowers or the long light stems of leaves. Pitt stayed outside in it because he wanted the cool feel of it on his face and the sight of the slowly dimming light across the sky. He had been inside all day, and hated it. And it was a satisfaction to work manually and see the garden begin to look cared for, manicured and husbanded. Charlotte did the small chores like taking the dead heads off the roses and pansies, lifting the tiny weeds, and Gracie swept the path, but they had too many other chores to attend to it every day, and the grass cutter was too heavy for them anyway.

He came in at last a little after nine o'clock when the overcast was bringing the dusk early. He took off his wet jacket and boots and sat down in his chair in the parlor, ignoring the fact that his trouser legs were damp also.

Charlotte was mending a dress of Jemima's. She put it down, poking the needle in carefully where she could find it again.

"What is it?" she asked, her face grave, her eyes on his.

He thought for a moment of evading the question and giving some trivial answer, but he wanted to share it. He did not want to make the decision alone, and she at least he could trust absolutely. With brief, painful words he told her.

She sat listening without moving her eyes from his face and her hands in her lap for once were completely motionless. She did not reach again for the needle or to wind wool or skein silks.

"What are you going to tell Mr. Drummond?" she said at last when he was finished.

"I don't know." He looked at her, trying to see any certainty in her face, if she had a vision of judgment he had not. "I don't know how deep he is in this brotherhood himself."

She thought for only an instant.

"If you don't tell him, you are making the judgment that you do not trust him."

"No," he said, denying it immediately. "No," he said again.

"I am simply not placing him in a position where he has to defy the Inner Circle if he is to continue with the Weems case as it is at the moment. Latimer may not be guilty of killing Weems."

"Only of corruption," she said bluntly, still sitting without moving.

"I don't even know that," he argued. "I only believe it from the case notes. They could all be misjudgments, or simply errors. If anyone went through all my cases they would find a lot that is open to criticism, and perhaps worse, if they wished to see it that way."

Charlotte seldom thought of things like means and opportunity, weapons, forensic evidence, but she understood motive, emotions, lies, all that was concerned purely with people.

"Rubbish," she said with a smile full of gentleness, her eyes so soft he could not take hurt. "Superintendent Latimer is corrupt, and you are afraid that Micah Drummond is too, or may become so. But you cannot make the choice for him, Thomas, you must give him the chance to do the right thing, whatever the consequences."

"The consequences may be very ugly." He shifted a little, sitting lower in his chair. "The Inner Circle is secret, powerful and ruthless. They have no forgiveness."

"Do you admire them?"

"Don't be ridiculous. I despise them more than almost anything else. They are worse than a simple garroter who kills people in the street; they seduce and corrupt minds and turn ambitious and foolish men into liars and corrupters of others." He stopped; his voice had become harsh and his hands were clenched on his knees with the violence of his feelings. He stared at Charlotte and saw her face intensely clearly in the lamplight, its high cheekbones and soft mouth, her eyes steady on his.

"Do you not think that Micah Drummond might hate them too, if he understood what they are?" she asked him. "Perhaps even more strongly than you do, since they have tried to soil him too."

"Perhaps," he agreed slowly.

"Then you must give him the opportunity to fight them." She leaned forward a little. "You cannot protect him from it, and I don't believe you should try. I should not thank you if you removed from me the chance to redeem myself from a terrible mistake of judgment."

He took her hand in his and held it gently.

"All right. You don't need to argue any further. I understand. I shall tell him tomorrow."

She lifted her other hand and touched his face very softly, smiling, her eyes bright. It was not necessary that she should speak.

However the following morning Pitt's intention was balked by a furore of excitement when he reached Bow Street. There were newspapers being passed from one person to another and cries of indignation and anger all around the entrance and the desk and the corridors.

"It's downright dishonest!" the desk sergeant said, his face bright pink.

"It's monstrous, that's what it is!" a constable said heatedly, holding the offending newspaper out in front of him. "It's lies! How do they get away with printing such things?"

"It's a conspiracy!" another constable agreed with outrage in his voice. "Ever since the Whitechapel murders they've been out to get us!"

"I wouldn't wonder if there's anarchists behind it," the desk sergeant added.

"What is it?" Pitt demanded, snatching one of the newspapers from a constable.

"There." The constable pointed with a rigid forefinger. "Look at that."

Pitt looked.

" 'Police brutality'!" he read. " 'Miss Beulah Giles, a victim of police harassment and brutal interrogation, was yesterday taken forcibly from her home to Scotland Yard where she was secretly interrogated by Superintendent Latimer in police attempts to defend themselves against charges of perjury on the park bench case.' " And it went on in the same vein about the shock and dismay to an innocent girl's feelings as she was removed from her home and family and subjected to insult and degradation in a desperate effort to force her to change her testimony and incriminate her friend.

Pitt pushed the paper back at the constable and reached for one of the others. The words were a trifle different, but the meaning was essentially the same. Beulah Giles had been the victim of police insult and intimidation. Everywhere people would rise to avenge the outrage. What was this new police force coming to when an English maiden was not safe from their assaults and abuse? Their entire existence must be questioned forthwith. Pitt swore, quietly and bitterly—an extraordinary circumstance for him; he very seldom lost his temper, and even more rarely did he use unseemly language.

CHAPTER
EIGHT

When Pitt had left the next morning, Charlotte went straight to her escritoire in the parlor and took out her pen, ink and paper. She wrote:

> Dear Emily,
>
> I hope you are feeling thoroughly well, and have no need of me at your forthcoming dinner party for that reason, nevertheless it is most important that I come. Thomas told me some extraordinarily serious things about his current case last evening, and I am determined to do all I can to help. I cannot remember having seen him so upset before in quite this way. He has nowhere else to turn, for the most wretched of reasons.
>
> And I know you will already have arranged how your table is to be, but I would like you to change it so as to place me next to both Lord Byam and Mr. Addison Carswell. Believe me I have excellent reasons for asking this, and I do know how inconvenient it will be—but both are being blackmailed and are suspects for murder. You know I do not exaggerate in such matters nor say it lightly.
>
> Naturally I shall tell you all you wish when I see you, however I think perhaps you had better burn this letter when you have read it. In the meantime I remain your loving sister,
>
> Charlotte

She folded it, put it in an envelope, wrote Emily's address on it, then she found a postage stamp which she licked and stuck on.

"Gracie," she called out.

She heard Gracie's feet scuttling down the passage and her head appeared around the door.

"Yes ma'am?"

"Will you take this letter and put it in the box for me, please? It is extremely urgent. I must go to Mrs. Radley's dinner party tomorrow evening, and it is terribly important that if possible I sit next to particular people, because they may have committed murder—one of them, I mean, not both."

Any other housemaid might have shrieked and fainted at this point, but Gracie was well used to such ideas and fully intended to help where she could. Her eyes widened in her thin little face and she stood more smartly to attention.

"Oh ma'am."

Charlotte knew she was longing to help as well, but she could think of nothing for her to do, beyond posting the letter. Judges and politicians were completely outside Gracie's knowledge, in fact she had probably never even seen such a person, let alone spoken to one.

"It was a moneylender who was killed," she added, just so her instructions were not so bare.

"Good," Gracie said instantly, then blushed. "Beggin' yer pardon, ma'am. But they in't nice people. Once they gets their 'ands on yer they don't never let go. Don't matter 'ow much as yer borrers, or 'ow little, yer never gets done payin' 'em back." She frowned, screwing up her face. "But ma'am, people what goes ter Mrs. Radley's dinner parties don't borrer from the likes o' moneylenders, do they?"

"One would not think so," Charlotte agreed. "But he was also a blackmailer, so one never knows. But you must keep all this to yourself, Gracie. It would be most dangerous to allow anyone else to think you know something. No careless words to the butcher's boy, or the fishmonger."

Gracie's chin came up and her eyes blazed.

"I don't speak to the errand boys or their likes, 'ceptin' to tell 'em their business," she said with heat. "I listens, 'cos that's me job, I might learn summink, but I don't never tell 'em nuffin'."

Charlotte smiled in spite of herself. "I apologize," she said humbly. "I really didn't imagine you did, I was simply warning from habit."

Gracie forgave her instantly, but with a little sniff as she took the letter, and a moment later Charlotte heard the front door open and close.

She also told Pitt that evening when he came home tired and hot and hungry. She made very light of it, simply saying that she would attend the dinner because both Byam and Carswell would be there, and she had received Emily's reply, delivered by hand, to say that arrangements had been remade and she would indeed sit at the table between the two people she had requested. She did not tell Pitt the dire threats that were also made, should Charlotte fail to tell Emily every single thing she knew about the case, proved or suspected. That really went without saying anyway.

"Be careful," Pitt said quickly, his eyes sharpening and his attention reawakened in spite of the oppressive heat and his real tiredness. "You are dealing with very powerful people. Don't imagine because they are unfailingly polite that they are as gentle in deed as they are in word."

"Of course not," she said quickly. "I shall merely listen and watch."

"Rubbish! You never kept silent in your life when your interest was engaged," he said with a twisted smile. "And neither will Emily."

"I—" she began, then caught his eye and her denial withered away. He knew perfectly well Emily would demand and Charlotte would relate everything she knew, in between the hairpins and the petticoats and the instructions to footmen, parlormaids and anyone else who was involved. "I shall not forget how serious it is," was the very best she could do and retain a shred of honesty. She passed him a glass of lemonade from the pantry (which was still cool, even in this weather) and a small piece of cake, small so as not to spoil his appetite for dinner. "Did you speak to Mr. Drummond?"

"Yes." He took the lemonade and the cake.

She looked at his face and saw the lines of weariness in it, the shadows under his eyes and the tightness around his mouth.

She slid her hand over his shoulder and touched his hair. It was thick and too long, and badly needed cutting. She kissed him very gently, and did not ask what Drummond had said.

He set the cake down, put both his arms around her and pulled her closer to him. They were still standing together, her head on his shoulder, when Jemima came in and put her arms around him too, not knowing why, simply wanting to be included.

The following evening was utterly different. Charlotte was collected in Emily's carriage so that she would have plenty of time to prepare herself with the help of Emily's maid, and immeasurably more important, to tell Emily everything there was to tell about the case.

"So you don't know if Lord Byam might have done it!" Emily exclaimed, putting the last touches to her hair while her maid was temporarily out of the room.

"No," Charlotte conceded. "We have only his word. The ridiculous thing is, why was the letter not there, and the paper incriminating him, and who has them now?"

"Or did they ever exist?" Emily added. "And if they did not, why did he call in Mr. Drummond and draw attention to himself? Is it all actually something to do with this wretched secret society, and perhaps nothing to do with moneylending or blackmail at all?"

"Thomas didn't even mention that. But why?" Charlotte sat in front of the mirror, pushing Emily along a little. They both looked their loveliest. Emily was in aquamarine satin stitched with tiny pearls, extremely expensive; but it was her party, and she wished to impress. After all, that was the entire purpose of it at the moment, enjoyment of personal acquaintance was incidental. Charlotte was in borrowed plumes again, this time hot apricot, and it looked far better on her than it had on Emily two summers ago. It had been extensively remade, both to bring the style more up to date and to add an inch or two for Charlotte's more handsome figure.

"Who knows?" Emily dismissed it, staring at her face in the glass and apparently finding it beyond further help, because either it was as she wished it, or she could think of nothing more to do. "Men are sometimes incredibly silly. They play such self-important games. There is nothing makes them feel so superior as having a secret, so if they don't have one they will invent it. Then everyone else wants to know it, simply because they don't already."

"You don't murder people over it," Charlotte pointed out.

"You might, if you didn't know it wasn't worth anything." Emily stood up and smoothed out her skirts. Her gown fitted very flatteringly and her condition was entirely disguised. "It sounds as if there might be a great deal of money involved, and far more important to some people, a lot of power."

"It is the police corruption I really care about," Charlotte said more gravely. "It distresses Thomas so much. I wish we could prove somehow that there is another answer, or at least that it was not one of the police who murdered Weems."

They went no further because they were interrupted by Emily's ladies' maid returning, and as soon as she had gone, Jack came in looking very dashing. He welcomed Charlotte, kissing her on the cheek in a brotherly fashion, then quickly his face clouded with concern.

"Emily, are you feeling worse again?"

"No, not at all," Emily assured him with ringing candor.

He still looked doubtful, his eyes puckered with anxiety. He glanced at Charlotte.

"She is here to detect," Emily said quickly.

Jack was not convinced. "No one in society has been murdered," he pointed out.

Emily walked over to him, her eyes very soft, a little smile on her lips. She stood in front of him and touched his cravat proprietorially with her finger.

"It is a blackmailer who is dead, and two of his victims are to dine with us tonight," she said sweetly.

Charlotte smiled to herself and looked back in the mirror, pretending to do something further to her hair, although there was nothing to do.

"Charlotte is going to observe, that is all." Emily raised her eyes and met Jack's with devastating sweetness.

"It is never 'all,' " Jack said dubiously, but he knew not to enter a battle he had no chance of winning.

Emily kissed him very lightly. "Thank you," she whispered, and after only a second's hesitation, turned and led the way out onto the landing and downstairs ready to receive her guests.

Among the first to arrive was Fanny Hilliard, looking extremely pretty if a trifle behind the fashion. After greeting her with genuine pleasure, Charlotte made the opportunity to look unobtrusively at her gown. She herself had altered a bodice here and there to adapt someone else's clothes, usually Emily's or Great-Aunt Vespasia's, in order to make a new dress for herself out of an old one of somebody else's. She saw the telltale needle holes and the fabric slightly across the weave where a waist had been made a great deal smaller than had originally been intended. Even a clever dress-maker could not completely disguise the fact that the bustle had been almost entirely recut, and a piece of toning fabric added to hide the alteration. No man would have known, but any woman who had done the same thing could see it.

She felt an instant empathy with her, and silently wished her well.

Her brother, James, who had escorted her, now gave her his arm into the withdrawing room, and Charlotte turned to welcome that very curious young man, Peter Valerius. He still looked untidy because of his beautiful hair, and a rather artistic disregard for conventional neckwear. His cravat was not only a little oversized, but instead of tying it loosely like the aesthetic set, he had apparently dressed in some haste, and it was tight, and crooked. Charlotte decided it was not an attempt to be Bohemian, simply a lack of interest in something he considered totally trivial.

"Good evening, Mr. Valerius," she said with a smile, because he reminded her a trifle of Pitt. "How agreeable to see you again."

"Good evening, Mrs. Pitt." He looked at her with interest. His eyes flew to Emily, noticed her very obviously improved health, and then came back to Charlotte again. He smiled, but made no comment, and Charlotte had a very strong idea he read her presence here as a matter of interest and not duty this time.

Ten minutes later Great-Aunt Vespasia came in. She was resplendent in ivory lace and a double row of pearls that was so beautiful one felt that even should all the lights fail at once, and leave the room in darkness, they would still shine with a luster of their own. Her face registered a benign surprise when she had greeted Emily and Jack, and moved on to Charlotte.

"Good evening, Great-Aunt Vespasia," Charlotte said enthusiastically.

"Good evening, my dear," Vespasia replied with slightly raised eyebrows. "Do not tell me Emily is unwell; she is in abundantly good health, as any fool can see." She regarded Charlotte closely. "And you have a warmth in your cheeks which I know of old. You are here meddling." She could not drop her dignity so far as to ask in what, or to request inclusion, but Charlotte knew what was in her mind, and bit her lips to hide her smile.

"I am waiting . . ." Vespasia warned.

Charlotte altered her expression immediately, making it as close to demure and innocent as she could.

"We have two possible murderers at the table," she said in a whisper.

"A conspiracy?" Vespasia did not change expression, only the brilliance of her eyes betrayed her.

"No—I mean either of two people might be guilty," Charlotte continued.

"Indeed?" Vespasia's eyebrows rose. "Is this still Thomas's miserable usurer in—where was it? Some unpleasant place."

"Clerkenwell. Yes. He was a blackmailer as well, remember."

"Of course I remember! I am not yet in my dotage. I assume Sholto Byam is one. Who, pray, is the other?"

"Mr. Addison Carswell."

"Good gracious. Why, may one ask?"

"He has a mistress."

Vespasia looked surprised. "That is hardly a matter for blackmail, my dear. Half the well-to-do men in London have mistresses, or have had—or will do. And that is a conservative estimate. If Mrs. Carswell is a well-bred woman with any sense of her own and her family's survival, she will take good care that she never finds out, and will continue her life as usual." Her face darkened for a moment. "You don't mean that he is spending a ridiculous amount of money on this person, whoever she is?"

"I don't know. It is possible, but Thomas didn't say so."

"Oh dear—then it may be worse. Is she married to someone who will take the matter ill, and be vindictive? That could be serious." She sighed. "How very foolish. No one is so high in society that a scandal cannot ruin him, if it is ugly enough. Look at Doll Zouche and that miserable business with Wilfred Scawen Blunt. Amusing in its fashion, but all quite unnecessary. Are there letters, do you know?"

"No I don't know. I don't think it has got that far yet, but I didn't ask Thomas. Perhaps he wasn't familiar with the Zouche case."

"He must be, my dear. Everyone is," Vespasia said with total assurance.

Charlotte blinked. "I'm not."

"Are you not? Well, Doll Zouche, daughter of Lord Fraser of Saltoun, and wife of the current Lord Zouche. They held a tournament—"

"Did you say a tournament?" Charlotte interrupted in amazement. "When did this happen, for heaven's sake?"

"In 1875," Vespasia said coolly. "Do you wish to hear it or not?"

"Oh yes! I just didn't know they had tournaments in 1875!"

Vespasia's face was almost straight. "They have tournaments whenever the 'romantic ideal' grips hold of them, and they have more money than they need, and more time than things to do with it."

"Go on," Charlotte prompted. "Doll Zouche?"

"She came as the Queen of Abyssinia—they proposed making a trip to that country the following summer. The culmination of the tournament was a sham fight in which Doll and others dressed as Christian ladies were attacked by Moorish marauders, Blunt being one of them. They were rescued by two knights on horseback— Lords Zouche and Mayo. What began in fun ended in earnest. Unfortunately she was having an affaire with both young Fraser and Lord Mayo, who wished to elope with her—which he ultimately did—and of course, Blunt."

Charlotte was speechless.

"On the day of the tournament," Vespasia concluded, "she quarreled with her husband, and galloped away on her favorite horse. Blunt was nearly cited in the ensuing divorce."

Charlotte's eyebrows shot up. "Only nearly?"

"That is what I said. But you may be sure Mr. Carswell will know of it!"

"Oh dear." Unconsciously Charlotte copied Vespasia's exact tone. "Thomas seemed to feel Mr. Carswell was very much in love, not merely a matter of—appetite."

"Who is she? Does he know?"

"Yes, but he did not tell me. He followed Mr. Carswell one day—over the river somewhere."

They were prevented from continuing the conversation any further by the arrival of Lord and Lady Byam and the necessity of greeting them. Charlotte found the color distinctly warm in her cheeks as wild speculations raced through her mind while she spoke politely to Lord Byam, and looked at his remarkable eyes. She felt acutely guilty. She was swapping politenesses with him, saying how nice it was to see him, and all the time her mind was wondering if he had stood with a gun in his hand and shot William Weems's head to pieces.

What was he thinking behind that sensitive, imaginative face and the formal words? Something equally wild and terrible? For that matter, what were any of them thinking? Could Eleanor Byam possibly feel as calm and sedate as she looked? She was dressed in black, which made her hair the more startling and her shoulders and throat whiter. She wore a necklace of onyx and diamonds, both unusual and very lovely. She was greeting Micah Drummond, and there was a faint flush of color creeping up her cheeks. She met his eyes with a directness not required or expected of such a ritual occasion.

Of course—she would know who he was, and that her husband had asked his help. Beneath the formal acknowledgments and inquiries for health, she would ache to know what he had learned. And presumably she knew both he and her husband were members of the Inner Circle, so his loyalty was assured. No—that was not

true: women were excluded. She would not know, so perhaps she
had no idea why Drummond should help, and consequently no
reason to believe he was anything more than a police officer with
breeding, a social equal, or something close. Perhaps "equal" was
overstating it; at least not hopelessly inferior, like Pitt, and almost
all the rest of the police force.

And what was Drummond thinking, behind the courteous expression and the pale, rather drawn face? Probably remembering
Pitt's confrontation over the secret brotherhood, the police corruption he must do something about because Pitt knew, and perhaps
wondering about his own role in it. Charlotte trusted her judgment
where he was concerned. She did not believe he was corrupt, not
when he faced the reality of it. He might well be blind, a little
naive; there was a quality of innocence in him which she had often
observed in some of the nicest men. They were inclined to trust
people no woman worth a fig would have trusted half as far as she
could have thrown them. Funny how men thought it was women
who were the innocents. In Charlotte's experience, most women,
underneath the daydreams and the trappings that gave a little
glamour, were eminently practical. The human race would hardly
have survived otherwise. Knights on white chargers had their place,
in dreams which were completely necessary to sweeten some of the
pills that must be swallowed, but one could divide off part of the
mind for such a purpose. In the end one knew quite well which
was which, and most women did not confuse the two.

Yes, *naive*, that was the word. She looked at him again, his tall
lean figure and rather quiet face. It was not wildly imaginative, but
without a shred of ill temper or undue vanity. He was looking at
Eleanor Byam with such gentleness, and a diffidence as if it mattered to him intensely what she thought, how she felt. How very
kind that he should be so concerned for her, so sensitive to her
fears . . .

Oh my goodness. How totally idiotic of her.

"What is it?" Vespasia had noticed and was staring at her with
interest.

"Nothing," Charlotte lied instinctively.

Vespasia snorted very slightly, like a well-bred horse.

"Poppycock. You have observed that your Mr. Drummond is more than a little in love with Lady Byam. Which will make life very difficult for him—whether Lord Byam is guilty or not."

"Oh dear." Charlotte sighed. "I wonder if Thomas has any idea?"

"I doubt it," Vespasia said with a tiny shake of her head. "I like him quite as much as any man I know—but he is as unobservant as most men over such things." She seemed unaware of her astounding admission that she, Lady Vespasia Cumming-Gould, held Thomas Pitt, policeman and gamekeeper's son, in an affection unsurpassed by any man, even of her own station and breeding.

Charlotte held her breath, and felt a tide of hot emotion surge up her face, and an overwhelming pride burst open inside her like a flower.

She swallowed hard, and tried to sound nonchalant.

"I imagine not," she said huskily. "I had better point it out to him. It may matter." And with that parting shot she made her way into the main withdrawing room to speak to more of the guests who had arrived in the intervening time.

A few moments later she found herself talking polite nonsense with Fanny Hilliard. It was nonsense because neither of them cared particularly about the sort of subjects it was good manners to discuss: the weather (which was of no interest whatever), fashion (which neither of them could afford to follow), current gossip (which neither of them was acquainted with, not being in the rank of society which was privy to such confidences, nor being in the places to observe it at first hand), or theater, (which they visited very seldom, for the same financial reasons).

Indeed the whole conversation was simply a device through which they could express a certain liking for each other. One could not simply stand and stare without exchanging some words, however pointless.

Charlotte was not in the least put out to see Fanny's eyes wander from hers several times, and a soft warmth come into them, and a trace of color up her cheeks as if her pulse were beating faster. She was quite aware that Fitz Fitzherbert was somewhere behind her and a little to her left.

Therefore she was not surprised when a few minutes later he

joined them, talking of equally mindless and silly subjects. His fair face reflected an inner laughter and a complete acceptance that their words were of no importance whatsoever, their thoughts of the greatest importance possible.

"How good of Mrs. Radley to invite me again," he said to both of them, including Charlotte equally, although she knew perfectly well she served only as a chaperon to make the exchange possible. "She is playing this extremely fairly, don't you think?"

Fanny smiled and looked up at him, not through her lashes— she was too candid for that, and too sincere in her feelings. Her eyes were wide and bright, and there was a vivid color in her cheeks.

"Indeed," she agreed, although Charlotte was not sure if Fanny had any idea what Fitz meant; no one had said anything about selection for Parliament, or Fitz's and Jack's rivalry.

"Have you spoken with Lord Anstiss?" Fitz went on. "He is one of the most interesting men I have met. I have no difficulty whatever in listening to him with rapt attention. It is so gratifying when the people to whom one has to be polite and flattering are so distinguished as to earn it naturally." He was looking at Fanny, his eyes never leaving her face.

She could not have been unaware of it as she gazed at the glass in Charlotte's hand, although probably she was not seeing it at all.

"I have spoken to him only briefly," she admitted. "I believe he is an expert in much of art, is that so?"

"Extremely," Fitz replied. "I wish I could remember all he said, so I could repeat it to you. His opinions were most enlightening— on almost everything."

"Oh please don't!" Fanny said quickly, looking up at him. "I should far rather hear your own." Then she realized she had been forward, and as on this occasion it mattered extremely to her what he should think, she colored furiously and looked away.

"You are very generous," he said quietly. "I am afraid my knowledge is pretty poor by comparison."

"I should not know how to reply to someone who knew everything," she said with a tiny smile. "I should feel very overwhelmed."

"Would you?"

"Although of course I should try not to show it," she added with a touch of spirit.

He laughed.

"So I shall not know whether I have impressed you or not?"

"I most profoundly hope not."

And so they continued, on the very outermost surface speaking of nothing that mattered, on the second surface, just a trifle below, flirting mildly as people do at parties when they find each other agreeable. And underneath they cared more and more deeply as all the unspoken things were understood between glances, through inflections of the voice and expressions of the face changing from laughter to self-awareness, wry knowledge of their own frailty, tenderness for the other, excitement because it was new and piquant, and fear because the hurt could cut so deeply.

When they were joined by Odelia Morden, her face pale, her glass clutched in clammy hands, Charlotte felt a stab of pity which took her by surprise. She had not liked Odelia, thinking her both cold and complacent. Now she watched her face and saw in it the sudden awareness of defeat, not necessarily of fact—Fitz was betrothed to her and to break the engagement would be an act of folly in the face of his ambitions—but she recognized in him now a laughter and a magic she had never seen for herself, and the pain of it cut very sharp. For the moment she was too stunned to fight.

Once her eyes met Fanny's and the color drained from Fanny's face as she understood. They looked at each other and the rest of the busy, chattering crowd faded from their awareness. Even Fitz himself seemed shadowy, his reality pushed to the edge of vision. They both understood precisely what the issue was. For the first time in his life Fitz was held by the same sort of enchantment that he had exercised over so many others, the charm that wakens all sorts of dreams, the feeling of warmth and the possibility of never being alone, of being understood in all that was best in oneself. It was too sweet ever to let go of entirely, no matter what the reality became.

Odelia saw something she had not realized before, and at the moment she understood it, she also knew it was beyond her reach.

Fanny realized she was in love with another woman's betrothed as she could probably not love anyone else. And he was socially

above her, and his ambition made their union impossible. If he
were to jilt Odelia he would not be forgiven.

And Fitz knew it also, but he did not accept it. Only the guilt
hurt as he perceived at least in part what he was doing to Odelia,
although he had not sought to feel as he did, nor was there anything he could do to govern it.

They were still all four standing motionless. Charlotte began
talking to cover the confusion and the pain, not because she imagined for an instant that anyone was listening to her or cared in the
slightest what she said. Then Regina Carswell stepped back and
almost bumped into them, turning to apologize.

Over her shoulder Fanny's startled gaze met that of Addison
Carswell.

"I'm so sorry," Regina said hastily, regaining her balance.
"Oh—Miss Hilliard, is it not? How pleasant to see you again."

Fanny gulped, all the color and excitement blanching out of
her face.

"G-good evening, Mrs. Carswell." She swallowed and coughed
as the air caught in her throat. "Good evening, Mr. Carswell."

"Good—good evening, Miss—er—Hilliard," Carswell said awkwardly. "I—I'm delighted to make your acquaintance—again."

Regina looked puzzled. Their discomposure was hardly accounted for by the triviality of the occasion. She sought for some
reason for it, without understanding in the slightest.

"I do apologize, Miss Hilliard, if I trod upon your gown. It was
most clumsy of me. I seem to have lost my balance."

"Not at all," Fanny said quickly. "You did not tread on me, I
assure you. I don't know what came over me."

"Perhaps you are a little warm?" Charlotte suggested, looking
at the tiny waist and wondering how much of it was owed to stays
and a good maid with one foot on the bedpost. "The garden is
quite charming, and we shall not be going in to dine for some
minutes yet."

"Oh how kind of you." Fanny grasped at the escape, her eyes
brimming with gratitude. "Yes I am sure that is the answer. I shall
take a little air."

"Shall I come with you?" Fitz offered, then realized he had
overstepped propriety. He was still with Odelia, at least in fact, if

not at heart. He blushed at his own most uncharacteristic awkwardness.

"Oh no—thank you." Fanny at least remembered herself so far as to decline, no matter how much she might have wished it; although Charlotte, looking at the quite sudden unhappiness in her eyes, thought perhaps she did not wish it after all.

Odelia opened her mouth to offer, then thought better of it.

Regina Carswell, who had daughters of her own and was quite used to such sudden feelings of faintness with all their causes, took charge of the situation.

"I shall come with you," she said firmly. "I could do with a moment's air myself. And if you feel faint, it is better that you should not be alone, just in case you trip."

"Oh please," Fanny said in something approaching distress. "I shall be perfectly all right, please believe me. It was only a moment—I should not dream of troubling you—"

"It is no trouble, my dear," Regina said with a smile which gave an unusual radiance to her otherwise ordinary face. "I have already contributed anything I can to the conversation, and I shall be no loss to it. Come—we shall have a few minutes in the air before going to the dining room." And taking Fanny's arm she excused them and gently but irresistibly escorted her towards the French doors at the far end of the room.

Carswell cleared his throat uncomfortably and stared at no one.

Charlotte was suddenly furious with him for having taken a young mistress and betraying a woman of such innate kindness as Regina. What was a little laughter and a pretty face, compared with the years shared, the understanding and the loyalty of his wife? Perhaps she was a little domestic at times, not always as glamorous and sometimes boring. For goodness sake, no doubt so was he.

"How very kind of Mrs. Carswell," she said with an edge to her voice, gazing at him very directly. "Surely the most precious of all virtues, don't you think?"

Odelia looked at her in amazement. The remark was totally uncalled for and she was confused by the vehemence of it, in fact by the making of it at all.

"Why—er—indeed," Carswell said uncomfortably. "Yes—to be sure."

Charlotte realized she had spoken unaccountably, but she had left herself nowhere to retreat.

"Was not Miss Hilliard at the Royal Academy exhibition?" she said apropos of nothing, simply to fill the silence.

"Indeed?" Odelia seized the straw to join in. "We also were there—" Suddenly she realized how the "we" was no longer true in the way it had been then, and her voice died away, thick with unhappiness, her face flushed.

"There were some very fine pictures, don't you think?" Charlotte was not insensitive to her pain; indeed she felt a pity for it which surprised her with its depth. She merely wanted to cover it for her so it was not added to by being public. "There was one of a bowl of lilies I found especially attractive."

"I don't recall it." Fitz dragged his attention back with an effort.

That was hardly surprising since Charlotte had invented it for something to say. However she now proceeded to describe the mythical picture in detail, and it carried over the time until everyone began to recover themselves and conversation resumed as normal. A few minutes later dinner was announced and they parted to find the person with whom they had been assigned to enter the dining room. It would be unpardonable to go in with the wrong person. It would throw everything out of order and be a social gaffe of the worst sort. There was the strictest etiquette in such things, and Charlotte went in on the arm of Peter Valerius.

At the table Emily had granted Charlotte's request, and she was seated between Addison Carswell, on her left, and Lord Byam to her right.

The first course was soup; the second fish, a choice of deviled whitebait or smelts. She picked delicately at it. Ladies were not expected to be able to eat everything served them, and indeed with the stays which were obligatory to attain the required figure, a waist of so many inches according to one's age, much eating would have been impossible.

Conversation was only slight to begin with, and upon the usual trivialities of style, theater, the weather and other inconsequential matters. Charlotte looked under her lashes first at Carswell, who was still pale. She observed that his hand with the fork raised to his lips shook very slightly. Then she turned her attention to Lord Byam, who was quite composed, at least on the outside. Whatever deep fears were troubling him, he had mastered his demeanor so that a relative stranger like herself could see nothing in his manner to betray it.

The entrées were served: curried eggs, sweetbreads or quenelles of rabbit. The remove course was simply iced asparagus.

With the game course the mood was changed quite suddenly and completely when Aunt Vespasia with casual innocence looked up from her plate and asked of the table in general:

"Does anyone know how poor Horatio Osmar is faring? It seems extraordinary to me, but I believe he is to sue the police for perjury, or something of the sort. Can that really be true?"

Charlotte slid the asparagus across her plate and nearly upset her wine.

Beside her Carswell was absolutely motionless, his fork in the air.

Fitz seemed unaware of any strain. Either that, or he was far more subtle than his manner suggested, or his charming, artless smile.

"Good gracious. I didn't know you could do such a thing. Wouldn't that open the door for anyone charged with an offense to suggest the police were lying?" His fair eyebrows rose. "The courts would never settle any charge at all, they would be so busy with claims and counterclaims as to who was telling the truth and who was not." He looked at Carswell. "You are a magistrate, sir; don't you agree?"

"I am afraid—" Carswell swallowed hard. "It—it is a subject upon which it would be improper for me to express an opinion."

At the far end of the table Drummond apparently did not hear them.

"But your opinion would be most interesting, and surely the most informed," Fitz protested. He looked around. "After all, who else among us knows about the law in such matters? But you are an expert."

Fanny Hilliard's face was very pink. She looked across at Carswell and there was anguish in her eyes, a sort of fierce, protective pain.

"I think what Mr. Carswell means is that it would be profoundly unethical for him to comment," she said quickly but very distinctly. She avoided Fitz's eyes.

Fitz heard the sharpness in her voice and he did not understand it. A shadow crossed his face but he continued with a light, easy voice, looking at Carswell.

"Oh is it? Are you involved with the case?"

Carswell at last put his fork down. He was very pale.

"Yes—yes I am. It was I who first heard the case."

"Good gracious," Vespasia said mildly, her eyebrows arched very high. "Will you be called to give an opinion as to whether the police were lying or not?"

"I have no way of knowing, Lady Cumming-Gould." He was beginning to regain his composure at last. "It would be quite pointless to ask me."

"I don't see how anyone can know, except the police themselves, and Osmar," Peter Valerius said with a twisted smile on his lips. "And they all have very considerable vested interests in the matter. What I don't understand is why he chose to contest it at all. Why didn't he just admit that he was behaving like a fool, and get it over with quietly, pay a small fine, which he would well afford, and be a bit more discreet in future?"

"It is a matter of reputation," Carswell said sharply. "The man has been charged publicly with indecency. It is not something most men would care to have said about them, surely you can understand that, sir? He is defending his reputation, which any Englishman has a right to do."

"I beg to disagree, sir." Valerius said it politely, but his face held none of the mildness of his words; his eyes were bright and the muscles of his jaw hard. "Immeasurably more people will hear of it now that he has chosen to contest it than ever would have had he merely paid the fine, and I don't believe that his taking up battle over it will change anyone's mind at all." He leaned forward a little. "Those who thought the police corrupt will have their beliefs confirmed, and those who thought the judiciary corrupt or inefficient in the face of privilege will retain that opinion."

His smile was full of sharp-edged humor. "The whole issue will be not whether Horatio Osmar was being vulgar on a park bench with a woman no one had ever heard of, or cares about except in principle, but whether our police and our judiciary are honest and efficient or not. And that, I think, is a question it were better not to raise."

"Sir!" Carswell exploded, his face bright pink. "You go too far!"

Peter Valerius's face barely changed expression. Only his eyebrows rose a little, and his voice remained perfectly level.

"Because it will cause a number of fears which are quite unfounded," he continued, "but for which we have no effective proof that will calm those doubts once they have been disturbed." A shadow of a smile crossed his face again and his eyes met Carswell's.

Carswell could not justifiably sustain his anger. He had leaped to a hasty and mistaken conclusion, but the offense was still hot and hard inside him. Charlotte wondered briefly and with a mixture of pity and resentment whether it was some guilt of his own that made him defend where there had been no attack.

She glanced at Peter Valerius again, found his clever eyes watching her, and knew he had seen the reflection of a new thought across her mind.

She turned to Carswell.

"Do you think Mr. Osmar will succeed in his suit against the police?" she asked with interest.

Carswell composed himself with an effort and turned to her with all the politeness he could manage.

"I have no idea, Mrs. Pitt. It is something at which I could make no guess of value."

"He has powerful friends." Vespasia regained the conversation with a stiff face reflecting her disapproval. "They may exert influence on his behalf."

Byam turned to her with slight surprise. "Surely that is natural, Lady Cumming-Gould? Would not anyone in such a position seek all the assistance available?"

"I do not know." The ghost of a smile crossed her silver-gray eyes. "I have never known anyone else in such a position. It seems both indiscreet to ask one's friends to defend one in such a matter, and unjust to attempt to malign the integrity of those who enforce the law, and have more than enough difficulty as it is."

"A novel view," Byam said thoughtfully, not exactly in criticism, but certainly not in agreement.

Valerius looked at her with new and sharpened regard. It was obvious in his face that quite suddenly she had assumed a different role; one to be taken seriously, even admired.

Carswell was still uncertain. He glanced at Byam, then at Vespasia, and ended by saying nothing.

"I hope, for the sake of the rest of us, that your view prevails," Charlotte said clearly, looking at Vespasia. "If the police are blackened in public esteem any further, it will destroy confidence in them to a degree where their efficiency, perhaps even their existence, will be jeopardized."

"I am sure your fears are unfounded, Mrs. Pitt," Carswell said stiffly. "I beg you, do not disturb yourself."

And from there the conversation became more general. The sweet course was served, and then the ices.

Finally after the fruit—pineapples, cherries, apricots and melons—the ladies excused themselves and retired to the withdrawing room to sit and discuss polite trivialities and exchange purely frivolous gossip. The men remained around the table to pass the port and smoke, and speak of the subjects that were too contentious or intellectual to be aired while the ladies were present.

When the gentlemen rejoined them again Charlotte found herself listening to Peter Valerius. They had begun to speak of usury, with Carswell still in their company. Charlotte had hoped it might produce some emotional response which she could judge, but Carswell had left them and the conversation had somehow turned to international finance.

"It is still usury," Valerius said with an intensity that held her attention in spite of her lack of interest in the subject. "A powerful industry invests in a small, backward country, a part of the empire, for example in Africa." He leaned towards her, his face sharp with the strength of his emotion. "The people begin to prosper, as there is work for many of them. They are able to sell their goods and in exchange buy imported luxuries, for which they soon develop not only a taste, but a dependence. Perhaps it even includes the raw materials or the machinery necessary for their new industry."

She could see no connection to the wretchedness of personal usury, and he must have observed it in her face. He resumed with greater urgency, his voice demanding her attention.

"The parent company expands the business, promising even better trade. The small country accepts. Suddenly life is better than they have ever known it. They have luxuries undreamed of before."

"Is that not good?" She sought to understand, but the cause of his anger eluded her.

"And the country is utterly dependent on the industry, and those who govern it," he continued, now oblivious of the rest of the room. Even Odelia's skirt brushing his elbow and thigh as she passed behind his back made no impression on him at all. She apologized and he did not hear her. He leaned closer to Charlotte. "Suddenly the price is altered. They pay less for the goods the country produces, they charge more for the materials they supply. The rate of interest on the money borrowed is increased. The small country is in difficulties. Profits disappear. They need more money to service their needs and keep the industry surviving. The loans are increasingly expensive. Perhaps they cease altogether, and then they have to turn to venture capital."

He must have seen from Charlotte's expression that she had no idea what that was.

"Instead of simply lending money at a rate of twenty percent, or so," he explained, his voice hard-edged, his face pale, "the rate of interest is higher, much higher, and the lender also demands one-third ownership in the business itself—forever."

"But that's monstrous," she protested. "It's . . . usury!"

A bitter smile lit his face.

"Of course it is!" he agreed. "Not man to man, but industry to nation. A few score profit, and tens of thousands suffer."

She nearly asked why people allowed such a thing to happen, but the answer was already in what he had told her. She sat for several minutes digesting in her mind what he had said, and he sat in front of her, watching her face, knowing he had no need to add anything further.

While Charlotte was absorbed with Peter Valerius, Micah Drummond was standing apart, next to the enormous curtains that hung swathed across the windows at the entrance to the balcony and the steps down to the garden. He found the chatter almost impossible to concentrate on and the small snatches of gossip and opinion were insufferable when so much clamored in his mind: doubts so ugly they stifled everything else that entered his thoughts; doubts about himself, his actions and judgments of the past, his motives of the present; his own honesty; and dark, crowding fear for the future.

The room was full of lights. The chandeliers glittered pendant from the ceiling, their crystal facets winking in the barest movement of air. Lights burned from all the gas brackets on the walls. Diamonds sparkled around throats, on arms and in hair, even on slender wrists, waved to emphasize a remark. Reflected light glanced from polished tables and on silver and in glass.

The soft buzz of voices was interrupted by laughter, the chink of goblets. It all looked so gay and unshadowed. But he longed to go outside to the solitude and the concealing darkness of the summer garden, where his face would not be read, no one else saw or remembered who spoke to whom, and where at least for a while he could be alone.

He stood undecided, and perhaps it would be more honest to say unable to make the decision to escape, in case he was observed. It was an entirely new experience for him to feel so racked by guilt, so uncertain of his own judgments. Of course he had made mistakes, but he had understood them, and they had not corroded his underlying belief in himself.

But this was entirely different. Why had he joined the secret brotherhood of the Inner Circle? He could remember Pitt's face as exactly as if he had only just left him, standing in his office looking tired, deep lines of strain around his mouth, and his eyes unhappy. Drummond had realized immediately that Pitt's distress was more than merely professional, but he had still been totally unprepared for what had followed. Pitt had not merely told him of corruption on the force, officers who were members of the Inner Circle and had been pressed by that secret brotherhood to use their professional power in the interests of members, but he had quietly but relentlessly asked him of his own concern with the brotherhood, and if he had been aware what hostage he was to their commands, and the penalties for disobedience. He had been civil, even gentle, but the train of doubt he had started in Drummond's mind was beyond evasion, as he had known it must be.

He could answer Pitt with innocence. No, he had never made any decision of even the slightest degree to comply with the brotherhood's wishes. But would that always be so? Was it so now? He had answered Byam's summons because Byam was a brother. He had interfered with the course of investigation in Clerkenwell, and put Pitt onto the case of William Weems's death, to suit the brotherhood. What else might he have done, unrealizing from whence the request originated? He racked his brain, and could not remember or decide.

And what might he yet do, if he discovered evidence that Byam was guilty, if not of Weems's murder, then of complicity in it, or of sheltering whoever had done it, or merely of concealing evidence? What would the brotherhood do if he did not comply? He remembered with a bitter chill the secret initiation, which he had simply thought colorful and a trifle absurd at the time. But looking back now, it had contained some very dark threats to those who betrayed a brother or revealed any of the group's secrets. He had thought them in a rather adolescent way romantic until now, insomuch as he had thought of them at all: the sorts of things boys got up to in the long holidays out of school when there was little to occupy the imagination but summer days and stories of adventure.

Now it seemed from Pitt as if the Inner Circle exercised a very real discipline on its errant members, and punishment was swift and extremely unpleasant. Would it be visited on him? Of course. Why not, if he failed in his duty to his oaths?

Even more unpleasant to him would be if he were asked to administer punishment upon another. Would he do it?

No!

Regina Carswell passed close to him, hesitated in her step as if to speak, then saw his face more closely and continued on her way. A sensitive woman.

But why would he not carry out such a punishment? He knew the answer before he was prepared to admit it.

Because a man must be free to follow his own conscience. No society of any sort, whatever its aims, however noble, must be allowed to dictate what a man believes to be right or wrong.

But that is not what the oath had said. And now that he saw it in plainer light, that was where he had made the mistake upon which all the others depended. He had sworn allegiance to people, not to an ideal, to something unknown which might change from what he believed to what he did not—and he had allowed himself no avenue of redress. That was what Pitt had pointed out to him.

He could see Byam and Lord Anstiss talking together, Anstiss standing square, a glass in his hand, his stocky body at ease, but not elegant. Beside him Byam stood a little sideways, his weight asymmetrically balanced, with a curious kind of grace, but there was a tension in him that showed in the angle of his head, his tight fingers around his goblet.

He was not close enough to hear their words, but he followed the emotion of the conversation from their expressions. Anstiss was speaking, his face full of animation, eyes wide and candid. He put his arm on Byam's affectionately.

Byam laughed, and for a moment the anxiety slipped from him and the weariness ironed out of his features. Drummond could see in him the young man he must have been twenty years ago before the tragedy of Laura Anstiss's infatuation and death. He and Anstiss were simply two friends who cared for each other, enjoyed each other's company with an open trust and fellowship like the best of brothers. They shared interests, hopes, laughter—until Anstiss's fragile, unstable wife had stepped between them, and her death had left pain and guilt.

Anstiss held his glass up to the light and said something.

Byam replied, and they both laughed.

Anstiss turned, his expression altered, hardening, and he said something to Byam.

The moment froze. They both stood motionless, the chandeliers blazing, the lights winking on the glasses. Then all the pain and the weariness returned to Byam's face. He set his glass down on the sideboard near him, made some reply to Anstiss, and walked away.

The dull color touched Anstiss's cheeks and he opened his mouth to reply, then changed his mind, but the fierce, suppressed emotion remained in his face.

Byam was walking over towards where Drummond was standing. He could see him clearly now. He did not look like a man who had just quarreled, rather like one who has resumed a familiar burden after a short respite, and not for the first time. He did not look bruised so much as unbearably tired.

Drummond watched him with a wild and painful mixture of emotions. He could never know what the exchange with Anstiss had been, but he could guess. He was sorry for Byam. He was a man in a frightening situation, through no fault of his own, a misjudgment of a woman's character which anyone might make, especially a youth. He had done what he saw as the honorable thing, and it had ended in a tragedy he could not possibly have foreseen. And he had suffered a guilt for it ever since.

Now he faced the very real possibility of being charged and even tried for murder because of it. If Pitt did not find the murderer, Byam could even be hanged. Would he call on the brotherhood to help him? Surely he would—and long before it reached trial. How would Drummond respond then? What could Byam ask? So far it had been entirely honorable, but then the danger was still very slight, only problematical. When it became real and within a matter of days, or even hours, and the shadow of Newgate and the dock touched him, might he not ask what was far less honorable?

Would others of the brotherhood exercise their power on his behalf? That was the question Drummond had been avoiding asking himself ever since Pitt spoke to him. Just how far would the Inner Circle go to protect its own? They had spoken of high moral values, and in the same breath of loyalty to each other above all. No one had thought to ask which principle governed when one could not observe them both, certainly Drummond had not. Now the dark and highly painful thought came to him that it might be the personal loyalty.

And what would he do then?

There was only one possible answer. He would betray the Inner Circle.

He drew in a deep breath. He felt better for having framed the question, and the answer, to himself.

A footman, less sensitive than Regina Carswell, interrupted his thoughts to offer him a glass. He refused with a tight smile. At the far side of the room Eleanor Byam was talking to Anstiss now. She looked stiff and very formal. He wondered about her relationship with Anstiss. Did she like or dislike him? Was she even jealous of the past so charged with emotion and in which she had no part? Did she resent Anstiss because it was his wife who had caused so much pain, and because his mere existence was a constant reminder to her husband of his guilt? Knowing so little made Drummond feel at a disadvantage.

And that was his last, and perhaps his own deepest, guilt: his feeling for Eleanor. It was far more powerful than he wished to admit, and acutely personal. Part of him wanted to protect Byam, for her sake; another uglier part would gladly have seen him removed, disgraced in her eyes, leaving her free to love elsewhere, in time.

Love. That was the word he had avoided saying even to himself.

He turned away from the room and walked past the great swathed curtain and out onto the balcony. He needed not only to be alone, but to be unseen by others. His face might too easily reveal him, and he could not force himself into communication now.

He did not know how long he stood staring into the soft radiance of the night, glimmering from the reflected lamps like a row of suspended moons along the street, tree branches gleaming where the rays caught them, leaves dancing and turning in the breeze.

At last he was interrupted by a voice, tentative and apologetic, but carrying an urgency that even embarrassment and the knowledge of intrusion would not curb.

"Mr. Drummond—"

He knew it instantly. It was Eleanor Byam. It was as if his thoughts had conjured her there, and he felt guilty for her presence, as if somehow she knew what was in his mind, and worse, his heart. He turned slowly to face her, trying to compose himself and his racing pulse.

"Yes—Lady Byam?"

"I'm—I'm sorry for disturbing you, when you seem to wish to be alone . . ." she began. It appeared she was finding it every bit as difficult as he.

"I merely wished for a little air," he lied, trying to ease her embarrassment.

"You are very generous." Her voice was lower and there was a touch of warmth in it now which caught his emotions like touching a fine cut on the skin. "Please do not be polite with me," she went on urgently. "It is a time when I must be honest with you, regardless of how painful it might be."

He was about to interrupt, but she did not allow him time.

"Something further has happened which disturbs me more than I know how to describe . . ." He longed to say something, even more to do something to comfort her. His instinct was to touch her, and it would have been unforgivable.

She plunged on through his desperate silence.

"Sir John Seaforth, a long-standing friend and colleague of Sholto's, came to visit yesterday evening. I merely saw him arrive and he looked angry but well in command of himself, and hopeful, as if he believed Sholto could make right whatever it was that so upset him." She seemed uncertain how to express herself. Drummond was acutely aware of her so close to him he could smell the faint perfume of geraniums and hear the whisper of taffeta as she breathed in and out.

"You saw him arrive?" he asked pointlessly.

She took it as a request for some explanation.

"Yes—Sholto was upstairs at the time, and I have known Sir John for many years myself. He was shown to the withdrawing room while the footman was sent to inform Sholto of his arrival. He spoke only a few words to me. He was quite clearly not in a mood to exchange small talk, and I was sensible of that. As soon as the footman returned to say Sholto would receive him in the library, he went to that room."

"Did Lord Byam tell you why he called?"

"No—he would not discuss it. I know it was very heated, because I crossed the hall some twenty minutes later to go upstairs,
and I heard their voices from the library. I could catch only the
occasional word, and the tone was so unpleasant I was embarrassed
that one of them might open the door and see me. I did not wish
either of them to know I had overheard what was obviously a most
violent quarrel. I caught the words *deceit* and *betrayal* used by Sir
John . . ." Her voice shook a little and she swallowed several times
before she continued. "I did not hear Sholto reply, but from the
raised voices immediately afterwards, Sir John was not in any way
appeased."

"You said he was a colleague." Drummond sought for something to say that might allay her fears, and found nothing. Now
only the truth would be any use, and the more he heard, the less
did that promise any comfort. "In the Treasury?"

"No—no, he is a member of Parliament, deeply concerned with
trade and financial matters."

"Did you hear any more of the discussions?"

"No. As I was coming down the stairs again Sir John was leaving. I did not wish to meet with him when he was so deeply angry
and it must be of the greatest embarrassment to him, since he had
undoubtedly quarreled bitterly with Sholto. I waited in the shadows
at the top of the stairs, and I saw Sholto bid him good-bye. They
were both very stiff and barely civil to one another. I think perhaps
had the footman not been there, they might not even have pretended so far."

"Did you ask Lord Byam the cause of his quarrel?"

"Yes—not immediately. He was too furious at the time, and . . ."
Her voice sank to little more than a whisper. "And I was afraid of
what his answer would be."

Drummond forgot himself at last. He took her hand in his and
felt her fingers tighten in a quick grasp as if he were a lifeline and
she feared drowning in her distress.

"What was his answer?" he said, closing his hand over hers also.

"He said it was a political difference about finance," she said
miserably.

"And do you not believe that?"

"No—I—Mr. Drummond—I fear something terrible has happened, that whatever Sholto is so afraid of has actually come to pass. I feel as if I have betrayed him myself, even to think of it, but it lies so deeply in me I can deny it to myself no longer. I fear Sir John knows of Laura Anstiss's death, and Sholto's part in it, innocent as it was—and he knows of Weems's blackmail."

She swallowed and struggled for a moment to regain her composure before going on. "I believe him mistaken, and quite terribly wrong, but I think he believes Sholto killed Weems. That is all I can imagine that would make him so fearfully enraged with Sholto, and Sholto unable to defend himself. You see he still does feel guilty over Laura's death, even though he had no possible idea she was so—so wild, and self-destructive."

She looked at Drummond earnestly. "He did not imagine anyone, least of all she, would fall so in love with him she would sooner die than live without him. It is surely not—not quite sane—is it? When one hardly knows someone, and has shared no . . . intimacy of even the slightest sort with her?"

"I think it is sane," he said slowly. "But perhaps it is a little . . ." He searched for a word that would not be too cruel, too dismissive of an emotion he was trying to understand only too sharply in himself. "A little weak," he said. "Life often gives one the feeling that it is beyond enduring at the time. But with courage, one does—one has to. Perhaps that is something Laura Anstiss had never learned."

"Poor Laura," she whispered. "How well you put it. It is as if you have known . . ." She drew in her breath quickly and looked away. "I'm sorry, that is intrusive. Thank you for being so—" She withdrew her hand. "So patient, Mr. Drummond. I feel better to have told you."

"I will do all I can, I promise you," he said quietly. "We have several others we suspect, whose motives are stronger than Lord Byam's—and who can give no account of where they were at the time."

"Have you?" There was a lift in her voice for the first time.

"Yes—yes. There is cause to have much hope."

"Thank you." And with a rustle of taffeta, she moved away back towards the room and the lights and the laughter.

At the end of the evening when the last guests had departed, Charlotte, Emily and Jack were seated in the withdrawing room. The
gas was turned low and the last glasses and small dishes were packed
up for the servants to take away and deal with before they too were
able to go to bed.

Emily turned to Jack. She was interested in Charlotte's affairs,
but his took precedence.

"Was the evening successful?" she asked eagerly. "You seemed
to be a long time in the library with Lord Anstiss. Did he ask you
a great deal?"

Jack smiled, wiping as if by magic the tiredness from his face.

"Yes," he said with deep satisfaction. "And he told me a great
deal which I did not know. He is an extraordinarily . . ." He looked
for the right word. ". . . magnetic man. His knowledge is vast, but
far more than that, he speaks with so much vitality and wit. And
I think his influence is greater than I first supposed."

"But he liked you?" Emily pressed with a fine grasp of what
was important. "What did he say? Jack, don't keep us in suspense!"

His smile broadened. "He invited me to join a most select
society which does a great deal of good work, often secretly. They
provide funds for many charities, strive to fight inequity and injus-
tice, even some of the more dangerous and ugly facets of crime."

"It sounds excellent!" Emily was enthusiastic. "Are you going
to join?"

"No!" Charlotte said with vehemence so sharp both Jack and
Emily turned to her with incredulity. "No," she said more mod-
erately. "You must know a great deal more about it before you join
anything."

"Charlotte! It is a society wholly dedicated to doing good,"
Emily said reasonably. "What could possibly be wrong with that?"
She turned around to Jack again. "Isn't it?"

"Yes of course it is," Jack agreed. "And from what Lord Anstiss
says, it would be the most powerful single step I could take to
ensure the support of those who really matter in the political and
social world."

Charlotte wanted to muster an argument, but all she could think of was Pitt's fears for Micah Drummond, his misery over the corruption he had uncovered, and the deeper corruption he so far only suspected.

"And what do they want from you in return?" she demanded. "What loyalty? What sacrifice of your independence, perhaps in time of your conscience?"

"Nothing." Jack was surprised and mildly amused. "It is a society for doing good, Charlotte!"

"But secret?" she persisted.

"Not secret," he corrected. "Discreet. Surely that is how charity should be, done quietly, modestly and without seeking recognition?"

"Yes." She was reluctant to admit it not because what he said was untrue, but because she feared so much more. "But Jack, there may be other things. Thomas is dealing with a society at the moment . . ."

Emily looked at her with skepticism. "He is investigating the murder of a usurer, you told me."

"Yes, but he has uncovered a society as well . . ." She was out of her depth and floundering. She was not prepared to tell them of the police corruption. It was too indefinite in form as yet, and too painful. In some basic way she felt it reflected on Pitt, on his profession, and she did not wish them to know if it could be avoided.

"London is full of societies," Jack said more quietly, aware that her concern for him was real. "This one is very honorable, I promise you."

"What is it called?"

"I don't know—Anstiss did not tell me."

"Be careful."

"I will be. I give you my word." He stood up. "Now it is past time Emily went to bed, and you too I am sure. Would you prefer to go home in the carriage now, or stay here until morning and go then? You are very welcome, you know, always."

"Thank you, but I will go now. I would prefer to be there when Thomas leaves in the morning."

Jack smiled and took Emily's hand in his. "Then good night, my dear."

Pitt listened as he had breakfast to all that Charlotte related to him of the evening before, which was only impressions of conversation, emotions and fears, and the conviction that Micah Drummond had learned to love Eleanor Byam, with all the pain and conflict that that meant. She did not mention Anstiss's invitation to Jack to join the society. She would not burden him with that yet.

Pitt did not say anything, but he knew she understood his silence. He kissed her, long and gently, and went out into the hot, dusty street to find an omnibus and travel slowly to Scotland Yard and resume his investigations of Latimer's cases. From there he spent a miserable day going from one old underworld source to another, through filthy alleys, up steps of rotting wood into rookeries where rats scuttled at the sound of his feet, squeaking, their claws rattling on the boards and their little eyes red in the shadows. Refuse lay heaped in slowly sagging piles and the gutters stank in the heat. He swatted ineffectually at some of the flies, and gave all his coppers to children who begged.

Finally in a small, crowded public alehouse called the Grinning Rat he sat opposite a little man with a twisted arm, broken when as a child he had been a sweep's boy and fallen inside one of the vast chimneys. It had healed badly, and been broken a second time when he slipped off a church roof, stealing the lead, and now it was deformed past help. He made his living by selling information.

"Joey." Pitt brought his wandering attention back from a large man with a protuberant belly hanging over grimy trousers and a tankard of ale in each hand.

Joey looked back at Pitt reluctantly.

"Yes, Mr. Pitt. I dunno wot yer wanna hear." His voice sank into a plaintive whine as he expected to be criticized. " 'E in't wot yer'd call reelly bad—just a bit kind o' selective abaht 'oo 'e does, like. Y' unnerstand?"

"No," Pitt said unhappily. "Explain to me, and there'll be half a guinea."

" 'Alf a guinea." Joey's face brightened.

"The truth," Pitt warned. "Not what you think I want to hear.

You don't know what I want, or don't want. If I discover you're telling me lies I'll come back and do you for everything in the book—I swear it."

Joey let out a wail of outrage.

"Be quiet!" Pitt warned sharply. "Do you want everyone in the place looking at you?"

"Yer an 'ard man," Joey complained.

"I am," Pitt agreed. "Now tell me."

And slowly Joey told Pitt what he most feared to hear. There was no explanation for Latimer's omission to press some of his cases, for not calling certain witnesses. Joey did not know of his having taken money for his decisions, but he had assumed it, because to him there was no other answer. Why else did men do things, unless of course it was from fear? But to Joey, policemen of Latimer's rank had nothing to fear. They were the powerful, the unassailable, the safe.

"Thank you," Pitt said with a bitter misery inside. He handed over the half guinea he had promised and left the Grinning Rat. Tomorrow he would go back to Clerkenwell and Sergeant Innes.

Of course there were still the ordinary debtors from Weems's first list, and perhaps Innes would turn up evidence against one of them. He half hoped for it, although he did not expect it; but perhaps a more conscious, sharper half would hate it even more should some desperate man struggling to survive prove to have shot Weems.

"Nothing," Innes said gloomily, his thin face tired and without any lift of hope anymore.

"Nothing on Weems's private life?" Pitt pressed pointlessly. "He must have had friends of some sort, surely? No women—not one?"

"Found nothin'," Innes said flatly. His eyes looked anxious, even guilty.

"What is it?" Pitt demanded. They were sitting in the small room, little more than a cubbyhole, where Innes kept his notes and papers on the Weems case. Innes was perched on the narrow windowsill, leaving the solitary chair for Pitt, as the senior officer, and his guest.

Innes looked even more uncomfortable.

"I know as 'ow Mr. Latimer gets 'is money, sir. It weren't borrered from Weems—"

Pitt would have been pleased, had not the look on Innes's face made it impossible. Whatever the answer was, it was no better than usury.

"Well?" he said more sharply than he had intended.

Innes took no offense, he understood.

"Gambling, sir. 'E gambles, very successfully, it seems."

"How do you know?"

"Discovered it by accident, sir. Was lookin' inter one of our local debtors, 'oo gambles. Come across proof as Mr. Latimer does—in a big way. An' 'e wins, no doubt about it. 'E knows 'is bare-knuckle fighters." His face was pinched with unhappiness. Apart from the brutality, bare-knuckle fighting was illegal and they both knew it; so would Latimer.

"I see," Pitt said slowly. He did not bother to ask if Innes was sure beyond any doubt. He would not have mentioned it until he was.

Innes was looking at him earnestly. Neither of them needed to explain the possibilities ahead. Latimer would be ruined if his gambling, and condoning an illegal sport, were known. Was that what Weems had blackmailed him over? That would account for his name on the second list.

It was a powerful motive for murder.

"What are we going to do, Mr. Pitt?" Innes said quietly. "You want me ter go ter Mr. Drummond, like?"

It was a generous offer, made at some cost, and Pitt felt a tiny spark of warmth because of it.

"No," he said with a bleak smile. "Thank you. I'll go."

"Yes sir."

CHAPTER
NINE

Pitt made no objection whatever when Charlotte said she would like to attend Emily's musical evening towards the end of that week. Indeed when she explained, by the way, as though she had assumed he knew it already, that the Carswells would be there, he was quite openly pleased.

They had no time to discuss it because he was leaving early to go to Clerkenwell. He and Innes must work on the very last of the debtors on Weems's first list. Little by little Innes had whittled it down, but there were still a dozen or so left who were not accounted for beyond doubt. It was still possible one of them might have gone to Cyrus Street late in the evening, been admitted, and seized the blunderbuss, found the powder, and loaded the gun. But neither of them believed it. Weems may have despised his clients, but he surely knew despair when he saw it, and over the years had learned that desperate people can be dangerous.

Today they planned to question Weems's errand runner, Windy Miller, yet again, although they expected little useful from him, and later perhaps his housekeeper, in case there were any details they had overlooked, any thread of knowledge however frail. But both of them were convinced that Weems's killer was someone on the second list—or else Byam himself, although Innes had not said so, because of course he still did not know of Byam, a fact which weighed heavily on Pitt's mind and disturbed his conscience increasingly.

Charlotte kissed him good-bye, and when he was gone immediately set about that housework which could not wait, so that she could leave in the late afternoon with a clear mind and no housewifely guilt.

By six o'clock she was sitting on the Hepplewhite chair in Emily's withdrawing room, wearing a rose-colored gown spread around her elegantly, and surrounded by about thirty other people also sitting upright, facing the grand piano where a very earnest young man was playing some extraordinarily beautiful, dark and sad music by Franz Liszt. Indeed it was so lovely Charlotte's attention was entirely taken by it and she forgot even to glance at Addison Carswell, Regina, one of the Misses Carswell, or at Herbert Fitzherbert and Odelia Morden, or Fanny Hilliard, whom she was surprised to see present. Then she realized precisely what political value Fanny had in the possible fall from grace of Herbert Fitzherbert and Emily's so gentle part in it.

However at the first interval Charlotte remembered her own reason for being here, cast aside self-indulgence and began to observe other people. One of the first she noticed was the Miss Carswell present; she did not know her name as she could not tell one from another. She was no more than seventeen or eighteen, a girl pretty in a usual sort of way, clear complexion, all pink and white, fair hair tending a little towards mouse, and an agreeable, good-tempered face of no particular character. No doubt if one knew her one would find the individuality, the beliefs and emotions which made her unique, the humor, the dreams, the small kindnesses.

She now stood a few yards away from her mother, effectively unchaperoned, and was speaking with some animation to a young man Charlotte could not remember seeing before; but obviously Miss Carswell had. Her face was full of interest, instead of the usual rather simpering response many young women had to a first approach from an eligible and attractive man. And the man was responding with warmth and a total involvement of his attention.

Charlotte smiled. It was a most promising situation, and she imagined it might well progress into a happy relationship, most young girls' profoundest ambition. So much the better if it could accompany a genuine affection as well, and this looked, from their faces, as if it did. How wise of Regina Carswell not to interrupt with quite unnecessary affectations of propriety.

Since the Carswells were the only ones present who in Charlotte's mind could possibly be considered suspects, she determined to engage at least one of them in conversation, as the only way in which she might learn something more than sheer observation would teach, which seemed to be precious little. Accordingly she rose to her feet and made her way between the small groups of people exchanging polite enthusiasm for the pianist, until she reached Regina Carswell.

"Good evening, Mrs. Carswell," she said with a smile. "How pleasant to see you again. I hope you are well?"

"Quite well, thank you," Regina replied courteously. "And you, Mrs. Pitt?"

"Oh in the best health, thank you. Isn't it a lovely summer? I cannot recall the weather being quite so agreeable for a long time. But I daresay it is, and the winter simply makes one forget."

"Indeed," Regina agreed. She was about to continue with some pleasant triviality when a rather large lady with diamonds strung across an ample bosom engineered her way past them, lifting her skirts slightly to avoid crushing either her own gown or Regina's. She gave Regina a strange smile, forcedly bright and rather fixed, then turned away quickly and grasped the arm of the woman next to her.

"Poor soul," she murmured in a stage whisper perfectly audible to at least the half dozen people closest to her.

"Poor soul?" her companion said curiously. "Why? Is she not in good health? I hear she has three daughters, but I know she is doing quite well with them."

"Oh I know that," the large lady said, dismissing the subject. "Poor creature," she added in a hiss. "So difficult. Especially when everyone knows."

"Knows what?" Her companion, dressed in a fashionable but particularly repulsive shade of green, was getting irritated by the suspense. "I've heard nothing."

"Oh you will do," the large lady assured her. "No doubt you will do. Far be it from me—of course—"

Regina looked puzzled and embarrassed, a slight tinge of pink in her cheeks.

Charlotte did not know whether to pretend she had not heard the exchange, although it was quite obvious they both had, or to acknowledge it candidly and say something dismissive. She looked at Regina's face to try to judge which would be the kindest. She saw only confusion. Perhaps it had to do with the ridiculous Osmar case. Charlotte chose to assume it did.

"It seems Mr. Horatio Osmar is bent on causing trouble everywhere," she said with an attempt at cheerfulness. "I should put it from your mind, if I were you. A lot of people with little knowledge and even less judgment tend to pass comment. It will all die away as soon as some fresh scandal breaks."

Regina still looked puzzled.

"I fail to see why they should pity me for the matter," she said, opening her eyes wide and smiling rather tentatively. "I am sure my husband behaved with judicial correctness. The police must have failed to produce a proper case against him, or he would not have dismissed it from court. And it has little reflection on me."

"They must be very hard put for scandal to gossip over," Charlotte agreed. "Silly creatures. Don't you find that an astoundingly unbecoming shade of green? I cannot recall when I have seen anything quite so displeasing!"

Regina relaxed into a smile at Charlotte's determination to dismiss the whole episode as meaningless and of no importance whatever.

"Quite horrible," she agreed warmly. "Were her maid of any use at all she would have advised her not to wear it."

"These yellow-greens are most trying, especially to a sallow complexion," Charlotte went on. "I cannot imagine who makes such a gown in the first place. I would have suggested a soft blue, I think. She is something of a plain woman to begin with."

Regina touched her arm gently with her hand. "My dear Mrs. Pitt, it was the large lady who was the real offender. I think it is she we should be picking apart!"

"You are right," Charlotte agreed with enthusiasm. "Where shall we begin? She should never wear diamonds on so large a bosom. All that glitter only draws attention to what is only too obvious anyway."

"Crystals," Regina said with a slight giggle. "They are not diamonds, you know."

"Of course," Charlotte amended. "Crystals. Some muted color, a little darker, would have been best—" She was about to continue when out of the corner of her eye she noticed another woman looking at Regina with a softness that verged on pity, and as soon as she met Charlotte's glance, she looked away quickly, her face pink, as though she had been caught staring at someone improperly dressed, an intrusive and embarrassing thing to do.

Charlotte lost her place in what she had been going to say.

"What is it?" Regina asked, quick to sense her discomfort, however momentary.

"Nothing," Charlotte lied instantly, then, knowing the lie pointless, said, "I saw someone with whom I had a mildly unpleasant altercation. But I had forgotten." She dismissed the second lie as of no matter. And then she rushed on with some other topic of total triviality, a piece of gossip she had picked up from Emily.

She returned to her seat again for the second long piece upon the piano, and enjoyed it rather less. It was a composer she was unfamiliar with, and the work seemed to lack emotion, or perhaps she was simply unable to concentrate. In the interval that followed she made her way to Emily, who had been talking to Fitz.

"You look concerned," Emily said hastily. "Have you found something?"

"I don't think so. What do you know of Horatio Osmar? Is he politically important?" Charlotte whispered back.

Emily's face puckered. "I don't think he matters in the slightest. Why?"

"People seem to be speaking of him."

"What on earth do you mean, 'seem to be'? Are they or not?"

"I don't know. I have seen people giving Mrs. Carswell the oddest looks, and I wondered if it were to do with Horatio Osmar."

"You are talking nonsense," Emily said sharply. "What has Regina Carswell to do with Horatio Osmar?"

"It was Addison Carswell who threw out the case," Charlotte said impatiently. "Thomas seems to think it was quite a corrupt thing to do. It was a perfectly good case."

Emily frowned. "Who was looking at Regina Carswell oddly?"

"I don't know—a fat woman with crystals all over her bosom."

"Lady Arnforth—that's absurd. She doesn't know anything about justice, and cares still less. It must be gossip, probably about love or immorality—or both."

"And Regina Carswell?" Charlotte said dubiously.

"I don't know. Maybe you misunderstood?"

At that point they were rejoined by Fitz, who had stepped aside for a moment to pursue some courtesy with a man known to have considerable political influence. A few moments before the man had been deep in conversation with Jack. Fitz had been attempting to catch up. Now he looked rueful, as if aware he had not succeeded. Only half his attention was on Emily, the rest still dwelt with far more emotion on Fanny Hilliard a few yards away, her face flushed, her eyes bright, her lovely hair piled high and wound with a spray of silk flowers.

A tall young man with bright blue eyes and a receding chin came by gracefully, bowed to Emily and Charlotte with rather more flair than was called for by the occasion, and put his hand on Fitz's shoulder.

"How are you, old fellow?" he said cheerfully. "Going to be our next member of Parliament, are you? Have to be civil to you, what?" He followed the line Fitz had been looking at the moment before, and saw Fanny Hilliard. "Pretty, eh?" he said with admiration. "None of that sort of thing for you, my lad. Not if you are to become a member of Her Majesty's government, in time. Have to be very careful, don't you know. Above suspicion, and all that, what."

Fitz stiffened and a flicker of anger crossed his normally good-natured, almost indolent face.

"Be careful of your tongue, Ferdy. Miss Hilliard's reputation is above question."

Ferdy's face reflected comic disbelief.

"Oh come on, old fellow! She looks quite the lady, I'll grant you. Anyone would be taken in—but she's old Carswell's mistress, and no better than she should be. Adventuress, what. Keeps her in some room somewhere to the south of the river. Fool of a man. You'd think he'd be more discreet—magistrate and all that."

"You're a liar," Fitz said from between gritted teeth, his skin suddenly white. "And if this were not too public a place, and someone else's house, I'd make you eat those words right here!"

"Steady, old man." Ferdy was taken aback. "Sorry if you fancy the gel, but I'm quite definitely right. Got it from an impeccable source; my uncle, Lord Bergholt, what. Quite definitely Carswell's mistress. It's poor Mrs. Carswell I feel sorry for. The old ass should have been more discreet about it. Doesn't matter what you do if you are discreet, but it's damn bad form to embarrass the wife, don't you know. Damn bad." And without waiting for any further reaction from Fitz he moved away, still shaking his head.

Fitz looked stunned, and indeed Charlotte herself felt as if she had been hit in the face by someone she had entirely trusted.

"I don't believe it," Emily gasped. For once she too was at a loss. "What a wicked thing to say." She swung around, about to speak, then saw Charlotte's face.

"Charlotte?"

Charlotte's mind was racing. Pitt had said he had followed Carswell to the south side of the river, and seen him meet with a young woman. He had not said it was Fanny Hilliard. But then why would he? He had not known at that time that she had ever heard of Fanny, let alone knew her.

"Charlotte," Emily said more sharply. "What is it?"

Charlotte collected herself with difficulty, her mind full of anger for the deception, and fury and pain for Fitz.

"Perhaps it is a matter of mistake," Charlotte said feebly, fishing for any excuse. "People do sometimes repeat the most witless things and get them wrong."

But before they could attempt to continue with such hopes, their attention was drawn to the group a few yards away where Fanny herself was standing, almost next to Odelia Morden. Fanny's cheeks were scarlet, burning with misery and humiliation, but in the terrible silence she made no denial, she said absolutely nothing at all.

"Miss Hilliard?" Odelia said quietly. There was no triumph in her, rather a strange bewilderment, as though already she knew her victory would be bitter.

Fanny's eyes lifted slowly and she stared at Fitz, as though everyone else's opinions were trifling things, pinpricks compared with the single great wound of his.

He was stunned, not perhaps by the revelation, the curious and appalled crowd in its glittering dress, but by Fanny's own silence. Her face was agonized, everyone saw it; but she made no denial, no excuse.

For a moment he stood as if he would go to her. The silence prickled so long it seemed the lights wavered; one could hear the crackle of taffeta as women breathed in and out in tight bodices. Far away a maid's hard heels tapped on an uncarpeted passageway.

Then Fanny turned and walked away through the other guests and out into the hall.

Emily took a step forward.

"I'll go," Charlotte said instantly, and before Emily could protest, she pushed past her, almost bumped into the large woman with the crystals, trod on Ferdy's foot as he opened his mouth to say something, and made her way into the hall just in time to see the footman hold Fanny's cloak for her. James Hilliard, white-faced and wretched, stood shifting from one foot to the other a few yards away, obviously shocked and totally at a loss.

Charlotte had no idea what she could possibly say that would redeem any part of the situation, but emotion rather than reason had impelled her out. She went straight to Fanny.

Fanny turned to face her, her cheeks were white and a blinding misery showed in her eyes.

"I apologize," she said in a husky whisper. "I have abused your hospitality."

"I didn't come for an apology," Charlotte said, brushing it aside. "I don't understand, but I can see that you are totally wretched, and I wished to find some way to help . . ."

"You can't! No one can. Please—just let me go, before anyone else comes out here—especially . . ." She could not bring herself to say Fitz's name, but Charlotte knew whom she meant.

"Of course," she conceded. "But please agree to meet me somewhere else, where we can speak alone."

"There is nothing you can do." Fanny's voice rose in desperation, afraid that any moment Fitz might come, or (what would be every bit as bad) Odelia.

"Tomorrow," Charlotte insisted. "Meet me—in the park near Rotten Row."

"I haven't a horse."

"Neither have I. Just be there."

"There is no purpose. There is nothing you can do!"

"Be there. At nine o'clock," Charlotte insisted. "Or I shall come and find you, and I do know where to find you." It was not actually true; she would have to ask Pitt where he had followed Carswell over the river.

"There is nothing . . ." Fanny began again, but James Hilliard was suddenly there, his shock at last melted enough for him to come and defend his sister from what he believed to be harassment.

"Mrs. Pitt—" he began sharply.

"Yes," Fanny agreed. "Tomorrow." She swiveled around to her brother. "Thank you, James. Please take me home."

He glanced quickly at Charlotte with a look of confusion, pain and anger, then put his arm around Fanny's shoulders and escorted her to the door.

Back in the withdrawing room the music had begun again and everyone was seated. They at least appeared to be listening, although underneath the carefully composed expressions imaginations were seething and words were falling over themselves ready to relay the choice piece of scandal the moment they were able. Pages would be scurrying all through society tomorrow morning, and those with telephone instruments would be feeling a magnificent superiority over their more backward friends.

"What did she say?" Emily demanded as soon as Charlotte sat down beside her.

"Nothing," Charlotte replied. "I shall see her tomorrow."

"It's too bad." Emily was considerably upset. "I was becoming very fond of her. And I really hoped she would marry Fitz—even if he is Jack's rival. I know that is not very consistent, but I like him."

"It is not in the least inconsistent," Charlotte said with a sudden hard insight. "No matter how much you like Fitz and Fanny, and I accept that you do, it is nothing compared with your love for Jack, and your belief that he will make an excellent member for Parliament. And if Fitz jilts Odelia for Fanny, even if her reputation is immaculate, it will be one of the very few mistakes that could cost him his chance of selection." She saw Emily's look of consternation, but continued anyway. "I don't believe for a moment you would, or could, cause that to happen, but don't tell me you will grieve if Fitz brings it upon himself."

Emily looked uncomfortable. "Of course I would not bring it about," she defended herself, but there was no outrage in her voice. "If I hope for it for Fitz and Fanny, it is because I know that love in a marriage is far more important than this particular opportunity for political candidacy. Really Charlotte, I am not nearly so conniving as you seem to think."

Charlotte smiled at her without withdrawing a word, then faced forward and gave her attention to the music.

The morning was bright with sunshine and a brisk, clean wind, and Charlotte was glad of a light cloak as she stood at the southern end of Rotten Row, the long earthen track beneath the trees stretching from the Royal Albert Memorial to Hyde Park Corner where ladies of the fashionable world, both of excellent reputation and of the very worst, rode on horseback to parade their skills, their outfits, and their personal charms.

As Charlotte waited a small group passed close to her, all dressed in precisely the clothes required by custom, tight-waisted jackets, some with high necks and beautiful pins of horse heads or stirrups at the collar, one with reveres to her jacket and a silver hunting horn pin in her dazzlingly white cravat.

Of course they all wore long riding gloves and carried crops with ornamented handles; she saw one of carved horn, and the light caught the head of another and shone silver for a bright moment.

Then the riders turned and set off at a canter, passing another group going in the opposite direction. The leader changed hands with her reins and crop in order to touch hands with her acquaintance in greeting, rather a daring maneuver at such a speed. Another leaned forward to pat her horse's neck, another quite unnecessary gesture performed solely to display the rider's skill.

Charlotte smiled to herself and walked a few paces to keep warm.

When at last she saw Fanny about twenty yards away, coming

from the Kensington Road, she thought for a moment it could not be her. She looked so unlike her previous self; the joy was emptied out of her, the grace gone from her step, all the vividness and life from her face. Whatever she had done, and why she had done it, all Charlotte could feel for her was a wrenching pity.

She went over to her quickly, almost at a run, taking the younger woman's hand in hers and holding it tightly.

"I don't know why you've come," Fanny said in a voice so husky Charlotte knew in a moment she had been weeping so long her throat ached. She could remember the same pain long ago, over other loves before Pitt, rejections that hurt abominably at the time, even though their faces were long faded from her memory now.

"I want to know the truth," she said simply. "Maybe there is something that can be done—and if there isn't, then I am still your friend."

The tears spilled down Fanny's cheeks as though the kindness were more than she could bear. She had steeled herself against condemnation, but this caught her unguarded.

For several seconds she fought to master herself.

Charlotte pulled out a wholly inadequate handkerchief and gave it to her, then hunted for another, and when she found it, passed that over too.

Fanny blew her nose and sniffed fiercely. It was extremely inelegant.

"Do you love Mr. Carswell?" Charlotte asked.

A ghost of a smile crossed Fanny's face, the tears brimmed over and slid unregarded down her cheeks. Her eyes were red rimmed, her skin blotched and she was barely recognizable as the glowingly pretty girl Charlotte had first seen, but it was of no importance now.

"Yes," she said hesitantly, then with a choking laugh. "Yes— I do."

Charlotte was taken aback, but she had committed herself too far to retreat.

"I would have sworn you were in love with Fitz."

"I am." Fanny sniffed. "I am—" She swallowed convulsively and reached for the sodden handkerchief again.

Trying to be practical, Charlotte reached into her reticule for yet another handkerchief and failed to find one. Resenting the extravagance, but feeling Fanny's pain too sharply to deny it, she fished very discreetly under her skirts and tore off a strip of her cotton petticoat.

"Blow your nose," she ordered. "And then explain yourself." She felt like Vespasia as she said it. Someone had to take command of the situation.

Fanny was too weary and too wretched to fight anymore.

"I love them both—quite differently," she said haltingly, in little more than a whisper.

"That's nonsense," Charlotte said briskly. "Unless you are just plain silly. You cannot for a moment imagine you can have the position of financial help from a man like Addison Carswell, deceiving his wife, who is a very nice woman and does not deserve it, and at the same time say you love Fitz."

"I do!" Fanny looked desperate, as if her only friend were threatening to abandon her. She blushed hard and made some last terrible decision. "Not the way you think. Addison Carswell is my father."

For a moment Charlotte was stunned. Then gradually a whole new picture took shape.

"Oh! You are illegitimate? I'm so sorry! How dreadfully painful for you."

"No I'm not. That is the whole point." Now that Fanny had at last committed herself to telling the truth, she was eager to tell it all. "Papa was married to my mother first—that is the whole awful thing of it." She looked at Charlotte with anguished eyes.

"Then your mother is dead?"

"No." It was little more than a whisper.

"Divorced?" Charlotte was amazed. Divorce was so terribly rare, and a fearful scandal. Divorced women were worse than dead in society. A man put his wife away only for the most heinous of reasons, like flagrant adultery. Mere disagreeability he ignored, and took a more pleasant mistress, spending only what time was absolutely necessary in his home, but continuing to provide for his wife, and whatever children there were, and keeping his social status intact. Such arrangements were kept discreet, and well understood. A woman only put her husband away if he deserted her, or beat her beyond anything even remotely reasonable. A little merited discipline was expected. And of course adultery was no reason for divorce, if committed by the man.

"No." Fanny's voice was sunk to a whisper.

"Then—I don't understand." Charlotte was totally confused.

"That's it," Fanny said desperately. "There was no divorce. My mother and father are still married."

"But—but what about Mrs. Carswell? I mean—Regina . . ." Suddenly Charlotte saw the awful truth. "Oh! You mean—you mean she is not married at all? Does she—?"

"No—no, she doesn't know," Fanny said quickly. "That is why I would not tell them the truth last night. That is why we neither of us can. Her marriage is bigamous. And her daughters—and her son—are bastards."

"Oh my heavens!" Charlotte was aghast. "Oh you poor creature."

"I can't betray him," Fanny said in anguish. "It would ruin him, and in so many ways, more terrible than that, it would ruin them too. Did you see Mabel with that young man yesterday evening? What chance would she have of marrying him—or anyone—if people knew?"

"None," Charlotte admitted. "But what about you?" Then she wished she had not said it. Fanny knew only too well what her future was now. "I'm sorry," Charlotte said quickly.

"I know." Fanny's hands closed around hers even more tightly. "Believe me, I've thought of it all since last night. I suppose I should have realized it would come out—I just thought it was all secret. Papa was so careful. He came to see me so very secretly. I don't know who found out, or how. But perhaps it was bound to have happened one day."

"Your brother? He seemed last night not to know."

"He didn't. He is younger than I and had no memory of Papa. Hilliard is my mother's maiden name, and she used that after—after they separated. She never told James the truth, and I saw no point to it. I did not tell him that in the last two years I have seen Papa again. When Mama became ill—very ill, not only in her body but in her mind, we needed help. I went and found Papa and told him of our state. He was full of sympathy, and perhaps a little guilt." She winced. "And he helped immediately. He provided an allowance for Mama and used his influence to get James a good position in the City. Of course, James does not know that." She smiled very slightly. "He was so very fond of me, so gentle and so nice to be with, I never once thought it was other than affection. I still don't."

"But you did not tell your brother?"

"No—nor will I now. He—he might betray Papa—to defend me—and that is something I am not prepared to do."

"That is very fine of you," Charlotte said with instant admiration.

Fanny smiled wanly. "It is also realistic. I love Papa; and I could not live with myself if I ruined his present family and brought such terrible misery upon them. But even if I did, who would admire me for it? People might see some justice in it—but justice is not what I want. I want Fitz—and that I cannot have. He would not love me for that, and I cannot tell him the truth." Again her eyes filled quite suddenly with tears and she turned away for a moment to regain her self-mastery.

This time Charlotte permitted her the dignity of silence, then gently put her hand on Fanny's arm.

"I would be very happy if you would permit me to be your friend," she said sincerely. "For the little that is worth. That is, if when you know me better, the things you do not know at the moment, you wish it."

Fanny put her other hand up and clasped Charlotte's fingers tightly.

"Please," she whispered huskily.

In his Bow Street office Micah Drummond paced the floor from the closed door to the window overlooking the hot, busy street, and back again, door to window, and again, too restless to sit. He was furious over the Osmar case. He poured all his frustration and unhappiness into his rage that this wretched man should call on his past friendships with ministers of state in order to make the courts ridiculous and impugn the honesty of the police. He had no doubt that it was done by the influence of the Inner Circle. Osmar had no importance himself. The fact that it was the brotherhood added to his own sense of guilt that he was part of it, and his growing fear as to its power and its purpose.

He was halfway facing the window when there was a sharp rap on the door. He spun around as if he had been caught in some wrongful act.

"Yes?"

The door opened and Urban came in. He was looking pleased, although there was still a shadow of irritation over his tight, amused smile.

"What is it?" Drummond said less courteously than usual.

Urban disregarded his manner; he was too full of his own news.

"We won," he said simply.

Drummond had not the slightest idea what he meant. "Won what?" he said irritably.

Urban was crestfallen, much of the triumph drained from his face.

"The case over Osmar."

"We can't have." Drummond was still confused. "It's already been dismissed!"

"Not the prosecution," Urban corrected with disappointed patience. "The case against the newspapers for slandering us over Latimer's interrogation of Beulah Giles."

"Oh!" Suddenly it came back to Drummond. He should have known straightaway; the issue had certainly been serious enough. He looked at Urban now and tried to make up for his omission. He forced his features into an expression of pleasure. "Thank heaven for that. I didn't think it was due for trial for months yet, surely?"

"It isn't," Urban agreed, mollified. "They settled out of court, paid us damages—and retracted all the charges of brutality."

"Then what was the reservation I saw in your face when you came in?" Drummond asked. "Were the damages poor?"

"No—they were excellent, and so they should be. It was a damned comprehensive slander, and they misquoted us, and even themselves," Urban replied heatedly. "It was a hysterical and completely irresponsible piece of journalism, and the other papers that picked it up didn't even bother to check their facts."

Drummond waited, his eyes wide.

Urban smiled, at himself. "That swine Osmar is still free to prance around saying he is innocent and without a stain on his character." He pushed his hands into his pockets. "Which doesn't matter in that he's hardly a major criminal, simply an elderly ass who fornicates in the public parks." His face darkened and his voice took on a graver note. "But he's also a man who uses personal influence and the obligations of past office to escape the consequences of acts he expects other people to answer to, if they are caught. He uses privilege to set the law aside when it suits him—and that is about as serious a crime against society as there can be. In some ways it's worse than murder." And with those passionate words he turned on his heel and went out, closing the door very quietly behind him. Drummond was left shaken so profoundly he stood in the middle of the floor with the sunlight shining around him and felt cold, the sounds of the street below like insects far away, his mind whirling.

By five o'clock he had determined what he must do, and half past nine saw him in a hansom cab on his way to Belgravia. He alighted in Belgrave Square and presented himself at number 21. The footman admitted him without question or comment except to tell him that Lord Byam had not yet returned home, but was expected.

"I'll wait," Drummond said without hesitation.

"Shall I inform Lady Byam you are here, sir?" the footman asked as he showed him not into the morning room, but into the library.

"It would be civil, but it is Lord Byam I wish to speak with," Drummond replied, walking past the man into the calm room lit with the late sun reflected in dappled patterns from the leaves at the window.

"Yes sir," the footman accepted expressionlessly. "May I bring you some refreshment? A whiskey, perhaps, or a brandy and soda, sir?"

"No thank you." Drummond felt awkward about accepting the hospitality of a man from whom he had come determined to demand some further explanation of his deepest trouble and the tragedy and fears arising from it.

"Very good, sir." The footman withdrew, closing the door behind him.

Drummond was too tense to sit. Over and over he had prepared in his mind what he would say, but still it was unsatisfactory. One moment it seemed too deferential, not direct enough, the next too shrill, as if he himself were frightened and unsure.

He was still wrestling with it and growing more and more torn with doubts, when five minutes later the door opened almost silently and Eleanor came in. She was dressed in soft blue-gray, the exact color of her eyes. The neckline plunged deeply and was filled with lace of a softer shade, and she wore two ropes of pearls almost to her waist. For the first instant he could only think how lovely she was. Standing in the doorway, her face a little flushed, one hand still on the knob, she was warm, elegant, graceful, everything that a man loved in a woman, everything that was gentle and strong, vulnerable and tender.

Then he realized it was a very formal gown, and he was terrified she was preparing to dine out, or to receive guests. This would mean when Byam arrived he would be in a hurry, and have no time for an extended interview, however pressing Drummond felt the matter. Eleanor must have come to explain this to him, and suggest he call another day.

"Mr. Drummond," she said urgently, closing the door behind her. "Sholto will not be here for at least half an hour. May I speak with you?" She was obviously agitated and in some distress. Her color was high and her eyes held his with an intensity that disturbed him profoundly.

"Of course."

She came towards him until they were both standing in the center of the floor, but she too seemed unable to sit.

"Has something—" she began, then stopped. She looked at him very directly. "Has something new happened in the case? Is that why you have come?"

For a wild moment he thought she was going to ask if he had come to arrest Byam. Had the thought entered her mind that Byam might be guilty? Or was it simply fear, and no confidence in justice?

"Nothing decisive," he answered. "And—nothing to implicate Lord Byam."

"Mr. Drummond—" She breathed in deeply. He could see the light on her pearls as her breast rose and fell. "Mr. Drummond, are you telling me the truth, or trying to shield me from a pain which I will eventually have to know?"

"I am telling you the truth," he said steadily. "I have come because I need to know more, not because I already know it."

She made as if to press him further, then changed her mind and moved away towards the mantelpiece, her back to him. There was no fire in the grate, the evening was too warm, but she stood next to it as if there were.

"You have come very opportunely," she said in a small voice, looking down at the brass fire tongs with their finely wrought handles. "There are things I—I need to tell you."

He waited. He longed to be able to help her, but there was nothing he could have done, even had propriety allowed.

She stayed motionless, still staring at the tongs.

"I have learned what the quarrel was which I overheard," she went on. Her face was sad and frightened. "I discovered by accident—at the dinner table—from a young man named Valerius. In the office he holds in the Treasury Sholto has to do with foreign loans to certain countries in the empire. He has the authority to permit them or refuse. He has always been very committed to giving whatever assistance is possible. In one instance he has quite suddenly and unaccountably reversed years of policy—" She stopped and at last looked up at him, her eyes darkly troubled.

Emotions raged through him, fury at his impotence to help her. He was bound by inability, convention, his own shyness and uncertainty. He loved her, that should be admitted; it was ridiculous to go on calling it by any other name. But for him to say anything, even to allow her to know it unspoken, would be inexcusable. She was desperately vulnerable. Her husband stood in jeopardy of his life and she had come to the one person who might be able to save him; she had come trusting. To abuse that trust because of his own passion would be despicable, the lowest and most vile of acts. His face scalded hot at even the thought of it.

And he felt an impossible anger with Byam himself, for the pain and the fear he was causing her, for his failure to explain, for having come to Drummond in the first place and involved him in this dilemma with all its confusion and distress.

And as great as any of these burned an overwhelming guilt because he had been asked by a brother, in trust, to help him when he was in desperate need—and he had failed to do so. Instead he had fallen in love with the man's wife.

He was also afraid, deeply and horribly afraid. What if Byam was guilty? What if Byam brought the pressure of the Inner Circle on Drummond to conceal that guilt? And if they were as ruthless as Pitt seemed to think, that was not an impossibility. How would he face Eleanor? He could not do it—how would he explain that to her? He would sound pompous, selfish, cowardly. She would despise him, and how that would hurt. But what was the alternative? To conceal murder, and perhaps allow an innocent man to be hanged for it, or at best, if it was unprovable, his reputation and career to be ruined.

Pitt would despise him for that. He would know. Pitt would always know in the end. And that too would hurt. In its own way it would hurt as much as any rejection by Eleanor. She might hate him, but she at least would know it was because he obeyed a higher honor. With Pitt it would be because he had betrayed himself and sunk to a level where Pitt could only despise him.

And how would the Inner Circle punish him? They would—of that he now had no doubt.

How could he have been so gullible, so naive and incredibly, blindly stupid? Because he had been flattered, thought about it too little, and seen only what he wanted to see, without thinking deeply or looking below the surface. Self-disgust added to the furor in his mind.

He must concentrate.

Eleanor was looking at him with clear, gray eyes, waiting for him to give some sensible, strong answer. What could he say? He must stop indulging in passions and try to concentrate his brain.

"Are you sure there is no good political reason for such a reversal?" he asked, seeking for time to clear his head and sort emotion from reason.

"Yes I am sure," she said unhappily. "That is what he quarreled with Sir John about. Had there been a political reason he would have told him of it, and Sir John would still have been disappointed, but he would have understood. They would not have parted with ill feeling. They have been friends and political allies for too long."

He named the only other cause he dared, and it had to be dismissed.

"And you are certain he has no personal motive, no financial one, for his decision." Then he feared she might think he believed Byam dishonest, and hurried on. "I say so only to dismiss it. It could not be that Sir John thought such a thing?"

"No." Her brows furrowed. "I cannot imagine that he did." There was a brief lift of hope in her voice, just for a moment. Ugly as the thought was, it was still better than the other one which lay like a stone in her mind. Then the lightness faded again. "No, Sholto has never had personal interests that would jeopardize his political impartiality. It would be less than totally honest in the best of circumstances, and in the worst might easily make his situation impossible." She looked away, out through the window at the leaves against the light. "His personal fortune comes from family estates in Huntingdonshire, and large holdings in Wales and Ireland. He has never taken any part in banking or commerce, and certainly not in importing or exporting."

"I see."

She lowered her eyes and her expression tightened again as though she was expecting a blow, perhaps self-inflicted, but only before fate could do it instead.

"No, Mr. Drummond, there is no easy, honorable answer that I can find, and believe me, I have racked my brain looking. And—and apart from all the explanations reason might try, the worst thing is that Sholto is so changed in himself." Suddenly she looked up and met his eyes so intensely and with such undisguised emotion he felt as if she had touched him physically. "He is afraid, he is every bit as afraid as I am. The only difference is that he knows what it is he fears, and I am only plagued by guesses."

There was no way to avoid it and retain a shred of honesty, and honesty mattered to him desperately where she was concerned. It was the one closeness permitted.

He forced out the words.

"What are your guesses?"

Her voice was full of pain. "That someone else has the letter and Weems's notes of Sholto's payments to him, and he is blackmailing him, just as Weems did. It must be the murderer, mustn't it?"

He could not deny it. "I can think of no one else."

She looked away again. "Why won't he tell me? That is what I cannot understand. I know all about Laura Anstiss, he has nothing to hide. It was foolish perhaps, a misjudgment of youth, but if he told me now that he is still being blackmailed, what is there to lose? I never blamed him for it." She moved her foot along the smooth brass fender as if fidgeting gave her some ease. "I wondered if in some way he was still defending Frederick Anstiss. Friendship can tie you so hard—and so close—and he still feels guilty . . ." She looked at him, puckering her brows. "But I don't see how, do you? If he told you that there was another blackmailer now, it would surely help your investigation, wouldn't it? It would at least be knowledge—and how would that hurt Frederick? He already knows more than we do about Laura's death. He saw her and he knew she was obsessed with Sholto—temporarily mad—however you wish to name it."

"I don't know," he admitted. "I don't understand. But sometimes old guilt, however unreasonable, can make us defend people . . ." He tailed off. It was not necessary to say all this. She knew it, and it availed little. It did not answer her fear.

"Do you believe he knows who it is?" He asked what they were both dreading.

She winced but did not look away.

"I have thought he might. And there is only one reason he would not tell you." Her voice sank even lower. "Because he means to confront the man himself. Mr. Drummond, I am so afraid he will. And that one of them will not live."

He reached for her without thinking of propriety or conscience, only of her anguish. He held her hands in his own.

"My dear. You must not think such a thing. It is ridiculous. If Lord Byam knows who it is, he will tell me and we will arrest the man quietly, discreetly, and he will have no opportunity to speak to anyone before his trial. And by then we will have found a way to make it in his own interests to be silent."

"Can you?" she whispered.

"Of course." He held her hands very gently. "That is why he called me in the beginning," he went on. "He would not be so hysterical now as to turn to violence himself. He never did harm Weems—he paid the miserable devil. Now when we know about Laura Anstiss's death, and there is Weems's murder to solve, he has even less reason to face the man personally. If he were violent, believe me, he would have acted long ago, not now."

There was no answering hope in her eyes. In fact she looked even more wretched with fear.

"Eleanor!" He was unaware of having used her name. "Eleanor—" He was about to ask what troubled her so terribly, when the answer came too glaringly to his mind. She had admitted the possibility that Byam himself had murdered Weems, and the blackmail now was not over anything so simple and relatively innocent as Laura Anstiss's death and his part in it. This was a blackmail he could not confess to Drummond and ask his help. Someone had seen him, someone knew. Or perhaps Weems had taken even more precautions than he had said, and somehow his protector was now avenging him.

"It is possible—isn't it?" she whispered, her face white. Then she lowered her eyes, slipping her hands out of his and clasping them together. "God forgive me for even having let such a thought into my mind."

He struggled through emotion for a thread of reason, something to cling onto to help him, and to help himself from taking her in his arms and holding her, abusing her trust and her distress. He forced the thought from him and let go of her hands, stepping back. Then he saw the sudden bleakness in her face.

"You find me disloyal," she said with hopelessness. "I cannot blame you."

"No. My dear—I—" He floundered, not knowing what to say, how to redeem himself without telling her the impossible truth. He stared helplessly.

She looked back at him, her eyes widening, then filling with wonder.

He blushed scarlet, knowing he had betrayed himself. There

were no possible words, no excuses. All he could do was assure her he would take no advantage. But how to do that and be believed, and retain some shred of her respect . . .

He looked at her, his face burning.

She was smiling.

Very gently she took his hand; her fingers were warm. She held it for a moment, then let it go.

He felt wildly close to her, as if she had kissed him, but sweeter than that, less the passion of an instant, longer lasting, and without haste or pity. He searched her eyes, and saw in them no fear, no fear at all, a world of regret, but no blame. Was it possible? He dared not think it. It must be thrust from his mind.

"There—there are other reasons," he began hesitantly. "Things to think of . . ." He went on, fumbling for a thread of continued, sensible thought. "If he had killed Weems, why did he not take the letter then—and the papers? If he could not find them, surely he would not have told us but simply taken the chance that we would not either. After all, he knew they were there and would look for them; we did not even know of their existence."

"Perhaps he did take them." She was playing devil's advocate because it must be done. "But he did not know of this other. person, if he exists, the one Weems gave a second copy to."

"That still does not make any sense," he answered with gathering conviction. "If he thought he had all the evidence pointing to him, he would not have sent for me. We would never have connected him with Weems, why on earth should we? And anyway, what purpose did it serve for Weems's mysterious other person to have evidence, if no one knew of it? I cannot see Weems as a man who wished his death avenged, but it makes every sense that he would create a safeguard that his life should not be taken. And that served only so long as every person who was a danger to him knew of its existence, and that it would be used if Weems came to any harm."

"Perhaps he did not believe Sholto any danger to him."

"Then why give a set of papers to this friend? And why keep the one set himself, which we know he did because Lord Byam told us of it?"

"Then if you did not find them, where are they?" she asked.

He was confounded. "I don't know. I can only presume the murderer took them. Although why he did not take the other list as well I don't understand."

"What other list?" Her dark brow puckered.

It was an error, but there was no way of retrieving it, and he was not even sure he wanted to. He hated keeping so much from her.

"Oh—of course, you don't know of that. There was a list of other people of better financial circumstances who were down as having borrowed large amounts—all of whom deny it."

Her eyes widened. "Were they blackmailed as well?"

"It seems so."

"And—and are they still being blackmailed?" Now there was a sharper fear in her and he understood it instantly.

He could not answer.

"No—" She breathed out. "You don't need to say it, it is there in your face. Sholto is the only one."

The silence lay between them. There was no need for either to spell out the reasoning. The only answer to all the questions pounding in their heads was that Byam had killed Weems, and had been seen by someone else, who was now blackmailing him, not over Laura Anstiss's death, but over the murder of Weems. And if only Byam knew who it was, then he might very easily murder him too. Why not; he had nothing else to lose, and freedom to win. It explained everything—it was the one possibility which did explain everything.

They were still standing facing each other when they heard the outside door open and the butler's voice welcoming Lord Byam.

Eleanor closed her eyes for a moment as if she had been struck, then stepped back from Drummond and went to the door. She met his eyes for an instant, then turned the latch and went out into the hall, leaving the door ajar. Drummond heard her voice plainly.

"Good evening, Sholto."

"Good evening, my dear." The clarity of his tone, the immediacy of it, brought his presence to Drummond more sharply than he would have thought possible. They had been speaking about him and the reality of his being, his mind, his intelligence, his volition had almost receded into an impersonal problem. Hearing his voice brought him back with a vividness that was like a shock of icy water.

"Mr. Drummond is here to see you," Eleanor went on. Perhaps they were simply the words anyone would have used, but they also sounded like a kind of warning, before he could say anything else, speak of his day, expose any anxieties or fears.

"Micah Drummond?" He sounded surprised. "Did he say what for?"

"No . . ."

"You hesitated."

"Did I? It is because I fear it cannot be good. If he had arrested someone he would have told me."

"Then I had better see him." Was his voice as edgy as Drummond thought? Was there fear in it, or simply irritation that a man he knew so slightly should have called at such an inconvenient hour? "Where is he?"

"In the library."

He made no answer that Drummond could hear. The next moment his footsteps sounded sharply across the flagged floor and the door swung open and he was there.

"I believe you called to see me." He closed the door behind him. He did not offer any refreshment or exchange the usual trivialities. Either he assumed Eleanor had already done so, or else he considered them irrelevant.

Drummond looked at him. He was pale and there were dark smudges of sleeplessness under his eyes. He was immaculately dressed, as always, but there was an air of distraction about him and it was all too obvious that the tension Eleanor had spoken of was in him. Every movement was tight, awkward, his muscles stiff, his attention strained.

"Yes," Drummond agreed, anger at the man evaporating, and now strongly mixed with pity. For the moment the fact that he was Eleanor's husband, and therefore the man who stood irrevocably between him and the woman he now loved, was immaterial, so unimportant as to have vanished from his thoughts.

"Do I take it that there have been new events, or discoveries?" Byam came across the room and stood close to the mantel, where Eleanor had been so shortly before.

"There are new questions," Drummond equivocated. He must not allow Byam to realize that Eleanor had confided in him. He could only view it as a kind of betrayal, even if he understood it as anxiety for him and a belief that she could help.

"Indeed?" Byam's black brows rose. "Then you had better ask them, since it is what you have come for. Although I cannot think of anything I have not already told you."

Drummond began with what he had intended to say before Eleanor had spoken to him.

"It regards that circle of which we are both members."

Byam's face tightened. "I hardly think this is the time, or the place, to discuss the business of the Circle—"

"You called me here in the name of the Circle," Drummond interrupted. "Therefore they are already included in anything we do."

Byam winced, as though what Drummond had said were in bad taste.

"I call on you as a brother in that circle to which we both belong, to help me in a certain matter." Drummond's own voice hardened and he saw Byam's look of astonishment, then extraordinary relief. It was short-lived. As soon as Drummond continued it disappeared. "In the matter of Horatio Osmar."

"Horatio Osmar? I don't know the man. He is not one of the same 'ring' as I."

"Nevertheless you know that he is a brother?" Drummond pressed.

"I do. Surely you don't wish something from him? The man is disgraced. Not openly, I grant, but we all know perfectly well he was guilty of behaving like a fool, and of being caught at it."

"And of asking the brotherhood to exercise favor in extricating him, and attempting to impugn the police in the process."

"That was unnecessary," Byam said with irritation. "He got out of the charge. He should have left it at that. Accusing the police of perjury was gratuitous. The man is a complete outsider."

"Indeed," Drummond agreed with feeling. "Nevertheless, the brotherhood assisted him in bringing the charge. Questions were raised in the House, and the Home Secretary himself set certain wheels in motion."

"I am aware of that. I was in the House at the time. I thought he was a fool then, but there was nothing I could do about it."

"Of course not." Drummond was watching him closely. The

subject did not distress him, but the underlying fear was only too apparent. His whole body was so stiff Drummond ached watching him. And he was abominably tired, as if he had not slept with any ease for weeks.

"Well?" Byam said with rising impatience. "What is it you want of me? It is not my concern."

"If the brotherhood will respond to Osmar's trivial and tedious case by raising questions in the House," Drummond answered, "and impugning the honesty of the police as they have done, what latitude do they have in matters of individual honor and integrity where more serious matters are involved?"

"I don't understand you." Byam's voice was getting sharper. "For heaven's sake, man, be plain!"

Drummond took a breath and met Byam's hollow eyes.

"If I discover incriminating evidence against you, will the brotherhood defend you against the police, and will it expect me to do the same?"

Byam was white as a ghost. He stared at Drummond as if he could scarcely believe him.

Drummond waited.

Byam spoke with difficulty, his voice catching in his throat.

"I—I have never thought in the matter. It will not arise—dangerous evidence perhaps, but not incriminating. I did not kill Weems." He seemed about to add something, then changed his mind and stood silently facing Drummond.

"Then why have you changed your decision about African financing?" Drummond asked.

Byam seemed so stunned, so deathly white, Drummond was afraid for a moment he was going to pass out. The dusk was growing in the room. The last of the sun's rays had faded away from the ceiling and now the faintly luminous air had gone. A bird sang in the branches beyond the window.

"How do you know that?" Byam said at last.

"I heard of it through a young man called Valerius." It was not a lie exactly, even if it was by intent.

Byam was too shocked for surprise or interest.

"Peter Valerius? He came and told you? Why, for God's sake? It is of no concern to you."

"Not directly," Drummond answered. "He told someone, who told me."

"Who?"

"I am not at liberty to say."

Byam turned away, weary, hiding his face and staring at the shelf of books and the corner.

"I suppose it hardly matters. It involves issues you are not aware of—trade, money . . ."

"Blackmail?"

Byam froze. The relief that had been in his face an instant before fled utterly. His body jerked as if he had been struck.

"Was it?" Drummond said very quietly, almost gently. "Has someone else found the papers Weems left? Byam, do you know who killed Weems?"

"No! No I don't!" It was a cry full of pain and despair. "Dear God I don't know. I have no idea at all."

"But whoever it is has Weems's notes, and is blackmailing you still?"

Byam's shoulders relaxed a fraction and he turned around, his eyes black in the last light through the window, a wraith of a smile on his lips, a smile of pain and self-mockery, as if he knew some terrible joke against himself.

"No—no. Weems's notes seem to have vanished into the air. I am beginning to think he never actually made any, he simply said he had to protect himself. Unnecessarily—I would never have attacked him physically, or any other way. The worst I would have done was tell him to go to hell. Someone else killed him, and I have not even the shred of an idea who."

"And the change of mind over the African money?"

Byam's face was still white. "The brotherhood," he said with stiff lips. "It is a favor for them. I cannot tell you why. It concerns many issues, international finance, risk, political situations I am not at liberty to discuss." His words were a mockery of Drummond's earlier ones, but there was no jeering in them, no triumph.

"They would ask that of you, knowing how you feel, your reputation in the matter, your conscience?" Drummond was horrified, although now he had no surprise left. "That is monstrous. What would happen to you if you refused them?"

There was no smile on Byam's face, only bleak, humorless despair.

"I don't know, and I am not in a position to put it to the test."

"But your honor," Drummond said involuntarily. "The agony of your own conscience. Do they imagine they have purchased your soul with some idiotic ritual oath? For God's sake, man, tell them to go to the devil! Not a great journey, if they would press you to act against your conscience in such a manner."

Byam looked away from him. "I cannot," he said in a level, hopeless voice. "There is much that you do not understand. They explained to me other reasons. It is not as much against my conscience as you believe, simply against my past record of belief, and what people expect of me. There are other factors—things I did not know of before . . ."

But Drummond did not believe him. He was overwhelmed with pity, and revulsion—and a terrible, dark fear of the circle he had entered so blindly so many years ago. Pitt had thought it evil, and he had barely scraped the surface. Why did a gamekeeper's son like Pitt have so infinitely more understanding of evil and its smiling, promising faces?

He felt cold throughout his body.

"I'm sorry," he said futilely, not knowing what he meant, simply that he was filled with a dragging heaviness and a sense of tragedy to come, and guilt.

He walked to the hall door and opened it.

"Thank you for your candor."

Byam looked up, his eyes black with pain, like a cornered creature. He said nothing.

Drummond went out and closed the door. In the hallway the butler handed him his cloak, hat and stick, then opened the door for him. He went out into the balmy air of the evening, oblivious to its sweetness.

CHAPTER
TEN

It was at a garden party, lawns, flower beds and dappled shade, parlormaids and footmen carrying trays of chilled champagne, women with parasols, that Charlotte observed the next event connected with Jack's pursuit of selection as candidate for Parliament. She had gone hoping to see something more of Lord Byam, but as it transpired neither he nor Lady Byam was present, although they had been expected. It was a glorious afternoon, if a trifle warm, and everyone was greatly involved in discussing the Eton and Harrow cricket match which was held annually between the two outstanding private schools for boys of excellent family.

The other great topic of conversation was the forthcoming regatta to be held at Henley, as usual. There was intense speculation as to who would win the cricket match, as many of the gentlemen had attended either one school or the other, and emotions were running high.

"My dear fellow," one elegantly dressed man said, leaning a little on his cane and staring at his companion, his top hat an inch or two askew. "The fact that Eton won last year is nothing whatsoever to go by. Hackfield was the best bat they ever had, and he has left and gone up to Cambridge. The whole side will disintegrate without him, don't you know."

They were standing beside a bed of delphiniums.

"Balderdash." His friend smiled indulgently, and stepped to one side to allow a lady in a large hat to pass by. The feather in its brim was touching his shoulder, but she was oblivious of it, being totally occupied gazing through her eyelashes at someone a few yards in the opposite direction. "Absolute tommyrot," the man continued. "Hackfield was merely the most showy. Nimmons was the real strength."

"Nimmons." The man in the top hat was patronizingly amused. "Scored a mere twenty runs, as I recall."

"Your recollection is colored by your desires, not to mention your loyalty." His friend was gently pleased with himself. "Twenty runs, and bowled out five of your side—for a total of thirty-three. And he's still very much there this year. Doesn't go up till 'ninety-one."

"Because he's a fool." But his face clouded as memory returned. Absentmindedly he put his empty goblet on the tray of an attendant footman and took a fresh one.

"Not with a ball in his hand, old chap—not with a ball," his companion retorted.

Charlotte could imagine the summer afternoon, the crowd sitting on benches or walking on the grass, the players all in white, the crack of leather on willow as the bat struck the ball, the cheering, the sun in the eye and in the face, the long lazy day, excited voices of boys calling out, cucumber sandwiches for tea. It was pleasant to think about, but she had no real wish to go. Her thoughts were filled with darker, more urgent matters. And it was part of a world she had never really belonged to, and in which Pitt, and that mattered more, had no place. It did cross her mind to wonder for an instant if he had played cricket as a boy. She could imagine it, not at a great school founded centuries ago and steeped in tradition, but on the village green, perhaps with a duck pond, and old men sitting outside the inn, and a dog or two lying in the sun.

She saw Regina Carswell with two of her daughters. The third, whom Charlotte had seen previously so obviously attracted to the young man at the musical soiree, was again speaking with him. This time she was walking by his side and involved in a murmured conversation of smiles and glances, and very considerable tenderness. It was such that in the present society and circumstances it was tantamount to a statement of intent. It would have to be a very remarkable incident now to alter the inevitable course.

Charlotte smiled, happy for her.

Beside her, Emily was equally indulgent. She had been lonely far too recently not to have a very real sympathy for the state.

"Is Jack going to join the secret society?" Charlotte asked abruptly.

Emily looked at her with a frown as a young woman passed by them holding a dish of strawberries and giggling at her companion, a short man in a military uniform who moved with a definite swagger.

"Why on earth did Miss Carswell make you think of that?" she asked.

"Because she is so obviously happy, and so are you," Charlotte continued. "And I wish more than almost anything that you should remain so."

Emily smiled at her warmly. "I love you for it, but if you think my happiness depends upon Jack being selected to stand for Parliament, you are mistaken." A shadow crossed her face. "I would have expected you to know me better. I admit I used to be ambitious socially, and I still get pleasure and amusement from it, but it is no more than that, I promise you. It is not my happiness." She tweaked her skirt off the grass to stop it being trodden on by a shortsighted gentleman with a cane. "I want Jack to succeed at something, of course. I love him, and how could he be happy if he whiled away his time in pursuits of no purpose? But if he does not get this nomination, there will be others."

"Good," Charlotte responded with emotion. "Because I feel very strongly indeed that he should not join any society whose membership is secret, and that requires oaths of loyalty that rob him of any of his freedom of conscience. Thomas has some knowledge of at least one of the societies in London, and it is very dangerous indeed, and very powerful." She became even more grave, determined that Emily should believe her. "Emily, do everything within your power to dissuade him, even if it causes a quarrel. It would be a small price to pay to keep him from such a group."

Emily stood still, turning to face Charlotte.

"You know something of importance that you are not telling me. I imagine it is to do with the murder of the usurer. I think you had better tell me now."

Charlotte looked at Emily's steady blue eyes. If she were to persuade her, nothing less than the truth would serve.

"Only indirectly," she replied, moving to one side as another footman passed by with a tray of glasses of chilled champagne. She lowered her voice still further; it would not do to be overheard. "In investigating some others who are being blackmailed, or might be—of course they deny it—he discovered that they all belong to one of the secret societies, and that the society demands of its members a loyalty ahead of their honor or conscience, even if that should be contrary to the law."

"How can it be? What do you mean?" Emily was worried, but still failed to understand.

"Police," Charlotte whispered fiercely. "Some of the members are police, and they have been corrupted, turned their backs on certain crimes . . ."

"But that is their own choice," Emily argued, unconsciously shifting her position a little and putting her hand to the small of her back. "What would the society do if they refused? Blackmail them? In those circumstances one would be very glad to be thrown out. And they run the risk of being reported for attempts at corruption."

"You have been standing long enough." Charlotte noticed the gesture and understood it with sympathy. She could well remember the backache of pregnancy. "Come, sit down. There is a seat over there." And without giving Emily time to reply, or to demur, she took her arm and walked over towards the wooden garden bench.

"I am afraid it is nothing so pleasant," she answered, smiling with artificial sweetness at a fat lady whose name she should remember. "They do not forgive betrayal, and that is apparently how they see it." They sat down and arranged their skirts. "And you seem to have forgotten that the membership is secret," she went on. "So you do not know if perhaps your own superior is a member also. Or your banker, your physician, your lawyer, the next police officer you should meet. Certain members, and Thomas does not know who, exercise discipline, which can be extremely nasty. Incriminating evidence may be placed where the police will find it, and scandal and prosecution may result."

Emily's face darkened. "Are you sure?"

"Yes. Thomas is very distressed by it."

"But it may not be the same society," Emily reasoned. "There are totally philanthropic organizations also, and from what Jack said, this one is extremely dedicated to good works. Their secrecy is a matter of not wishing to boast, and because certain kinds of justice can be effected only if their enemies are unaware of who fights their cause. Lord Anstiss is a member, because it was he who invited Jack to join."

"Of course yours may not be the same society as Thomas is concerned with," Charlotte agreed. "Is 'may not' good enough for you?"

"No . . ."

Before she could add anything further she was interrupted with great good humor by a lady with a magnolia-trimmed hat and a booming voice. She greeted Emily effusively as if they had been the closest of friends, was introduced to Charlotte with a beaming smile, then proceeded to monopolize the conversation with memories of a function she and Emily had recently attended.

Charlotte excused herself, catching Emily's eye and nodding politely to the lady with the magnolias. Then she rose and walked along the path towards the gazebo and a magnificent bed of azaleas.

Her next encounter took her totally by surprise. She had seen Great-Aunt Vespasia in the distance and, anticipating the pleasure of speaking to her, had set out across the grass, lifting her skirts with one hand to avoid soiling them. She was within two or three yards of her when she saw that she would interrupt a meeting that was about to take place. Vespasia was very upright, her shoulders slender and stiff under exquisite pale pink silk and Chantilly lace, a magnificent triple rope of pearls hanging to her waist. She was wearing a hat almost as big as a cart wheel, lifted rakishly at one side, her silver hair coiled to perfection, luminous pearls dropping from her ears, her chin high.

The woman approaching her was also of a good height, but very lush of figure, with creamy white skin and auburn hair. Her features were lovely in a very classic manner and she was gorgeously dressed to flatter the striking attributes with which nature had endowed her. And from the expression on her face she was not unaware of the stir she caused. There was a supreme confidence in her and not quite an arrogance, but most definitely an enjoyment of her power.

The middle-aged man beside Vespasia, clean shaven with a ruddy face and broad brow, affected introductions between the two women well within Charlotte's hearing.

"Lady Cumming-Gould, may I present Mrs. Lillie Langtry—"

Vespasia's eyes widened, her silver brows arched and her very slightly aquiline nose flared infinitesimally.

"To seek permission now seems a trifle late," she said with only the barest edge to her voice, and a definite lift of amusement.

The man flushed. "I—er—" he stammered, caught off guard. He had thought well of himself. Most people had envied him his acquaintance with the Jersey Lily. Indeed he had bragged about it to some effect.

Vespasia turned to Mrs. Langtry. She inclined her head with very deliberate graciousness. She had been the greatest beauty of her day, and she deferred to no one on that score.

"How do you do, Mrs. Langtry," she said coolly. She was an upstart. She might be the Prince of Wales's mistress, and Lord knew who else's, and have beauty and even wit, but Vespasia would not be introduced to her as if she could in a few years climb to that eminence Vespasia had taken a lifetime to achieve. That required also intelligence, patience, dignity and discretion. "I hope you are finding the London season enjoyable?" she added.

Mrs. Langtry was taken aback.

"How do you do, Lady Cumming-Gould. Indeed, thank you, it is most enjoyable. But it is not my first season, you know. Indeed, far from it."

Vespasia's eyebrows rose even higher. "Indeed?" she said without interest. One would have thought from her expression she had never heard of Lillie Langtry. She looked her up and down, her eyes lingering for a moment on her neck and waistline, where so often age tells most unkindly. "No—of course not," she amended.

"It must be simply that our paths have not crossed." She did not say "nor are they likely to in the future," but it hung in the air delicately suggested.

Lillie Langtry was the most famous of London beauties sprung from nowhere, and she had been rebuffed before and had overridden it with grace. She was not going to be stopped in her triumph by one elderly lady, no matter who.

She smiled tolerantly. "No, perhaps not," she agreed. "Do you dine very often at Marlborough House?" She was referring to the Prince of Wales and his friends, as they all knew.

Vespasia was not going to be bested. She smiled equally icily.

"Not quite my generation," she murmured, implying that they were Mrs. Langtry's, although they were at least a decade older.

Mrs. Langtry flushed, but battle had been joined, and she did not retreat either.

"Too much dancing, perhaps?" Mrs. Langtry looked at Aunt Vespasia's silver-topped cane.

Vespasia's eyes glittered. "I care for the waltz, a delightful dance, and the lancers and the quadrille. But I fear some of the modern dances are not to my liking—the cancan, for example . . ." She left her distaste hanging in the air.

Mrs. Langtry's lips tightened. The cancan's scandalous reputation was well known. It was performed by prostitutes and women of other unspeakable occupations in places like Paris, and even there it was illegal. "You dine with Her Majesty, perhaps?" she suggested, still smiling. They both knew that ever since Prince Albert had died twenty-eight years before, the Queen had ceased to entertain. Her mourning was so profound as to have caused open criticism in the land that she did not do her duty as monarch.

Vespasia raised her eyebrows. "Oh no, my dear. Her Majesty does not entertain anymore." Then she added gently, "I am surprised you did not know that. But still—perhaps . . ." She left it trailing in the air, too unkind to speak aloud.

Mrs. Langtry drew in her breath but at last a retort failed her and she forced a wintry smile, relying on beauty and youth alone, which were sure cards in any game. And certainly she was an exceptionally beautiful woman.

Vespasia had filled her time richly and she did not rue its passing, or regret that which was past. She inclined her head graciously.

"Most—interesting—to have met you, Mrs. Langtry." And she swept away before victory could in any way be turned into defeat, leaving Charlotte to bring up the rear as she chose.

She caught up with Vespasia, opening her mouth to comment, then changing her mind and assuming an air of total innocence as though she had observed none of the exchange. Charlotte swapped a little polite conversation, suppressing her laughter and seeing the bravado in Vespasia's eye.

Then balancing a glass of champagne and wishing she knew how to manage a cake elegantly at the same time, and knowing she did not, she made her way to where Emily was talking animatedly with Fitzherbert and Lord Anstiss. Odelia Morden stood desultorily a little to one side, her blush-pink gown and parasol delicate as apple blossoms, white ribbons on her hat and white gloves immaculate. She looked more feminine even than Emily. Charlotte felt a little twist of sorrow for her. She seemed isolated, uncertain what to say or to do.

Charlotte joined the group. Fitz made way for her quickly as though she had rescued him from a sudden silence.

"How nice to see you, Mrs. Pitt. I am sure you are acquainted with Lord Anstiss?"

"Indeed." Charlotte dropped the slightest of curtseys. "Good afternoon, Lord Anstiss."

"Good afternoon, Mrs. Pitt." He smiled back at her. He was a more dynamic man than she had remembered. She was aware not merely of an acute intelligence in his glance, but of an energy within him, a restlessness of interest seeking new knowledge, hungry for experience, curious and powerful, and a needle-sharp humor. He was not a man she would have challenged. The thought of him as a friend was exciting, as an enemy something which raised a prickle of fear.

Apparently she had interrupted a conversation. It was resumed without niceties, and she was absorbed into it easily, which was in itself a kind of compliment.

"We made up a party to see it," Fitz was saying with a smile. "I must admit I was most keen. Madame Bernhardt has such a reputation . . ."

"I believe she is to do Joan of Arc next year," Anstiss said, his eyes bright. "In French." He glanced at Odelia.

"I should enjoy that," she said quickly. "I think my French is well enough."

"I am sure." He inclined his head very slightly. "After all, we are familiar with the story, and there is something extremely satisfying about watching a drama well played out towards a predestined end of which we are acutely aware. It has a piquancy."

She seemed aware that he had a meaning deeper than that on the surface, but not what it might be.

"I did see Henry Irving last week," Fitz offered cheerfully. "He was quite excellent, I thought. Captured the audience completely."

"Indeed." Anstiss seemed unconvinced. "Mrs. Pitt? Have you seen anything of interest lately?"

"Not at the theater, my lord." She suppressed a smile, but saw the quick leap of humor in his eyes. Then as quickly it was gone, and he turned to Fitz again.

"I imagine you will be marrying soon?" He looked in Odelia's direction. "Are you planning the Grand Tour as a honeymoon? You could leave in a month or two and still be returned long before a general election." He shrugged. "Unfortunately one must think of such things. I apologize for raising the subject. It seems indelicate, but however graceful and amateur we may wish to appear, politics is a very professional affair, if we wish to succeed." His words were pleasant, his voice quite light, but there was steel beneath it, and Fitz was not the only one to realize it. An answer was required, if he wished Anstiss to consider him for selection.

Beside Charlotte, Emily drew in her breath sharply.

Fitz raised his eyes slowly, his face losing the casual interest and the ease disappearing. Odelia waited motionless, except that her fingers curled tightly on the handle of her parasol.

"Of course," he said slowly. "The art is to make the work look like a hobby, an interest undertaken for its own sake, and the skill like an art, something a gentleman might do to fill his time."

"Oh quite," Anstiss agreed with a smile that touched only his lips; his eyes did not flicker. "But we have enough dilettante politicians already. We need men who are committed."

The last trace of lightness disappeared from Fitz's eyes. He knew he could no longer evade making an irretrievable statement, a date he would have to abide by, regardless of either his own emotions or Odelia's.

Anstiss was waiting.

Emily opened her mouth to prompt Fitz, then changed her mind, realizing she would intrude in something too serious for such comment to be anything but misplaced.

"I—" Fitz began, then stopped, his face pale. He turned himself to meet Odelia's gaze. It was a long, painful look, his face puckered in a mixture of apology and shame.

No one else moved, but Anstiss's brows darkened and the skin across his cheekbones became tighter.

Fitz drew in his breath slowly. The ghost of a smile returned to his lips, but it was bravado. There was no joy in it.

"I value my career, such as it is, and I wish to serve politics wholeheartedly, if I am given the opportunity, but I do not intend to allow it to dictate my personal arrangements, or those of my family. I shall marry when it best suits all those who are concerned." He met Anstiss's eyes squarely, although there was still regret and courtesy in his voice. "I hope that does not sound less than civil. It is not meant to."

There was no answering warmth in Anstiss. His brows drew together, his lips narrowed.

Emily looked at Fitz, then at Odelia. A slow wave of emotion spread up her face, compassion, anxiety, and suddenly Charlotte knew it was not unmixed with guilt. So much hung in the balance, the inflections of Fitz's words, whether he had the courage or the depth of feeling to cast away all that he was so close to winning, Anstiss's reaction, Odelia's—and on all of it depended Jack's future as well.

Emily avoided Charlotte's eyes and stepped forward, taking Odelia's arm.

"Come, let us leave them to talk politics. Tell me of your own thoughts—would you care to do the Grand Tour? I did, you know, and there is much that is fascinating, and I would not have missed, but my goodness it can be uncomfortable at times. I found I am not cut out for physical adventure. Do you know, in Africa I saw—" And the grisly account of what she saw was lost as the two of them drifted away, leaving Fitz alone with Anstiss and Charlotte.

"Very tactful," Anstiss said dryly without glancing at Emily's back, although his meaning was quite apparent. "A woman of considerable poise—most necessary for a man who has any hope of surviving in politics." There was no compromise in his eyes, hard, bleak light gray. "I take it from your reluctance that you have reservations about marrying Miss Morden? Surely you are not still thinking of that wretched Hilliard girl? Very pretty, but not remotely possible as a wife."

A flash of anger sparked in Fitz's face.

Anstiss ignored it. He had no need to tread warily. He held the patronage and he knew it.

"Whatever her morality, Fitzherbert—and it is open to question, even at the most charitable interpretation—her reputation is ruined."

"I beg to differ," Fitz said with freezing civility. "There has been a little whispering, largely by the idle and ill informed."

"By society," Anstiss snapped. "And whatever your opinion of them, or of their intelligence, you would do well to remember it is they who will put you in Parliament—or keep you out!"

A pink flush spread up Fitz's cheeks, but he was stubborn in his convictions.

"I do not wish to owe my success to those who would grant it me at the same time as they tear down the reputation of a young woman about whom they know nothing."

"My dear Fitzherbert, they know she was publicly accused of being Carswell's mistress, and she made not the slightest effort to deny it. On the contrary, she said nothing at all, and fled the scene—which is a confession of guilt. Not even a fool would deny that."

Fitz's face was unyielding, but he had no argument. Whatever his belief, the facts were as Anstiss had said. He was painfully unhappy, but he refused to give ground. He stood upright, head high, lips tight.

"Can you give me a date when you will marry Miss Morden?" Anstiss said levelly, his voice courteous and cold. "Keep Miss Hilliard as a mistress if you wish, only for God's sake be discreet about it. And wait a couple of years—she'll still be in the business."

"That is not my standard of morality, sir," Fitz said stiffly. His face was hot as he was hideously aware of how pompous he sounded, and how offensive, but unable to retreat. "I am surprised that you should suggest such a thing."

Anstiss smiled sourly. "It is not mine either, Fitzherbert. But then I have no amorous interest in Miss Hilliard. You have made it apparent that you do. I am telling you that is the only arrangement with such a woman that society will accept."

Fitz stood ramrod straight.

"We shall see." He bowed. "Good day, sir."

"Good-bye," Anstiss replied with the faintest inclination of his head. The dismissal was unmistakable and absolute.

Fitz turned away. With a glance at Anstiss by way of excusing herself, Charlotte followed Fitz through the crowd, as he trod on skirts, brushed past people balancing glasses and plates, till he stood next to a glorious rosebush trailing flowers over an ornamental arch.

There he stopped and faced her.

"I hope you haven't come to argue me out of it? No—of course you haven't. You are Mrs. Radley's sister."

"I am also Fanny's friend," Charlotte said with chill.

He blushed. "I'm sorry. That was appallingly rude, and quite unjustified. I have no one to blame but myself, for any of it. And I've treated Odelia abominably. I hope her father will break off our engagement officially, and say that I have consorted with an unsuitable woman and proved myself unworthy of his daughter. Otherwise her reputation . . ." He left the rest unsaid. They both knew the ugly speculations that followed when a man jilted a young woman. There was the inevitable whisper that he had discovered she was not above suspicion.

"That will damage your own reputation," Charlotte pointed out. "And untruly."

"Not untruly. I have consorted with totally unsuitable women."

"Have you?"

"Fanny . . ."

"You haven't consorted with her—you have met her only socially in a way we all have."

"I will have consorted with her by then—if you will be good enough to tell me where I may find her? You said across the river."

"I don't know where, but I can find out, if you are sure. She did not deny her relationship with Mr. Carswell, you know."

He was very pale.

"I know."

A few yards to the left a large gentleman in a hussar's uniform gave a roar of laughter and slapped the shoulders of a slender young man with a large mustache. Behind them two ladies laughed vacuously.

"What Lord Anstiss says is true," Charlotte went on carefully. But there was a growing hope in her, quite unreasonable and against all her common sense. What happiness could there be for Fitz and Fanny Hilliard? Even if he was rash enough to marry her, and she accepted him, that would not lift her to his social status. His friends would never look upon her as one of them. Whatever they supposed the truth to be, they would remember the charges, and that she had not denied them. She was a loose woman, and he a fool for marrying her. And Anstiss had made it plain that selection for Parliament was ended. Fanny would have to realize what it would cost him. And knowing Fanny better than Fitz did, Charlotte thought she would not marry him at that price.

The hussar hailed someone he knew and went striding over, crying out loudly.

"And consider it from Fanny's view," Charlotte went on. "If she loves you, she will not accept you at such a price to you. What happiness would that give her?"

He stared at her, not with the derision she had expected, but with suddenly candid eyes and a dawning brilliance in them.

"You think she loves me? You do. And far more to the point,

310 • BELGRAVE SQUARE

Mrs. Pitt, you think her a woman of selflessness and such honor that she would prize my welfare and my reputation above her own, and her security as my wife." Impulsively he put his hands on her shoulders and kissed her cheek. "Bless you, Mrs. Pitt, for a devious and unconventional woman. Now you will find out for me where I may call upon Fanny, because having gone this far you cannot now abandon me. And you will do your brother-in-law a favor, because he is an excellent fellow, and will make a fine member of Parliament, thoroughly acceptable to his lordship, having a wife above criticism, intelligent, tactful, charming and I suspect extremely clever. And her reputation is spotless."

"I will find out," she agreed with a rueful smile. "But I will ask Fanny if she wishes to receive you."

"No—don't do that. She will refuse. Allow me to press my own suit. I give you my word I will not harass her. And she has a brother to protect her—just tell me where I may call. For heaven's sake, Mrs. Pitt, I am gentleman enough not to pay my attentions where they are unwanted."

Charlotte bit her lip to suppress her amusement.

"Have they ever been unwanted, Mr. Fitzherbert?"

A little of the natural color returned to his face. He was being teased, and he could see it.

"Not often," he admitted with a spark of the old humor. "But I think I'll know it if I see it. Promise me."

"I promise," she conceded. "Now I must return to Emily and see what progresses. I shall send the address to her, and you may fetch it there."

And with that he was content. He thanked her again and she excused herself and threaded her way back to where Emily was talking about climate to a retired colonel with a bristling mustache and stentorian opinions about India.

While Charlotte was attending the garden party, Pitt returned to the job he hated of further investigating Samuel Urban. It was something he could not avoid, whatever his personal liking for the man or his desire to believe him guilty of no more than misjudgment, and seeking a second and forbidden income in a manner which would have been perfectly legal had he not been in the police. It was far preferable in his mind to Latimer's gambling and condoning of bare-knuckle fistfighting. But bitter experience had taught him that people otherwise law abiding and in many ways likable could, when frightened enough, caught without time to think, commit murder. And often men he despised for cruelty, indifference to others' pain or humiliation, were nevertheless capable of coolness of thought which avoided the need for violence. Not that they abhorred it but because they understood the terrible consequences for themselves.

It was little use retracing his steps over Urban's old cases until he knew of something else to look for. He had found no unexplainable irregularities the first time, and he knew where the extra money came from. Whether he had used his office to further the cause of the Inner Circle or not could wait for another time. Pitt thought not. He remembered how angry Urban had been over the Osmar case, and the influence he believed the Circle had brought to bear on that. And the very fact that he had betrayed them so far as to tell Pitt of their existence and his own membership was proof which way his loyalties lay.

In fact the more Pitt thought of him, the deeper was his liking for Urban personally, and his conviction that the Inner Circle had not succeeded in corrupting him to its uses. His disobedience had been the reason his name was on the list in the first place.

Then why was Carswell's name there? He had succumbed. He had dismissed Osmar's case. And what about Latimer? He needed to know more.

Where to find it?

He began with the music halls where Urban might have been seeking more remunerative employment, if he was telling the truth about the night Weems was killed. They were tawdry in the daylight: stages dusty, backdrops unreal; all the glamour lent by music, shadows and spotlights was gone, leaving a curious nakedness. It took him all day tramping from one hall to another, questioning reluctant management, which was very much on its dignity, protesting uprightness, moral probity and reputations not helped by having the like of Pitt hanging around asking questions. Yes of course they inquired into the backgrounds of everyone they hired.

It was regrettably necessary to employ people to keep order, human nature being as it was, but they took on only men of the best character. It was grossly unfair that anyone should suggest otherwise.

Pitt brushed aside their arguments. He was not on this occasion interested in the general excellence of the establishment, only had they recently interviewed a man answering the description he gave.

Unfortunately three managers said they had. But in each case the description was so general it could have been Urban, or any of a thousand others. It only highlighted the impossibility of proving Urban innocent, unless the managers were faced with the actual man, and their memories were clear enough to make a positive identification.

Finally he went back to the hall in Stepney where he knew Urban had worked and asked to see the manager. A large man with thin hair scraped across the top of his head, and graying at the temples, came out to see him. He was well dressed, and it flashed through Pitt's mind that he possibly owned the building as well as ran it.

"Yes, Inspector? My name is Caulfield, Hosea Caulfield. What can I do for you?" he asked agreeably. His voice was light and his diction a little sibilant. "Always help the police, if I can. What is it this time? Not that bouncer fellow again, is it? Getting hisself into trouble? Police were 'ere asking about him."

"Yes it is," Pitt answered, watching the man's face, noticing the way he stood. There was something about him that puzzled, something not what he expected.

"Oh dear." Caulfield rubbed his hands together as if he were cold, although it was midsummer and humid. "I feared as much, since the other officer was here. But I can't help you." He shook his head. "He never came back. Scarpered, you might say. Suspicious that, in itself."

Pitt struggled to place what it was in the man that troubled him. He had spoken to enough music hall managers. They were all civil, but they were not fond of the police, and were better pleased to see him leave than arrive. But Caulfield was almost eager. He stood on the balls of his feet and under his fair brows his eyes were sharp on Pitt's face. He was waiting for something, and it was not for Pitt to go. He wanted something first. Was it to receive information, or to give it?

To give it. Pitt could tell him nothing he could not have found out from Innes, and by general inquiry. And there was some emotion in him far stronger than fear, at least than fear of Pitt.

"What is it I can tell you, Inspector?" Caulfield urged, his face eager, his manner wavering between the dignified and deferential, as though he was uncertain of his role. "I know very little of the man, except he did his job well. Never gave me any trouble. Although he was an odd one." He shook his head, then when Pitt was silent, pursued his thoughts regardless. "Struck up some strange friendships, or perhaps acquaintances would be a better term for it. I suppose a music hall is a good place for meeting people casually, unobserved, as it were, if you know what I mean?" He looked at Pitt questioningly.

Pitt found himself disliking him, and instinct fought with reason. He was being unfair. The man was probably anxious for his livelihood. There had already been one policeman inquiring about his employees. If he now suspected there had been some criminal activity on his premises he had every reason to be worried. An innocent man would behave this way.

Caulfield was watching Pitt's face closely.

"Do you want to see the room he used?" he asked, licking his lips.

"Used?" Pitt said with a frown. "For what purpose?"

Caulfield looked uncomfortable.

"Well—perhaps 'room' is a bit of a grand term for it." He shrugged elaborately. "More of a cubbyhole, really. He—he asked to keep things now and then." He looked sideways at Pitt rapidly then away again. "So of course I said 'e could. No harm in obliging." He seemed to feel some need to explain himself as he led Pitt along a narrow, airless corridor and unlocked the door of a room very spartanly furnished with a wooden table, an unframed glass on the wall above it, two wooden chairs and a set of cupboards against the far wall, several tall enough to serve as wardrobes, and an uncurtained window looking into the blind wall of the next building.

"We use it for changing rooms for extra artistes," Caulfield explained, waving his arm vaguely at the table.

Pitt said nothing.

Caulfield seemed to feel compelled to go on talking, his face growing pinker.

"Your man used that cupboard at the end there." He pointed with a well-manicured hand.

Pitt looked, but did not move towards it.

Caulfield took a deep breath and licked his lips again. "I suppose you'll be wanting to take a look inside?"

Pitt raised his eyebrows.

"Is there something in it?"

"I—well—I, er . . ." Caulfield was plainly caught in some embarrassment. Why? If he had looked that was not hard to understand. It was his cupboard and the man to whom he had lent its use had gone without warning. It would be usual to look and see if he had left anything behind. Such an act needed no explanation and certainly no apology.

Pitt regarded him unblinkingly and Caulfield colored.

"No," he denied. "I don't know if there's anything there. I just thought—you bein' police, and interested in the man, like, you'd want to see."

"I do," Pitt agreed, certain now that he would find something. It was unfair to be angry with the manager. It should have been Urban; it was Urban who had been greedy for the pictures and Urban who had gone moonlighting to get the money. No one had pushed him into ruining his career, certainly not this curiously uncomfortable man with his red face and constantly moving hands. "By the way, why was the room locked? There hardly seems anything worth stealing."

Again Caulfield was thrown off balance. He shifted his feet.

"I—er—well—habit, I suppose. Sometimes people leave things . . ." He tailed off. "Do you want to see in the cupboard? Don't mean to be uncivil, sir, but I do have duties . . ."

"Of course." Pitt went over to the corner and opened the cupboard door. Inside was a large parcel, about two feet by three feet tall, but barely two inches thick, and wrapped in brown paper tied with string. He did not need to undo it to know what it was.

For once Caulfield kept silent. There was not even an indrawn breath of surprise.

"Did he often leave pictures here?" Pitt asked.

Caulfield hesitated.

"Well?" Pitt asked.

"He often had parcels that size with 'im," Caulfield said nervously. "He didn't say what they were, an' I didn't ask. It did cross my mind as he was an artist, maybe, an' that was why 'e needed the work extra."

"An artist carrying his pictures about with him to work at a music hall?" Pitt sounded dubious.

"Well—yes." Caulfield rose to his feet and his eyes were very wide as he gazed at Pitt. " 'E did come with one picture sometimes, an' leave with a different one."

"How do you know? At first you didn't even know they were pictures. You said 'parcels.' "

"Well—I mean—the parcel 'e left with was a different size. An' I just supposed they were pictures cause o' the shape." His voice grew sharper with irritation. "An'—an' he carried them very careful, like. And because he asked to keep 'em safe, I took it as they was of value to 'im. What else could they be?"

Slowly Pitt undid the string and the paper and disclosed a large, very ornate, carved and gilded frame, containing nothing but a bare wood backing.

"Frames?" he said with a lift of bleak astonishment in his voice.

"Well I never!" The response was not wholly convincing. "What'd 'e do that for? I wonder what 'appened to the picture? Looks like there was one, don't it?"

"It does," Pitt conceded reluctantly. The frame was far from new and the backing was dark with age. It was probably the frame and backing from an old work of value. He ran his fingers over it and felt the smooth surfaces. He was not sure, but he thought it was probably gold leafed, not merely gilt paint.

"You reckon it's stolen?" Caulfield said from close behind him.

"A stolen picture frame?" Pitt said with surprise.

"Well obviously there was a picture in it. Whoever it was he sold it to didn't want the frame."

"Or maybe he found an old frame for someone and brought it for them?" Pitt suggested, not believing it himself for a moment.

"Well it's your business," Caulfield said resignedly. "You do as you like. I got my own affairs to run. If you seen what you need, maybe you'll take that with you and I'll call it an end to the matter."

Pitt picked up the frame and rewrapped it.

"Yes, I'll take it."

"I'll want a paper," Caulfield warned. "Just to protect me, like. I don't want some other police officer comin' 'ere and saying I kept it or sold it for myself." This time he looked Pitt squarely in the face.

Pitt understood. What he meant was that he wanted proof that Pitt had found it, so he would be obliged to report it to his senior. That was the purpose of it, to make sure Urban was implicated. In what? Art theft, forgery, fencing stolen works—bribery with paintings for an officer who was prepared to turn his back now and again on theft? He was chilled inside. The Inner Circle again? Urban had defied them a second time by pressing for prosecution in the Osmar case. He had invited a more severe discipline than merely his name on Weems's list. Was this it?

A loathing for the manager welled up inside him, although he knew it was unreasonable. Very probably the man was caught by the Inner Circle himself.

"That's quite fair," he said with a smile over bared teeth. "I shall take the matter back to Bow Street and report it to Mr. Urban; he's head of the uniformed men there. I'll tell him you are most cooperative. I daresay no one will bother you any further."

Caulfield drew in his breath sharply, his eyes wide. He was about to protest, then remembered just in time that he was not supposed to know who his employee had been. He had almost betrayed himself. With care he ironed out the expression from his face and forced himself to smile back at Pitt, a bare glimmer of triumph in his eyes for at least one snare avoided.

"Yes of course. I'm obliged. Now the paper, if you please? Just for my safeguard, you understand."

"Oh I understand," Pitt said viciously. "I understand perfectly. You'd better bring me a pen and paper."

Caulfield inclined his head. "Of course, right away, Officer."

While Pitt was in Stepney struggling with the question of Urban and the Inner Circle, Charlotte sought for Fanny's address and sent it to Emily so she might give it to Fitz. Then after a day spent in furious housework, baking bread and cakes more than anyone wanted, and ironing everything she could reach, laundered or not, she finally came to a decision the following morning. She confided to Gracie what she was going to do, and then set out in her best summer day dress and coat against a rising wind. She hired a hansom cab to take her to the magistrate's court where Addison Carswell was accustomed to preside.

She had already written him a very carefully worded letter reminding him who she was, and that she had befriended Fanny Hilliard and grown fond of her on the several occasions on which they had met, so much so that Fanny had confided in her some of her present troubles. Therefore she would be most grateful if in the interests of compassion, Mr. Carswell would do her the honor of taking luncheon with her, so they might discuss how best to be of assistance to that charming but unfortunate young woman, for whom it seemed they both had some affection.

It was not intended as a threat—apart from anything else she would not have betrayed Fanny's confidence in her—but on the other hand she did not wish Carswell simply to send a note to decline and say that he wished her well, but he had not the time to indulge in luncheons, much as he might care to.

She had been quite shameless in asking Emily for the means to pay both for the hansom ride there and back, and for luncheon at a public restaurant should Carswell accept, and not offer to pay for them both. She had also written to Emily and had Gracie post the letter on the previous evening. She had been unequivocal.

Dear Emily,

I am sure you are quite as desirous as I am that all should work out as well as possible between Fitz and Fanny Hilliard, albeit our interests are not precisely the same, but perhaps close—I do care very much that Jack should be selected for Parliament, and I am sure he will succeed when he is there. However you know as well as I that in the process poor Fanny seems to have suffered greatly. She is innocent of the charge, for which you will have to accept my word—one day I may be able to tell you the truth, which is quite remarkable. In the meantime I am going to do what I can to set matters right—for which I shall need a small sum, sufficient to take a hansom cab into the city, and back again, and treat a certain gentleman to luncheon, in an effort to get him to assist by making the truth known— to Fitz at least, if no one else.

I trust totally that you will help, therefore I shall take the money from my housekeeping, and rely on you to re-place it.

Your loving sister, Charlotte

She sat in the hansom with every confidence that at least the mechanics of her plan would work. What was far more in the balance was whether she would find the words to persuade Addison Carswell to jeopardize everything he possessed in order to help Fanny, especially when there was no certainty that it was what Fanny herself wished.

In fact, as she jolted along, Charlotte began to have doubts that what she was doing was wise. She could not foresee the out-come, but she was perfectly sure Fanny loved Fitz and desired that he should know the truth about her and Carswell, and that Fanny herself would not tell him.

She reached the courthouse long before she was ready, and was obliged to alight, pay the cabby and either stand on the pavement and cause people to wonder and perhaps be accosted by peddlers, newsboys shouting the scandal of the latest case, or beggars in need of assistance she could not afford to give, or else to go straight in.

She wrapped her coat a little tighter around her, not because it was cold, but instinctively in a kind of protection, as though she was chilled and vulnerable, and ascended the steps.

Inside the courthouse was busy and impersonal. There were many nervous women clutching coats and shawls around them-selves, pale faced, watching every passerby, hesitant to speak and yet seemingly wishing to. Shabby men waited, hands in pockets, eyes furtive. Bailiffs and clerks hurried past carrying piles of papers, gowns flying, wigs making them look either important or slightly ridiculous, depending on one's own purpose and fears.

Charlotte spoke to one who was going a little less swiftly.

"Excuse me, sir—"

He swung to a stop, turning on his heel and staring at her with brisk arrogance.

"Yes ma'am?" He wore wire-rimmed pince-nez and blinked at her through them.

"I have a letter to deliver urgently to Mr. Addison Carswell." She stated her business without preamble. "To whom may I give it to make certain it reaches him before luncheon?"

"He is in court, ma'am!"

"I assumed that, or I would have attempted to give it to him myself." She held his eyes without flickering and he seemed somewhat taken aback. It was not what he expected from young women, or indeed any women at all.

"It is important," she said firmly.

"Is it personal, ma'am?" He was still dubious.

"It is personal to Mr. Carswell," she replied with a very slight edge to her voice, hoping it would put him off asking anything further about it. "Not to me."

"Indeed. Then I will take it for you." He held out his hand.

"Before luncheon," she repeated, passing it to him.

"Certainly," he agreed, taking it and putting it in his pocket, then with a nod proceeding on his way.

There was nothing further she could do but find a seat and compose herself to wait for an answer. Usually she enjoyed watching people, their faces, their clothes, their attitudes towards one another, and speculating in her imagination as to what they were like, their occupations, relationships. But in this place there was so much anxiety, hopelessness and underlying fear that it was too harrowing. She sat instead and whiled away the time wondering about Lord and Lady Byam, and Lady Byam's relationship with Micah Drummond, and what manner of person Lord Anstiss might be if one knew him as a friend and were not overawed by him, indeed how Laura Anstiss had seen him!

She was quite lost in this when the lawyer's clerk returned and stood in front of her with rather more courtesy than previously.

"Mrs. Pitt? Mr. Carswell requested me to give you this." And he held out an envelope for her.

"Thank you." She took it, surprised to find her fingers clumsy and shaking a little. She waited until he was gone again, bustling away full of importance, before she pulled her gloves off and tore it open. She read:

> Dear Mrs. Pitt,
>
> I fear I can contribute very little to Miss Hilliard's happiness, but I shall be pleased to meet you and hope you will be my guest for luncheon at midday. If you request a clerk to bring you to my chambers I shall escort you to a suitable establishment where we may dine. I request that you will be punctual, because as you may appreciate, my time is circumscribed by the necessities of the court.
>
> Faithfully yours, Addison Carswell

She folded it and put it in her reticule. She had thought to carry a fob watch her father had given her many years ago, against the possibility of having to keep an exact appointment and not being easily within sight of a public clock.

At five minutes before twelve she sought a clerk and was conducted to Carswell's chambers, and at noon precisely he emerged looking composed but extremely pale. He saw her immediately and his features set, his chin hardened and his mouth thinned into a straight line.

Charlotte was not surprised, although it was an unpleasant feeling. She had worded her request in such a way that he might well think she meant to blackmail him. And indeed if William Weems had done so before, then he could hardly be blamed for such a fear.

"Good day, Mrs. Pitt," he said levelly. "I am obliged to you for being punctual. May I escort you to luncheon? There is an excellent chophouse 'round the corner where we may sit discreetly without being overheard, and they will serve us without delay." He did not offer her his arm.

"Thank you, that would be very satisfactory," she accepted, unreasonably annoyed by an assumption on his part which she had just admitted was quite fair. She walked out, head high, precisely in step with him.

The chophouse was as he had said, noisy, busy with people at almost every table, mostly men and all in dark and sober dress. Waiters passed nimbly, swinging trays on their shoulders and setting dishes and tankards down with flair. When Charlotte and Carswell were seated and Carswell had ordered for them both, he came to the point without the pretense of courtesies. She had no time to look around her any further, which would normally have been most interesting. She had never been in a chophouse before. She assumed the other tables were filled with lawyers and their clients all talking earnestly, heads bent.

"You mentioned Miss Hilliard, Mrs. Pitt," he said coldly. "And that you had formed an affection for her. I am quite aware of what unkind gossip has said of her, and it is not something I propose to discuss with you. I am extremely sorry it has happened." His eyes were miserable but there was no evasion in them, no flinching from her. "But I know of nothing I can do to repair it. I am sure you are aware that denial would accomplish nothing."

She felt a considerable pity for him, and no dislike. Even more urgent to her, she had a very real regard for Regina, and knew very well the situation of the other daughters, and their hopes of marriage, indeed their need for it. But she also felt for Fanny, who was being pushed into a position where she alone suffered.

She steeled herself and took the irretrievable step.

"I would not expect you to deny it easily, Mr. Carswell," she said with a tiny smile. "It is a miserable thing to have people believe, especially since it cannot but hurt your wife and your daughters, and ruin Miss Hilliard in society—which I know is not everything. The circle of people who have heard the rumor is small enough, and there may be other alliances open to her, in time . . ."

She took a deep breath and went on. "And ugly as it is, it is far better than the truth." She saw him pale, but his expression barely changed and his eyes never left hers. She knew from the icy hardness in them that he was now quite certain in his mind that she had come to extort money. The contempt in him could almost be felt across the white-clothed table and the knives and forks.

He remained silent.

She was about to continue when the waiter brought them their meals and set them down.

Carswell thanked him grimly and dismissed him.

"I am sure you have some point, Mrs. Pitt. I would be obliged if you would reach it."

A flicker of anger moved in her.

"I know that Fanny is your daughter, Mr. Carswell. I do not expect you to tell the world so; it would ruin your—your present wife and your other daughters, and Fanny herself would never wish that. Which indeed you know, since she left all that she hoped for and retreated to her home in disgrace, rather than explain herself and tell anyone, even Herbert Fitzherbert."

He was staring at her without blinking. At the table behind him a young man was waving a legal document in the air, its red seal catching the light, its ribbons flapping. A waiter passed by with two tankards of ale on a tray.

"What is it you want of me, Mrs. Pitt?" Carswell asked her between clenched teeth.

"I want you to consider telling Herbert Fitzherbert the truth," she replied. "He loves Fanny, and is prepared to marry her in spite of the scandal, but she will not trust even him and defend herself. I find it very hard that he will always think her a woman of no virtue, and in time it may come to sour his regard for her and cause suspicion between them. He has forfeited his opportunity to Parliament; his love for her is of greater value to him. But I fear she will not tell him the truth herself, in order to protect you, and she will not marry him as long as he does not know it but believes her your mistress."

She picked up her glass by the stem, and then put it down again.

"Also her brother deserves to know. Why should she endure his contempt as well? She will become quite isolated and believed immoral by those she cares for most, and all to protect you and your new family. Is that something you can live with happily, Mr. Carswell?"

His face was pink, his eyes wretched. He fought off the most horrible decision a moment longer by facing the lesser.

"And what is your intent, Mrs. Pitt? Why do you concern yourself with this? You have known Fanny only a very short time. I find it hard to believe your emotion is so engaged."

"I am aware of what you suppose, Mr. Carswell, and given your connection with Weems it is not unreasonable." She saw his face blanch and a look of incredulity come over it. Then slowly realization came to him. "Pitt—Mrs. Pitt? You cannot be . . ."

All the world of social differences was there in his unspoken words: the gulf between Charlotte as Emily's sister, receiving society, dancing, dining, visiting the opera; and as the wife of Pitt, a policeman calling at people's houses to ask about the murder of a usurer in the back streets of Clerkenwell.

She swallowed back the sharp defense that came leaping to her tongue. With icy dignity, still less now would she permit him to think she would stoop to blackmail.

"I am," she agreed. "And yes my emotion is engaged on Fanny's behalf. It seems someone's needs to be. Yours is not."

He flushed hotly.

"That is unfair, Mrs. Pitt! Surely you must have some idea what it would do to my present family if such a thing were to become known? They are totally innocent, just as innocent of any wrong as Fanny. I have four daughters and a son. Would you have them ruined for Fanny's sake?" His voice shook a little and Charlotte realized with sudden pity how appallingly difficult it was for him to be telling such intimate details of his life to someone who was not only a stranger, but an unsympathetic one.

"It is my error," he went on, looking not at her but at his plate. Neither of them could eat. "I married Fanny's mother when I was twenty and she seventeen. We thought we loved each other. She was so very pretty, full of life and laughter . . ." For a moment his face softened. "Like Fanny herself." He sighed. "For four years everything was happy; Fanny was born, and then James. Then when James was still a baby, Lucy changed completely. She became in-

fatuated with a dance teacher, of all things. I suppose I was absorbed in my work. I was an aspiring lawyer then, trying to take
all the cases I could, and finding it hard to make sufficient money
to keep us well—and I was ambitious."

Charlotte took a bite of her meal, but her attention was undi-
vided.

"I left her too much alone, I accept. And I was not yet in that
place in society or income where I could offer her the pastimes she
wished." He shrugged. "She left her home and went off with the
dancing master, taking the children with her."

Charlotte was stunned. She knew the law regarding errant wives
and their children.

"Did you not require that she at least leave the children in
your custody?" she asked in surprise. "Even if you did not wish her
back."

He blushed. "No. I thought of it—and the embarrassment of
admitting that my wife had run off with a dancing master. It hurt
that I should lose my children, but what could I offer them? A
nurse to care for them while I was working. She loved them and
was a good mother."

"And the dancing master?"

"It did not last." There was pity both in his face and in his
voice. "In two years he died of typhus, which was perhaps less
cruel than if he had deserted her. She was living in the house off
the Kennington Road, which he owned, and it became hers." He
colored with awareness of guilt. "Of course I should have divorced
her, but I was ashamed of the scandal. And since I was in law, my
friends would have known and I could not bear their pity. I could
not afford to entertain, and with two nursing children Lucy had
not had the inclination to accept invitations which we could not
return. They did not know I was married, and so I simply said
nothing."

"What about her parents?" Charlotte asked.

"Lucy was an orphan. Her guardian, an elderly uncle, had
nothing more to do with her personally after our marriage. He
considered finding her a husband a discharge to his duty towards
her."

"And you did not take her back? Or your children?"

"Neither Lucy nor I had any desire to live under one roof anymore. And it would have been cruel and pointless for me to demand the children. I had no wife at that time who could raise them, and as I have already admitted, I did not wish the world to know of my unfortunate relationship." He looked up at her, his eyes soft in spite of the misery in them. "And by then I had met Regina, and learned to love her in a way I had not loved Lucy. I was desperate she should not know of any earlier marriage. Her parents would never have looked upon me favorably. It was hard enough to persuade them I could provide for her adequately as it was . . ." He stopped, looking up at her.

It was not an attractive story and he was painfully aware of it, yet she could very easily understand how it had happened. Told in the space of a few minutes it was bereft of the shock, the sense of humiliation and loneliness; the young man full of overwhelming inadequacy, fearing ridicule, coming home tired to the house where so shortly before he had been met by wife and children, now finding only servants, polite, distant and unsympathetic.

At last he had simply denied it, pushed it from his mind. Then when happiness had offered itself in the form of Regina, he had grasped it, paying the necessary price. And now twenty-three years later the price had suddenly become so very much higher, and not only he had to pay it, but Fanny—or else Regina and his other children.

"Did you pay Weems?" she asked without warning.

His face was slack with surprise.

"No. As God is my judge, I never even knew the man."

"But you let Horatio Osmar off. You threw the case out without calling Beulah Giles."

"That had nothing to do with Fanny or my first marriage—or with Weems or his murder."

"No." She was about to add that it had everything to do with the secret society of the Inner Circle, when Pitt's warning about their power rang sharply in her mind, and she bit the words back. "No," she said again. "I did not think so, but I had to ask. What are you going to do about Fanny and Herbert Fitzherbert?"

"What are you going to do, Mrs. Pitt?"

"Nothing. I have already done all I can. It is your decision."

"Fitzherbert may betray me, in Fanny's interest—and his own."

"He may. But if he does he will lose Fanny's love forever, and he is quite intelligent enough to know that."

"I must think."

"Please do not leave it long. Once Fanny has refused him he may believe her and not ask again."

"You press me hard, Mrs. Pitt."

For the first time she smiled. "Yes. It is a very hard matter. I daresay Mrs. Carswell—by that I mean Regina—may find it very difficult to accept that your marriage to her is bigamous." She saw him wince but carried on. "But I think she might find it no more painful than the thought that you have been currently having an affair with a girl Fanny's age. Surely when faced with two such awful alternatives, there is something to be said for the truth—and before the lie can bite too deep with its pain."

"Do you believe that? How would you feel, Mrs. Pitt, to discover that your husband was not your husband at all, and that your beloved children were illegitimate?"

"I cannot think how dreadful I should feel, Mr. Carswell. Or how angry and how confused and betrayed. But I think I might find it easier to forgive than the thought that my husband had loved and been intimate with a girl not much older than my own daughter."

He smiled very bleakly. "How very aspiring to the genteel, Mrs. Pitt. I might even say working class. A lady would accept such a thing as part of life, and as long as it was not forced upon her attention or made public to her embarrassment, she would scarcely observe it at all. Indeed, a lady of refined tastes might very well be glad her husband satisfied his less pleasing appetites elsewhere without troubling her, and causing her to bear a larger family than she wished, or her health could support."

"Then I am quite definitely of a distinctly lower class, Mr. Carswell," she said with crisp satisfaction. "If that is the guide by which to judge. And I would not be surprised if Mrs. Carswell is as well. But the decision is yours." And with that she bent to eat some of her almost cold pork chop, and drink a little of the really very good wine.

"I will speak to Fitzherbert," he said at last, just before they rose to leave. "And to James."

"Thank you," she accepted, matter-of-factly, as if he had passed the salt. But inside she felt a little swift, singing happiness, very small, very bright.

In the days after the garden party at which Fitz had made it only too apparent that he did not intend to marry Odelia, and had virtually defied Lord Anstiss, Jack Radley became very slowly and painfully aware of just what such an act had cost him.

Nothing was said. No overt comments were made and Jack did not hear Anstiss himself make any remark at all, and he saw him on several social occasions. The first thing he came across was at his club, where he overheard quite by chance two men he knew slightly, discussing Fitz and shaking their heads over the fact that he had been blackballed from another club of which one of them was a member.

"Good heavens, George. Herbert Fitzherbert? Really!" The man's blond eyebrows rose in amazement. "Whatever for? Always thought he was a pretty decent chap—one of us, and all that."

"So did I," his friend agreed. "That's what made it stick in my mind."

"Sure it was Fitzherbert?"

" 'Course I'm sure. Take me for a fool, Albert?"

"Whatever for? Not because that girl Morden jilted him, surely? Don't care what he did, you don't blackball a fellow for that sort of thing. Good God, if they started doing that, there'd be precious few of us left, what."

"No, of course not. Something else. Don't know what exactly. Word went out. That's all I know. But I'll tell you this: White's follows—and then all the other clubs worth belonging to."

"You think so? But what's he done?"

"Doesn't really matter, poor fellow. Don't need to know, people just follow suit. Too bad. Liked him. Nice chap, always agreeable, and generous."

"Can't be that Hilliard girl, can it?"

"Don't be an ass. Who the devil cares if a fellow sees a lady of dubious reputation? Long as you don't insult your wife, or expect decent people to treat her like one of the family . . ."

"Oh really? Does the Prince of Wales know that?"

"What? Oh—Mrs. Langtry? Well what the Marlborough House set do isn't really the pattern for all of us. Can't get away with it just because they do. Anyway, all he did, as I hear, was flirt with the girl a bit. No harm in that. No—no, it's something else. No idea what."

Jack did not know that it was Anstiss, but he feared it. He remembered the anger in his eyes, the sudden hard line of his mouth. It had changed from being an amiable, intelligent face into one that held a ruthlessness that was final.

He heard other remarks, saw the change in people's expressions when Fitz's name was mentioned.

"It is a curious comment on one's acquaintances," he said to Emily and Charlotte one afternoon as they were sitting in Charlotte's garden in the sun. They had called briefly to tell her of their change in plans. He smiled with an uncharacteristic twist of cynicism. "I think I can almost divide them into two classes: those I admire and those I don't, according to their reactions. It is a very sour thing to discover how many people are prepared to condemn a man without knowing even what it is he is supposed to have done, let alone whether he is guilty of it or not."

"You shouldn't be surprised, my dear," Emily said with a sad little grimace. "Society is all about influence and fashion. Someone with influence has blackballed Fitz, and suddenly he is no longer fashionable. Everyone, or almost everyone, is a follower, trying desperately to climb a little higher. And since no one knows where they are going, it is imperative one follows the right people."

Charlotte shot her a glance to see if she were as bitter as her words, but saw the flicker of amusement in her eyes, and was reassured that it was a tolerant understanding and not a matter of self-pity, or worse, of hatred.

"What are you going to do?" Charlotte asked, looking at Jack.

"Tell Lord Anstiss that I will seek selection, but that I will not enter the society to which he has invited me," Jack answered with sudden deep seriousness. And looking at him more closely Charlotte saw the gravity in him, and a flicker of fear. She knew then that he believed it was Anstiss at the back of Fitz's disfavor. They were all aware of his real power, not the money, the philanthropy, the open counsel, patronage and hospitality, but the influence that made or broke people according to his wish. He was a friend one could not do without, he was also an enemy one could not afford.

"He will not like it," Charlotte said quietly, but inside she was immensely relieved. No hope of failure Anstiss could threaten was anything like the horror that the Inner Circle visited on its members, the twisting of conscience, the tearing of loyalties, the secrecy and uncertainty, not knowing who to trust, and thus in the end the distrust of everyone, and the final utter loneliness.

"I know," Jack agreed. "And I don't know whether it is the same secret society that Thomas mentioned, but just in case, I should prefer not to."

"But you will still stand?"

"Of course. But independently, if that is the price." His smile was a little bleak. Perhaps already he had some idea that indeed that was the price, and in the end without the help of Anstiss and people like him, he would have no better a chance than Fitz.

Charlotte felt an overwhelming rush of sadness for all that he might have accomplished, and a pride in him that he would not do it at such a cost. She glanced across at Emily, and saw the answering pride in her eyes, and a happiness that was brighter than ambition, even for the opportunity to serve.

"I'm glad," Charlotte said quietly. "No one can please everyone. It is very important indeed to know whose approval matters in the end."

CHAPTER
ELEVEN

Pitt stood in Micah Drummond's office in the hazy sun. It was mid-afternoon and he had come to the point in his thoughts when he could no longer put off asking Drummond further about Byam. He was sinking in a morass of facts and suppositions, few of which he could fit into any coherent order. He did not even know fully how Weems had been killed, let alone by whom. Someone had visited him that night, found the blunderbuss and the powder, either seen or brought with him the coins, and had loaded the gun and fired it. But why had Weems sat still and permitted him to do that? From all he had learned, it seemed that Weems was a cautious man and well familiar with the danger he might be in from desperate clients pushed beyond endurance.

Drummond was standing by the window as he so often did. Pitt, hands in his pockets, was close to the desk, his thoughts still racing.

Surely Weems's other occupation as a blackmailer would have made him even more careful still? The bars on the door to the single entrance testified to that. Who would he permit to visit him at that hour, and for what purpose?

If they knew that, Pitt felt they would be a great deal closer to knowing who killed him.

And why? Was it debt? That seemed less and less likely. Or blackmail? If blackmail, then was it Byam, in a double bluff, or Carswell, or Urban, or Latimer? He thought not Urban, for all the excellent motive. Or was that simply because he liked the man? He had not yet told anyone about the picture frame in the Stepney music hall.

Charlotte was convinced it was not Carswell, and he was disposed to agree. Latimer? Or Byam himself, after all?

Or was it not blackmail, but some other motive, a more deep and ugly personal reason to do with Weems. Or perhaps his death was simply a necessary part of some other plan, and someone else was the real victim.

If that was true, they might be as far from a solution now as they had been when Byam first sent for them, which was a frightening thought.

"What is it?" Drummond said aloud, his face creased with anxiety. This case troubled him as very few before, and in an entirely different way. Pitt understood it, but he could do nothing to ease it; in fact it was probable he would make it worse.

He hitched himself sideways a little to sit on the desk. It was a very disrespectful attitude, but neither of them noticed. Drummond was sitting on the windowsill, his back to the sun.

"What if the motive was not debt or blackmail, but something else?" Pitt said aloud. "What if it was part of something personal . . ."

Drummond frowned. "But you said you had already investigated that, and you could find no personal relationships at all. He had no family of any sort, his only employees were the errand runner and the housekeeper, neither of whom seemed suspects, and no connection with any woman that you could find. Who would feel violently enough about him to kill him? There isn't even an heir."

"He must have had a collaborator of some sort," Pitt pointed out. "He didn't learn all his blackmail information himself. Someone told him."

Drummond looked up quickly, his eyes sharp.

"A backer? Perhaps Weems was only the person who actually contacted the victims and took the money, but he paid it on to someone else?" He straightened up a fraction as new hope caught him. "And that person murdered him? Maybe he got greedy, or even threatened a little pressure of his own, do you think?"

"He may have got greedy," Pitt said slowly. "He'd be a fool to try twisting the arm of whoever it is; and I don't have the feeling that Weems was a fool. He wouldn't have lasted long in that business if he were."

Drummond bit his lip. "No—but greedy. He wouldn't have been in the business in the first place otherwise."

Pitt smiled. "I'll grant you that."

Drummond went on thoughtfully. "But if as you say Weems got his information from someone else, we have to find out who it was. In fact we ought to find out anyway. That someone will surely take up the blackmail—" He stopped, comprehension of something coming into his face and as quickly being masked.

But Pitt saw it.

"Again," he finished for him. "And is he? Is someone being blackmailed again?"

Drummond hesitated.

Pitt saw his indecision and understood it. He had every compassion with Drummond's feelings for Eleanor Byam, and thus the complex emotions over Byam himself, but he could not permit it to interfere with their pursuit of the truth.

"Byam," he said aloud.

"I believe so." Drummond did not look at him.

Pitt thought for a few moments before continuing.

"Byam," he said at last. "I wonder why him, and so far as we know, not the others."

Drummond lifted his face. "You have an idea?"

"Perhaps . . ."

"Well what is it? For heaven's sake don't equivocate. It's not like you, and it doesn't serve anyone."

Pitt smiled for an instant, then was totally serious.

"What if Anstiss did not forgive him as openly and generously as Byam supposed? What if in fact he never got over Laura's death, and above all her betrayal of him—and he is taking a subtle and vicious revenge on Byam for it?"

"But why now?" Drummond asked, his brows drawn together in doubt. "Laura Anstiss has been dead for twenty years, and Anstiss himself always knew the truth about it."

"I don't know," Pitt confessed. "Perhaps something happened that they haven't told us."

"What, for example? A quarrel Byam would know about himself, and then he would hardly have drawn us in."

"If he realized Anstiss was behind it," Pitt argued. "Perhaps Weems was used as a cover precisely to prevent that."

"Have you found any connection between Anstiss and Weems?" Drummond asked slowly. "Anything at all?"

"No—but it occurs to me that we may have been looking in the wrong area for the motive to murder Weems. It's worth considering."

Drummond remained silent for several moments, his face dark with thought.

Pitt waited some time before he interrupted him.

"Is it still money?" he said at last.

"What?"

"That Byam is being blackmailed for this time?"

"I think not," Drummond said miserably. He drew in a deep breath then let it out. "I think this time it is influence in office—a matter of changing his mind over certain foreign investments and loans. At least it seems likely, from what Lady Byam says. I don't know."

"You asked him?"

"Of course I asked him." Drummond colored very faintly. "He said it was partly a political decision, pressed upon him by fellow members of the Inner Circle, and for reasons he could not explain to me, but he said he was persuaded by them. He denied it was blackmail."

"But you did not believe him?"

"No—I don't think so. I'm not sure. But you'll have to prove some connection between Anstiss and Weems, to make that even remotely believable. I can't see Lord Anstiss as a petty blackmailer behind a wretch like Weems. How would he even come to know Weems in the first place?"

Pitt hitched himself a little further onto the desk.

"Maybe Weems found him. After all Weems had the love letter Laura Anstiss wrote to Byam. Maybe he tried to sell it to Anstiss first."

"Then surely Anstiss would have killed him then, if he were going to do it at all," Drummond reasoned. "No Pitt, I can't see it. I agree there is someone behind Weems, apart from the servant who came up with the letter, someone who provided his other information." He looked up suddenly. "Maybe one of Weems's debtors? Perhaps some wretched beggar was desperate and paid off his debts in information?"

It was a good idea. It made sense.

"One of the larger debtors," Pitt elaborated slowly. "Someone who knew about Fanny Hilliard and Carswell, and that Urban was working at the music hall in Stepney—and Latimer was taking payoffs from the bare-knuckle fighters, and gambling on them . . ."

"Not necessarily one person." Drummond was enthusiastic now. "It could have been several people. Once Weems got the idea of accepting repayment in information he may have suggested it to other people himself. It would be a permanent source of income for him—never repayable in capital, always interest."

"Makes you wonder why no one killed him sooner, doesn't it?" Pitt said harshly.

"But how to find these sources of information, or at least prove they exist, other than by deduction." Drummond pulled a face. "Not that it necessarily brings us any closer to finding out who killed him. There are times when I would dearly like to abandon the whole case—I really don't care who killed the miserable swine."

"Did we ever?" Pitt said grimly. "All we set out to do was to prove it was not Byam, didn't we?"

Drummond's face tightened, but it was guilt, not anger. There was no need for him to reply, and denial was impossible. He looked up at Pitt.

"What are you going to do?"

"Go and see Byam again, and try to find out more about this letter and precisely where it came from."

"You think it matters?"

"It might. I should have paid more attention to it in the beginning. I'd like to find this servant who gave it to Weems and see who else might have known about it, and why we didn't find it among Weems's possessions. It was worth far too much for him to have parted with it."

"Maybe he sold it," Drummond suggested. "It could have got him a nice profit. Or more likely the murderer took it, along with his record of Byam's dealings. He would very probably have kept the two things together, since they were part of the same business." He bit his lip. "I know—that points to Byam again."

"Except that if he had both the original letter and Weems's notes, he would not have come to you—and who is blackmailing him now, and with what?"

"With having murdered Weems, of course," Drummond said miserably. "Don't creep all 'round it, Pitt."

Pitt said nothing, but stood up off the desk. He glanced at Drummond from the doorway.

"Tell me," Drummond asked.

"I will," Pitt promised, and went out into the corridor and downstairs.

It was pointless expecting to find Byam at home before the early evening. Accordingly it was after six when Pitt arrived at Belgrave Square and the footman let him in. Byam received him within a few minutes; there was no pretense that he had better or more important things to take his time.

They stood together in the library, Pitt by the window with his back to the light, Byam against the mantel facing him. Even the golden glow of early evening could not entirely soften the lines of fear and sleeplessness and the shadows around his eyes.

"What have you learned?" he asked, still with the same courtesy in his voice, although it was strained and his body was stiff under his immaculate clothes. He looked thinner.

"A great deal, sir." He felt sorry for the man because his suffering was so plainly visible in spite of all his efforts to appear normal, and even though he knew Byam might well be guilty of bringing most of it upon himself, indeed he might even have caused it directly. "But there are still facts missing before we can fit it all together to make sense of it," he went on.

"You don't know who killed Weems?" There was a flicker of hope in Byam, but it died almost before he had finished speaking.

"I'm not sure, but I think I am far closer than before."

Byam's face tightened but he did not ask again.

"What can I do to help?" he said instead.

"You told me in the beginning, or at least you told Mr. Drummond, that Weems's original weapon against you was a letter written by Lady Anstiss to you, which unfortunately had fallen into the hands of a maid, who was related to Weems."

"That's right. Presumably she showed it to him, or told him of it, and he saw the financial possibilities for himself."

"And Weems took it from her, because presumably you knew he had it or you would not have paid him?" Pitt went on.

Byam was very pale. "Yes. He had half of it. He showed it to me."

"We didn't find it."

"No. I assume if you had you would not be asking me these questions. What can I tell you that is of any purpose now?"

"Do you know the name of this servant?"

Byam was quite motionless, but his eyes widened. "No—can it matter?"

"It may."

"For heaven's sake why?"

"Do you believe that whoever stole the letter did so by chance, sir?"

Byam's face drained of every last vestige of blood. He swayed on his feet so that for a moment it seemed almost as if he might fall. He put his tongue over dry lips and made no sound.

Pitt waited, wondering if he would say something, anything at all to reveal what terrible thought had come to him. But the seconds ticked by and still he said nothing.

"The maid?" Pitt prompted at last. "She may have told someone else. Perhaps if she married, her husband might be a greedy or ruthless man?"

"I—I have—I have no idea," Byam said at last. "It was twenty years ago. You will have to ask in Lord Anstiss's house. Perhaps his butler has some record of past servants—or the housekeeper? Do you really think it could be that? It seems . . . farfetched."

"It is farfetched that a man like Weems should have the means to blackmail a person of your position and standing," Pitt pointed out. It was somewhat less than honest, but he did not wish Byam to have any idea that he suspected Anstiss, even as a remote possibility.

Byam smiled bitterly, but he seemed to accept it as an answer.

"Then you'd better go and see Lord Anstiss's butler," he said, as if weariness had suddenly overcome him and he were exhausted with it all. "I presume you know his address?"

"Not of the country house, sir, which is where I suppose I will find the appropriate butler?"

"No, not at this time of the year. Some domestic staff stay in the country, housekeepers probably, and maids, and so on, and a cook of sorts, and naturally all the outside staff, but the butler and valet travel with his lordship. You'll find the butler in London."

"Thank you. I shall call upon him and see if he has any record."

"Please God you find something useful! This matter is—" he stopped, either not wanting to put words to it, or not finding any powerful enough to express his emotions.

"Thank you, sir," Pitt said quietly.

"Is that all?"

"Yes, thank you sir, for the time being." And Pitt excused himself and left Byam standing by the cold grate, staring outside at the garden and the fading light.

He preferred to visit Anstiss's house during the day, when his lordship would more probably be out. He was not an easy man to bluff, or a man who would accept a partial explanation.

However on this occasion, although it was ten o'clock in the morning, Anstiss was at home, and he received Pitt in the morning room of his very elegant and imposing house. The style was Queen Anne, gracious and substantial, but with all the clean brilliance of that period. The curtains were forest-green velvet, the wood mahogany, and the one ornament Pitt had time to observe was an Irish silver chalice of utter simplicity and a beauty so exceptional he found it hard to refrain from staring at it, in spite of the urgency of his business and the fact that Anstiss made him less sure of himself than usual.

Anstiss stood beside a mahogany table with a large bronze of horses and surveyed Pitt with mild curiosity.

"What can I do for you, Inspector?" His blue-gray eyes were unflinching and he seemed vaguely amused. Certainly there was no apprehension in him at all. He was a spectator of this petty tragedy, no more.

Pitt had to treat him as if he knew nothing whatever about any part of the affair, except what anyone might know from the head-lines in the newspapers.

"I am investigating the murder of a blackmailer, my lord," Pitt began.

"How unpleasant. But I imagine such people frequently come to an untimely end." Anstiss was still only very superficially inter-ested. He was being polite, but it would be safe to assume that his courtesy would last only briefly if there were not something a great deal more relevant following soon.

"They don't often press their fortune far enough to endanger their own lives," Pitt answered. Ridiculously he found his mouth dry. "This one was successful for quite a long time. He obtained his information from servants who had chanced to learn something personal about their employers, and chosen to try to take advantage of it."

Anstiss's face darkened with contempt.

"If you expect my pity, you will be disappointed, Inspector. Such people deserve to be hoist on their own petard."

"No sir." Pitt shook his head. "I find it hard to care who killed him myself. But it is my duty, and we cannot permit private persons to become executioners, no matter how hardly tempted. This judg-ment may be one we concur with, but what about the next?"

"I take your point, Inspector, you do not need to labor it. What has all this to do with me?"

"One of the servants in question once worked in your country house." He watched closely to see if there was a flicker in Anstiss's face, anything that would tell him he had caught a nerve.

There was nothing.

"Indeed? Are you sure? I am not being blackmailed, Inspector." He made no protestations and there was humor in his face, not anxiety.

"I'm very glad." Pitt smiled back. "It is someone who was a guest in your home some time ago."

"Oh? Who is that?"

It was Anstiss's first error, and not a serious one.

"I am sure, my lord, you will understand if I do not answer that," Pitt said smoothly. "I must treat such information in confidence."

"Of course." Anstiss shrugged. "Foolish of me to have asked. I was not thinking. It was a sense of guilt. I feel responsible that a guest of mine should suffer such an offense." He shifted his weight a little and relaxed, but he did not invite Pitt to sit. One did not entertain policemen as if they were social acquaintances. "How can I help? You said it was some time ago?"

"Yes. Several years. If I could speak to your butler he may have either records, or if not, then some memory of past servants. He may even know where they may be found now."

"It's possible," Anstiss agreed. "But don't hold much hope, Inspector Pitt. Some servants stay a long time, of course, indeed all their lives, but many others move position often, and this one sounds most unsatisfactory. The sort of person you are speaking of may well have passed from one place to another, always downward, and in quite a short space have ended up on the streets, or by this time dead. Still, by all means speak to Waterson if you like. I'll call him." And without waiting for any better instruction he moved to the bell rope and rang it.

Waterson proved a dignified man with a dry and individual humor in his face, and Pitt liked him immediately. On Anstiss's instruction he conducted Pitt to his pantry, where he offered him a cup of tea with biscuits, an unusually civilized concern to a policeman. Then he recalled as well as he was able all the upstairs servants in the country house approximately twenty years previously.

He was tall and lean with a fine head of white hair. Were it not for his deferential and unobtrusive manner, one might have taken him for the aristocratic owner of the house. His features had a refinement Anstiss's lacked, but neither the strength nor the blazing intelligence. Seeing them side by side one would never have failed to see that Anstiss was the leader designed by nature as well as by society.

"Probably a housemaid or a ladies' maid," Pitt prompted, sipping his tea. It was hot and delicately flavored and was served in porcelain cups.

"That would be about the time of Lady Anstiss's death," Waterson said slowly, his eyes on the ceiling as he leaned back in his chair. "Not a time easily forgotten. Let me see . . . we had young Daisy Cotterill then, she's still with us—head laundress now. And Bessie Markham. She married a footman from somewhere or other. Left us, of course. We've got one of her daughters as tweeny now." He frowned in concentration. "The other one I can recall would be Liza Cobb. Yes, she left shortly after that. Said it was something to do with family. Happens sometimes, of course, but not often a girl can afford to give up a good place just because her family has difficulties." He looked up at Pitt. "Usually her job is the more important then—a little guaranteed money. Not a particularly satisfactory girl, not got her mind on her duty. Sights set on something better. Yes, Liza Cobb could be your girl."

"Thank you very much, Mr. Waterson. Have you any idea how I might find her?"

Waterson's blue eyes opened wider. "Now?"

"If you please?" Pitt took the last biscuit. They were remarkably good.

"Well, let me see . . ." Waterson looked up at the ceiling again and concentrated for several minutes. "I don't know myself, but it is possible Mrs. Fothergill, the housekeeper at number twenty-five, may know. I believe she was some sort of cousin. If you wish, I will write you a note of introduction."

"That is very civil of you," Pitt said with surprise and gratitude. "Really very civil."

He spent another quarter of an hour sharing a little harmless gossip with Waterson, who seemed to have an ungentlemanly interest in detection, about which he was embarrassed, but it did little to dim his delight. Then Pitt took his leave and visited the house across the street Waterson had indicated. There he found Mrs. Fothergill, who was able with much shaking of her head and

tutting to redirect him to yet another possible source of information as to Liza Cobb's present whereabouts.

Actually it took him till the following noon before he found
her behind the counter in an insalubrious fishmonger's off Bilings-
gate. She was a large woman with raw hands and a coarse face
which might have been handsome twenty years ago, but was now
rough-skinned, fleshy and arrogant. He knew instantly that he had
the right person. There was a look about her that reminded him
sickeningly of the half of Weems's face which the gold coins had
left more or less intact.

He stood in front of the counter between the scales and the
wooden slab and knife on which the fish were cut, and wondered
how to approach her. If he were too direct she would simply leave.
The door to the interior of the shop was behind her, and the
counter between her and Pitt.

Perhaps she was as greedy as her relative.

"Good afternoon, ma'am," he said with a courtesy that came
hard to him.

"Arternoon," she said with slight suspicion. People did not
customarily address her so.

"I represent the law," he said more or less truthfully. Then as
he saw the dislike in her pale eyes, "It is a matter of finding the
heir, or heiress, to a gentleman recently deceased," he went on.
Yes, it was the eyes that were like Weems. "And if I may say so,
ma'am, you bear such a resemblance to the gentleman in question, I think my search ends right here."

"I ain't lorst anyone," she said, but the edge was gone from
her voice. " 'Oo's dead?"

"A Mr. William Weems, of Clerkenwell."

Her face hardened again and she glanced angrily at the queue
of women beginning to form behind Pitt, faces curious. " 'E were
murdered," she said accusingly. " 'Ere! 'Oo are yer? I don't know
nuffin' abaht it. I don't get nuffin' 'cause 'e's dead."

"There's his house," Pitt said truthfully. "It seems you may be
his only relative, Miss—er, Miss Cobb?"

She thought for several seconds, then eventually the vision of
the house became too strong.

"Yeah, I'm Liza Cobb."

"Naturally I have one or two questions to ask you," Pitt continued.

"I don't know nuffin' abaht 'is death." She glared not at him but at the women behind him. " 'Ere—you keep your ears to yerself," she said loudly.

"I have nothing to ask you about Mr. Weems's death," Pitt replied soothingly. "What I want to ask you goes back long before that. May we speak somewhere a little more private?"

"Yeah, we better 'ad. Too many 'round 'ere can't mind their own business."

"Well I'm sure I don't care if you got relations wot was murdered," the first woman said with a sniff. "But you keep a civil tongue in yer 'ead, Liza Cobb, or I'll get me fish elsewhere. I will."

"Yer comes 'ere 'cause I give yer tick when no one else will, Maisie Stillwell, an' don't yer ferget it neither!" Liza Cobb spat back at her. She turned and cried out shrilly for someone to come and take her place at the counter, then led him into a hot, stale-smelling back room.

"Well?"

"Twenty years ago you were in service in Lord Anstiss's country house?"

"Yeah—must'a bin abaht then. Why?"

"You found a letter from Lady Anstiss to Lord Byam, who was a guest there?"

"Not exactly," she said guardedly. "But what if I 'ad?"

"Then what did happen—exactly?"

"W'en Lady Anstiss died, Rose, 'er ladies' maid, took some of 'er things, they gave 'em 'er, there weren't nuffin' wrong in it," she answered. "Well w'en Rose died, abaht three year ago, them things passed ter me. All rolled up inside them, like, were this letter. Love letter, summink fierce." Her broad lip curled in a sneer. "Din't know decent folk wrote letters like that to each other."

"How did you come to give it to Weems?"

Her eyes were sharp and clever. "I din't give it ter 'im. Least not all of it. It were in two pages, like. I sold 'im one, an' kept the other."

Pitt felt a prickle of excitement.

"You kept the other one yourself?"

She was watching him closely.

"Yeah—why? Yer want ter see it? It'll corst yer—yer can take a copy, fer five guineas."

"Is that what Weems paid you?"

"Why?"

"Curious. It's a fair price. Let me see it. If I think it's worth it, I'll pay you five guineas."

"Let's see the color o' yer money. Yer don't look like yer got five guineas."

Pitt had come prepared to buy information, although he had not expected to spend it all on one person. But he was increasingly certain that this letter was at the heart of the case. He fished in his pocket and found a gold guinea, six half guineas and a handful of crowns, shillings and sixpences. He held his hand half open so she could see them but not reach them.

"I'll get it for yer," she said, her eyes keen, and she disappeared into the back room. Several minutes later she returned with a piece of paper in her hand. She held out her other hand for the money.

Pitt gave it to her, counting it out carefully, and then quickly took the paper. He unfolded it and saw written in a strong, emotionally charged hand:

Sholto, my love,

We have shared a rare and high passion which most of the world will never know as we do. It must never be lost, or denied us. When I look back on our hours together, they hold all that is most exquisite to the body, and the soul. I will permit no one to tear it from me.

Have courage! Fear nothing, and keep our secret in your heart. Turn it over and over, as I do, in the long hours alone. Dream of times past, and times to come.

There was no more, no signature. Apparently there had been at least one other page, and it was missing.

Pitt kept it in his hand. It was a passionate letter, nothing

344 • BELGRAVE SQUARE

modest in it or waiting to be wooed. Indeed it seemed Laura Anstiss
had been a woman of violent emotions, self-assured, willful, not
even considering that her love might not be equally returned.

He began to see how indeed she might have been so stunned
by rejection that it temporarily unbalanced her mind and threw
her into a state of melancholia. If Byam had ever received that
letter, he would have been far less surprised at her suicide.

" 'Ere—gimme it back!" Liza Cobb said sharply. "Yer read it."

Had Laura Anstiss lived in a world of her own fantasy? The
letter implied they had been lovers in a very physical sense. Anyone reading it would assume so. Had Anstiss seen either this, or
some other like it?

"No," he said levelly. "It is evidence in a murder case. I'll
keep it for now."

"Yer thievin' swine!" She lunged forward at him, but he was
taller and heavier than she. He held out his other hand in a loose
fist and she met it hard and retreated with ugly surprise in her face.
"It's mine," she said between closed teeth.

"It was apparently never sent, so it belongs to Lady Anstiss,"
he contradicted. "And since she is dead, presumably to her heirs."

Her lip curled in a sneer. "Yer goin' ter give it ter 'is lordship,
are yer? I'll bet—at a price. The more fool you! D'yer fink if it were
that easy I wouldn't 'a done that meself? I know 'im. You don't.
'E'll never pay yer. 'Orsewhip yer more like."

"I'm going to give it to the police," he said with a tight smile.
"Which I am—Inspector Pitt of Bow Street. When the case is
finished, if you'd like to come to Bow Street, you can try to claim
it back." And he turned on his heel and marched out, hearing her
string of epithets and curses following him.

He walked briskly, pushing past the now wildly curious crowd.
He was glad that the corner of small, open square lay across his
way; the sight of the leaves against the sky was a clean and uncom-
plicated thing after the greed and the rage of the fishmonger's shop
and the woman in it. Reading the letter gave him a much clearer
picture of why Byam had paid Weems for over two years. It was
not the innocent passion he had implied, at least not in Laura
Anstiss's mind, and would not be read as such by any impartial
person now.

If Frederick Anstiss hated Byam it would not be surprising. It would take a man of superhuman forgiveness not to feel betrayed by such emotions in his wife for his best and most trusted friend, and guest under his roof.

The square was crossed diagonally by a path and there were two couples strolling along, heads close in conversation, and a third couple standing facing each other in what was unmistakably an angry exchange. The man in a high winged collar was very pink in the face and clutched his cane fiercely, twitching it now and again, jabbing at the air. The woman was equally heated, but there was a certain air of enjoyment in her, and it served only to exacerbate her companion's rage. After a few moments more he turned on his heel and strode off, and then as he passed a flower bush he lifted the cane high and sliced off a small branch in sheer temper. The action was so sudden and unforeseen it took Pitt by surprise.

Then startlingly he had a picture in his mind of Lord Anstiss standing in front of Weems's desk in his office while Weems read that damning letter aloud, jeering, demanding money, and a stick going up in the air without warning, striking Weems on the side of the head, robbing him of his senses long enough for Anstiss to take up the blunderbuss, fill the powder pan and load it with gold coins, and fire it.

Or it might have been anyone else, any gentleman who quite normally carried a stick or a cane, and any other provocation. But the letter stayed in his mind, and the image of Anstiss's face.

Had Weems, after two years of successful blackmail of Byam, tried his hand with Anstiss, and met a very different man; a man not plagued by guilt, but still burning with injury, humiliation and a long-hidden and unsatisfied hatred?

But why should he hide the hatred, if indeed he felt it? Friends drift apart; it would need no explanation, and Byam of all people would understand. He would never tell anyone the truth, in his own interest if not in Anstiss's.

Pitt quickened his step.

Or was this the first time Anstiss had realized his wife's guilt? Perhaps until then he had accepted Byam's word for the innocence of the affair, that it was simply an unwise friendship into which she alone had imagined love?

No one had thought to ask where Anstiss was on the night Weems was shot. He had never been a suspect; he was the injured party, not the offender.

The injured party.

He slowed down again unconsciously, the spring going out of his step. That was true. Anstiss was the one wronged. He had done nothing whatever to indicate a hatred of Byam or a desire to do anything but forget the whole matter. He did not seem a man to act in rage so uncontrollable as to commit murder.

No. If it was he who had struck Weems, and then shot him, there must have been a more powerful motive than simply to avoid paying a few guineas in blackmail over a letter which branded his long-dead wife as an adulteress.

He was well beyond the square now and walking quickly along the street towards the thoroughfare where he could get an omnibus home. It was early, but he wanted to speak to Charlotte.

The omnibus seemed ages in coming, and when it did, was hot and crowded. He sat squashed between two large ladies with shopping baskets, but he was unaware of them as he thought more and more of Anstiss and the terrible wound to his pride of his wife so obsessed with Byam. It was a passionate, immodest letter. There was something willful, almost commanding about it. It changed his view of Laura Anstiss entirely. He had imagined her as fragile, utterly feminine with a haunting beauty, and her suicide as a solitary grief, hugged to herself, a terrible loneliness. But the letter sounded far more robust, almost domineering, as though she expected to be obeyed, in fact had little doubt of it. Was she really such a spoilt beauty? Pitt thought he would not have liked her.

Perhaps Byam had been secretly nonplussed and had rejected her fairly roughly after once succumbing to physical temptation. That would explain his guilt even after so many years. He had betrayed Anstiss by making love to Laura, and then when he discovered her nature more fully, had rejected her pretty abruptly.

He reached home still preoccupied with his thoughts, and threw the door open. He called Charlotte's name, and there was no answer. He went down the corridor and through the kitchen out into the garden.

"Thomas!" Charlotte swung around from the roses where she

was snapping off the dead flower heads. "What has happened? Are you all right?"

He looked around. "Where are the children?"

"At school, of course. It's only three o'clock. What is it?"

"Oh—yes, of course it is. I want to talk to you."

She passed him the raffia trug for the flower heads and he took it obediently, holding it for her to continue.

"What about?" she asked, clipping off another head.

"Lord Anstiss."

She must have caught the urgency in his voice. She stopped what she was doing, her hands motionless above the next rose. She looked at him.

"You think he is behind your secret society?" She put the secateurs in the basket and abandoned the task. "I think you are probably right. We had better go inside and talk about it."

"No," he said honestly, although even as he said it it ceased to be true. "I think he might have murdered Weems, but I am not totally sure why. I have bits of motives, but they none of them seem quite strong enough."

She frowned, standing still by the rose bed. "Well, he surely wouldn't kill someone just so the police would find the notes incriminating Mr. Carswell, and the police officers, even if he did want to take away the references to Lord Byam, who was his friend—and presumably in good favor with the society. He must be clever enough to think of a better way of doing that." She shook her head. "One that wouldn't be so dangerous to himself, or so extreme. It seems rather hysterical to me—and he certainly is not a panicky man, I am as sure of that as I am of anything about anyone. I would say he is cold-blooded, and quite in control of himself at all times. Wouldn't you?"

"Yes—but we could be mistaken. Sometimes very deep emotions lie under an outwardly calm face and manner." He followed as she led the way inside and set the trug down on the kitchen table. Without asking she put the kettle on the hob and reached for cups and the teapot.

"Lord Byam might panic," she replied. "I still don't think Anstiss would. But I know that is not proof of anything. And he would need a very good reason indeed to do something so dangerous."

"I know." He sat down at the table.

"Have you had luncheon?" she asked.

"No."

Automatically she took bread, butter, cheese and rich, fruity pickle from the cupboard.

"Byam is still being blackmailed," he went on thoughtfully.

"For money?" she asked, spreading the bread.

"Not directly, so far as I can see. According to Lady Byam he has changed his mind very radically over the government policy in lending moneys to certain small countries in the empire, in Africa. One of his longtime friends and colleagues called recently and they had a fearful quarrel. He accused Byam of having betrayed his principles. Byam is in a very poor state, sleeping badly and looks like a ghost."

She stopped what she was doing, her hands in the air.

"Peter Valerius—" she said.

"Peter Valerius is blackmailing him?" Pitt asked with disbelief.

"No, no! He told me about venture capital."

"What are you talking about? Why are you interested in venture capital, and what is it?"

"I'm not." She took the kettle off the hob and poured the water over the tea, letting it steep. "He told me because honestly I think he'd tell anyone who would have the good manners to listen, or the inability to escape. It is a sort of money you can get, at a terrible usury, when no one else will lend you money and you are desperate. I mean industries and countries and the like, not little personal debtors." She turned around to face him. It was not easy to explain because she understood it only very little herself. "If you have a big industry and you have run out of money, perhaps your costs have gone up and your profits have gone down, and your ordinary banker won't help—that is someone like Byam—then you may go to someone who will lend you venture capital, at a very high rate of interest, and the price of a third of your company, forever—which may be where Anstiss comes in—maybe? But if you are desperate and will lose everything—perhaps you are a small country and your whole trade is tied up in one export—your people are starving . . ."

"All right," he said quickly. "I understand. But I have no idea if Anstiss has anything to do with venture capital."

"Well if that is what Byam is being blackmailed for, then it seems someone has."

He bit into the bread and pickle, hungry in spite of the thoughts running faster and faster in his brain.

"I need to know a great deal more about Anstiss," he said with his mouth full.

"Well where was he when Weems was killed?" she began. With one hand she poured his tea and passed him the mug.

"I don't know—but I think it is past time I found out." He ate the rest of his bread and held out his hand for the tea. As soon as he was finished he meant to go and find this Peter Valerius. He needed to know if Anstiss had profited from Byam's Treasury decision. "Where does Valerius work?" he asked her. "He does work, I suppose?"

"I haven't any idea. But Jack probably knows. You could ask him."

Pitt stood up. "I will." He kissed her quickly. "Thank you."

He took a hansom to Emily's house and was fortunate that Jack was at home. From him he learned where to find Peter Valerius, and by quarter to five he was striding along Piccadilly with him, dodging around slower pedestrians, leaping off the pavement over the gutter and back again, avoiding hooves and carriage wheels with considerable skill, coattails flying.

"Of course that is off the top of my head," Valerius warned cheerfully. "You will want some sort of documentary proof."

"If I'm right, I will," Pitt replied, increasing his pace to keep up.

Valerius jumped back onto the curb with alacrity. A horse swerved sideways and the coachman shouted a string of ungentlemanly imprecations at him.

"My apologies!" Valerius called over his shoulder. He grinned at Pitt. "Anstiss is the prime mover behind a lot of financial dealings, and the major shareholder in a few merchant banking interests. He, and his associates, stand to make a fortune, and not a small one, if certain African interests have to go to venture capital. A single year's interest repayments alone would keep most of us for life, let alone a third share in the company and all its profits in perpetuity." His face tightened and a look of anger close to hatred came into his eyes. "Never mind they are robbing blind a small country of people caught in a vise of borrowing, price fixing, and trade wars, and not sophisticated or powerful enough to fight."

Pitt caught him by the arm and pulled him back as he was about to launch off the pavement into a cross street almost under the hooves of a hansom.

"Thank you," Valerius said absently. "It's one of the most monstrous damned crimes going on, but no one seems to care."

Pitt had no argument to offer and no comfort. He refused to make some polite platitude.

The hansom passed and they crossed the street, Pitt watching both ways for traffic, and just reaching the far side as an open carriage swept by at a reckless speed.

"Idiot," Pitt said between his teeth at the driver.

"It will be traceable." Valerius went on with his own train of thought. "I'll get you the proof." He lengthened his step yet again, his coat flying. Meandering pedestrians who were simply taking the air and showing off moved aside with more haste than dignity, a dandy with a monocle muttering under his breath and two pretty women stopping to stare with interest.

"Thank you," Pitt said with appreciation. "Can you bring it to me in Bow Street?"

"Of course I can. How long will you be there?"

"Tonight?"

Valerius grinned. "Of course tonight. In a hurry, aren't you?"

"Yes."

"Excellent. Then I'll see you in Bow Street." And with a wave he swung around and raced off down Half Moon Street and disappeared.

With a new sense of hope Pitt made his way to Bow Street.

Once there he went straight up to Micah Drummond's office and knocked on the door. As soon as he was inside he knew something was wrong. Drummond looked profoundly unhappy. His face was pale, his features drawn, and there was fury in every angle of his body.

"What is it?" Pitt said immediately. "Byam?"

"No, Latimer, the swine. The man is a complete outsider!"

From a man like Drummond that was the ultimate condemnation. To be an outsider was to be lost beyond recall. Pitt was taken aback.

"What has he done?" His mind raced through possibilities and came up with nothing damning enough to warrant such contempt.

Drummond was staring at him.

"Where have you been?" he demanded.

"I think I may be close to the end of the Weems case," Pitt replied. "It's nothing to do with Latimer."

"I didn't think it was." Drummond turned back to the window. "Damn him!"

"Is it about the bare-knuckle fighting?"

Drummond turned around, his face lifting with hope. "What bare-knuckle fighting?"

"He gambles on it. That's where his money comes from—not from Weems. Didn't I tell you?"

"No you didn't! Don't be this ingenuous, Pitt. Nor did you tell me about Urban's moonlighting at a music hall in Stepney, and having possible stolen works of art."

Pitt felt a sudden coldness inside him. "Then how do you know?"

"Because Latimer told me, of course!"

"About Urban? Why, for—" But before he could finish the questions, he understood. The Inner Circle. Latimer had showed his ultimate obedience by betraying Urban, becoming his executioner for the brotherhood. Drummond knew it, and this was the reason for his rage. "I see," Pitt said aloud.

"Do you?" Drummond demanded, his face white, his eyes blazing. "Do you? It's that hellish Inner Circle."

"I know."

For moments they stood staring at each other, then Drummond's eyes dulled into misery again and the fire went out of him.

"Yes—of course you do." He sat down behind the desk and waved towards the chair opposite. "There's one good thing. That self-important idiot Osmar has done it again, and been caught beyond question this time—in a public railway carriage on the Waterloo line, of all things." His eyes held a flash of humor. "And by an elderly lady of unquestionable reputation and veracity. No one will doubt the Dowager Lady Webber when she says his behavior was unpardonable and his dress inadequate for public wear. And the young woman likewise, and her profession only too apparent. He'll have no defense this time."

In other circumstances Pitt would have laughed. Now all he could raise was a hard smile.

"What did you come for?" Drummond asked.

Pitt told him all he either knew or believed about Lord Anstiss, his suppositions about Weems and the letter, Charlotte's information concerning venture capital and his subsequent meeting with Peter Valerius.

"Do you have this letter?" Drummond asked, frowning.

Pitt drew it out of his pocket and passed it to him.

Drummond took it and read it slowly, his brows drawing down, his face darkening as he came to the end. He looked up, puzzled and oddly disappointed.

"Somehow this is not how I imagined Laura Anstiss." He smiled very briefly. "Which is foolish. It hardly matters, but I . . ." He seemed unable to find the words, or else was embarrassed by his emotion and its irrelevance.

"Nor I," Pitt agreed. "It's a forceful letter, and perhaps even a little indelicate."

"That's it," Drummond agreed quickly. "And it seems Byam was a good deal less than honest with us. From this it sounds as if they were indisputably lovers, which he said they were not. I'm not surprised he still feels guilt over her."

Pitt looked at Drummond's face, the letter lying on the desk between them. He knew Drummond was faintly repelled by it, as he had been himself, and had not wished to say so.

"I think Weems may have decided to try his hand with Anstiss as well," Pitt said. "After all, it had worked successfully for him with Byam. For two years he had had a nice little addition to his income."

Drummond regarded him steadily without interruption.

"But this time he found a very different mettle of man," Pitt went on. "Anstiss lost his temper and struck him with his stick. If we go to Anstiss's house and find his cane, I think there may well be blood or hair on it."

Drummond pursed his lips but there was agreement in his eyes.

"And then when Weems was temporarily unconscious," Pitt continued, "he saw the opportunity—probably Weems had already let him know he was blackmailing Byam—so he loaded the blunderbuss and killed Weems. Then he took the papers incriminating Byam, and Weems's half of the letter, perhaps not even realizing there was another half. He left the second list incriminating the errant members of the Inner Circle, of which he is a master, in order to discipline them. I daresay he knew their secrets through the Inner Circle as well. With this situation he would take over the blackmail of Byam himself, and force him to change his Treasury decisions and allow Anstiss to step in with his venture capital. The profit would be enormous."

Drummond sat without speaking for several moments, then at last he looked up. There was no conviction in his eyes.

"It seems to me you are trying too hard, Pitt. There are too many motives for Anstiss, and all of them too small to move an intelligent and self-controlled man to murder, especially one who already has power, wealth and position. I can easily believe he would take advantage of Weems's death and Byam's vulnerability to extend the blackmail and force Byam to change his political decisions on African loans. But I can't see him committing cold-blooded murder to bring it about. And honestly, even with proof that he profited, I don't think we would convince any jury of it. In fact I don't think we'd even get the public prosecutor to bring the charge."

Pitt refused to give up.

"Perhaps Anstiss had not seen the letter until Weems showed it to him," he suggested. "And we don't know what was in his half, but if it was in the same vein as the half we have, he may have struck out in rage then, and his prime motive might have been to have revenge on Byam. Especially if Byam told him what he told you—that he was never Laura Anstiss's lover, that it was simply a sudden infatuation she had for him, and he broke it off when he realized how serious she was. If Anstiss had accepted that all these years and forgiven him in that belief, to see proof in Laura's own hand, if he was also deeply in love with her . . ."

He stopped. It was not necessary to fill in the rest. Infatuation was one offense; to be cuckolded in one's own house quite another.

Drummond's face tightened.

"That I can believe. If he had always accepted Byam's innocence, and his wife's virtue, if not her love, then it would come as a very violent shock to him, enough to make him lose all control, at least for long enough to strike out at Weems's smiling face, and then kill him, and get rid of the one other person who knew of it—and destroy Byam as the perpetrator. But can you prove any of it?"

"I don't know." Pitt shook his head. "Valerius will bring proof of the financial connection, which will be sufficient to go and question him. Then we can find the stick, or prove he has recently lost one. I don't suppose we'll ever find the blunderbuss, or that he will have kept Weems's half of the letter."

"The main thing will be to see if we can place him in Cyrus Street," Drummond pointed out. "Or if he can prove he was somewhere else. When do you expect this Valerius?"

"Some time this evening."

"No more accurate than that?"

"No—he said it would not take him long, but I did not press him to a particular hour."

Drummond rose to his feet slowly, as though his body were stiff.

"Then I'll go and see Byam, at least tell the poor devil he is no longer suspected. He will be very shocked if it is Anstiss. They have been friends most of their lives."

"He won't be so very shocked when he realizes Anstiss has read Laura's letters," Pitt said dryly.

Drummond made no comment, but picked up his hat from the stand at the door, and his cane from the rack below.

Drummond walked well over a mile before he hailed a hansom and directed it towards Belgrave Square. It was a cool evening with a breeze off the river and the mist was rising. By dusk it could well be foggy. He needed time to think, although all the time in the world would not alter the facts. He would be able to give Eleanor the one thing she really wished: her husband's innocence, even his release from the second blackmail. Drummond would always know what the letter contained, the evidence that Byam's involvement with Laura Anstiss was not as innocent as he had claimed, but he would not tell her that.

He passed a group of ladies and tilted his hat politely as they inclined their heads.

What Byam chose to tell Eleanor was his affair, and if she guessed he had lied it was still between them. She might well put it from her mind and forgive him. It had been twenty years ago, and before he knew her.

Then Drummond would never see her again, unless their paths crossed socially, and he was torn as to whether he even wanted that or not. It was a decision he would not make now.

An acquaintance passed in an open carriage and he acknowledged him absently. Why was it when you most wished to be alone that you passed so many people you knew?

He hailed a hansom and climbed in.

Belgrave Square came all too quickly. He alighted and paid. There was nothing more to decide, nothing more to think about. He went up the steps and pulled the bell.

The butler let him in and mistook his grave face for a portent of bad news.

"Shall I call Lord Byam, sir?" he said grimly.

Drummond forced a pleasanter look.

"If you please. I have word he will wish to hear."

"Indeed, sir." The man's eyebrows rose. "I am very relieved." And after conducting Drummond to the library, he disappeared about his errand.

The fire was lit this evening, in spite of its being summer and still many hours of daylight left. The mist was heavier now and there was a dampness to the air outside. The fire's glow was welcome. Automatically Drummond went over to it.

Byam came almost immediately. Drummond was half glad Eleanor had not come with him. It would be easier, and perhaps more appropriate, if he were able to tell Byam without her there.

"What have you heard?" Byam did not even pretend to courtesies. His face was pale with spots of color high in his cheeks and his eyes looked feverish. He had closed the door behind him, cutting off the servants, Eleanor and the rest of the house. "Do you know who killed Weems?"

"Yes, I believe I do," Drummond replied. He was taken by surprise that Byam should have asked so bluntly. He had expected to govern the conversation himself, to approach the subject and choose his words.

Byam tried to be casual, but his body under its elegant clothes was rigid and he drew his breath as though his lungs were compressed and his throat tight.

"Is it—is it anyone I have—have heard of?" He cleared his throat. "I mean was it someone else he was blackmailing? Or one of his ordinary debtors?" He made half a move as if to go to one of the silver-topped decanters on the side table, then stopped.

"It appears to be someone he was blackmailing," Drummond answered. "But you will appreciate, we have not arrested him yet, so I prefer not to say more. I came to tell you as soon as I could that you need no longer worry about your own safety or reputation."

"Good. I—I am obliged to you." Byam swallowed. "You have behaved with great consideration, Drummond. I am sensible of your generosity."

Drummond was embarrassed, painfully aware of his emotions as well as his acts, things of which he profoundly hoped Byam had no notion.

"I assume you will arrest him?" Byam went on, more to fill the silence than from any apparent interest.

"Tomorrow," Drummond replied. "We still require some documentary evidence."

Byam moved jerkily and made as if to speak, then remained silent. He seemed very little relieved, considering the weight of the

news Drummond had just brought, almost as if it were peripheral
to his real anguish.

"We know you are not guilty," Drummond said again, just in
case somehow he had not grasped that his ordeal was over.

Byam forced a smile. It was ghastly.

"Yes—yes, I am very grateful."

"And the blackmail will end," Drummond added, trying to
bring the man some ease.

"Of course. Weems . . ."

"No—I mean the second blackmail—to change your mind on
the lending policy in the African empire states and drive them
to venture capital. It was the same man, and his arrest will end
it all."

Byam stood motionless.

"I—I thought it was one of Weems's associates," he said very
quietly. "Whoever he left his papers with, to safeguard himself."

"No—it was his murderer," Drummond corrected. "When he
killed Weems he took the letter, and blackmailed you with it. Only
this time not for a few guineas, but for political corruption and the
infinitely greater prizes that would bring." He realized as he said it
that freedom from suspicion, even from that pressure, was only part
of Byam's need. He would never undo the decisions he had made
in office, or the guilt for having set his personal reputation ahead
of his political honor.

"I'm sorry," Drummond said quietly. It was not an apology.

Byam was ashen, as if every vestige of blood had drained from
his face.

"And Weems was blackmailing the murderer also, you say?"

"Yes."

"For money?"

"Presumably. But it didn't work. The man killed him."

Byam swayed on his feet. He forced the words between dry lips.

"And—took the—letter?"

"Yes." Drummond was afraid Byam was going to faint, he
looked so ill.

"How—how did you discover . . . ?" Byam stammered.

"It was the letter, actually," Drummond replied. "Pitt found
half of it. Can I get you something? Brandy?"

"No—no! Please leave me. I am . . ." He coughed and gasped for breath. "I—I am obliged." Drummond stood helpless for a moment longer, then went to the door and found the butler standing outside in the hall.

"I think Lord Byam is not well," he said hastily. "Perhaps you had better go and see if you can be of assistance."

"Yes sir." And without waiting to hand him his hat and stick, simply indicating the footman, the butler did as he was told. Drummond took the things from the footman's hand and went outside into the foggy, clammy evening, already growing dim.

Pitt met Drummond at eight o'clock the following morning. The mist had not yet cleared and the streets were damp, their footsteps echoing when they alighted from the hansom and walked across the pavement and up the steps to Lord Anstiss's house. Drummond rang the bell.

It was several chilly minutes before a footman answered, looking surprised and more than a little confused to see two people he did not know on the step at this hour.

"I'm sorry sir," he apologized. "Lord Anstiss is not yet receiving visitors."

Pitt showed him his police identification.

"He will see us," he insisted, gently pushing past the man.

"No 'e won't, sir!" The footman was clearly extremely unhappy. "Not at this hour, 'e won't!"

Drummond followed them in and unconsciously glanced at the hall stand where two sticks and an umbrella rested. Pitt picked up both sticks and turned them over in his hand, looking at the lower ends of the shafts.

" 'Ere!" the footman said sharply. "You can't do that! Them is 'is lordship's. Give 'em ter me!"

"Are they Lord Anstiss's sticks?" Pitt asked, still holding them. "Are you sure?"

" 'Course I'm sure! Give 'em ter me!"

Drummond waited, deeply unhappy, visions of dismissal and disgrace in his mind, should they prove mistaken.

But Pitt seemed very certain.

"Don't worry," he said to the footman more gently. "They are evidence—at least this one is."

"Is it?" Drummond demanded. "Have you found something? You're sure?"

Pitt's face did not lose its grim expression, but the line around his mouth eased a little. "Yes—there's a dark stain ingrained in the wood of the shaft, reddish brown." He looked at the footman. "We must see Lord Anstiss. This is not your fault. We are police and you have no choice but to call his lordship. We will wait at the bottom of the stairs."

"Dammit, Pitt!" Drummond said under his breath. "He's not going to run away!"

Pitt gave him a dour look, but did not move.

The footman hesitated a moment, looking questioningly at Drummond.

"You'd better go and waken him," Drummond agreed. The die was cast and there was no retreating now.

Obediently the footman went upstairs, and came down again within the space of three minutes, his face pink and worried.

"I can't get in, sir, and neither can I make 'is lordship answer me. Is there summink wrong, sir? 'Ad I better fetch Mr. Waterson?"

"No—we'll go up," Pitt said quickly, without giving Drummond time to suggest any alternative. He glanced at the footman. "You're a big lad, come with us in case we need to force the door."

"Oh, I can't do that!"

"Yes you can if you're told to." Pitt strode up the stairs two at a time and the others followed hard on his heels. "Which way?" he asked at the top.

"Left, sir." The footman squeezed in front and went along to the first door in the east wing. "This one, sir. But it's locked."

Pitt turned the handle. It was indeed locked.

"Lord Anstiss!" he said loudly.

There was no answer.

"Come on!" he ordered.

He, Drummond and the footman put their shoulders to it and together all three of them threw their weight at it. It took them four attempts before the lock burst and they half fell inside. The footman stumbled across the dim room towards the curtains and drew them back. Then he turned and stared at the bed. He gave a shriek and swayed a moment before falling to the floor in a dead faint.

"God Almighty!" Drummond said in a strangled voice.

Pitt felt his stomach lurch, but he went forward and stood by the side of the bed staring down at it.

Sholto Byam and Frederick Anstiss lay side by side in the big four-poster, both naked. Anstiss was drenched in blood, his throat cut from side to side, his head lying awkwardly at a half angle, his eyes wide in horror. Byam was beside him, more composed, as if he had expected death, even welcomed it, and his haggard features were ironed out, all the anguish gone at last. A broad-bladed knife lay beside him and both his wrists were gashed. The surrounding area of the bed was dark red with deep-soaked blood, as if once the act was done he had not moved but lain there almost at peace while his life poured away.

Somewhere behind them in the doorway a housemaid was screaming hysterically over and over again, but the footman was incapable of helping her. There was a sound of running feet.

On the pillow beside Byam's head was a letter addressed not to Drummond but to Pitt. He reached over and picked it up.

By now you probably know the truth. Micah Drummond told me you had found the other half of the letter to me, and you know it was not Laura who wrote it, but Frederick. Laura did not love me, poor woman. I will never forget the night she came and found Frederick and me together, in bed.

Many women might have kept such a secret, but she would not. He and I killed her, and gave out the story that it was an accident. We kept the suicide idea in case anyone did not believe that she had slipped. It was better than the truth, and of course it was what I told Drummond when that devil Weems began to blackmail me.

But when he tried it on Frederick it was a different thing—the letter was in Frederick's hand, and when Weems realized that, however he did, perhaps he had some letter or agreement to meet, then of course Frederick had to kill him. Weems knew the truth, not only about us, but presumably he guessed we had killed Laura as well.

Whether or not Frederick would have betrayed me when he was arrested, I don't know—and perhaps it hardly matters now. I have loved him all these years, and he professed to love me—that he could have blackmailed me for the African loans and corrupted the best thing I did is beyond my ability to bear, or to forgive.

He has ruined me, and all I believed in, both love and honor. I shall see that he dies with such a scandal London will never forget it.

There is nothing more to be said, this is the end of it all.

Sholto Byam

Pitt passed it across to Drummond.

Drummond read it slowly then looked up, his face ashen.

"God, what a mess."

Beyond the doorway Waterson, gray-faced, was standing like a man stricken. Someone had taken the housemaid away. The footman was still on the floor.

"You'd better go and tell Lady Byam," Pitt said quietly. "It will come better from you than anyone else. I'll clear up here."

Drummond hesitated only a moment, guilt, realization and pity fighting in him.

"There's nothing else to do," Pitt assured him. "It is all finished here—we must care for the living now."

Drummond took his hand and squeezed it fiercely for a moment, wringing it so hard he bruised the flesh, then swung around on his heel and went out.

Pitt turned back to the bed, and very gently pulled up the bedspread to cover the faces of the dead.

ABOUT THE AUTHOR

Anne Perry is the author of the acclaimed Victorian mystery series featuring Thomas and Charlotte Pitt, which includes *Silence in Hanover Close* and *Highgate Rise*. She is also the author of *The Face of a Stranger* and *A Dangerous Mourning*, featuring Inspector William Monk.

Anne Perry lives in Portmahomack in the Scottish Highlands.